SPECIAL MESSAGE TO READERS

THE ULVERSCROFT FOUNDATION

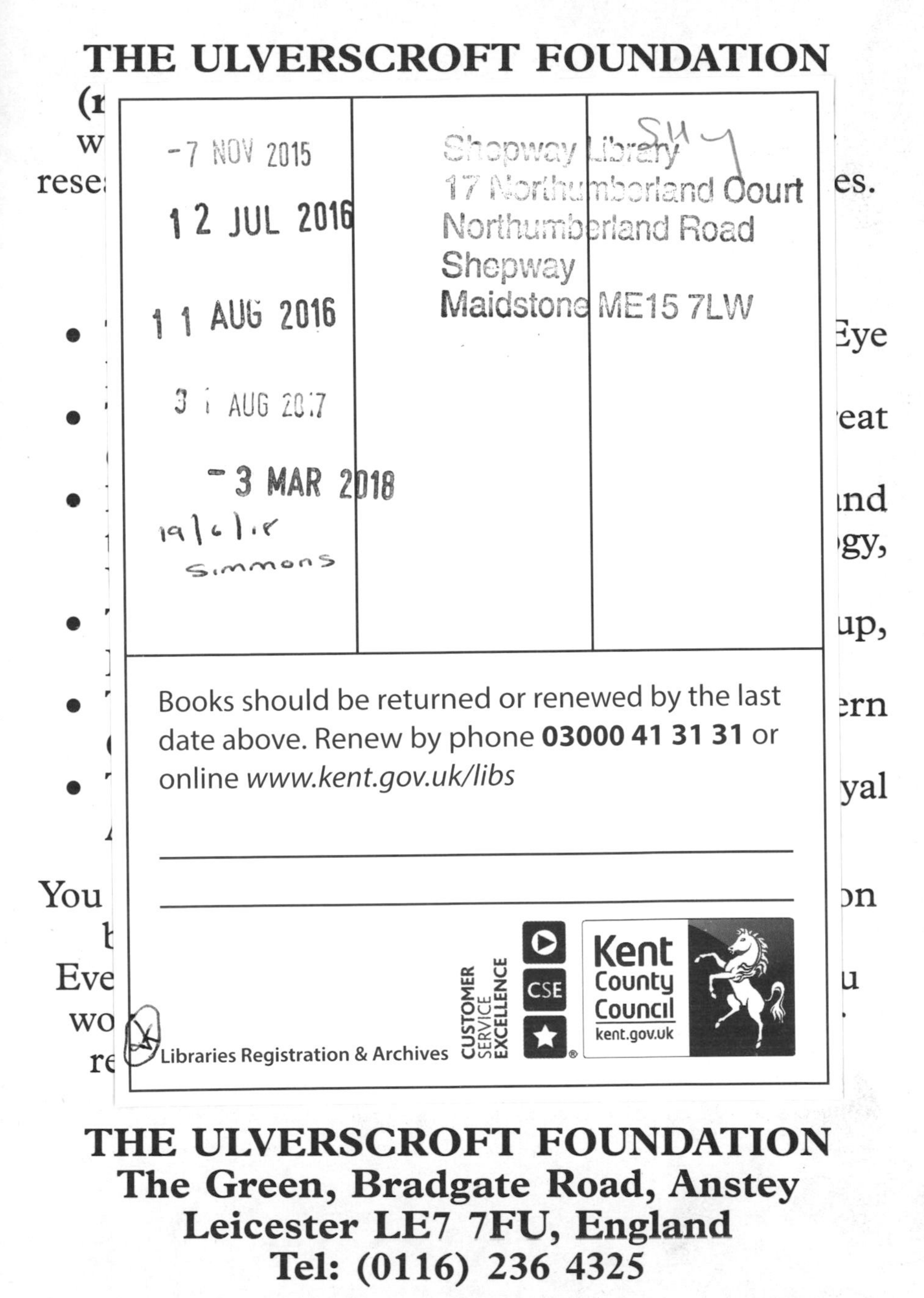

THE ULVERSCROFT FOUNDATION
The Green, Bradgate Road, Anstey
Leicester LE7 7FU, England
Tel: (0116) 236 4325

website: …ft.com

SPECIAL MESSAGE TO READERS

THE ULVERSCROFT FOUNDATION

(registered UK charity number 264873)

was established in 1972 to provide funds for research, diagnosis and treatment of eye diseases. Examples of major projects funded by the Ulverscroft Foundation are:—

- The Children's Eye Unit at Moorfields Eye Hospital, London
- The Ulverscroft Children's Eye Unit at Great Ormond Street Hospital for Sick Children
- Funding research into eye diseases and treatment at the Department of Ophthalmology, University of Leicester
- The Ulverscroft Vision Research Group, Institute of Child Health
- Twin operating theatres at the Western Ophthalmic Hospital, London
- The Chair of Ophthalmology at the Royal Australian College of Ophthalmologists

You can help further the work of the Foundation by making a donation or leaving a legacy. Every contribution is gratefully received. If you would like to help support the Foundation or require further information, please contact:

THE ULVERSCROFT FOUNDATION
The Green, Bradgate Road, Anstey
Leicester LE7 7FU, England
Tel: (0116) 236 4325

website: www.foundation.ulverscroft.com

THE BISHOP'S SECRET

A man is murdered: shot through the heart. In the quiet cathedral city of Beorminster, so unusual an event can only bring on dizzying excitement. People gather by the dozen on street corners and in public-houses, where they attempt to thrash out the problem — and develop their most intricate theories over their beer. But then there appears in Beorminster the strangest figure: an elderly, weather-beaten man with the quick, alert eye of a fowl. For all he looks and speaks like a sailor, he calls himself a missionary. His name is Ben Baltic — and he is a detective . . .

Books by Fergus Hume
Published by Ulverscroft:

THE MYSTERY OF A HANSOM CAB

FERGUS HUME

THE BISHOP'S SECRET

Complete and Unabridged

ULVERSCROFT
Leicester

First published in Great Britain in 1900

This Large Print Edition
published 2015

A catalogue record for this book is available from the British Library.

ISBN 978–1–4448–2579–4

Published by
F. A. Thorpe (Publishing)
Anstey, Leicestershire

Set by Words & Graphics Ltd.
Anstey, Leicestershire
Printed and bound in Great Britain by
T. J. International Ltd., Padstow, Cornwall

This book is printed on acid-free paper

Table of Contents

1

'Enter Mrs Pansey as Chorus'

Of late years an anonymous mathematician has declared that in the British Isles the female population is seven times greater than the male; therefore, in these days is fulfilled the scriptural prophecy that seven women shall lay hold of one man and entreat to be called by his name. Miss Daisy Norsham, a veteran Belgravian spinster, decided, after some disappointing seasons, that this text was particularly applicable to London. Doubtful, therefore, of securing a husband at the rate of one chance in seven, or dissatisfied at the prospect of a seventh share in a man, she resolved upon trying her matrimonial fortunes in the country. She was plain, this lady, as she was poor; nor could she rightly be said to be in the first flush of maidenhood. In all matters other than that of man-catching she was shallow past belief. Still, she did hope, by dint of some brisk campaigning in the diocese of Beorminster, to capture a whole man unto herself.

Her first step was to wheedle an invitation

out of Mrs Pansey, an archdeacon's widow — then on a philanthropic visit to town — and she arrived, towards the end of July, in the pleasant cathedral city of Beorminster, in time to attend a reception at the bishop's palace. Thus the autumn manœuvres of Miss Norsham opened most auspiciously.

Mrs Pansey, with whom this elderly worshipper of Hymen had elected to stay during her visit, was a gruff woman, with a scowl, who 'looked all nose and eyebrows.' Few ecclesiastical matrons were so well known in the diocese of Beorminster as was Mrs Pansey; not many, it must be confessed, were so ardently hated, for there were few pies indeed in which this dear lady had not a finger; few keyholes through which her eye did not peer. Her memory and her tongue, severally and combined, had ruined half the reputations in the county. In short, she was a renowned social bully, and like most bullies she gained her ends by scaring the lives out of meeker and better-bred people than herself. These latter feared her 'scenes' as she rejoiced in them, and as she knew the pasts of her friends from their cradle upwards, she usually contrived, by a pitiless use of her famous memory, to put to rout anyone so ill-advised as to attempt a stand against her domineering authority. When her tall, gaunt figure

— invariably arrayed in the blackest of black silks — was sighted in a room, those present either scuttled out of the way or judiciously held their peace, for everyone knew Mrs Pansey's talent for twisting the simplest observation into some evil shape calculated to get its author into trouble. She excelled in this particular method of making mischief. Possessed of ample means and ample leisure, both of these helped her materially to build up her reputation of a philanthropic bully. She literally swooped down upon the poor, taking one and all in charge to be fed, physicked, worked and guided according to her own ideas. In return for benefits conferred, she demanded an unconditional surrender of free will. Nobody was to have an opinion but Mrs Pansey; nobody knew what was good for them unless their ideas coincided with those of their patroness — which they never did. Mrs Pansey had never been a mother, yet, in her own opinion, there was nothing about children she did not know. She had not studied medicine, therefore she dubbed the doctors a pack of fools, saying she could cure where they failed. Be they tinkers, tailors, soldiers, sailors, Mrs Pansey invariably knew more about their vocations than they themselves did or were ever likely to do. In short, this celebrated lady — for her reputation was more than local — was what the American so succinctly terms a 'she-boss'; and in a less enlightened age she would indubitably have been ducked in the Beorflete river as a meddlesome, scolding, clattering jade. Indeed, had anyone been so brave as to ignore the flight of time and thus suppress her, the righteousness of the act would most assuredly have remained unquestioned.

Now, as Miss Norsham wanted, for her own purposes, to 'know the ropes,' she was fortunate to come within the gloom of Mrs Pansey's silken robes. For Mrs Pansey certainly knew everyone, if she did not know everything, and whomsoever she chaperoned had to be received by Beorminster society, whether Beorminster society liked it or not. All *protégées* of Mrs Pansey sheltered under the ægis of her terrible reputation, and woe to the daring person who did not accept them as the most charming, the cleverest, and in every way the most desirable of their sex. But in the memory of man, no one had ever sustained battle against Mrs Pansey, and so this feminine Selkirk remained monarch of all she surveyed, and ruled over a community consisting mainly of canons, vicars and curates, with their respective wives and offsprings. There were times when her subjects made use of language not precisely ecclesiastic, and not infrequently Mrs Pansey's name was mentally included in the Commination Service.

Thus it chanced that Daisy, the spinster, found herself in Mrs Pansey's carriage on her way to the episcopalian reception, extremely well pleased with herself, her dress, her position, and her social guardian angel. The elder lady was impressively gloomy in her usual black silk, fashioned after the early Victorian mode, when elegance invariably gave place to utility. Her headgear dated back to the later Georgian epoch. It consisted mainly of a gauze turban twinkling with jet ornaments. Her bosom was defended by a cuirass of cold-looking steel beads, finished off at the throat by a gigantic brooch, containing the portrait and hair of the late archdeacon. Her skirts were lengthy and voluminous, so that they swept the floor with a creepy rustle like the frou-frou of a brocaded spectre. She wore black silk mittens, and on either bony wrist a band of black velvet clasped with a large cameo set hideously in pale gold. Thus attired — a veritable caricature by Leech — this survival of a prehistoric age sat rigidly upright and mangled the reputations of all and sundry.

Miss Norsham, in all but age, was very

modern indeed. Her neck was lean; her arms were thin. She made up for lack of quality by display of quantity. In her *décolleté* costume she appeared as if composed of bones and diamonds. The diamonds represented the bulk of Miss Norsham's wealth, and she used them not only for the adornment of her uncomely person, but for the deception of any possible suitor into the belief that she was well dowered. She affected gauzy fabrics and fluttering baby ribbons, so that her dress was as the fleecy flakes of snow clinging to a well-preserved ruin.

For the rest she had really beautiful eyes, a somewhat elastic mouth, and a straight nose well powdered to gloss over its chronic redness. Her teeth were genuine and she cultivated what society novelists term silvery peals of laughter. In every way she accentuated or obliterated nature in her efforts to render herself attractive.

Ichabod was writ large on her powdered brow, and it needed no great foresight to foresee the speedy approach of acidulated spinsterhood. But, to do her justice, this regrettable state of single blessedness was far from being her own fault. If her good fortune had but equalled her courage and energy she should have relinquished celibacy years ago.

'Oh, dear — dear Mrs Pansey,' said the

younger lady, strong in adjectives and interjections and reduplication of both, 'is the bishop very, very sweet?'

'He's sweet enough as bishops go,' growled Mrs Pansey, in her deep-toned voice. 'He might be better, and he might be worse. There is too much Popish superstition and worship of idols about him for my taste. If the departed can smell,' added the lady, with an illustrative sniff, 'the late archdeacon must turn in his grave when those priests of Baal and Dagon burn incense at the morning service. Still, Bishop Pendle has his good points, although he *is* a time-server and a sycophant.'

'Is he one of the Lancashire Pendles, dear Mrs Pansey?'

'A twenty-fifth cousin or thereabouts. He says he is a nearer relation, but I know much more about it than he does. If you want an ornamental bishop with good legs for gaiters, and a portly figure for an apron, Dr Pendle's the man. But as a God-fearing priest' (with a groan), 'a simple worshipper' (groan) 'and a lowly, repentant sinner' (groan), 'he leaves much — much to be desired.'

'Oh, Mrs Pansey, the dear bishop a sinner?'

'Why not?' cried Mrs Pansey, ferociously; 'aren't we all miserable sinners? Dr Pendle's a human worm, just as you are — as I am. You may dress him in lawn sleeves and a mitre, and make pagan genuflections before his throne, but he is only a worm for all that.'

'What about his wife?' asked Daisy, to avert further expansion of this text.

'A poor thing, my dear, with a dilated heart and not as much blood in her body as would fill a thimble. She ought to be in a hospital, and would be, too, if I had my way. Lolling all day long on a sofa, and taking glasses of champagne between doses of iron and extract of beef; then giving receptions and wearing herself out. How he ever came to marry the white-faced doll I can't imagine. She was a Mrs Creagth when she caught him.'

'Oh, really! a widow?'

'Of course, of course. You don't suppose she's a bigamist even though he's a fool, do you?' and the eyebrows went up and down in the most alarming manner. 'The bishop — he was a London curate then — married her some eight-and-twenty years ago, and I daresay he has repented of it ever since. They have three children — George' (with a whisk of her fan at the mention of each name), 'who is a good-looking idiot in a line regiment; Gabriel, a curate as white-faced as his mother, and no doubt afflicted as she is with heart trouble. He was in Whitechapel, but his father put him in a curacy here — it was sheer nepotism. Then there is Lucy; she is the best of the bunch, which is not saying much. They've engaged her to young Sir Harry Brace, and now they are giving this reception to celebrate having inveigled him into the match.'

'Engaged?' sighed the fair Daisy, enviously. 'Oh, do tell me if this girl is really, really pretty.'

'Humph,' said the eyebrows, 'a pale, washed-out rag of a creature — but what can you expect from such a mother? No brains, no style, no conversation; always a simpering, weak-eyed rag baby. Oh, my dear, what fools men are!'

'Ah, you may well say that, dear Mrs Pansey,' assented the spinster, thinking wrathfully of this unknown girl who had succeeded where she had failed. 'Is it a very, very good match?'

'Ten thousand a year and a fine estate, my dear. Sir Harry is a nice young fellow, but a fool. An absentee landlord, too,' grumbled Mrs Pansey, resentfully. 'Always running over the world poking his nose into what doesn't concern him, like the Wandering Jew or the *Flying Dutchman*. Ah, my dear, husbands are not what they used to be. The late archdeacon never left his fireside while I was there. I knew better than to let him go to

Paris or Pekin, or some of those sinks of iniquity. Cook and Gaze indeed!' snorted Mrs Pansey, indignantly; 'I would abolish them by Act of Parliament. They turn men into so many Satans walking to and fro upon the earth. Oh, the immorality of these latter days! No wonder the end of all things is predicted.'

Miss Norsham paid little attention to the latter portion of this diatribe. As Sir Harry Brace was out of the matrimonial market it conveyed no information likely to be of use to her in the coming campaign. She wished to be informed as to the number and the names of eligible men, and forewarned with regard to possible rivals.

'And who is really and truly the most beautiful girl in Beorminster?' she asked abruptly.

'Mab Arden,' replied Mrs Pansey, promptly. 'There, now,' with an emphatic blow of her fan, 'she is pretty, if you like, though I daresay there is more art than nature about her.'

'Who is Mab Arden, dear Mrs Pansey?'

'She is Miss Whichello's niece, that's who she is.'

'Whichello? Oh, good gracious me! what a very, very funny name. Is Miss Whichello a foreigner?'

'Foreigner? Bah!' cried Mrs Pansey, like a stentorian ram, 'she belongs to a good old English family, and, in my opinion, she disgraces them thoroughly. A meddlesome old maid, who wants to foist her niece on to George Pendle; and she's likely to succeed, too,' added the lady, rubbing her nose with a vexed air, 'for the young ass is in love with Mab, although she is three years older than he is. Mr Cargrim also likes the girl, though I daresay it is money with him.'

'Really! Mr Cargrim?'

'Yes, he is the bishop's chaplain; a Jesuit in disguise I call him, with his moping and mowing and sneaky ways. Butter wouldn't melt in his mouth; oh, dear no! I gave my opinion about him pretty plainly to Dr Graham, I can tell you, and Graham's the only man with brains in this city of fools.'

'Is Dr Graham young?' asked Miss Norsham, in the faint hope that Mrs Pansey's list of inhabitants might include a wealthy bachelor.

'Young? He's sixty, if you call that young, and in his second childhood. An Atheist, too. Tom Payn, Colonel Ingersoll, Viscount Amberly — those are his gods, the pagan! I'd burn him on a tar-barrel if I had my way. It's a pity we don't stick to some customs of our ancestors.'

'Oh, dear me, are there no young men at all?'

'Plenty, and all idiots. Brainless officers,

whose wives would have to ride on a baggage-waggon; silly young squires, whose ideal of womanhood is a brazen barmaid; and simpering curates, put into the Church as the fools of their respective families. I don't know what men are coming to,' groaned Mrs Pansey. 'The late archdeacon was clever and pious; he honoured and obeyed me as the marriage service says a man should do. I was the light of the dear man's eyes.'

Had Mrs Pansey stated that she had been the terror of the late archdeacon's life she would have been vastly nearer the truth, but such a remark never occurred to her. Although she had bullied and badgered the wretched little man until he had seized the first opportunity of finding in the grave the peace denied him in life, she really and truly believed that she had been a model wife. The egotism of first person singular was so firmly ingrained in the woman that she could not conceive what a scourge she was to mankind in general; what a trial she had been to her poor departed husband in particular. If the late Archdeacon Pansey had not died he would doubtless have become a missionary to some cannibal tribe in the South Seas in the hope that his tough helpmate would be converted into 'long-pig.' But, unluckily for Beorminster, he was dead and his relict was a mourning widow, who constantly referred to her victim as a perfect husband. And yet Mrs Pansey considered that Anthony Trollope's celebrated Mrs Proudie was an overdrawn character.

As to Miss Norsham, she was in the depths of despair, for, if Mrs Pansey was to be believed, there was no eligible husband for her in Beorminster. It was with a heavy heart that the spinster entered the palace, and it was with the courage born of desperation that she perked up and smiled on the gay crowd she found within.

2

The Bishop is Wanted

The episcopalian residence, situate some distance from the city, was a mediæval building, enshrined in the remnant of a royal chase, and in its perfect quiet and loneliness resembled the palace of the Sleeping Beauty. Its composite architecture was of many centuries and many styles, for bishop after bishop had pulled down portions and added others, had levelled a tower here and erected a wing there, until the result was a jumble of divers designs, incongruous but picturesque. Time had mellowed the various parts into one rich coloured whole of perfect beauty, and elevated on a green rise, surrounded by broad stone terraces, with towers and oriels and turrets and machicolated battlements; clothed with ivy, buried amid ancient trees, it looked like the realisation of a poet's dream. Only long ages and many changing epochs; only home-loving prelates, ample monies, and architects of genius, could have created so beautiful and unique a fabric. It was the admiration of transatlantic tourists with a twang; the desire of millionaires. Aladdin's industrious genii would have failed to build such a masterpiece, unless their masters had arranged to inhabit it five centuries or so after construction. Time had created it, as Time would destroy it, but at present it was in perfect preservation, and figured in steel-plate engravings as one of the stately homes of England. No wonder the mitre of Beorminster was a coveted prize, when its gainer could dwell in so noble and matchless a mansion.

As the present prelate was an up-to-date bishop, abreast of his time and fond of his creature comforts, the interior of the palace was modernised completely in accordance with the luxurious demands of nineteenth-century civilisation. The stately reception-rooms — thrown open on this night to what the *Beorminster Weekly Chronicle,* strong in foreign tongues, tautologically called 'the *élite* and *crème de la crème* of the diocese' — were brilliantly illuminated by electric lamps and furnished magnificently throughout, in keeping with their palatial appearance. The ceilings were painted in the Italian style, with decently-clothed Olympian deities; the floors were of parquetry, polished so highly, and reflecting so truthfully, that the guests seemed to be walking, in some magical way, upon still water. Noble windows, extending from floor to roof, were draped with purple curtains, and stood open to the quiet moonlit world without; between these, tall mirrors flashed back gems and colours, moving figures and floods of amber radiance, and enhanced by reduplicated reflections the size of the rooms. Amid all this splendour of warmth and tints and light moved the numerous guests of the bishop. Almost every invitation had been accepted, for the receptions at the palace were on a large and liberal scale, particularly as regards eating and drinking. Dr Pendle, in addition to his official salary, possessed a handsome income, and spent it in the lavish style of a Cardinal Wolsey. He was wise enough to know how the outward and visible signs of prosperity and dignity affect the popular imagination, and frequently invited the clergy and laity to feast at the table of Mother Church, to show that she could dispense loaves and fishes with the best, and vie with Court and Society in the splendour and hospitality of her entertainments. As he approved of an imposing ritual at the cathedral, so he affected a magnificent way of living at the palace. Mrs Pansey and many others declared that Dr Pendle's aims in that direction were Romish. Perhaps they were, but he could scarcely have followed a better example, since the Church of Peter owes much of its power to a judicious employment of riches and ritual, and a dexterous gratification of the lust of the eye. The Anglican Church is more dignified now than she was in the days of the Georges, and very rightly, too, since God's ministers should not be the poorest or meanest of men.

Naturally, as the host was clerical and the building ecclesiastical, the clergy predominated at this entertainment. The bishop and the dean were the only prelates of their rank present, but there were archdeacons, and canons and rectors, and a plentiful supply of curates, all, in their own opinion, bishops in embryo. The shape and expression of the many faces were various — ascetic, worldly, pale, red, round, thin, fat, oval; each one revealed the character of its owner. Some lean, bent forms were those of men filled with the fire of religion for its own sake; others, stout, jolly gentlemen in comfortable livings, loved the loaves and fishes of the Church as much as her precepts. The descendants of Friar Tuck and the Vicar of Bray were here, as well as those who would have been Wycliffes and Latimers had the fires of Smithfield still been alight. Obsequious curates bowed down to pompous prebendaries; bluff rectors chatted on cordial terms with suave archdeacons; and in the fold of the Church there were no black sheep on this great occasion. The shepherds and pastors of the Beorminster flock were polite, entertaining, amusing, and not too masterful, so that the general air was quite arcadian.

The laity also formed a strong force. There were lords magnificently condescending to commoners; M.P.s who talked politics, and M.P.s who had had enough of that sort of thing at St Stephen's and didn't; hearty squires from adjacent county seats; prim bankers, with whom the said squires were anxious to be on good terms, since they were the priests of Mammon; officers from near garrison towns, gay and lighthearted, who devoted themselves to the fairer portion of the company; and a sprinkling of barristers, literary men, hardy explorers, and such like minnows among Tritons. Last, but not least, the Mayor of Beorminster was present and posed as a modern Whittington — half commercial wealth, half municipal dignity. If some envious Anarchist had exploded a dynamite bomb in the vicinity of the palace on that night, the greatest, the most intellectual, the richest people of the county would have come to an untimely end, and then the realm of England, like the people themselves, would have gone to pieces. The *Beorminster Chronicle* reporter — also present with a flimsy book and a restless little pencil — worked up this idea on the spot into a glowing paragraph.

Very ungallantly the ladies have been left to the last; but now the last shall be first, although it is difficult to do the subject justice. The matrons of surrounding parishes, the ladies of Beorminster society, the damsels of town and country, were all present in their best attire, chattering and smiling, and becking and bowing, after the observant and diplomatic ways of their sex. Such white shoulders! such pretty faces! such Parisian toilettes! such dresses of obviously home manufacture never were seen in one company. The married ladies whispered scandal behind their fans, and in a Christian spirit shot out the lip of scorn at their social enemies; the young maidens sought for marriageable men, and lurked in darkish corners for the better ensnaring of impressionable males. Cupid unseen mingled in the throng and shot his arrows right and left, not always with the best result, as many post-nuptial experiences showed. There was talk of the gentle art of needlework, of the latest bazaar and the agreeable address delivered thereat by Mr Cargrim; the epicene pastime of lawn tennis was touched upon; and ardent young persons discussed how near they could go to Giant Pope's cave without getting into the clutches of its occupant. The young men talked golfing, parish work, horses, church, male millinery, polo and shooting; the young ladies chatted about Paris fashions and provincial adaptations thereof, the London season, the latest engagement, and the necessity of reviving the flirtatious game of croquet. Black coats, coloured dresses, flashing jewels, many-hued flowers, — the restless crowd resembled a bed of gaudy tulips tossed by the wind. And all this chattering, laughing, clattering, glittering mass of well-bred, well-groomed humanity moved, and swayed, and gyrated under the white glare of the electric lamps. Urbs in Rus; Belgravia in the Provinces; Vanity Fair amid the cornfields; no wonder this entertainment of Bishop and Mrs Pendle was the event of the Beorminster year.

Like an agreeable Jupiter amid adoring mortals, the bishop, with his chaplain in attendance, moved through the rooms, bestowing a word here, a smile there, and a hearty welcome on all. A fine-looking man was the Bishop of Beorminster; as stately in appearance as any prelate drawn by Du Maurier. He was over six feet, and carried himself in a soldierly fashion, as became a leader of the Church Militant. His legs were all that could be desired to fill out episcopalian gaiters; and his bland, clean-shaven face beamed with smiles and benignity. But Bishop Pendle was not the mere figure-head Mrs Pansey's malice declared him to be; he had great administrative powers, great organising capabilities, and controlled his diocese in a way which did equal credit to his heart and head. As he chatted with his guests and did the honours of the palace, he seemed to be the happiest of men, and well worthy of his exalted post. With a splendid position, a charming wife, a fine family, an obedient flock of clergy and laity, the bishop's lines were cast in pleasant places. There was not even the proverbial crumpled rose-leaf to render uncomfortable the bed he had made for himself. He was like an ecclesiastical Jacob — blessed above all men.

'Well, bishop!' said Dr Graham, a meagre sceptic, who did not believe in the endurance of human felicity, 'I congratulate you.'

'On my daughter's engagement?' asked the prelate, smiling pleasantly.

'On everything. Your position, your family, your health, your easy conscience; all is too smooth, too well with you. It can't last, your lordship, it can't last,' and the doctor shook his bald head, as no doubt Solon did at Crœsus when he snubbed that too-fortunate monarch.

'I am indeed blessed in the condition of life to which God has been pleased to call me.'

'No doubt! No doubt! But remember Polycrates, bishop, and throw your ring into the sea.'

'My dear Dr Graham,' said the bishop, rather stiffly, 'I do not believe in such paganism. God has blessed me beyond my deserts, no doubt, and I thank Him in all reverence for His kindly care.'

'Hum! Hum!' muttered Graham, shaking his head. 'When men thank fortune for her gifts she usually turns her back on them.'

'I am no believer in such superstitions, doctor.'

'Well, well, bishop, you have tempted the gods, let us see what they will do.'

'Gods or God, doctor?' demanded the bishop, with magnificent displeasure.

'Whichever you like, my lord; whichever you like.'

The bishop was nettled and rather chilled by this pessimism. He felt that it was his duty as a Churchman to administer a rebuke; but Dr Graham's pagan views were well known, and a correction, however dexterously administered, would only lead to an argument. A controversy with Graham was no joke, as he was as subtle as Socrates in discovering and attacking his adversary's weak points; so, not judging the present a fitting occasion to risk a fall, the bishop smoothed away an incipient frown, and blandly smiling, moved on, followed by his chaplain. Graham looked grimly after this modern Cardinal Wolsey.

'I have never,' soliloquised the sceptic, 'I have never known a man without his skeleton. I wonder if you have one, my lord. You look cheerful, you seem thoroughly happy; but you are too fortunate. If you have not a skeleton now, I feel convinced you will have to build a cupboard for one shortly. You thank blind fortune under the alias of God? Well! well! we shall see the result of your thanks. Wolsey! Napoleon! Bismarck! they all fell when most prosperous. Hum! hum! hum!'

Dr Graham had no reason to make this speech, beyond his belief — founded upon experience — that calms are always succeeded by storms. At present the bishop stood under a serene sky; and in no quarter could Graham descry the gathering of the tempest he prophesied. But for all that he had a premonition that evil days were at hand; and, sceptic as he was, he could not shake off the uneasy feeling. His mother had been a Highland woman, and the Celt is said to be gifted with second sight. Perhaps Graham inherited the maternal gift of forecasting the future, for he glanced ominously at the stately form of his host, and shook his head. He thought the bishop was too confident of continuous sunshine.

In the meantime, Dr Pendle, quite free from such forebodings, unfortunately came within speaking distance of Mrs Pansey, who, in her bell of St Paul's voice, was talking to a group of meek listeners. Daisy Norsham had long ago seized upon Gabriel Pendle, and was chatting with him on the edge of the circle, quite heedless of her chaperon's monologue. When Mrs Pansey saw the bishop she swooped down on him before he could get out of the way, which he would have done had courtesy permitted it. Mrs Pansey was the one person Dr Pendle dreaded, and if the late archdeacon had been alive he would have encouraged the missionary project with all his heart. 'To every man his own fear.' Mrs Pansey was the bishop's.

'Bishop!' cried the lady, in her most impressive archidiaconal manner, 'about that public-house, The Derby Winner, it must be removed.'

Cargrim, who was deferentially smiling at his lordship's elbow, cast a swift glance at Gabriel when he heard Mrs Pansey's remark. He had a belief — founded upon spying — that Gabriel knew too much about the public-house mentioned, which was in his district; and this belief was strengthened when he saw the young man start at the sound of the name. Instinctively he kept his eyes on Gabriel's face, which looked disturbed and anxious; too much so for social requirements.

'It must be removed,' repeated the bishop, gently; 'and why, Mrs Pansey?'

'Why, bishop? You ask why? Because it is a hot-bed of vice and betting and gambling; that's why!'

'But I really cannot see — I have not the power — '

'It's near the cathedral, too,' interrupted Mrs Pansey, whose manners left much to be desired. 'Scandalous!

'When God erects a house of prayer,

'The devil builds a chapel there.

'Isn't it your duty to eradicate plague-spots, bishop?'

Before Dr Pendle could answer this rude question, a servant approached and spoke in a whisper to his master. The bishop looked surprised.

'A man to see me at this hour — at this time,' said he, repeating the message aloud. 'Who is he? What is his name?'

'I don't know, your lordship. He refused to give his name, but he insists upon seeing your lordship at once.'

'I can't see him!' said the bishop, sharply; 'let him call to-morrow.'

'My lord, he says it is a matter of life and death.'

Dr Pendle frowned. 'Most unbecoming language!' he murmured. 'Perhaps it may be as well to humour him. Where is he?'

'In the entrance hall, your lordship!'

'Take him into the library and say I will see him shortly. Most unusual,' said the bishop to himself. Then added aloud, 'Mrs Pansey, I am called away for a moment; pray excuse me.'

'We must talk about The Derby Winner later on,' said Mrs Pansey, determinedly.

'Oh, yes! — that is — really — I'll see.'

'Shall I accompany your lordship?' murmured Cargrim, officiously.

'No, Mr Cargrim, it is not necessary. I must see this man as he speaks so strongly, but I daresay he is only some pertinacious person who thinks that a bishop should be at the complete disposal of the public — the exacting public!'

With this somewhat petulant speech Dr Pendle walked away, not sorry to find an opportunity of slipping out of a noisy argument with Mrs Pansey. That lady's parting words were that she should expect him back in ten minutes to settle the question of The Derby Winner; or rather to hear how she intended to settle it. Cargrim, pleased at being left behind, since it gave him a chance of watching Gabriel, urged Mrs Pansey to further discussion of the question, and had the satisfaction of seeing that such discussion visibly disconcerted the curate.

And Dr Pendle? In all innocence he left the reception-rooms to speak with his untoward visitor in the library; but although he knew it not, he was entering upon a dark and tortuous path, the end of which he was not destined to see for many a long day. Dr Graham's premonition was likely to prove true, for in the serene sky under which the bishop had moved for so long, a tempest was gathering fast. He should have taken the doctor's advice and have sacrificed his ring like Polycrates, but, as in the case of that old pagan, the gods might have tossed back the gift and pursued their relentless aims. The bishop had no thoughts like these. As yet he had no skeleton, but the man in the library was about to open a cupboard and let out its grisly tenant to haunt prosperous Bishop Pendle. To him, as to all men, evil had come at the appointed hour.

3

The Unforeseen Happens

'I fear,' said Cargrim, with a gentle sigh, 'I fear you are right about that public-house, Mrs Pansey.'

The chaplain made this remark to renew the discussion, and if possible bring Gabriel into verbal conflict with the lady. He had a great idea of managing people by getting them under his thumb, and so far quite deserved Mrs Pansey's epithet of a Jesuit. Of late — as Cargrim knew by a steady use of his pale blue eyes — the curate had been visiting The Derby Winner, ostensibly on parochial business connected with the ill-health of Mrs Mosk, the landlord's wife. But there was a handsome daughter of the invalid who acted as barmaid, and Gabriel was a young and inflammable man; so, putting this and that together, the chaplain thought he discovered the germs of a scandal. Hence his interest in Mrs Pansey's proposed reforms.

'Right!' echoed the archidiaconal widow, loudly, 'of course I am right. The Derby Winner is a nest of hawks. William Mosk would have disgraced heathen Rome in its worst days; as for his daughter — well!' Mrs Pansey threw a world of horror into the ejaculation.

'Miss Mosk is a well-conducted young lady,' said Gabriel, growing red and injudicious.

'Lady!' bellowed Mrs Pansey, shaking her fan; 'and since when have brazen, painted barmaids become ladies, Mr Pendle?'

'She is most attentive to her sick mother,' protested the curate, wincing.

'No doubt, sir. I presume even Jezebel had some redeeming qualities. Rubbish! humbug! don't tell me! Can good come out of Nazareth?'

'Good did come out of Nazareth, Mrs Pansey.'

'That is enough, Mr Pendle; do not pollute young ears with blasphemy. And you the son of a bishop — the curate of a parish! Remember what is to be the portion of mockers, sir. What happened to the men who threw stones at David?'

'Oh, but really, dear Mrs Pansey, you know Mr Pendle is not throwing stones.'

'People who live in glass houses dare not, my dear. I doubt your interest in this young person, Mr Pendle. She is one who tires her head and paints her face, lying in wait for comely youths that she may destroy them. She — '

'Excuse me, Mrs Pansey!' cried Gabriel, with an angry look, 'you speak too freely and too ignorantly. The Derby Winner is a well-conducted house, for Mrs Mosk looks after it personally, and her daughter is an excellent young woman. I do not defend the father, but I hope to bring him to a sense of his errors in time. There is a charity which thinketh no evil, Mrs Pansey,' and with great heat Gabriel, forgetting his manners, walked off without taking leave of either the lady or Miss Norsham. Mrs Pansey tossed her turban and snorted, but seeing very plainly that she had gone too far, held for once her virulent tongue. Cargrim rubbed his hands and laughed softly.

'Our young friend talks warmly, Mrs Pansey. The natural chivalry of youth, my dear lady — nothing more.'

'I'll make it my business to assure myself that it *is* nothing more,' said Mrs Pansey, in low tones. 'I fear very much that the misguided young man has fallen into the lures of this daughter of Heth. Do you know anything about her, Mr Cargrim?'

Too wise to commit himself to speech, the chaplain cast up his pale eyes and looked volumes. This was quite enough for Mrs Pansey; she scented evil like a social vulture, and taking Cargrim's arm dragged him away to find out all the bad she could about The Derby Winner and its too-attractive barmaid.

Left to herself, Miss Norsham seized upon Dean Alder, to whom she had been lately introduced, and played with the artillery of her eyes on that unattractive churchman. Mr Dean was old and wizen, but he was unmarried and rich, so Miss Norsham thought it might be worth her while to play Vivien to this clerical Merlin. His weak point, — speedily discovered, — was archæology, and she was soon listening to a dry description of his researches into Beorminster municipal chronicles. But it was desperately hard work to fix her attention.

'Beorminster,' explained the pedantic dean, not unmoved by his listener's artificial charms, 'is derived from two Anglo-Saxon words — Bëorh, a hill, and mynster, the church of a monastery. Anciently, our city was called Bëorhmynster, 'the church of the hill,' for, as you can see, my dear young lady, our cathedral is built on the top of a considerable rise, and thence gained its name. The townsfolk were formerly vassals, and even serfs, of the monastery which was destroyed by Henry VIII; but the Reformation brought about by that king put an end to the abbot's power. The head of the Bëorhmynster monastery was a mitred abbot — '

'And Bishop Pendle is a mitred bishop,' interposed the fair Daisy, to show the quickness of her understanding, and thereby displaying her ignorance.

'All bishops are mitred,' said Dr Alder, testily; 'a crozier and a mitre are the symbols of their high office. But the Romish abbots of Bëorhmynster were not bishops although they were mitred prelates.'

'Oh, how very, very amusing,' cried Daisy, suppressing a yawn. 'And the name of the river, dear Mr Dean? Does Beorflete mean 'the church of the hill' too?'

'Certainly not, Miss Norsham. 'Flete,' formerly 'fleot,' is a Scandinavian word and signifies 'a flood,' 'a stream,' 'a channel.' Bëorhfleot, or — as we now erroneously call it — Beorflete, means, in the vulgar tongue, the flood or stream of the hill. Even in Normandy the word fleot has been corrupted, for the town now called Harfleur was formerly correctly designated 'Havoflete.' But I am afraid you find this information dull, Miss Norsham!'

This last remark was occasioned by Daisy yawning. It is true that she held a fan, and had politely hidden her mouth when yawning; unfortunately, the fan was of transparent material, and Daisy quite forgot that Mr Dean could see the yawn, which he certainly did. In some confusion she extricated herself from an awkward situation by protesting that she was not tired but hungry, and suggested that Dr Alder should continue his instructive conversation at supper. Mollified by this dexterous evasion, which he saw no reason to disbelieve, the dean politely escorted his companion to the regions of champagne and chicken, both of which aided the lady to sustain further doses of dry-as-dust facts dug out of a monastic past by the persevering Dr Alder. It was in this artful fashion that the town mouse strove to ensnare the church mouse, and succeeded so well that when Mr Dean went home to his lonely house he concluded that it was just as well the monastic institution of celibacy had been abolished.

On leaving Mrs Pansey in disgust, Gabriel proceeded with considerable heat into the next room, where his mother held her court as hostess. Mrs Pendle was a pale, slight, small-framed woman with golden hair, languid eyes, and a languid manner. Owing to her delicate health she could not stand for any length of time, and therefore occupied a large and comfortable arm-chair. Her daughter Lucy, who resembled her closely in looks, but who had more colour in her face, stood near at hand talking to her lover. Both ladies were dressed in white silk, with few ornaments, and looked more like sisters than mother and daughter. Certainly Mrs Pendle appeared surprisingly young to be the parent of a grown-up family, but her continuance of youth was not due to art, as Mrs Pansey averred, but to the quiet and undisturbed life which her frail health compelled her to lead. The bishop was tenderly attached to her, and even at this late stage of their married life behaved towards her more like a lover than a husband. He warded off all worries and troubles from her; he surrounded her with pleasant people, and made her life luxurious and peaceful by every means obtainable in the way of money and influence. It was no wonder that Mrs Pendle, treading the Primrose Path with a devoted and congenial companion, appeared still young. She looked as fair and fragile as a peri, and as free from mortal cares.

'Is that you, Gabriel?' she said in a low, soft voice, smiling gently on her younger and favourite son. 'You look disturbed, my dear boy!'

'Mrs Pansey!' said Gabriel, and considering that the name furnished all necessary information, sat down near his mother and took one of her delicate hands in his own to smooth and fondle.

'Oh, indeed! Mrs Pansey!' echoed the bishop's wife, smiling still more; and with a slight shrug cast an amused look at Lucy, who in her turn caught Sir Harry's merry eyes and laughed outright.

'Old catamaran!' said Brace, loudly.

'Oh, Harry! Hush!' interposed Lucy, with an anxious glance. 'You shouldn't.'

'Why not? But for the present company I would say something much stronger.'

'I wish you would,' said Gabriel, easing his stiff collar with one finger; 'my cloth forbids me to abuse Mrs Pansey properly.'

'What has she been doing now, Gabriel?'

'Ordering the bishop to have The Derby Winner removed, mother.'

'The Derby Winner,' repeated Mrs Pendle, in puzzled tones; 'is that a horse?'

'A public-house, mother; it is in my district, and I have been lately visiting the wife of the landlord, who is very ill. Mrs Pansey wants the house closed and the woman turned out into the streets, so far as I can make out!'

'The Derby Winner is my property,' said Sir Harry, bluffly, 'and it sha'n't be shut up for a dozen Mrs Panseys.'

'Think of a dozen Mrs Panseys,' murmured Lucy, pensively.

'Think of Bedlam and Pandemonium, my

dear! Thank goodness Mrs Pansey is the sole specimen of her kind. Nature broke the mould when that clacking nuisance was turned out. She — '

'Harry! you really must not speak so loud. Mrs Pansey might hear. Come with me, dear. I must look after our guests, for I am sure mother is tired.'

'I *am* tired,' assented Mrs Pendle, with a faint sigh. 'Thank you, Lucy, I willingly make you my representative. Gabriel will stay beside me.'

'Here is Miss Tancred,' observed Harry Brace, in an undertone.

'Oh, she must not come near mother,' whispered Lucy, in alarm. 'Take her to the supper-room, Harry.'

'But she'll tell me the story of how she lost her purse at the Army and Navy Stores, Lucy.'

'You can bear hearing it better than mother can. Besides, she'll not finish it; she never does.'

Sir Harry groaned, but like an obedient lover intercepted a withered old dame who was the greatest bore in the town. She usually told a digressive story about a lost purse, but hitherto had never succeeded in getting to the point, if there was one. Accepting the suggestion of supper with alacrity, she drifted away on Sir Harry's arm, and no doubt mentioned the famous purse before he managed to fill her mouth and stop her prosing.

Lucy, who had a quiet humour of her own in spite of her demure looks, laughed at the dejection and martyrdom of Sir Harry; and taking the eagerly-proffered arm of a callow lieutenant, ostentatiously and hopelessly in love with her, went away to play her part of deputy hostess. She moved from group to group, and everywhere received smiles and congratulations, for she was a general favourite, and, with the exception of Mrs Pansey, everyone approved of her engagement. Behind a floral screen a band of musicians, who called themselves the Yellow Hungarians, and individually possessed the most unpronounceable names, played the last waltz, a smooth, swinging melody which made the younger guests long for a dance. In fact, the callow lieutenant boldly suggested that a waltz should be attempted, with himself and Lucy to set the example; but his companion snubbed him unmercifully for his boldness, and afterwards restored his spirits by taking him to the supper-room. Here they found Miss Tancred in the full flow of her purse story; so Lucy, having pity on her lover, bestowed her escort on the old lady as a listener, and enjoyed supper at an isolated table with Sir Harry. The sucking Wellington could have murdered Brace with pleasure, and very nearly did murder Miss Tancred, for he plied her so constantly with delicacies that she got indigestion, and was thereby unable to finish about the purse.

Gabriel and his mother were not long left alone, for shortly there approached a brisk old lady, daintily dressed, who looked like a fairy godmother. She had a keen face, bright eyes like those of a squirrel, and in gesture and walk and glance was as restless as that animal. This piece of alacrity was Miss Whichello, who was the aunt of Mab Arden, the beloved of George Pendle. Mab was with her, and, gracious and tall, looked as majestic as any queen, as she paced in her stately manner by the old lady's side. Her beauty was that of Juno, for she was imperial and a trifle haughty in her manner. With dark hair, dark eyes, and dark complexion, she looked like an Oriental princess, quite different in appearance to her apple-cheeked, silvery-haired aunt. There was something Jewish about her rich, eastern beauty, and she might have been painted in her yellow dress as Esther or Rebecca, or even as Jael who slew Sisera on the going down of the sun.

'Well, good folks,' said the brisk little lady

in a brisk little voice, 'and how are you both? Tired, Mrs Pendle? Of course, what else can you expect with late hours and your delicacies. I don't believe in these social gatherings.'

'Your presence here contradicts that assertion,' said Gabriel, giving up his chair.

'Oh, I am a martyr to duty. I came because Mab must be amused!'

'I only hope she is not disappointed,' said Mrs Pendle, kindly, for she knew how things were between her eldest son and the girl. 'I am sorry George is not here, my dear.'

'I did not expect him to be,' replied Mab, in her grave, contralto voice, and with a blush; 'he told me that he would not be able to get leave from his colonel.'

'Ha! his colonel knows what is good for young men,' cried Miss Whichello; 'work and diet both in moderate quantities. My dear Mrs Pendle, if you only saw those people in the supper-room! — simply digging their graves with their teeth. I pity the majority of them to-morrow morning.'

'Have you had supper, Miss Whichello?' asked Gabriel.

'Oh, yes! a biscuit and a glass of weak whisky and water; quite enough, too. Mab here has been drinking champagne recklessly.'

'Only half a glass, aunt; don't take away my character!'

‘My dear, if you take half a glass, you may as well finish the bottle for the harm it does you. Champagne is poison; much or little, it is rank poison.’

‘Come away, Miss Arden, and let us poison ourselves,’ suggested the curate.

‘It wouldn’t do you any harm, Mrs Pendle,’ cried the little old lady. ‘You are too pale, and champagne, in your case, would pick you up. Iron and slight stimulants are what *you* need. I am afraid you are not careful what you eat.’

‘I am not a dietitian, Miss Whichello.’

‘I am, my dear ma’am; and look at me — sixty-two, and as brisk as a bee. I don’t know the meaning of the word illness. In a good hour be it spoken,’ added Miss Whichello, thinking she was tempting the gods. ‘By the way, what is this about his lordship being ill?’

‘The bishop ill!’ faltered Mrs Pendle, half rising. ‘He was perfectly well when I saw him last. Oh, dear me, what is this?’

‘He’s ill now, in the library, at all events.’

‘Wait, mother,’ said Gabriel, hastily. ‘I will see my father. Don’t rise; don’t worry yourself; pray be calm.’

Gabriel walked quickly to the library, rather astonished to hear that his father was indisposed, for the bishop had never had a day’s illness in his life. He saw by the demeanour of the guests that the indisposition of their host was known, for already an uneasy feeling prevailed, and several people were departing. The door of the library was closed and locked. Cargrim was standing sentinel beside it, evidently irate at being excluded.

'You can't go in, Pendle,' said the chaplain, quickly. 'Dr Graham is with his lordship.'

'Is this sudden illness serious?'

'I don't know. His lordship refuses to see anyone but the doctor. He won't even admit me,' said Cargrim, in an injured tone.

'What has caused it?' asked Gabriel, in dismay.

'I don't know!' replied Cargrim, a second time. 'His lordship saw some stranger who departed ten minutes ago. Then he sent for Dr Graham! I presume this stranger is responsible for the bishop's illness.'

4

The Curiosity of Mr Cargrim

Like that famous banquet, when Macbeth entertained unawares the ghost of gracious Duncan, the bishop's reception broke up in the most admired disorder. It was not Dr Pendle's wish that the entertainment should be cut short on his account, but the rumour — magnified greatly — of his sudden illness so dispirited his guests that they made haste to depart; and within an hour the palace was emptied of all save its usual inhabitants. Dr Graham in attendance on the bishop was the only stranger who remained, for Lucy sent away even Sir Harry, although he begged hard to stay in the hope of making himself useful. And the most unpleasant part of the whole incident was, that no one seemed to know the reason of Bishop Pendle's unexpected indisposition.

'He was quite well when I saw him last,' repeated poor Mrs Pendle over and over again. 'And I never knew him to be ill before. What does it all mean?'

'Perhaps papa's visitor brought him bad

news,' suggested Lucy, who was hovering round her mother with smelling-salts and a fan.

Mrs Pendle shook her head in much distress. 'Your father has no secrets from me,' she said decisively, 'and, from all I know, it is impossible that any news can have upset him so much.'

'Dr Graham may be able to explain,' said Gabriel.

'I don't want Dr Graham's explanation,' whimpered Mrs Pendle, tearfully. 'I dislike of all things to hear from a stranger what should be told to myself. As your father's wife, he has no right to shut me out of his confidence — and the library,' finished Mrs Pendle, with an aggrieved afterthought.

Certainly the bishop's conduct was very strange, and would have upset even a less nervous woman than Mrs Pendle. Neither of her children could comfort her in any way, for, ignorant themselves of what had occurred, they could make no suggestions. Fortunately, at this moment, Dr Graham, with a reassuring smile on his face, made his appearance, and proceeded to set their minds at ease.

'Tut! tut! my dear lady!' he said briskly, advancing on Mrs Pendle, 'what is all this?'

'The bishop — '

'The bishop is suffering from a slight

indisposition brought on by too much exertion in entertaining. He will be all right to-morrow.'

'This visitor has had nothing to do with papa's illness, then?'

'No, Miss Lucy. The visitor was only a decayed clergyman in search of help.'

'Cannot I see my husband?' was the anxious question of the bishop's wife.

Graham shrugged his shoulders, and looked doubtfully at the poor lady. 'Better not, Mrs Pendle,' he said judiciously. 'I have given him a soothing draught, and now he is about to lie down. There is no occasion for you to worry in the least. To-morrow morning you will be laughing over this needless alarm. I suggest that you should go to bed and take a stiff dose of valerian to sooth those shaky nerves of yours. Miss Lucy will see to that.'

'I should like to see the bishop,' persisted Mrs Pendle, whose instinct told her that the doctor was deceiving her.

'Well! well!' said he, good-humouredly, 'a wilful woman will have her own way. I know you won't sleep a wink unless your mind is set at rest, so you *shall* see the bishop. Take my arm, please.'

'I can walk by myself, thank you!' replied Mrs Pendle, testily; and nerved to unusual exertion by anxiety, she walked towards the library, followed by the bishop's family and his chaplain, which latter watched this scene with close attention.

'She'll collapse after this,' said Dr Graham, in an undertone to Lucy; 'you'll have a wakeful night, I fear.'

'I don't mind that, doctor, so long as there is no real cause for alarm.'

'I give you my word of honour, Miss Lucy, that this is a case of much ado about nothing.'

'Let us hope that such is the case,' said Cargrim, the Jesuit, in his softest tones, whereupon Graham looked at him with a pronounced expression of dislike.

'As a man, I don't tell lies; as a doctor, I never make false reports,' said he, coldly; 'there is no need for your pious hopes, Mr Cargrim.'

The bishop was seated at his desk scribbling idly on his blotting-pad, and rose to his feet with a look of alarm when his wife and family entered. His usually ruddy colour had disappeared, and he was white-faced and haggard in appearance; looking like a man who had received a severe shock, and who had not yet recovered from it. On seeing his wife, he smiled reassuringly, but with an obvious effort, and hastened to conduct her to the chair he had vacated.

'Now, my dear,' he said, when she was seated, 'this will never do.'

'I am so anxious, George!'

'There is no need to be anxious,' retorted the bishop, in reproving tones. 'I have been doing too much work of late, and unexpectedly I was seized with a faintness. Graham's medicine and a night's rest will restore me to my usual strength.'

'It's not your heart, I trust, George?'

'His heart!' jested the doctor. 'His lordship's heart is as sound as his digestion.'

'We thought you might have been upset by bad news, papa.'

'I have had no bad news, Lucy. I am only a trifle overcome by late hours and fatigue. Take your mother to bed; and you, my dear,' added the bishop, kissing his wife, 'don't worry yourself unnecessarily. Good-night, and good sleep.'

'Some valerian for your nerves, bishop — '

'I have taken something for my nerves, Amy. Rest is all I need just now.'

Thus reassured, Mrs Pendle submitted to be led from the library by Lucy. She was followed by Gabriel, who was now quite easy in his mind about his father. Cargrim and Graham remained, but the bishop, taking no notice of their presence, looked at the door through which his wife and children had vanished, and uttered a sound something between a sigh and a groan.

Dr Graham looked anxiously at him, and the look was intercepted by Cargrim, who at once made up his mind that there was something seriously wrong, which both Graham and the bishop desired to conceal. The doctor noted the curious expression in the chaplain's eyes, and with bluff good-humour — which was assumed, as he disliked the man — proceeded to turn him out of the library. Cargrim — bent on discovering the truth — protested, in his usual cat-like way, against this sudden dismissal.

'I should be happy to sit up all night with his lordship,' he declared.

'Sit up with your grandmother!' cried Graham, gruffly. 'Go to bed, sir, and don't make mountains out of molehills.'

'Good-night, my lord,' said Cargrim, softly. 'I trust you will find yourself fully restored in the morning.'

'Thank you, Mr Cargrim; good-night!'

When the chaplain sidled out of the room, Dr Graham rubbed his hands and turned briskly towards his patient, who was standing as still as any stone, staring in a hypnotised sort of way at the reading lamp on the desk.

'Come, my lord,' said he, touching the bishop on the shoulder, 'you must take your composing draught and get to bed. You'll be all right in the morning.'

'I trust so!' replied Pendle, with a groan.

'Of course, bishop, if you won't tell me what is the matter with you, I can't cure you.'

'I am upset, doctor, that is all.'

'You have had a severe nervous shock,' said Graham, sharply, 'and it will take some time for you to recover from it. This visitor brought you bad news, I suppose?'

'No!' said the bishop, wincing, 'he did not.'

'Well! well! keep your own secrets. I can do no more, so I'll say good-night,' and he held out his hand.

Dr Pendle took it and retained it within his own for a moment. 'Your allusion to the ring of Polycrates, Graham!'

'What of it?'

'I should throw my ring into the sea also. That is all.'

'Ha! ha! You'll have to travel a considerable distance to reach the sea, bishop. Good-night; good-night,' and Graham, smiling in his dry way, took himself out of the room. As he glanced back at the door he saw that the bishop was again staring dully at the reading lamp. Graham shook his head at the sight, and closed the door.

'It is mind, not matter,' he thought, as he put on hat and coat in the hall; 'the cupboard's open and the skeleton is out. My premonition was true — true. Æsculapius forgive me that I should be so superstitious. The bishop has had a shock. What is it? what is it? That visitor brought bad news! Hum! Hum! Better to throw physic to the dogs in his case. Mind diseased: secret trouble: my punishment is greater than I can bear. Put this and that together; there is something serious the matter. Well! well! I'm no Paul Pry.'

'Is his lordship better?' said the soft voice of Cargrim at his elbow.

Graham wheeled round. 'Much better; good-night,' he replied curtly, and was off in a moment.

Michael Cargrim, the chaplain, was a dangerous man. He was thin and pale, with light blue eyes and sleek fair hair; and as weak physically as he was strong mentally. In his neat clerical garb, with a slight stoop and meek smile, he looked a harmless, commonplace young curate of the tabby cat kind. No one could be more tactful and ingratiating than Mr Cargrim, and he was greatly admired by the old ladies and young girls of Beorminster; but the men, one and all — even his clerical brethren — disliked and distrusted him, although there was no apparent reason for their doing so. Perhaps his too-deferential manners and pronounced effeminacy, which made him shun manly sports, had something to do with his masculine unpopularity; but, from the bishop downward, he was certainly no favourite, and in every male breast he constantly inspired a desire to kick him. The clergy of the diocese maintained towards him a kind of 'Dr Fell' attitude, and none of them had more to do with him than they could help. With all the will in the world, with all the desire to interpret brotherly love in its most liberal sense, the Beorminster Levites found it impossible to like Mr Cargrim. Hence he was a kind of clerical Ishmael, and as dangerous within as he looked harmless without.

How such a viper came to warm itself on the bishop's hearth no one could say. Mrs Pansey herself did not know in what particular way Mr Cargrim had wriggled himself — so she expressed it — into his present snug position. But, to speak frankly, there was no wriggling in the matter, and had the bishop felt himself called upon to explain his business to anyone, he could have given a very reasonable account of the election of Cargrim to the post of chaplain. The young man was the son of an old schoolfellow, to whom Pendle had been much attached, and from whom, in the earlier part of his career, he had received many kindnesses. This schoolfellow — he was a banker — had become a bankrupt, a beggar, finally a suicide, through no fault of his own, and when dying, had commended his wife and son to the bishop's care. Cargrim was then fifteen years of age, and being clever and calculating, even as a youth, had determined to utilise the bishop's affection for his father to its fullest extent. He was clever, as has been stated; he was also ambitious and unscrupulous; therefore he resolved to enter the profession in which Dr Pendle's influence would be of most value. For this reason, and not because he felt a call to the work, he entered holy orders. The result of his wisdom was soon apparent, for after a short career as a curate in London, he was appointed chaplain to the Bishop of Beorminster.

So far, so good. The position, for a young man of twenty-eight, was by no means a bad one; the more so as it gave him a capital opportunity of gaining a better one by watching for the vacancy of a rich preferment and getting it from his patron by asking directly and immediately for it. Cargrim had in his eye the rectorship of a wealthy, easy-going parish, not far from Beorminster, which was in the gift of the bishop. The present holder was aged and infirm, and given so much to indulgence in port wine, that the chances were he might expire within a few months, and then, as the chaplain hoped, the next rector would be the Reverend Michael Cargrim. Once that firm position was obtained, he could bend his energies to developing into an archdeacon, a dean, even into a bishop, should his craft and fortune serve him as he intended they should. But in all these ambitious dreams there was nothing of religion, or of conscience, or of self-denial. If ever there was a square peg which tried to adapt itself to a round hole, Michael Cargrim, allegorically speaking, was that article.

With all his love for the father, Dr Pendle could never bring himself to like the son, and determined in his own mind to confer a benefice on him when possible, if only to get rid of him; but not the rich one of Heathcroft, which was the delectable land of Cargrim's desire. The bishop intended to bestow that on Gabriel; and Cargrim, in his sneaky way, had gained some inkling of this intention. Afraid of losing his wished-for prize, he was bent upon forcing Dr Pendle into presenting him with the living of Heathcroft; and to accomplish this amiable purpose with the more certainty he had conceived the plan of somehow getting the bishop into his power.

Hitherto — so open and stainless was Dr Pendle's life — he had not succeeded in his aims; but now matters looked more promising, for the bishop appeared to possess a secret which he guarded even from the knowledge of his wife. What this secret might be, Cargrim could not guess, in spite of his anxiety to do so, but he intended in one way or another to discover it and utilise it for the furtherance and attainment of his own selfish ends. By gaining such forbidden knowledge he hoped to get Dr Pendle well under his thumb; and once there the prelate could be kept in that uncomfortable position until he gratified Mr Cargrim's ambition. For a humble chaplain to have the whip-hand of a powerful ecclesiastic was a glorious and easy way for a meritorious young man to succeed in his profession. Having come to this conclusion, which did more credit to his head than to his heart, Cargrim sought out the servant who had summoned the bishop to see the stranger. A full acquaintance with the circumstances of the visit was necessary to the development of the Reverend Michael's ingenious little plot.

'This is a sad thing about his lordship's indisposition,' said he to the man in the most casual way, for it would not do to let the servant know that he was being questioned for a doubtful purpose.

'Yes, sir,' replied the man. ''Tis mos' extraordinary. I never knowed his lordship took ill before. I suppose that gentleman brought bad news, sir.'

'Possibly, John, possibly. Was this gentleman a short man with light hair? I fancy I saw him.'

'Lor', no, Mr Cargrim. He was tall and lean as a rake; looked like a military gentleman, sir; and I don't know as I'd call him gentry either,' added John, half to himself. 'He wasn't what he thought he was.'

'A decayed clergyman, John?' inquired Cargrim, remembering Graham's description.

'There was lots of decay but no clergy about him, sir. I fancy I knows a parson when I sees one. Clergymen don't have scars on their cheekses as I knows of.'

'Oh, indeed!' said Cargrim, mentally noting that the doctor had spoken falsely. 'So he had a scar?'

'A red scar, sir, on the right cheek, from his temple to the corner of his mouth. He was as dark as pitch in looks, with a military moustache, and two black eyes like gimblets. His clothes was shabby, and his looks was horrid. Bad-tempered too, sir, I should say, for when he was with his lordship I 'eard his voice quite angry like. It ain't no clergy as 'ud speak like that to our bishop, Mr Cargrim.'

'And his lordship was taken ill when this visitor departed, John?'

'Right off, sir. When I got back to the library after showing him out I found his lordship gas'ly pale.'

'And his paleness was caused by the noisy conduct of this man?'

'Couldn't have bin caused by anything else, sir.'

'Dear me! dear me! this is much to be deplored,' sighed Cargrim, in his softest manner. 'And a clergyman too.'

'Beggin' your pardon, sir, he weren't no clergyman,' cried John, who was an old servant and took liberties; 'he was more like a tramp or a gipsy. I wouldn't have left him near the plate, I know.'

'We must not judge too harshly, John. Perhaps this poor man was in trouble.'

'He didn't look like it, Mr Cargrim. He went in and came out quite cocky like. I wonder his lordship didn't send for the police.'

'His lordship is too kind-hearted, John. This stranger had a scar, you say?'

'Yes, sir; a red scar on the right cheek.'

'Dear me! no doubt he has been in the wars. Good-night, John. Let us hope that his lordship will be better after a night's rest.'

'Good-night, sir!'

The chaplain walked away with a satisfied smile on his meek face.

'I must find the man with the scar,' he thought, 'and then — who knows.'

5

The Derby Winner

As its name denotes, Beorminster was built on a hill, or, to speak more precisely, on an eminence elevated slightly above the surrounding plain. In former times it had been surrounded by aguish marshes which had rendered the town unhealthy, but now that modern enterprise had drained the fenlands, Beorminster was as salubrious a town as could be found in England. The rich, black mud of the former bogs now yielded luxuriant harvests, and in autumn the city, with its mass of red-roofed houses climbing upward to the cathedral, was islanded in a golden ocean of wheat and rye and bearded barley. For the purposes of defence, the town had been built originally on the slopes of the hill, under the very shadow of the minster, and round its base the massive old walls yet remained, which had squeezed the city into a huddled mass of uncomfortable dwellings within its narrow girdle. But now oppidan life extended beyond these walls; and houses, streets, villas and gardens spread into the plain on all sides. Broad, white roads ran to Southberry Junction, ten miles away; to manufacturing Irongrip, the smoke of whose furnaces could be seen on the horizon; and to many a tiny hamlet and sleepy town buried amid the rich meadowlands and golden cornfields. And high above all lorded the stately cathedral, with its trio of mighty towers, whence, morning and evening, melodious bells pealed through the peaceful lands.

Beyond the walls the modern town was made up of broad streets and handsome shops. On its outskirts appeared comfortable villas and stately manors, gardens and woody parks, in which dwelt the aristocracy of Beorminster. But the old town, with its tall houses and narrow lanes, was given over to the plebeians, save in the Cathedral Close, where dwelt the canons, the dean, the archdeacon, and a few old-fashioned folk who remained by preference in their ancestral dwellings. From this close, which surrounded the open space, wherein the cathedral was built, narrow streets trickled down to the walls, and here was the Seven Dials, the Whitechapel, the very worst corner of Beorminster. The Beorminster police declared that this network of lanes and alleys and malodorous *cul-de-sacs* was as dangerous a neighbourhood as any London slum, and they were particularly emphatic in denouncing the public-house known as The Derby Winner, and kept by a certain William Mosk, who was a sporting scoundrel and a horsey scamp. This ill-famed hostel was placed at the foot of the hill, in what had once been the main street, and being near the Eastgate, caught in its web most of the thirsty passers-by who entered the city proper, either for sight-seeing or business. It affected a kind of spurious respectability, which was all on the outside, for within it was as iniquitous a den as could well be conceived, and was usually filled with horse-copers and sporting characters, who made bets, and talked racing, and rode or drove fiery steeds, and who lived on, and swindled through, the noblest of all animals. Mr Mosk, a lean light-weight, who wore loud check suits, tight in the legs and short in the waist, was the presiding deity of this Inferno, and as the Ormuz to this Ahrimanes, Gabriel Pendle was the curate of the district, charged with the almost hopeless task of reforming his sporting parishioners. And all this, with considerable irony, was placed almost in the shadow of the cathedral towers.

Not a neighbourhood for Mr Cargrim to venture into, since many sights therein must have displeased his exact tastes; yet two days after the reception at the palace the chaplain might have been seen daintily picking his way over the cobble-stone pavements. As he walked he thought, and his thoughts were busy with the circumstances which had led him to venture his saintly person so near the spider's web of The Derby Winner. The bishop, London, curiosity, Gabriel, this unpleasant neighbourhood — so ran the links of his chain of thought.

The day following his unexpected illness brought no relief to the bishop, at all events to outward seeming, for he was paler and more haggard than ever in looks, and as dour as a bear in manner. With Mrs Pendle he strove to be his usual cheerful self, but with small success, as occasionally he would steal an anxious look at her, and heave deep sighs expressive of much inward trouble. All this was noted by Cargrim, who carefully strove, by sympathetic looks and dexterous remarks, to bring his superior to the much-desired point of unburdening his mind. Gabriel had returned to his lodgings near the Eastgate, and to his hopeless task of civilising his degraded centaurs. Lucy, after the manner of maids in love, was building air-castles with Sir Harry's assistance, and Mrs Pendle kept her usual watch on her weak heart and fluctuating pulse. The bishop thus escaped their particular notice, and it was mainly Cargrim who saw how distraught and anxious he was. As for Dr Graham, he had departed after a second unsatisfactory visit, swearing that he could do nothing with a man who refused to make a confidant of his doctor. Bishop Pendle was therefore wholly at the mercy of his suspicious chaplain, to be spied upon, to be questioned, to be watched, and to be made a prey of in his first weak moment. But the worried man, filled with some unknown anxiety, was quite oblivious to Cargrim's manœuvres.

For some time the chaplain, in spite of all his watchfulness, failed to come upon anything tangible likely to explain what was in the bishop's mind. He walked about restlessly, he brooded continuously, and instead of devoting himself to his work in his usual regular way, occupied himself for long hours in scribbling figures on his blotting-paper, and muttering at times in anxious tones. Cargrim examined the blotting-paper, and strained his ears to gather the sense of the mutterings, but in neither case could he gain any clue to the bishop's actual trouble. At length — it was on the morning of the second day after the reception — Dr Pendle abruptly announced that he was going up to London that very afternoon, and would go alone. The emphasis he laid on this last statement still further roused Cargrim's curiosity.

'Shall I not accompany your lordship?' he asked, as the bishop restlessly paced the library.

'No, Mr Cargrim, why should you?' said the bishop, abruptly and testily.

'Your lordship seems ill, and I thought — '

'There is no need for you to think, sir. I am not well, and my visit to London is in connection with my health.'

'Or with your secret!' thought the chaplain, deferentially bowing.

'I have every confidence in Dr Graham,' continued Pendle, 'but it is my intention to consult a specialist. I need not go into details, Mr Cargrim, as they will not interest you.'

'Oh, your lordship, your health is my constant thought.'

'Your anxiety is commendable, but needless,' responded the bishop, dryly. 'I am due at Southberry this Sunday, I believe.'

'There is a confirmation at St Mark's, your lordship.'

'Very good; you can make the necessary arrangements, Mr Cargrim. To-day is Thursday. I shall return to-morrow night, and shall rest on Saturday until the evening, when I shall ride over to Southberry, attend at St Mark's, and return on Sunday night.'

'Does not your lordship desire my attendance?' asked Cargrim, although he knew that he was the morning preacher in the cathedral on Sunday.

'No,' answered Dr Pendle, curtly, 'I shall go and return alone.'

The bishop looked at Cargrim, and Cargrim looked at the bishop, each striving to read the other's thoughts, then the latter turned away with a frown, and the former, much exercised in his mind, advanced towards the door of the library. Dr Pendle called him back.

'Not a word about my health to Mrs Pendle,' he said sharply.

'Certainly not, your lordship; you can rely upon my discretion in every way,' replied the chaplain, with emphasis, and glided away as soft-footed as any panther, and as dangerous.

'I wonder what the fellow suspects,' thought the bishop when alone. 'I can see that he is filled with curiosity, but he can never find out the truth, or even guess at it. I am safe enough from him. All the same, I'll have a fool for my next chaplain. Fools are easier to deal with.'

Cargrim would have given much to have overheard this speech, but as the door and several passages were between him and the talker, he was ignorant of the incriminating remarks the bishop had let slip. Still baffled, but still curious, he busied himself with attending to some business of the See which did not require the personal supervision of Dr Pendle, and when that prelate took his departure for London by the three o'clock train, Cargrim attended him to the station, full of meekness and irritating attentions. It was with a feeling of relief that the bishop saw his officious chaplain left behind on the platform. He had a secret, and with the uneasiness of a loaded conscience, fancied that everyone saw that he had something to conceal — particularly Cargrim. In the presence of that good young man, this spiritual lord, high-placed and powerful, felt that he resembled an insect under a microscope, and that Cargrim had his eye to the instrument. Conscience made a coward of the bishop, but in the case of his chaplain his uneasy feelings were in some degree justified.

On leaving the railway station, which was on the outskirts of the modern town, Cargrim took his way through the brisk population which thronged the streets, and wondered in what manner he could benefit by the absence of his superior. As he could not learn the truth from Dr Pendle himself, he thought that he might discover it from an investigation of the bishop's desk. For this purpose he returned to the palace forthwith, and on the plea of business, shut himself up in the library. Dr Pendle was a careless man, and never locked up any drawers, even those which contained his private papers. Cargrim, who was too much of a sneak to feel honourable scruples, went through these carefully, but in spite of all his predisposition to malignity was unable to find any grounds for suspecting Dr Pendle to be in any serious trouble. At the end of an hour he found himself as ignorant as ever, and made only one discovery of any note, which was that the bishop had taken his cheque-book with him to London.

To many people this would have seemed a natural circumstance, as most men with banking accounts take their cheque-books with them when going on a journey. But Cargrim knew that the bishop usually preferred to fill his pockets with loose cash when absent for a short time, and this deviation from his ordinary habits appeared to be suspicious.

'Hum!' thought the chaplain, rubbing his chin, 'I wonder if that so-called clergyman wanted money. If he had wished for a small sum, the bishop could easily have given it to him out of the cash-box. Going by this reasoning, he must have wanted a lot of money, which argues blackmail. Hum! Has he taken both cheque-books, or only one?'

The reason of this last query was that Bishop Pendle had accounts in two different banks. One in Beorminster, as became the bishop of the See, the other in London, in accordance with the dignity of a spiritual lord of Parliament. A further search showed Mr Cargrim that the Beorminster cheque-book had been left behind.

'Hum!' said the chaplain again, 'that man must have gone back to London. Dr Pendle is going to meet him there and draw money from his Town bank to pay what he demands. I'll have a look at the butts of that cheque-book when it comes back; the amount of the cheque may prove much. I may even find out the name of this stranger.'

But all this, as Cargrim very well knew, was pure theory. The bishop might have taken his cheque-book to London for other reasons than paying blackmail to the stranger, for it was not even certain that there was any such extortion in the question. Dr Pendle was worried, it was true, and after the departure of his strange visitor he had been taken ill, but these facts proved nothing; and after twisting and turning them in every way, and connecting and disconnecting them with the absence of the London cheque-book, Mr Cargrim was forced to acknowledge that he was beaten for the time being. Then he fancied he might extract some information from Gabriel relative to his father's departure for London, for Mr Cargrim was too astute to believe in the 'consulting a specialist' excuse. Still, this might serve as a peg whereon to hang his inquiries and develop further information, so the chaplain, after meditating over his five-o'clock cup of tea, took his way to the Eastgate, in order to put Gabriel unawares into the witness-box. Yet, for all these doings and suspicions Cargrim had no very good reason, save his own desire to get Dr Pendle under his thumb. He was groping in the dark, he had not a shred of evidence to suppose that the uneasiness of the bishop was connected with anything criminal; nevertheless, the chaplain put himself so far out of his usual habits as to venture into the unsavoury neighbourhood wherein stood The Derby Winner. Truly this man's cobweb spinning was of a very dangerous character when he took so much trouble to weave the web.

As in Excelsior, the shades of night were falling fast, when Cargrim found himself at the door of the curate's lodging. Here he met with a check, for Gabriel's landlady informed him that Mr Pendle was not at home, and she did not know where he was or when he would be back. Cargrim made the sweetest excuses for troubling the good lady, left a message that he would call again, and returned along Monk Street on his way back to the palace through the new town. By going in this direction he passed The Derby Winner — not without intention — for it was this young man's belief that Gabriel might be haunting the public-house to see Mrs Mosk or — as was more probable to the malignant chaplain — her handsome daughter.

As he came abreast of The Derby Winner it was not too dark but that he could see a tall man standing in the doorway. Cargrim at first fancied that this might be Gabriel, and paced slowly along so as to seize an opportunity of addressing him. But when he came almost within touching distance, he found himself face to face with a dark-looking gipsy, fiery-eyed and dangerous in appearance. He had a lean, cruel face, a hawk's beak for a nose, and black, black hair streaked with grey; but what mostly attracted Cargrim's attention was a red streak which traversed the right cheek of the man from ear to mouth. At once he recalled John's description — 'A military-looking gentleman with a scar on the right cheek.' He thought, 'Hum! this, then, is the bishop's visitor.'

6

The Man With the Scar

This engaging individual looked at Cargrim with a fierce air. He was not sober, and had just reached the quarrelsome stage of intoxication, which means objection to everyone and everything. Consequently he cocked his hat defiantly at the curate; and although he blocked up the doorway, made no motion to stand aside. Cargrim was not ill pleased at this obstinacy, as it gave him an opportunity of entering into conversation with the so-called decayed clergyman, who was as unlike a parson as a rabbit is like a terrier.

'Do you know if Mr Pendle is within, my friend?' asked the chaplain, with bland politeness.

The stranger started at the mention of the name. His face grew paler, his scar waxed redder, and with all his Dutch courage there was a look of alarm visible in his cold eyes.

'I don't know,' said he, insolently, yet with a certain refinement of speech. 'I shouldn't think it likely that a pot-house like this would be patronised by a bishop.'

'Pardon me, sir, I speak of Mr Gabriel Pendle, the son of his lordship.'

'Then pardon me, sir,' mimicked the man, 'if I say that I know nothing of the son of his lordship; and what's more, I'm d—d if I want to.'

'I see! You are more fortunate in knowing his lordship himself,' said the chaplain, with great simplicity.

The stranger plucked at his worn sleeve with a look of irony. 'Do I look as though I were acquainted with bishops?' said he, scoffingly. 'Is this the kind of coat likely to be admitted into episcopalian palaces?'

'Yet it was admitted, sir. If I am not mistaken you called at the palace two nights ago.'

'Did you see me?'

'Certainly I saw you,' replied Cargrim, salving his conscience with the Jesuitic saying that the end justifies the means. 'And I was informed that you were a decayed clergyman seeking assistance.'

'I have been most things in my time,' observed the stranger, gloomily, 'but not a parson. You are one, I perceive.'

Cargrim bowed. 'I am the chaplain of Bishop Pendle.'

'And the busybody of Beorminster, I

should say,' rejoined the man with a sneer. 'See here, my friend,' and he rapped Cargrim on the breast with a shapely hand, 'if you interfere in what does not concern you, there will be trouble. I saw Dr Pendle on private business, and as such it has nothing to do with you. Hold your tongue, you black crow, and keep away from me,' cried the stranger, with sudden ferocity, 'or I'll knock your head off. Now you know,' and with a fierce glance the man moved out of the doorway and sauntered round the corner before Cargrim could make up his mind how to resent this insolence.

'Hum!' said he to himself, with a glance at the tall retiring figure, 'that is a nice friend for a bishop to have. He's a jail-bird if I mistake not; and he is afraid of my finding out his business with Pendle. Birds of a feather,' sighed Mr Cargrim, entering the hotel. 'I fear, I sadly fear that his lordship is but a whited sepulchre. A look into the bishop's past might show me many things of moment,' and the fat living of Heathcroft seemed almost within Cargrim's grasp as he came to this conclusion.

'Now then, sir,' interrupted a sharp but pleasant female voice, 'and what may you want?'

Mr Cargrim wheeled round to answer this

question, and found himself face to face with a bar, glittering with brass and crystal and bright-hued liquors in fat glass barrels; also with an extremely handsome young woman, dressed in an astonishing variety of colours. She was high-coloured and frank-eyed, with a great quantity of very black hair twisted into many amazing shapes on the top of her head. In manner she was as brisk as a bee and as restless as a butterfly; and being adorned with a vast quantity of bracelets, and lockets, and brooches, all of gaudy patterns, jingled at every movement. This young lady was Miss Bell Mosk, whom the frequenters of The Derby Winner called 'a dashing beauty,' and Mrs Pansey 'a painted jade.' With her glittering ornaments, her bright blue dress, her high colour, and general air of vivacity, she glowed and twinkled in the lamp-light like some gorgeous-plumaged parrot; and her free speech and constant chatter might have been ascribed to the same bird.

'Miss Mosk, I believe,' said the polite Cargrim, marvelling that this gaudy female should be the refined Gabriel's notion of feminine perfection.

'I am Miss Mosk,' replied Bell, taking a comprehensive view of the sleek, black-clothed parson. 'What can I do for you?'

'I am Mr Cargrim, the bishop's chaplain,

Miss Mosk, and I wish to see Mr Pendle — Mr Gabriel Pendle.'

Bell flushed as red as the reddest cabbage rose, and with downcast eyes wiped the counter briskly with a duster. 'Why should you come here to ask for Mr Pendle?' said she, in guarded tones.

'I called at his lodgings, Miss Mosk, and I was informed that he was visiting a sick person here.'

'My mother!' replied Bell, not knowing what an amazing lie the chaplain was telling. 'Yes! Mr Pendle comes often to see — my mother.'

'Is he here now?' asked Cargrim, noticing the hesitancy at the end of her sentence; 'because I wish to speak with him on business.'

'He is upstairs. I daresay he'll be down soon.'

'Oh, don't disturb him for my sake, I beg. But if you will permit me I shall go up and see Mrs Mosk.'

'Here comes Mr Pendle now,' said Bell, abruptly, and withdrew into the interior of the bar as Gabriel appeared at the end of the passage. He started and seemed uneasy when he recognised the chaplain.

'Cargrim!' he cried, hurrying forward. 'Why are you here?' and he gave a nervous glance in the direction of the bar; a glance which the chaplain saw and understood, but discreetly left unnoticed.

'I wish to see you,' he replied, with great simplicity; 'they told me at your lodgings that you might be here, so — '

'Why!' interrupted Gabriel, sharply, 'I left no message to that effect.'

Cargrim saw that he had made a mistake. 'I speak generally, my dear friend — generally,' he said in some haste. 'Your worthy landlady mentioned several houses in which you were in the habit of seeing sick people — amongst others this hotel.'

'Mrs Mosk is very ill. I have been seeing her,' said Gabriel, shortly.

'Ay! ay! you have been seeing Mrs Mosk!'

Gabriel changed colour and cast another glance towards the bar, for the significance of Cargrim's speech was not lost on him. 'Do you wish to speak with me?' he asked coldly.

'I should esteem it a favour if you would allow me a few words,' said Cargrim, politely. 'I'll wait for you — outside,' and in his turn the chaplain looked towards the bar.

'Thank you, I can come with you now,' was Gabriel's reply, made with a burning desire to knock Cargrim down. 'Miss Mosk, I am glad to find that your mother is easier in her mind.'

'It's all due to you, Mr Pendle,' said Bell, moving forward with a toss of her head directed especially at Mr Cargrim. 'Your visits do mother a great deal of good.'

'I am sure they do,' said the chaplain, not able to forego giving the girl a scratch of his claws. 'Mr Pendle's visits here must be delightful to everybody.'

'I daresay,' retorted Bell, with heightened colour, 'other people's visits would not be so welcome.'

'Perhaps not, Miss Mosk. Mr Pendle has many amiable qualities to recommend him. He is a general and deserved favourite.'

'Come, come, Cargrim,' interposed Gabriel, anxiously, for the fair Bell's temper was rapidly getting the better of her; 'if you are ready we shall go. Good evening, Miss Mosk.'

'Good evening, Mr Pendle,' said the barmaid, and directed a spiteful look at Cargrim, for she saw plainly that he had intentionally deprived her of a confidential conversation with Gabriel. The chaplain received the look — which he quite understood — with an amused smile and a bland inclination of the head. As he walked out arm-in-arm with the reluctant Pendle, Bell banged the pewters and glasses about with considerable energy, for the significant demeanour of Cargrim annoyed her so much that she felt a great inclination to throw something at his head. But then, Miss Mosk was a high-spirited girl and believed in actions rather than speech, even though she possessed a fair command of the latter.

'Well, Cargrim,' said Gabriel, when he found himself in the street with his uncongenial companion, 'what is it?'

'It's about the bishop.'

'My father! Is there anything the matter with him?'

'I fear so. He told me that he was going to London.'

'What of that?' said Gabriel, impatiently. 'He told me the same thing yesterday. Has he gone?'

'He left by the afternoon train. Do you know the object of his visit to London?'

'No. What is his object?'

'He goes to consult a specialist about his health.'

'What!' cried Gabriel, anxiously. 'Is he ill?'

'I think so; some nervous trouble brought on by worry.'

'By worry! Has my father anything on his mind likely to worry him to that extent?'

Cargrim coughed significantly. 'I think so,' said he again. 'He has not been himself since the visit of that stranger to the palace. I fancy the man must have brought bad news.'

'Did the bishop tell you so?'

'No; but I am observant, you know.'

Privately, Gabriel considered that Cargrim was a great deal too observant, and also of a meddlesome nature, else why had he come to spy out matters which did not concern him? Needless to say, Gabriel was thinking of Bell at this moment. However, he made no comment on the chaplain's speech, but merely remarked that doubtless the bishop had his own reasons for keeping silent, and advised Cargrim to wait until he was consulted in connection with the matter, before troubling himself unnecessarily about it. 'My father knows his own business best,' finished Gabriel, stiffly, 'if you will forgive my speaking so plainly.'

'Certainly, certainly, Pendle; but I owe a great deal to your father, and I would do much to save him from annoyance. By the way,' with an abrupt change of subject, 'do you know that I saw the stranger who called at the palace two nights ago during the reception?'

'When? Where?'

'At that hotel, this evening. He looks a dangerous man.'

Gabriel shrugged his shoulders. 'It seems to me, Cargrim, that you are making a mountain out of a mole hill. A stranger sees my father, and afterwards you meet him at a public-house; there is nothing strange in that.'

'You forget,' hinted Cargrim, sweetly, 'this man caused your father's illness.'

'We can't be sure of that; and in any case, my father is quite clever enough to deal with his own affairs. I see no reason why you should have hunted me out to talk such nonsense. Good-night, Cargrim,' and with a curt nod the curate stalked away, considerably annoyed by the meddlesome spirit manifested by the chaplain. He had never liked the man, and, now that he was in this interfering mood, liked him less than ever. It would be as well, thought Gabriel, that Mr Cargrim should be dismissed from his confidential office as soon as possible. Otherwise he might cause trouble, and Gabriel mentally thought of the high-coloured young lady in the bar. His conscience was not at ease regarding his admiration for her; and he dreaded lest the officious Cargrim should talk about her to the bishop. Altogether the chaplain, like a hornet, had annoyed both Dr Pendle and his son; and the bishop in London and Gabriel in Beorminster were anything but well disposed towards this clerical busybody, who minded everyone's business instead of his own. It is such people who stir up muddy water and cause mischief.

Meanwhile, the busybody looked after the

curate with an evil smile; and, gratified at having aroused such irritation as the abrupt parting signified, turned back to The Derby Winner. He had seen Bell, he had spoken to Gabriel, he had even secured an unsatisfactory conversation with the unknown man. Now he wished to question Mrs Mosk and acquaint himself with her nature and attitude. Also he desired to question her concerning the military stranger; and with this resolve presented himself again before Miss Mosk, smiling and undaunted.

'What is it?' asked the young lady, who had been nursing her grievances.

'A mere trifle, Miss Mosk; I wish to see your mother.'

'Why?' was Bell's blunt demand.

'My reasons are for Mrs Mosk's ears alone.'

'Oh, are they? Well, I'm afraid you can't see my mother. In the first place, she's too ill to receive anyone; and in the second, my father does not like clergymen.'

'Dear! dear! not even Mr Pendle?'

'Mr Pendle is an exception,' retorted Bell, blushing, and again fell to wiping the counter in a fury, so as to keep her hands from Mr Cargrim's ears.

'I wish to see Mrs Mosk particularly,' reiterated Cargrim, who was bent upon carrying his point. 'If not, your father will do.'

'My father is absent in Southberry. Why do you want to see my mother?'

'I'll tell her that myself — with your permission,' said Cargrim, suavely.

'You sha'n't, then,' cried Bell, and flung down her duster with sparkling eyes.

'In that case I must go away,' replied Cargrim, seeing he was beaten, 'and I thank you, Miss Mosk, for your politeness. By the way,' he added, as he half returned, 'will you tell that gentleman with the scar on the cheek that I wish to see him also?'

'Seems to me you wish to see everybody about here,' said Bell, scornfully. 'I'll tell Mr Jentham if you like. Now go away; I'm busy.'

'Jentham!' repeated Cargrim, as he walked homeward. 'Now, I wonder if I'll find that name in the bishop's cheque-book.'

7

An Interesting Conversation

When Mr Cargrim took an idea into his head it was not easy to get it out again, and to this resolute obstinacy he owed no small part of his success. He was like the famous drop of water and would wear away any human stone, however hard it might be.

Again and again, when baffled, he returned with gentle persistence to the object he had in view, and however strong of will his adversary happened to be, that will was bound, in the long run, to yield to the incessant attacks of the chaplain. At the present moment he desired to have an interview with Mrs Mosk, and he was determined to obtain one in spite of Bell's refusal. However, he had no time to waste on the persuasive method, as he wished to see the invalid before the bishop returned. To achieve this end he enlisted the services of Mrs Pansey.

That good lady sometimes indulged in a species of persecution she termed district-visiting, which usually consisted in her thrusting herself at untoward times into poor people's houses and asking them questions about their private affairs. When she had learned all she wished to know, and had given her advice in the tone of a command not to be disobeyed, she would retire, leaving the evidence of her trail behind her in the shape of a nauseous little tract with an abusive title. It was no use any poor creature refusing to see Mrs Pansey, for she forced herself into the most private chambers, and never would retire unless she thought fit to do so of her own will. It was for this reason that Cargrim suggested the good lady should call upon Mrs Mosk, for he knew well that neither the father, nor the daughter, nor the whole assembled domestics of the hotel, would be able to stop her from making her way to the bedside of the invalid; and in the devastated rear of Mrs Pansey the chaplain intended to follow.

His principal object in seeing Mrs Mosk was to discover what she knew about the man called Jentham. He was lodging at The Derby Winner, as Cargrim ascertained by later inquiry, and it was probable that the inmates of the hotel knew something as to the reasons of his stay in Beorminster. Mr Mosk, being as obstinate as a mule, was not likely to tell Cargrim anything he desired to learn. Bell, detesting the chaplain, as she took no pains to conceal, would probably refuse to hold a conversation with him; but Mrs Mosk, being weak-minded and ill, might be led by dexterous questioning to tell all she knew. And what she did know might, in Cargrim's opinion, throw more light on Jentham's connection with the bishop. Therefore, the next morning, Cargrim called on the archdeacon's widow to inveigle her into persecuting Mrs Mosk with a call. Mrs Pansey, with all her acuteness, could not see that she was being made use of — luckily for Cargrim.

'I hear the poor woman is very ill,' sighed the chaplain, after he had introduced the subject, 'and I fear that her daughter does not give her all the attention an invalid should have.'

'The Jezebel!' growled Mrs Pansey. 'What can you expect from that flaunting hussy?'

'She is a human being, Mrs Pansey, and I expect at least human feelings.'

'Can you get blood out of a stone, Mr Cargrim? No, you can't. Is that red-cheeked Dutch doll a pelican to pluck her breast for the benefit of her mother? No, indeed! I daresay she passes her sinful hours drinking with young men. I'd whip her at a cart's tail if I had my way.'

'Gabriel Pendle is trying to bring the girl to

a sense of her errors.'

'Rubbish! She's trying to bring him to the altar, more like. I'll go with you, Mr Cargrim, and see the minx. I have long thought that it is my duty to reprove her and warn her mother of such goings-on. As for that weak-minded young Pendle,' cried Mrs Pansey, shaking her head furiously, 'I pity his infatuation; but what can you expect from such a mother as his mother? Can a fool produce sense? No!'

'I am afraid you will find the young woman difficult to deal with.'

'That makes me all the more determined to see her, Mr Cargrim. I'll tell her the truth for once in her life. Marry young Pendle indeed!' snorted the good lady. 'I'll let her see.'

'Speak to her mother first,' urged Cargrim, who wished his visit to be less warlike, as more conducive to success.

'I'll speak to both of them. I daresay one is as bad as the other. I must have that public-house removed; it's an eye-sore to Beorminster — a curse to the place. It ought to be pulled down and the site ploughed up and sown with salt. Come with me, Mr Cargrim, and you shall see how I deal with iniquity. I hope I know what is due to myself.'

'Where is Miss Norsham?' asked the chaplain, when they fell into more general conversation on their way to The Derby Winner.

'Husband-hunting. Dean Alder is showing her the tombs in the cathedral. Tombs, indeed! It's the altar she's interested in.'

'My dear lady, the dean is too old to marry!'

'He is not too old to be made a fool of, Mr Cargrim. As for Daisy Norsham, she'd marry Methuselah to take away the shame of being single. Not that the match with Alder will be out of the way, for she's no chicken herself.'

'I rather thought Mr Dean had an eye to Miss Whichello.'

'Stuff!' rejoined Mrs Pansey, with a sniff. 'She's far too much taken up with dieting people to think of marrying them. She actually weighs out the food on the table when meals are on. No wonder that poor girl Mab is thin.'

'But she isn't too thin for her height, Mrs Pansey. She seems to me to be well covered.'

'You didn't notice her at the palace, then,' snapped the widow, avoiding a direct reply. 'She wore a low-necked dress which made me blush. I don't know what girls are coming to. They'd go about like so many Eves if they could.'

'Oh, Mrs Pansey!' remonstrated the chaplain, in a shocked tone.

'Well, it's in the Bible, isn't it, man? You aren't going to say Holy Writ is indecent, are you?'

'Well, really, Mrs Pansey, clergyman as I am, I must say that there are parts of the Bible unfit for the use of schools.'

'To the pure all things are pure, Mr Cargrim; you have an impure mind, I fear. Remember the Thirty-Nine Articles and speak becomingly of holy things. However, let that pass,' added Mrs Pansey, in livelier tones. 'Here we are, and there's that hussy hanging out from an upper window like the Jezebel she is.'

This remark was directed against Bell, who, apparently in her mother's room, was at the window amusing herself by watching the passers-by. When she saw Mrs Pansey and the chaplain stalking along in black garments, and looking like two birds of prey, she hastily withdrew, and by the time they arrived at the hotel was at the doorway to receive them, with fixed bayonets.

'Young woman,' said Mrs Pansey, severely, 'I have come to see your mother,' and she cast a disapproving look on Bell's gay pink dress.

'She is not well enough to see either you or Mr Cargrim,' said Bell, coolly.

'All the more reason that Mr Cargrim, as a

clergyman, should look after her soul, my good girl.'

'Thank you, Mr Pendle is doing that.'

'Indeed! Mr Pendle, then, combines business with pleasure.'

Bell quite understood the insinuation conveyed in this last speech, and, firing up, would have come to high words with the visitors but that her father made his appearance, and, as she did not wish to draw forth remarks from Mrs Pansey about Gabriel in his hearing, she discreetly held her tongue. However, as Mrs Pansey swept by in triumph, followed by Cargrim, she looked daggers at them both, and bounced into the bar, where she drew beer for thirsty customers in a flaming temper. She dearly desired a duel of words with the formidable visitor.

Mosk was a lean, tall man with a pimpled face and a military moustache. He knew Mrs Pansey, and, like most other people, detested her with all his heart; but she was, as he thought, a great friend of Sir Harry Brace, who was his landlord, so for diplomatic reasons he greeted her with all deference, hat in hand.

'I have come with Mr Cargrim to see your wife, Mr Mosk,' said the visitor.

'Thank you, ma'am, I'm sure it's very kind

of you,' replied Mosk, who had a husky voice suggestive of beer. 'She'll be honoured to see you, I'm sure. This way, ma'am.'

'Is she very ill?' demanded the chaplain, as they followed Mosk to the back of the hotel and up a narrow staircase.

'She ain't well, sir, but I can't say as she's dying. We do all we can to make her easy.'

'Ho!' from Mrs Pansey. 'I hope your daughter acts towards her mother like as a daughter should.'

'I'd like to see the person as says she don't,' cried Mr Mosk, with sudden anger. 'I'd knock his head off. Bell's a good girl; none better.'

'Let us hope your trust in her is justified,' sighed the mischief-maker, and passed into the sickroom, leaving Mosk with an uneasy feeling that something was wrong. If the man had a tender spot in his heart it was for his handsome daughter; and it was with a vague fear that, after presenting his wife to her visitors, he went downstairs to the bar. Mrs Pansey had a genius for making mischief by a timely word.

'Bell,' said he, gruffly, 'what's that old cat hinting at?'

'What about?' asked Bell, tossing her head till all her ornaments jingled, and wiping the counter furiously.

'About you! She don't think I should trust you.'

'What right has she to talk about me, I'd like to know!' cried Bell, getting as red as a peony. 'I've never done anything that anyone can say a word against me.'

'Who said you had?' snapped her father; 'but that old cat hints.'

'Let her keep her hints to herself, then. Because I'm young and good-looking she wants to take my character away. Nasty old puss that she is!'

'That's just it, my gal. You're too young and good-looking to escape folks' talking; and I hear that young Mr Pendle comes round when I'm away.'

'Who says he doesn't, father? It's to see mother; he's a parson, ain't he?'

'Yes! and he's gentry too. I won't have him paying attention to you.'

'You'd better wait till he does,' flashed out Bell. 'I can take care of myself, I hope.'

'If I catch him talking other than religion to you I'll choke him in his own collar,' cried Mr Mosk, with a scowl; 'so now you know.'

'I know as you're talking nonsense, father. Time enough for you to interfere when there's cause. Now you clear out and let me get on with my work.'

Reassured by the girl's manner, Mosk

began to think that Mrs Pansey's hints were all moonshine, and after cooling himself with a glass of beer, went away to look into his betting-book with some horsey pals. In the meantime, Mrs Pansey was persecuting his wife, a meek, nervous little woman, who was propped up with pillows in a large bed, and seemed to be quite overwhelmed by the honour of Mrs Pansey's call.

'So you are weak in the back, are you?' said the visitor, in loud tones. 'If you are, what right have you to marry and bring feeble children into the world?'

'Bell isn't feeble,' said Mrs Mosk, weakly. 'She's a fine set-up gal.'

'Set-up and stuck-up,' retorted Mrs Pansey. 'I tell you what, my good woman, you ought to be downstairs looking after her.'

'Lord! mum, there ain't nothing wrong, I do devoutly hope.'

'Nothing as yet; but you shouldn't have young gentlemen about the place.'

'I can't help it, mum,' said Mrs Mosk, beginning to cry. 'I'm sure we must earn our living somehow. This is an 'otel, isn't it? and Mosk's a pop'lar character, ain't he? I'm sure it's hard enough to make ends meet as it is; we owe rent for half a year and can't pay — and won't pay,' wailed Mrs Mosk, 'unless my 'usband comes 'ome on Skinflint.'

'Comes home on Skinflint, woman, what do you mean?'

'Skinflint's a 'orse, mum, as Mosk 'ave put his shirt on.'

Mrs Pansey wagged her plumes and groaned. 'I'm sadly afraid your husband is a son of perdition, Mrs Mosk. Put his shirt on Skinflint, indeed!'

'He's a good man to me, anyhow,' cried Mrs Mosk, plucking up spirit.

'Drink and betting,' continued Mrs Pansey, pretending not to hear this feeble defiance. 'What can we expect from a man who drinks and bets?'

'And associates with bad characters,' put in Cargrim, seizing his chance.

'That he don't, sir,' said Mrs Mosk, with energy. 'May I beg of you to put a name to one of 'em?'

'Jentham,' said the chaplain, softly. 'Who is Jentham, Mrs Mosk?'

'I know no more nor a babe unborn, sir. He's bin 'ere two weeks, and I did see him twice afore my back got so bad as to force me to bed. But I don't see why you calls him bad, sir. He pays his way.'

'Oh,' groaned Mrs Pansey, 'is it the chief end of man to pay his way?'

'It is with us, mum,' retorted Mrs Mosk, meekly; 'there ain't no denying of it. And Mr

Jentham do pay proper though he *is* a gipsy.'
'He's a gipsy, is he?' said Cargrim, alertly.
'So he says, sir; and I knows as he goes sometimes to that camp of gipsies on Southberry Heath.'
'Where does he get his money from?'
'Better not inquire into that, Mr Cargrim,' said Mrs Pansey, with a sniff.
'Oh, Mr Jentham's honest, I'm sure, mum. He's bin at the gold diggin's and 'ave made a trifle of money. Indeed, I don't know where he ain't been, sir. The four pints of the compass is all plain sailing to 'im; and his 'airbreadth escapes is too h'awful. I shivers and shudders when I 'ears em.'
'What is he doing here?'
'He's on business; but I don't know what kind. Oh, he knows 'ow to 'old 'is tongue, does Jentham.'
'He is a gipsy, he consorts with gipsies, he has money, and no one knows where he comes from,' summed up Cargrim. 'I think, Mrs Pansey, we may regard this man as a dangerous character.'
'I shouldn't be surprised to hear he was an Anarchist,' said Mrs Pansey, who knew nothing about the man. 'Well, Mrs Mosk, I hope we've cheered you up. I'll go now. Read this tract,' bestowing a grimy little pamphlet, 'and don't see too much of Mr Pendle.'

'But he comforts me,' said poor Mrs Mosk; 'he reads beautiful.'

Mrs Pansey grunted. Bold as she was she did not like to speak quite plainly to the woman, as too-free speech might inculpate Gabriel and bring the bishop to the rescue. Besides, Mrs Pansey had no evidence to bring forward to prove that Gabriel was in love with Bell Mosk. Therefore she said nothing, but, like the mariner's parrot, thought the more. Shaking out her dark skirts she rose to go, with another grunt full of unspoken suspicions.

'Good-day, Mrs Mosk,' said she, pausing at the door. 'When you are low-spirited send for me to cheer you up.'

Mrs Mosk attempted a curtsey in bed, which was a failure owing to her sitting position; but Mrs Pansey did not see the attempt, as she was already half-way down the stairs, followed by Cargrim. The chaplain had learned a trifle more about the mysterious Jentham and was quite satisfied with his visit; but he was more puzzled than ever. A tramp, a gipsy, an adventurer — what had such a creature in common with Bishop Pendle? To Mr Cargrim's eye the affair of the visit began to assume the proportions of a criminal case. But all the information he had gathered proved nothing, so it only remained to wait for the bishop's return and see what discoveries he could make in that direction. If Jentham's name was in the cheque-book the chaplain would be satisfied that there was an understanding between the pair; and then his next move would be to learn what the understanding was. When he discovered that, he had no doubt but that he would have Dr Pendle under his thumb, which would be a good thing for Mr Cargrim and an unpleasant position for the bishop.

Mrs Pansey stalked down to the bar, and seeing Bell therein, silently placed a little tract on the counter. No sooner had she left the house than Bell snatched up the tract, and rushing to the door flung it after the good lady.

'You need it more than I do,' she cried, and bounced into the house again.

It was with a quiver of rage that Mrs Pansey turned to the chaplain. She was almost past speech, but with some difficulty and much choking managed to convey her feelings in two words.

'The creature!' gasped Mrs Pansey, and shook her skirts as if to rid herself of some taint contracted at The Derby Winner.

8

On Saturday Night

The bishop returned on Saturday morning instead of on Friday night as arranged, and was much more cheerful than when he left, a state of mind which irritated Cargrim in no small degree, and also perplexed him not a little. If Dr Pendle's connection with Jentham was dangerous he should still be ill at ease and anxious, instead of which he was almost his old genial self when he joined his wife and Lucy at their afternoon tea. Sir Harry was not present, but Mr Cargrim supplied his place, an exchange which was not at all to Lucy's mind. The Pendles treated the chaplain always with a certain reserve, and the only person who really thought him the good young man he appeared to be, was the bishop's wife. But kindly Mrs Pendle was the most innocent of mortals, and all geese were swans to her. She had not the necessary faculty of seeing through a brick wall with which nature had gifted Mrs Pansey in so extraordinary a degree.

As a rule, Mr Cargrim did not come to afternoon tea, but on this occasion he presented himself; ostensibly to welcome back his patron, in reality to watch him. Also he was determined, at the very first opportunity, to introduce the name of Jentham and observe what effect it had on the bishop. With these little plans in his mind the chaplain crept about the tea-table like a tame cat, and handed round cake and bread with his most winning smile. His pale face was even more inexpressive than usual, and none could have guessed, from outward appearance, his malicious intents — least of all the trio he was with. They were too upright themselves to suspect evil in others.

'I am so glad to see you are better, bishop,' said Mrs Pendle, languidly trifling with a cup of tea. 'Your journey has done you good.'

'Change of air, change of air, my dear. A wonderful restorative.'

'Your business was all right, I hope?'

'Oh, yes! Indeed, I hardly went up on business, and what I did do was a mere trifle,' replied the bishop, smoothing his apron. 'Has Gabriel been here to-day?' he added, obviously desirous of turning the conversation.

'Twice!' said Lucy, who presided over the tea-table; 'and the second time he told mamma that he had received a letter from George.'

'Ay, ay! a letter from George. Is he quite well, Lucy?'

'We shall see that for ourselves this evening, papa. George is coming to Beorminster, and will be here about ten o'clock to-night.'

'How vexing!' exclaimed Dr Pendle. 'I intended going over to Southberry this evening, but I can't miss seeing George.'

'Ride over to-morrow morning, bishop,' suggested his wife.

'Sunday morning, my dear!'

'Well, papa!' said Lucy, smiling, 'you are not a strict Sabbatarian, you know.'

'I am not so good as I ought to be, my dear,' said Dr Pendle, playfully pinching her pretty ear. 'Well! well! I must see George. I'll go to-morrow morning at eight o'clock. You'll send a telegram to Mr Vasser to that effect, if you please, Mr Cargrim. Say that I regret not being able to come to-night.'

'Certainly, my lord. In any case, I am going in to Beorminster this evening.'

'You are usually more stay-at-home, Mr Cargrim. Thank you, Lucy, I will take another cup of tea.'

'I do not care for going out at night as a rule, my lord,' observed the chaplain, in his most sanctimonious tone, 'but duty calls me into Beorminster. I am desirous of comforting poor sick Mrs Mosk at The Derby Winner.'

'Oh, that is Gabriel's pet invalid,' cried

Lucy, peering into the teapot; 'he says Mrs Mosk is a very good woman.'

'Let us hope so,' observed the bishop, stirring his new cup of tea. 'I do not wish to be uncharitable, my dear, but if Mrs Pansey is to be believed, that public-house is not conducted so carefully as it should be.'

'But *is* Mrs Pansey to be believed, bishop?' asked his wife, smiling.

'I don't think she would tell a deliberate falsehood, my love.'

'All the same, she might exaggerate little into much,' said Lucy, with a pretty grimace. 'What is your opinion of this hotel, Mr Cargrim?'

The chaplain saw his opportunity and seized it at once. 'My dear Miss Pendle,' he said, showing all his teeth, 'as The Derby Winner is the property of Sir Harry Brace I wish I could speak well of it, but candour compels me to confess that it is a badly-conducted house.'

'Tut! tut!' said the bishop, 'what is this? You don't say so.'

'Harry shall shut it up at once,' cried Lucy, the pretty Puritan.

'It is a resort of bad characters, I fear,' sighed Cargrim, 'and Mrs Mosk, being an invalid, is not able to keep them away.'

'What about the landlord, Mr Cargrim?'

'Aha!' replied the chaplain, turning towards Mrs Pendle, who had asked this question, 'he is a man of lax morals. His boon companion is a tramp called Jentham!'

'Jentham!' repeated Dr Pendle, in so complacent a tone that Cargrim, with some vexation, saw that he did not associate the name with his visitor; 'and who is Jentham?'

'I hardly know,' said the chaplain, making another attempt; 'he is a tramp, as I have reason to believe, and consorts with gipsies. I saw him myself the other day — a tall, lean man with a scar.'

The bishop rose, and walking over to the tea-table placed his cup carefully thereon. 'With a scar,' he repeated in low tones. 'A man with a scar — Jentham — indeed! What do you know of this person, Mr Cargrim?'

'Absolutely nothing,' rejoined the chaplain, with a satisfied glance at the uneasy face of his questioner. 'He is a gipsy; he stays at The Derby Winner and pays regularly for his lodgings; and his name is Jentham. I know no more.'

'I don't suppose there is more to know,' cried Lucy, lightly.

'If there is, the police may find out, Miss Pendle.'

The bishop frowned. 'As the man, so far as we know, has done nothing against the laws,' said he, quickly, 'I see no reason why the police should be mentioned in connection with him. Evidently, from what Mr Cargrim says, he is a rolling stone, and probably will not remain much longer in Beorminster. Let us hope that he will take himself and his bad influence away from our city. In the meantime, it is hardly worth our while to discuss a person of so little importance.'

In this skilful way the bishop put an end to the conversation, and Cargrim, fearful of rousing his suspicions, did not dare to resume it. In a little while, after a few kind words to his wife, Dr Pendle left the drawing-room for his study. As he passed out, Cargrim noticed that the haggard look had come back to his face, and once or twice he glanced anxiously at his wife. In his turn Cargrim examined Mrs Pendle, but saw nothing in her manner likely to indicate that she shared the uneasiness of her husband, or knew the cause of his secret anxiety. She looked calm and content, and there was a gentle smile in her weary eyes. Evidently the bishop's mind was set at rest by her placid looks, for it was with a sigh of relief that he left the room. Cargrim noted the look and heard the sigh, but was wholly in the dark regarding their meaning.

'Though I daresay they have to do with Jentham and this secret,' he thought, when bowing himself out of the drawing-room. 'Whatever the matter may be, Dr Pendle is evidently most anxious to keep his wife from knowing of it. All the better.' He rubbed his hands together with a satisfied smirk. 'Such anxiety shows that the secret is worth learning. Sooner or later I shall find it out, and then I can insist upon being the rector of Heathcroft. I have no time to lose, so I shall go to The Derby Winner to-night and see if I can induce this mysterious Jentham to speak out. He looks a drunken dog, so a glass of wine may unloosen his tongue.'

From this speech it can be seen that Mr Cargrim was true to his Jesuitic instincts, and thought no action dishonourable so long as it aided him to gain his ends. He was a methodical scoundrel, too, and arranged the details of his scheme with the utmost circumspection. For instance, prior to seeing the man with the scar, he thought it advisable to find out if the bishop had drawn a large sum of money while in London for the purpose of bribing the creature to silence. Therefore, before leaving the palace, he made several attempts to examine the cheque-book. But Dr Pendle remained constantly at his desk in the library, and although the plotter actually saw the cheque-book at the elbow of his proposed victim, he was unable, without any good reason, to pick it up and satisfy his curiosity. He was therefore obliged to defer any attempt to obtain it until the next day, as the bishop would probably leave it behind him when he rode over to Southberry. This failure vexed the chaplain, as he wished to be forearmed in his interview with Jentham, but, as there was no help for it, he was obliged to put the cart before the horse — in other words, to learn what he could from the man first and settle the bribery question by a peep into the cheque-book afterwards. The ingenious Mr Cargrim was by no means pleased with this slip-slop method of conducting business. There was method in his villainy.

That evening, after despatching the telegram to Southberry, the chaplain repaired to The Derby Winner and found it largely patronised by a noisy and thirsty crowd. The weather was tropical, the workmen of Beorminster had received their wages, so they were converting the coin of the realm into beer and whisky as speedily as possible. The night was calm and comparatively cool with the spreading darkness, and the majority of the inhabitants were seated outside their doors gossiping and taking the air. Children were playing in the street, their shrill voices at times interrupting the continuous chatter of the women; and The Derby Winner, flaring with gas, was stuffed as full as it could hold with artizans, workmen, Irish harvesters and stablemen, all more or less exhilarated with alcohol. It was by no means a scene into which the fastidious Cargrim would have ventured of his own free will, but his desire to pump Jentham was greater than his sense of disgust, and he walked briskly into the hotel, to where Mr Mosk and Bell were dispensing drinks as fast as they were able. The crowd, having an inherent respect for the clergy, as became the inhabitants of a cathedral city, opened out to let him pass, and there was much less swearing and drinking when his black coat and clerical collar came into view. Mosk saw that the appearance of the chaplain was detrimental to business, and resenting his presence gave him but a surly greeting. As to Bell, she tossed her head, shot a withering glance of defiance at the bland new-comer, and withdrew to the far end of the bar.

'My friend,' said Cargrim, in his softest tones, 'I have come to see your wife and inquire how she is.'

'She's well enough,' growled Mosk, pushing a foaming tankard towards an expectant navvy, 'and what's more, sir, she's asleep, sir, so you can't see her.'

'I should be sorry to disturb her, Mr Mosk, so I will postpone my visit till a more fitted occasion. You seem to be busy to-night.'

'So busy that I've got no time for talking, sir.'

'Far be it from me to distract your attention, my worthy friend,' was the chaplain's bland reply, 'but with your permission I will remain in this corner and enjoy the humours of the scene.'

Mosk inwardly cursed the visitor for making this modest request, as he detested parsons on account of their aptitude to make teetotalers of his customers. He was a brute in his way, and a Radical to boot, so if he had dared he would have driven forth Cargrim with a few choice oaths. But as his visitor was the chaplain of the ecclesiastical sovereign of Beorminster, and was acquainted with Sir Harry Brace, the owner of the hotel, and further, as Mosk could not pay his rent and was already in bad odour with his landlord, he judged it wise to be diplomatic, lest a word from Cargrim to the bishop and Sir Harry should make matters worse. He therefore grudgingly gave the required permission.

'Though this ain't a sight fit for the likes of you, sir,' he grumbled, waving his hand. 'This lot smells and they swears, and they gets rowdy in their cups, so I won't answer as they won't offend you.'

'My duty has carried me into much more

unsavoury localities, my friend. The worse the place the more is my presence, as a clergyman, necessary.'

'You ain't going to preach, sir?' cried Mosk, in alarm.

'No! that would indeed be casting pearls before swine,' replied Cargrim, in his cool tones. 'But I will observe and reflect.'

The landlord looked uneasy. 'I know as the place is rough,' he said apologetically, 'but 'tain't my fault. You won't go talking to Sir Harry, I hope, sir, and take the bread out of my mouth?'

'Make your mind easy, Mosk. It is not my place to carry tales to your landlord; and I am aware that the lower orders cannot conduct themselves with decorum, especially on Saturday night. I repine that such a scene should be possible in a Christian land, but I don't blame you for its existence.'

'That's all right, sir,' said Mosk, with a sigh of relief. 'I'm rough but honest, whatever lies may be told to the contrary. If I can't pay my rent, that ain't my fault, I hope, as it ain't to be expected as I can do miracles.'

'The age of miracles is past, my worthy friend,' replied Cargrim, in conciliatory tones. 'We must not expect the impossible nowadays. By the way' — with a sudden change — 'have you a man called Jentham here?'

‘Yes, I have,’ growled Mosk, looking suspiciously at his questioner. ‘What do you know of him, sir?’

‘Nothing; but I take an interest in him as he seems to be one who has known better days.’

‘He don’t know them now, at all events, Mr Cargrim. He owes me money for this last week, he does. He paid all right at fust, but he don’t pay now.’

‘Indeed,’ said the chaplain, pricking up his ears, ‘he owes you money?’

‘That he does; more nor two quid, sir. But he says he’ll pay me soon.’

‘Ah! he says he’ll pay you soon,’ repeated Cargrim; ‘he expects to receive money, then?’

‘I s’pose so, tho’ Lord knows! — I beg pardon, sir — tho’ goodness knows where it’s coming from. He don’t work or get wages as I can see.’

‘I think I know,’ thought Cargrim; then added aloud, ‘Is the man here?’

‘In the coffee-room yonder, sir. Half drunk he is, and lying like a good one. The yarns he reels off is wonderful.’

‘No doubt; a man like that must be interesting to listen to. With your permission, Mr Mosk, I’ll go into the coffee-room.’

‘Straight ahead, sir. Will you take something

to drink, if I may make so bold, Mr Cargrim?'

'No, my friend, no; thank you all the same,' and with a nod Cargrim pushed his way into the coffee-room to see the man with the scar.

9

An Exciting Adventure

Mr Cargrim found a considerable number of people in the coffee-room, and these, with tankards and glasses before them, were listening to the conversation of Jentham. Tobacco smoke filled the apartment with a thick atmosphere of fog, through which the gas-lights flared in a nebulous fashion, and rendered the air so hot that it was difficult to breathe in spite of the windows being open. At the head of the long table sat Jentham, drinking brandy-and-soda, and speaking in his cracked, refined voice with considerable spirit, his rat-like, quick eyes glittering the while with alcoholic lustre. He seemed to be considerably under the influence of drink, and his voice ran up and down from bass to treble as he became excited in narrating his adventures.

Whether these were true or false Cargrim could not determine; for although the man trenched again and again on the marvellous, he certainly seemed to be fully acquainted with what he was talking about, and related the most wonderful stories in a thoroughly dramatic fashion. Like Ulysses, he knew men and cities, and appeared to have travelled as much as that famous globe-trotter. In his narration he passed from China to Chili, sailed north to the Pole, steamed south to the Horn, described the paradise of the South Seas, and discoursed about the wild wastes of snowy Siberia. The capitals of Europe appeared to be as familiar to him as the chair he was seated in; and the steppes of Russia, the deserts of Africa, the sheep runs of Australia were all mentioned in turn, as adventure after adventure fell from his lips. And mixed up with these geographical accounts were thrilling tales of treasure-hunting, of escapes from savages, of perilous deeds in the secret places of great cities; and details of blood, and war, and lust, and hate, all told in a fiercely dramatic fashion. The man was a tramp, a gipsy, a ragged, penniless rollingstone; but in his own way he was a genius. Cargrim wondered, with all his bravery, and endurance, and resource, that he had not made his fortune. The eloquent scamp seemed to wonder also.

'For,' said he, striking the table with his fist, 'I have never been able to hold what I won. I've been a millionaire twice over, but the gold wouldn't stay; it drifted away, it was swept away, it vanished, like Macbeth's witches, into thin air. Look at me, you country cabbages! I've reigned a king amongst savages. A poor sort of king, say you; but a king's a king, say I; and king I have been. Yet here I am, sitting in a Beorminster gutter, but I don't stay in it. By —,' he confirmed his purpose with an oath, 'not I. I've got my plans laid, and they'll lift me up to the stars yet.'

'Hev you the money, mister?' inquired a sceptical listener.

'What's that to you?' cried Jentham, and finished his drink. 'Yes, I have money!' He set down his empty glass with a bang. 'At least I know where to get it. Bah! you fools, one can get blood out of a stone if one knows how to go about it. I know! I know! My Tom Tiddler's ground isn't far from your holy township,' and he began to sing, —

'Southberry Heath's Tom Tiddler's ground,
Gold and silver are there to be found.
It's dropped by the priest, picked up by the knave,
For the one is a coward, the other is brave.
More brandy, waiter; make it stiff, sonny! stiff! stiff! stiff!'

The man's wild speech and rude song were unintelligible to his stupid, drink-bemused audience; but the keen brain of the schemer lurking near the door picked up their sense at once. Dr Pendle was the priest who was to drop the money on Southberry Heath, and Jentham the knave who was to pick it up. As certainly as though the man had given chapter and verse, Cargrim understood his enigmatic stave. His mind flashed back to the memory that Dr Pendle intended to ride over to Southberry in the morning, across the heath. Without doubt he had agreed to meet there this man who boasted that he could get blood out of a stone, and the object of the meeting was to bribe him to silence. But however loosely Jentham alluded to his intention of picking up gold, he was cunning enough, with all his excitement, to hold his tongue as to how he could work such a miracle. Undoubtedly there was a secret between Dr Pendle and this scamp; but what it might be, Cargrim could by no means guess. Was Jentham a disreputable relation of the bishop's? Had Dr Pendle committed a crime in his youth for which he was now being blackmailed? What could be the nature of the secret which gave this unscrupulous blackguard a hold on a dignitary of the Church? Cargrim's brain was quite bewildered by his conjectures.

Hitherto Jentham had been in the blabbing stage of intoxication, but after another glass of drink he relapsed into a sullen, silent condition, and with his eyes on the table pulled fiercely at his pipe, so that his wicked face looked out like that of a devil from amid the rolling clouds of smoke. His audience waited open-mouthed for more stories, but as their entertainer seemed too moody to tell them any more, they began to talk amongst themselves, principally about horses and dogs. It was now growing late, and the most respectable of the crowd were moving homeward. Cargrim felt that to keep up the dignity of his cloth he should depart also; for several looks of surprise were cast in his direction. But Jentham and his wild speeches fascinated him, and he lurked in his corner, watching the sullen face of the man until the two were left the sole occupants of the room. Then Jentham looked up to call the waiter to bring him a final drink, and his eyes met those of Mr Cargrim. After a keen glance he suddenly broke into a peal of discordant laughter, which died away into a savage and menacing growl.

'Hallo!' he grumbled, 'here is the busybody of Beorminster. And what may you want, Mr Paul Pry?'

'A little civility in the first place, my worthy friend,' said Cargrim, in silky tones, for he did not relish the insolent tone of the satirical scamp.

'I am no friend to spies!'

'How dare you speak to me like that, fellow?'

'You call me a fellow and I'll knock your head off,' cried Jentham, rising with a savage look in his eyes. 'If you aren't a spy why do you come sneaking round here?'

'I came to see Mrs Mosk,' explained the chaplain, in a mighty dignified manner, 'but she is asleep, so I could not see her. In passing the door of this room I heard you relating your adventures, and I naturally stopped to listen.'

'To hear if I had anything to say about my visit to your bishop, I suppose?' growled Jentham, unpleasantly. 'I have a great mind to tell him how you watch me, you infernal devil-dodger!'

'Respect my cloth, sir.'

'Begin by respecting it yourself, d— you. What would his lordship of Beorminster say if he knew you were here?'

'His lordship does know.'

Jentham started. 'Perhaps he sent you?' he said, looking doubtful.

'No, he did not,' contradicted Cargrim, who saw that nothing was to be learned while the man was thus bemused with drink. 'I have told you the reason of my presence here. And as I am here, I warn you, as a clergyman, not to drink any more. You have already had more than enough.'

Jentham was staggered by the boldness of the chaplain, and stared at him open-mouthed; then recovering his speech, he poured forth such a volley of vile words at Cargrim that the chaplain stepped to the door and called the landlord. He felt that it was time for him to assert himself.

'This man is drunk, Mosk,' said he, sharply, 'and if you keep such a creature on your premises you will get into trouble.'

'Creature yourself!' cried Jentham, advancing towards Cargrim. 'I'll wring your neck if you use such language to me. I've killed fifty better men than you in my time. Mosk!' he turned with a snarl on the landlord, 'get me a drink of brandy.'

'I think you've had enough, Mr Jentham,' said the landlord, with a glance at Cargrim, 'and you know you owe me money.'

'Curse you, what of that?' raved Jentham, stamping. 'Do you think I'll not pay you?'

'I've not seen the colour of your money lately.'

'You'll see it when I choose. I'll have hundreds of pounds next week — hundreds;' and he broke out fiercely, 'get me more brandy; don't mind that devil-dodger.'

'Go to bed,' said Mosk, retiring, 'go to bed.'

Jentham ran after him with an angry cry, so Cargrim, feeling himself somewhat out of place in this pot-house row, nodded to Mosk and left the hotel with as much dignity as he could muster. As he went, the burden of Jentham's last speech — 'hundreds of pounds! hundreds of pounds!' — rang in his ears; and more than ever he desired to examine the bishop's cheque-book, in order to ascertain the exact sum. The secret, he thought, must indeed be a precious one when the cost of its preservation ran into three figures.

When Cargrim emerged into the street it was still filled with people, as ten o'clock was just chiming from the cathedral tower. The gossipers had retired within, and lights were gleaming in the upper windows of the houses; but knots of neighbours still stood about here and there, talking and laughing loudly. Cargrim strolled slowly down the street towards the Eastgate, musing over his late experience, and enjoying the coolness of the night air after the sultry atmosphere of the coffee-room. The sky was now brilliant with stars, and a silver moon rolled aloft in the blue arch, shedding down floods of light on the town, and investing its commonplace aspect with something of romance. The streets were radiant with the cold, clear lustre; the shadows cast by the houses lay black as Indian ink on the ground; and the laughter and noise of the passers-by seemed woefully out of place in this magical white world.

Cargrim was alive to the beauty of the night, but was too much taken up with his thoughts to pay much attention to its mingled mystery of shadow and light. As he took his musing way through the wide streets of the modern town, he was suddenly brought to a standstill by hearing the voice of Jentham some distance away. Evidently the man had quarrelled with the landlord, and had been turned out of the hotel, for he came rolling along in a lurching, drunken manner, roaring out a wild and savage ditty, picked up, no doubt, in some land at the back of beyond.

'Oh, I have treked the eight world climes,
And sailed the seven seas:
I've made my pile a hundred times,
And chucked the lot on sprees.

But when my ship comes home, my lads,
Why, curse me, don't I know
The spot that's worth, the blooming earth,
The spot where I shall go.

They call it Callao! for oh, it's Callao.
For on no condition

Is extradition
Allowed in Callao.'

Jentham roared and ranted the fierce old chanty with as much gusto and noise as though he were camping in the waste lands to which the song applied, instead of disturbing the peace of a quiet English town. As his thin form came swinging along in the silver light, men and women drew back with looks of alarm to let him pass, and Cargrim, not wishing to have trouble with the drunken bully, slipped into the shadow of a house until he passed. As usual, there was no policeman visible, and Jentham went bellowing and storming through the quiet summer night like the dissolute ruffian he was. He was making for the country in the direction of the palace, and wondering if he intended to force his way into the house to threaten Dr Pendle, the chaplain followed immediately behind. But he was careful to keep out of sight, as Jentham was in just the excited frame of mind to draw a knife: and Cargrim, knowing his lawless nature, had little doubt but that he had one concealed in his boot or trouser belt. The delicate coward shivered at the idea of a rough-and-tumble encounter with an armed buccaneer.

On went Jentham, swinging his arms with

mad gestures, and followed by the black shadow of the chaplain, until the two were clear of the town. Then the gipsy turned down a shadowy lane, cut through a footpath, and when he emerged again into the broad roadway, found himself opposite the iron gates of the episcopalian park. Here he stopped singing and shook his fist at them.

'Come out, you devil-dodger!' he bellowed savagely. 'Come out and give me money, or I'll shame you before the whole town, you clerical hypocrite.' Then he took a pull at a pocket-flask.

Cargrim listened eagerly in the hope of hearing something definite, and Jentham gathered himself together for further denunciation of the bishop, when round the corner tripped two women, towards whom his drunken attention was at once attracted. With a hoarse chuckle he reeled towards them.

'Come along m' beauty,' he hiccuped, stretching out his arms, 'here's your haven. Wine and women! I love them both.'

The women both shrieked, and rushed along the road, pursued by the ruffian. Just as he laid rude hands on the last one, a young man came racing along the footpath and swung into the middle of the road. The next moment Jentham lay sprawling on his back, and the lady assaulted was clinging to the arm of her preserver.

'Why, it's Mab!' said the young man, in surprise.

'George!' cried Miss Arden, and burst into tears. 'Oh, George!'

'Curse you both!' growled Jentham, rising slowly. 'I'll be even with you for that blow, my lad.'

'I'll kick you into the next field if you don't clear out,' retorted George Pendle. 'Did he hurt you, Mab?'

'No! no! but I was afraid. I was at Mrs Tear's, and was coming home with Ellen, when that man jumped on to us. Oh! oh! oh!'

'The villain!' cried Captain Pendle; 'who is he?'

It was at this moment that, all danger being over, Cargrim judged it judicious to emerge from his retreat. He came forward hurriedly, as though he had just arrived on the scene.

'What is the matter?' he exclaimed. 'I heard a scream. What, Captain Pendle! Miss Arden! This is indeed a surprise.'

'Captain Pendle!' cried Jentham. 'The son of the bishop. Curse him!'

George whirled his stick and made a dash at the creature, but was restrained by Mab, who implored him not to provoke further quarrels.

George took her arm within his own, gave a

curt nod to the chaplain, whom he suspected had seen more of the affray than he chose to admit, and flung a word to Jentham.

'Clear out, you dog!' he said, 'or I'll hand you over to the police. Come, Mab, yonder is Ellen waiting for you. We'll join her, and I shall see you both home.'

Jentham stood looking after the three figures with a scowl. 'You'll hand me over to the police, George Pendle, will you?' he muttered, loud enough for Cargrim to overhear. 'Take care I don't do the same thing to your father,' and like a noisome and dangerous animal he crept back in the shadow of the hedge and disappeared.

'Aha!' chuckled Cargrim, as he walked towards the park gates, 'it has to do with the police, then, my lord bishop. So much the better for me, so much the worse for you.'

10

Morning Service in the Minster

The cathedral is the glory of Beorminster, of the county, and, indeed, of all England, since no churches surpass it in size and splendour, save the minsters of York and Canterbury. Founded and endowed by Henry II in 1184 for the glory of God, it is dedicated to the blessed Saint Wulf of Osserton, a holy hermit of Saxon times, who was killed by the heathen Danes. Bishop Gandolf designed the building in the picturesque style of Anglo-Norman architecture; and as the original plans have been closely adhered to by successive prelates, the vast fabric is the finest example extant of the Norman superiority in architectural science. It was begun by Gandolf in 1185, and finished at the beginning of the present century; therefore, as it took six hundred years in building, every portion of it is executed in the most perfect manner. It is renowned both for its beauty and sanctity, and forms one of the most splendid memorials of architectural art and earnest faith to be found even in England, that land of fine churches.

The great central tower rises to the height of two hundred feet in square massiveness, and from this point springs a slender and graceful spire to another hundred feet, so that next to Salisbury, the great archetype of this special class of ecclesiastical architecture, it is the tallest spire in England. Two square towers, richly ornamented, embellish the western front, and beneath the great window over the central entrance is a series of canopied arches. The church is cruciform in shape, and is built of Portland stone, the whole being richly ornamented with pinnacles, buttresses, crocketted spires and elaborate tracery. Statues of saints, kings, queens and bishops are placed in niches along the northern and southern fronts, and the western front itself is sculptured with scenes from Holy Scripture in the quaint grotesque style of mediæval art. No ivy is permitted to conceal the beauties of the building; and elevated in the clear air, far above the smoke of the town, it looks as fresh and white and clean cut as though it had been erected only within the last few years. Spared by Henry VIII and the iconoclastic rage of the Puritans, Time alone has dealt with it; and Time has mellowed the whole to a pale amber hue which adds greatly to the beauty of the mighty fane. Beorminster Cathedral is a poem in stone.

Within, the nave and transepts are lofty and imposing, with innumerable arches springing from massive marble pillars. The rood screen is ornate, with figures of saints and patriarchs; the pavement is diversified with brasses and carved marble slabs, and several Crusaders' tombs adorn the side chapels. The many windows are mostly of stained glass, since these were not destroyed by the Puritans; and when the sun shines on a summer's day the twilight interior is dyed with rich hues and quaint patterns. As the Bishop of Beorminster is a High Churchman the altar is magnificently decorated, and during service, what with the light and colour and brilliancy, the vast building seems — unlike the dead aspect of many of its kind — to be filled with life and movement and living faith. A Romanist might well imagine that he was attending one of the magnificent and imposing services of his own faith, save that the uttered words are spoken in the mother tongue.

As became a city whose whole existence depended upon the central shrine, the services at the cathedral were invariably well attended. The preaching attracted some, the fine music many, and the imposing ritual introduced by Bishop Pendle went a great way towards bringing worshippers to the altar. A cold, frigid, undecorated service, appealing more to the intellect than the senses, would not have drawn together so vast and attentive a congregation; but the warmth and colour and musical fervour of the new ritual lured the most careless within the walls of the sacred building. Bishop Pendle was right in his estimate of human nature; for when the senses are enthralled by colour and sound, and vast spaces, and symbolic decorations the reverential feeling thus engendered prepares the mind for the reception of the sublime truths of Christianity. A pure faith and a gorgeous ritual are not so incompatible as many people think. God should be worshipped with pomp and splendour; we should bring to His service all that we can invent in the way of art and beauty. If God has prepared for those who believe the splendid habitation of the New Jerusalem with its gates of pearl and its streets of gold, why should we, His creatures, stint our gifts in His service, and debar the beautiful things, which He inspires us to create with brain and hand, from use in His holy temple? 'Out of the fulness of the heart the mouth speaketh,' and out of the fulness of the hand the giver should give. '*Date et dabitur!*' The great Luther was right in applying this saying to the church.

One of the congregation at St Wulf's on this particular morning was Captain George Pendle, and he came less for the service than in the hope — after the manner of those in love — of meeting with Mab Arden. During the reading of the lessons his eyes were roving here and there in search of that beloved face, but much to his dismay he could not see it. Finally, on a chair near a pillar, he caught sight of Miss Whichello in her poke bonnet and black silk cloak, but she was alone, and there were no bright eyes beside her to send a glance in the direction of George. Having ascertained beyond all doubt that Mab was not in the church, and believing that she was unwell after the shock of Jentham's attack on the previous night, George withdrew his attention from the congregation, and settled himself to listen attentively to the anthem. It was worthy of the cathedral, and higher praise cannot be given. 'I have blotted out as a thick cloud,' sang the boy soloist in a clear sweet treble, 'I have blotted out thy transgressions, and as a cloud thy sins.' Then came the triumphant cry of the choir, borne on the rich waves of sound rolling from the organ, 'Return unto me, for I have redeemed thee.' The lofty roof reverberated with the melodious thunder, and the silvery altoes pierced through the great volume of sound like arrows of song. 'Return! Return! Return!' called the choristers louder and higher and clearer, and ended, with a magnificent burst of harmony, with the sublime proclamation, 'The Lord hath redeemed Jacob, and glorified himself in Israel!' When the white-robed singers resumed their seats, the organ still continued to peal forth triumphant notes, which died away in gentle murmurs. It was like the passing by of a tempest; the stilling of the ocean after a storm.

Mr Cargrim preached the sermon, and, with a vivid recollection of his present enterprise, waxed eloquent on the ominous text, 'Be sure thy sin will find thee out.' His belief that the bishop was guilty of some crime, for the concealment of which he intended to bribe Jentham, had been strengthened by an examination on that very morning of the cheque-book. Dr Pendle had departed on horseback for Southberry after an early breakfast, and after hurriedly despatching his own, Cargrim had hastened to the library. Here, as he expected, he found the cheque-book carelessly left in an unlocked drawer of the desk, and on looking over it he found that one of the butts had been torn out. The previous butt bore a date immediately preceding that of Dr Pendle's departure for London, so Cargrim had little difficulty in concluding that the bishop had drawn the next cheque in London, and had torn out the butt to which it had been attached. This showed, as the chaplain very truly thought, that Dr Pendle was desirous of concealing not only the amount of the cheque — since he had kept no note of the sum on the butt — but of hiding the fact that the cheque had been drawn at all. This conduct, coupled with the fact of Jentham's allusion to Tom Tiddler's ground, and his snatch of extempore song, confirmed Cargrim in his suspicions that Pendle had visited London for the purpose of drawing out a large sum of money, and intended to pay the same over to Jentham that very night on Southberry Heath. With this in his mind it was no wonder that Cargrim preached a stirring sermon. He repeated his warning text over and over again; he illustrated it in the most brilliant fashion; and his appeals to those who had secret sins, to confess them at once, were quite heartrending in their pathos. As most of his congregation had their own little peccadilloes to worry over, Mr Cargrim's sermon made them quite uneasy, and created a decided sensation, much to his own gratification. If Bishop Pendle had only been seated on his throne to hear that sermon, Cargrim would have been thoroughly satisfied. But, alas! the bishop — worthy man — was confirming innocent sinners at Southberry, and thus lost any chance he might have had of profiting by his chaplain's eloquence.

However, the congregation could not be supposed to know the secret source of the chaplain's eloquence, and his withering denunciations were supposed to arise from a consciousness of his own pure and open heart. The female admirers of Cargrim particularly dwelt in after-church gossip on this presumed cause of the excellent sermon they had heard, and when the preacher appeared he was congratulated on all sides. Miss Tancred for once forgot her purse story, and absolutely squeaked, in the highest of keys, in her efforts to make the young man understand the amount of pleasure he had given her. Even Mrs Pansey was pleased to express her approval of so well chosen a text, and looked significantly at several of her friends as she remarked that she hoped they would take its warning to heart.

George came upon his father's chaplain, grinning like a heathen idol, in the midst of a tempestuous ocean of petticoats, and the bland way in which he sniffed up the incense of praise showed how grateful such homage was to his vain nature. At that moment he saw himself a future bishop, and that at no very great distance of time. Indeed, had the election of such a prelate been in the hands of his admirers, he would have been elevated that very moment to the nearest vacant episcopalian throne. Captain Pendle looked on contemptuously at this priest-worship.

'The sneaking cad!' he thought, sneering at the excellent Cargrim. 'I dare say he thinks he is the greatest man in Beorminster just now. He looks as though butter wouldn't melt in his mouth.'

There was no love lost between the chaplain and the captain, for on several occasions the latter had found Cargrim a slippery customer, and lax in his notions of honour; while the curate, knowing that he had not been clever enough to hoodwink George, hated him with all the fervour and malice of his petty soul. However, he hoped soon to have the power to wound Captain Pendle through his father, so he could afford to smile blandly in response to the young soldier's contemptuous look. And he smiled more than ever when brisk Miss Whichello, with her small face, ruddy as a winter apple, marched up and joined in the congratulations.

'In future I shall call you Boanerges, Mr Cargrim,' she cried, her bright little eyes dancing. 'You quite frightened me. I looked into my mind to see what sins I had committed.'

'And found none, I'm sure,' said the courtly chaplain.

'You would have found one if you had looked long enough,' growled Mrs Pansey, who hated the old maid as a rival practitioner amongst the poor, 'and that is, you did not bring your niece to hear the sermon. I don't call such carelessness Christianity.'

'Don't look at my sins through a microscope, Mrs Pansey. I did not bring Mab because she is not well.'

'Oh, really, dear Miss Winchello,' chimed in Daisy Norsham. 'Why, I thought that your sweet niece looked the very picture of health. All those strong, tall women do; not like poor little me.'

'You need dieting,' retorted Miss Whichello, with a disparaging glance. 'Your face is pale and pasty; if it isn't powder, it's bad digestion.'

'Miss Whichello!' cried the outraged spinster.

'I'm an old woman, my dear, and you must allow me to speak my mind. I'm sure Mrs Pansey always does.'

'You need not be so very unpleasant! No, really!'

'The truth is always unpleasant,' said Mrs Pansey, who could not forbear a thrust even at her own guest, 'but Miss Whichello doesn't often hear it,' with a dig at her rival. 'Come away, Daisy. Mr Cargrim, next time you preach take for your text, 'The tongue is a two-edged sword.''

'Do, Mr Cargrim,' cried Miss Whichello, darting an angry glance at Mrs Pansey, 'and illustrate it with the one to whom it particularly applies.'

'Ladies! ladies!' remonstrated Cargrim, while both combatants ruffled their plumes like two fighting cocks, and the more timid of the spectators scuttled out of the way. How the situation would have ended it is impossible to say, as the two ladies were equally matched, but George saved it by advancing to greet Miss Whichello. When the little woman saw him, she darted forward and shook his hand with unfeigned warmth.

'My dear Captain Pendle,' she cried, 'I am so glad to see you; and thank you for your noble conduct of last night.'

'Why, Miss Whichello, it was nothing,' murmured the modest hero.

'Indeed, I must say it was very valiant,' said Cargrim, graciously. 'Do you know, ladies, that Miss Arden was attacked last night by a tramp and Captain Pendle knocked him down?'

'Oh, really! how very sweet!' cried Daisy, casting an admiring look on George's handsome face, which appealed to her appreciation of manly beauty.

'What was Miss Arden doing to place herself in the position of being attacked by a tramp?' asked Mrs Pansey, in a hard voice. 'This must be looked into.'

'Thank you, Mrs Pansey, I have looked into it myself,' said Miss Whichello. 'Captain Pendle, come home with me to luncheon and tell me all about it; Mr Cargrim, you come also.'

Both gentlemen bowed and accepted, the former because he wished to see Mab, the latter because he knew that Captain Pendle did not want him to come. As Miss Whichello moved off with her two guests, Mrs Pansey exclaimed in a loud voice, —

'Poor young men! Luncheon indeed! They will be starved. I know for a fact that she weighs out the food in scales.' Then, having had the last word, she went home in triumph.

11

Miss Whichello's Luncheon-Party

The little lady trotted briskly across the square, and guided her guests to a quaint old house squeezed into one corner of it. Here she had been born some sixty-odd years before; here she had lived her life of spinsterhood, save for an occasional visit to London; and here she hoped to die, although at present she kept Death at a safe distance by hygienic means and dietary treatment. The house was a queer survival of three centuries, with a pattern of black oak beams let into a white-washed front. Its roof shot up into a high gable at an acute angle, and was tiled with red clay squares, mellowed by Time to the hue of rusty iron. A long lattice with diamond panes, and geraniums in flower-pots behind them, extended across the lower storey; two little jutting windows, also of the criss-cross pattern, looked like two eyes in the second storey; and high up in the third, the casement of the attic peered out coyly from under the eaves. At the top of a flight of immaculately white steps there was a squat little door painted green and adorned with a brass knocker burnished to the colour of fine gold. The railings of iron round the area were also coloured green, and the appearance of the whole exterior was as spotless and neat as Miss Whichello herself. It was an ideal house for a dainty old spinster such as she was, and rested in the very shadow of the Bishop Gandolf's cathedral like the nest of a bright-eyed wren.

'Mab, my dear!' cried the wren herself, as she led the gentlemen into the drawing-room, 'I have brought Captain Pendle and Mr Cargrim to luncheon.'

Mab arose out of a deep chair and laid aside the book she was reading. 'I saw you crossing the square, Captain Pendle,' she said, shaking his hand. 'Mr Cargrim, I am glad to see you.'

'Are you not glad to see me?' whispered George, in low tones.

'Do you need me to tell you so?' was Mab's reply, with a smile, and that smile answered his question.

'Oh, my dear, such a heavenly sermon!' cried Miss Whichello, fluttering about the room; 'it went to my very heart.'

'It could not have gone to a better place,' replied the chaplain, in the gentle voice which George particularly detested. 'I am sorry to hear you have suffered from your alarm last night, Miss Arden.'

'My nerves received rather a shock, Mr Cargrim, and I had such a bad headache that I decided to remain at home. I must receive your sermon second-hand from my aunt.'

'Why not first-hand from me?' said Cargrim, insinuatingly, whereupon Captain George pulled his moustache and looked savage.

'Oh, I won't tax your good nature so far,' rejoined Mab, laughing. 'What is it, aunty?' for the wren was still fluttering and restless.

'My dear, you must content yourself with Captain Pendle till luncheon, for I want Mr Cargrim to come into the garden and see my fig tree; real figs grow on it, Mr Cargrim,' said Miss Whichello, solemnly, 'the very first figs that have ever ripened in Beorminster.'

'I am glad it is not a barren fig tree,' said Cargrim, introducing a scriptural allusion in his most clerical manner.

'Barren indeed! it has five figs on it. Really, sitting under its shade one would fancy one was in Palestine. Do come, Mr Cargrim,' and Miss Whichello fluttered through the door like an escaping bird.

'With pleasure; the more so, as I know we shall not be missed.'

'Damn!' muttered Captain Pendle, when

the door closed on Cargrim's smile and insinuating looks.

'Captain Pendle!' exclaimed Miss Arden, becomingly shocked.

'Captain Pendle indeed!' said the young man, slipping his arm round Mab; 'and why not George?'

'I thought Mr Cargrim might hear.'

'He ought to; like the ass, his ears are long enough.'

'Still, he is anything but an ass — George.'

'If he isn't an ass he's a beast,' rejoined Pendle, promptly, 'and it comes to much the same thing.'

'Well, you need not swear at him.'

'If I didn't swear I'd kick him, Mab; and think of the scandal to the Church. Cargrim's a sneaking, time-serving sycophant. I wonder my father can endure him; I can't!'

'I don't like him myself,' confessed Mab, as they seated themselves in the window-seat.

'I should — think — not!' cried Captain George, in so deliberate and disgusted a tone that Mab laughed. Whereat he kissed her and was reproved, so that both betook themselves to argument as to the righteousness or unrighteousness of kissing on a Sunday.

George Pendle was a tall, slim, and very good-looking young man in every sense of the word. He was as fair as Mab was dark, with bright blue eyes and a bronzed skin, against which his smartly-pointed moustache appeared by contrast almost white. With his upright figure, his alert military air, and merry smile, he looked an extremely handsome and desirable lover; and so Mab thought, although she reproved him with orthodox modesty for snatching a kiss unasked. But if men had to request favours of this sort, there would not be much kissing in the world. Moreover, stolen kisses, like stolen fruit, have a piquant flavour of their own.

The quaint old drawing-room, with its low ceiling and twilight atmosphere, was certainly an ideal place for love-making. It was furnished with chairs, and tables, and couches, which had done duty in the days of Miss Whichello's grandparents; and if the carpet was old, so much the better, for its once brilliant tints had faded into soft hues more restful to the eye. In one corner stood the grandfather of all pianos, with a front of drawn green silk fluted to a central button; beside it a prim canterbury, filled with primly-bound books of yellow-paged music, containing, 'The Battle of the Prague,' 'The Maiden's Prayer,' 'Cherry Ripe,' and 'The Canary Bird's Quadrilles.' Such tinkling melodies had been the delight of Miss Whichello's youth, and — as she had a fine finger for the piano (her own observation) — she sometimes tinkled them now on the jingling old piano when old friends came to see her. Also there were Chippendale cupboards with glass doors, filled with a most wonderful collection of old china — older even than their owner; Chinese jars heaped up with dried rose leaves spreading around a perfume of dead summers; bright silken screens from far Japan; foot-stools and fender-stools worked in worsted which tripped up the unwary; and a number of oil-paintings valuable rather for age than beauty. None of your modern flimsy drawing-rooms was Miss Whichello's, but a dear, delightful, cosy room full of faded splendours and relics of the dead and gone so dearly beloved. From the yellow silk fire-screen swinging on a rosewood pole, to the drowsy old canary chirping feebly in his brass cage at the window, all was old-world and marvellously proper and genteel. Withal, a quiet, perfumed room, delightful to make love in, to the most beautiful woman in the world, as Captain George Pendle knew very well.

'Though it really isn't proper for you to kiss me,' observed Mab, folding her slender hands on her white gown. 'You know we are not engaged.'

'I know nothing of the sort, my dearest prude. You are the only woman I ever intend to marry. Have you any objections? If so, I should like to hear them.'

'I am two years older than you, George.'

'A man is as old as he looks, a woman as she feels. I am quite convinced, Miss Arden, that you feel nineteen years of age, so the disparity rests rather on my shoulders than on yours.'

'You don't look old,' laughed Mab, letting her hand lie in that of her lover's.

'But I feel old — old enough to marry you, my dear. What is your next objection?'

'Your father does not know that you love me.'

'My mother does; Lucy does; and with two women to persuade him, my dear, kind old father will gladly consent to the match.'

'I have no money.'

'My dearest, neither have I. Two negatives make an affirmative, and that affirmative is to be uttered by you when I ask if I may tell the bishop that you are willing to become a soldier's wife.'

'Oh, George!' cried Mab, anxiously, 'it is a very serious matter. You know how particular your father is about birth and family. My parents are dead; I never knew them; for my father died before I was born, and my mother followed him to the grave when I was a year old. If my dear mother's sister had not taken charge of me and brought me up, I should very likely have gone on the parish; for — as aunty says — my parents were paupers.'

'My lovely pauper, what is all this to me? Here is your answer to all the nonsense you have been talking,' and George, with the proverbial boldness of a soldier, laid a fond kiss on the charming face so near to his own.

'Oh, George!' began the scandalised Mab, for the fifth time at least, and was about to reprove her audacious lover again, when Miss Whichello bustled into the room, followed by the black shadow of the parson. George and Mab sprang apart with alacrity, and each wondered, while admiring the cathedral opposite, if Miss Whichello or Cargrim had heard the sound of that stolen kiss. Apparently the dear, unsuspecting old Jenny Wren had not, for she hopped up to the pair in her bird-like fashion, and took George's arm.

'Come, good people,' she said briskly, 'luncheon is ready; and so are your appetites, I've no doubt. Mr Cargrim, take in my niece.'

In five minutes the quartette were seated round a small table in Miss Whichello's small dining-room. The apartment was filled with oak furniture black with age and wondrously carved; the curtains and carpet and cushions were of faded crimson rep, and as the gaily-striped sun-blinds were down, the whole was enwrapped in a sober brown atmosphere restful to the eye and cool to the skin. The oval table was covered with a snow-white cloth, on which sparkled silver and crystal round a Nankin porcelain bowl of blue and white filled with deep red roses. The dinner-plates were of thin china, painted with sprawling dragons in yellow and green; the food, in spite of Mrs Pansey's report, was plentiful and dainty, and the wines came from the stock laid down by the father of the hostess in the days when dignitaries of the Church knew what good wine was. It is true that a neat pair of brass scales was placed beside Miss Whichello, but she used them to weigh out such portions of food as she judged to be needful for herself, and did not mar her hospitality by interfering with the appetites of her guests. The repast was tempting, the company congenial, and the two young men enjoyed themselves greatly. Miss Whichello was an entertainer worth knowing, if only for her cook.

'Mab, my dear,' cried the lively old lady, 'I am ashamed of your appetite. Don't you feel better for your morning's rest?'

'Much better, thank you, aunty, but it is too hot to eat.'

'Try some salad, my love; it is cool and green, and excellent for the blood. If I had my way, people should eat more green stuff than they do.'

'Like so many Nebuchadnezzars,' suggested Cargrim, always scriptural.

'Well, some kinds of grass are edible, you know, Mr Cargrim; although we need not go on all fours to eat them as he did.'

'So many people would need to revert to their natural characters of animals if that custom came in,' said George, smiling.

'A certain great poet remarked that everyone had a portion of the nature of some animal,' observed Cargrim, 'especially women.'

'Then Mrs Pansey is a magpie,' cried Mab, with an arch look at her aunt.

'She is a magpie, and a fox, and a laughing hyæna, my dear.'

'Oh, aunty, what a trinity!'

'I suppose, Cargrim, all you black-coated parsons are rooks,' said George.

'No doubt, captain; and you soldiers are lions.'

'Aunty is a Jenny Wren!'

'And Mab is a white peacock,' said Miss Whichello, with a nod.

'Captain Pendle, protect me,' laughed Miss Arden. 'I decline to be called a peacock.'

'You are a golden bird of paradise, Miss Arden.'

'Ah, that is a pretty compliment, Captain

Pendle. Thank you!'

While George laughed, Cargrim, rather tired of these zoological comparisons, strove to change the subject by an allusion to the adventure of the previous night. 'The man who attacked you was certainly a wolf,' he said decisively.

'Who was the man?' asked Miss Whichello, carefully weighing herself some cheese.

'Some tramp who had been in the wars,' replied George, carelessly; 'a discharged soldier, I daresay. At least, he had a long red scar on his villainous-looking face. I saw it in the moonlight, marking him as with the brand of Cain.'

'A scar!' repeated Miss Whichello, in so altered a tone that Cargrim stared at her, and hastened to explain further, so as to learn, if possible, the meaning of her strange look.

'A scar on the right cheek,' he said slowly, 'from the ear to the mouth.'

'What kind of a looking man is he?' asked the old lady, pushing away her plate with a nervous gesture.

'Something like a gipsy — lean, tall and swarthy, with jet-black eyes and an evil expression. He talks like an educated person.'

'You seem to know all about him, Cargrim,' said Captain Pendle, in some surprise, while Miss Whichello, her rosy face pale and scared, sat silently staring at the tablecloth.

'I have several times been to an hotel called The Derby Winner,' explained the chaplain, 'to see a sick woman; and there I came across this scamp several times. He stays there, I believe!'

'What is his name?' asked Miss Whichello, hoarsely.

'Jentham, I have been informed.'

'Jentham! I don't know the name.'

'I don't suppose you know the man either, aunty?'

'No, my love,' replied Miss Whichello, in a low voice. 'I don't suppose I know the man either. Is he still at The Derby Winner, Mr Cargrim?'

'I believe so; he portions his time between that hotel and a gipsy camp on Southberry Common.'

'What is he doing here?'

'Really, my dear lady, I do not know.'

'Aunty, one would think you knew the man,' said Mab, amazed at her aunt's emotion.

'No, Mab, I do not,' said Miss Whichello, vehemently; more so than the remark warranted. 'But if he attacks people on the high road he should certainly be shut up. Well, good people,' she added, with an attempt at her former lively manner, 'if you are finished we will return to the drawing-room.'

All attempts to restore the earlier harmony of the visit failed, for the conversation languished and Miss Whichello was silent and distraught. The young men shortly took their leave, and the old lady seemed glad to be rid of them. Outside, George and Cargrim separated, as neither was anxious for the other's company. As the chaplain walked to the palace he reflected on the strange conduct of Miss Whichello.

'She knows something about Jentham,' he thought. 'I wonder if she has a secret also.'

12

Bell Mosk Pays a Visit

Although the palace was so near Beorminster, and the sphere of Gabriel's labours lay in the vicinity of the cathedral, Bishop Pendle did not judge it wise that his youngest son should dwell beneath the paternal roof. To teach him independence, to strengthen his will and character, and because he considered that a clergyman should, to a certain extent, share the lot of those amongst whom he laboured, the bishop arranged that Gabriel should inhabit lodgings in the old town, not far from The Derby Winner. It was by reason of this contiguity that Gabriel became acquainted with the handsome barmaid of the hotel, and as he was a more weak-natured man than his father dreamed of, it soon came about that he fell in love with the girl. Matters between them had gone much further than even Cargrim with all his suspicions guessed, for in the skilful hands of Miss Mosk the curate was as clay, and for some time he had been engaged to his charmer. No one knew this, not even Mrs Mosk, for the fair Bell was quite capable of keeping a secret; but Gabriel was firmly bound to her by honour, and Bell possessed a ring, which she kept in the drawer of her looking-glass and wore in secret, as symbolic of an engagement she did not dare to reveal.

On Sunday evening she arrayed herself in her best garments, and putting on this ring, told her mother that she was going to church. At first Mrs Mosk feebly objected, as her husband was away in Southberry and would not be back all night; but as Bell declared that she wanted some amusement after working hard at pulling beer all the week, Mrs Mosk gave way. She did not approve of Bell's mention of evening service as amusement, but she did approve of her going to church, so when the young lady had exhibited herself to the invalid in all her finery, she went away in the greatest good-humour. As the evening was hot, she had put on a dress of pale blue muslin adorned with white ribbons, a straw hat with many flowers and feathers, and to finish off her costume, her gloves and shoes and sunshade were white. As these cool colours rather toned down the extreme red of her healthy complexion, she really looked very well; and when Gabriel saw her seated in a pew near the pulpit, behaving as demurely as a cat that is after cream, he could not but think how pretty and pious she was. It was probably the first time that piety had ever been associated with Bell's character, although she was not a bad girl on the whole; but that Gabriel should gift her with such a quality showed how green and innocent he was as regards the sex.

The church in which he preached was an ancient building at the foot of the hill, crowned by the cathedral. It was built of rough, grey stone, in the Norman style of architecture, and very little had been done to adorn it either within or without, as the worshippers were few and poor, and Low Church in their tendencies. Those who liked pomp and colour and ritual could find all three in the minster, so there was no necessity to hold elaborate services in this grey, cold, little chapel. In her heart Bell preferred the cathedral with its music and choir, its many celebrants and fashionable congregation, but out of diplomacy she came to sit under Gabriel and follow him as her spiritual guide. Nevertheless, she thought less of him in this capacity, than as a future husband likely to raise her to a position worthy of her beauty and merits, of both of which she entertained a most excellent opinion.

As usual, the pews were half empty, but Gabriel, being a devout parson, performed the service with much earnestness. He read the lessons, lent his voice to the assistance of the meagre choir, and preached a short but sensible discourse which pleased everyone. Bell did not hear much of it, for her mind was busy with hopes that Gabriel would shortly induce his father to receive her as a daughter-in-law. It is true that she saw difficulties in the way, but, to a clever woman like herself, she did not think them unconquerable. Having gone so far as to engage herself to the young man, she was determined to go to the whole length and benefit as much as possible for her sacrifice — as she thought it — of accepting the somewhat trying position of a curate's wife. With her bold good looks and aggressive love of dress and amusement, Bell was hardly the type likely to do credit to a parsonage. But any doubts on that score never entered her vain mind.

When the service was over, and the sparse congregation had dwindled away, she went round to the vestry and asked Jarper, the cross old verger, if she could see Mr Pendle. Jarper, who took a paternal interest in the curate, and did not like Miss Mosk over much, since she stinted him of his full measure of beer when he patronised her father's hotel, replied in surly tones that Mr

Pendle was tired and would see no one.

'But I must see him,' persisted Bell, who was as obstinate as a mule. 'My mother is very ill.'

'Then why don't ye stay t'ome and look arter her?'

'She sent me out to ask Mr Pendle to see her, and I want none of your insolence, Jacob Jarper.'

'Don't 'ee be bold, Miss Mosk. I hev bin verger here these sixty year, I hev, an' I don't want to be told my duty by sich as you.'

'Such as me indeed!' cried Bell, with a flash of the paternal temper. 'If I wasn't a lady I'd give you a piece of my mind.'

'He! he!' chuckled Jarper, 'pears as yer all ladies by your own way of showin'. Not that y'ain't 'andsome — far be it from me to say as you ain't — but Muster Pendle — well, that's a different matter.'

At this moment Gabriel put an end to what threatened to develop into a quarrel by appearing at the vestry door. On learning that Mrs Mosk wished to see him, he readily consented to accompany Bell, but as he had some business to attend to at the church before he went, he asked Bell to wait for a few minutes.

'I'll be some little time, Jarper,' said he kindly to the sour old verger, 'so if you give me the keys I'll lock up and you can go home to your supper.'

'I *am* hungry, Muster Pendle,' confessed Jarper, 'an' it ain't at my time of life as old folk shud starve. I've locked up the hull church 'ceptin' the vestry door, an' 'eres th' key oft. Be careful with the light an' put it out, Muster Pendle, for if you burns down the church, what good is fine sermons, I'd like to know?'

'It will be all right, Jarper. I'll give you the key to-morrow. Good-night!'

'Good-night, Jarper!' chimed in Bell, in her most stately manner.

'Thankee, Muster Pendle, good-night, but I don't want no beer fro' you this evening, Miss Bell Mosk,' growled the old man, and chuckling over this exhibition of wit he hobbled away to his supper.

'These common people are most insolent,' said Bell, with an affectation of fine ladyism. 'Let us go into the vestry, Gabriel, I wish to speak to you. Oh, you needn't look so scared; there's nobody about, now that old Dot-and-carry-one has gone' — this last in allusion to Jarper's lameness.

'Bell, please, don't use such language,' remonstrated Gabriel, as he conducted her into the vestry; 'someone might hear.'

'I don't care if someone does,' retorted Miss Mosk, taking a chair near the flaring, spluttering gas jet, 'but I tell you there is no one about. I wouldn't be here alone with you if there were. I'm as careful of my own reputation as I am of yours, I can tell you.'

'Is your mother ill again?' asked Gabriel, arranging some sheets of paper on the table and changing the conversation.

'Oh, she's no better and no worse. But you'd better come and see her, so that folks won't be talking of my having spoken to you. A cat can't look at a jug in this town without they think she's after the cream.'

'You wish to speak with me, Bell?'

'Yes, I do; come and sit 'longside of me.'

Gabriel, being very much in love, obeyed with the greatest willingness, and when he sat down under the gas jet would have taken Bell in his arms, but that she evaded his clasp. 'There's no time for anything of that sort, my dear,' said she sharply; 'we've got to talk business, you and I, we have.'

'Business! About our engagement?'

'You've hit it, Gabriel; that's the business I wish to understand. How long is this sort of thing going on?'

'What sort of thing?'

'Now, don't pretend to misunderstand me,' cried Bell, with acerbity, 'or you and I shall fall out of the cart. What sort of thing indeed! Why, my engagement to you being kept secret; your pretending to visit mother when it's me you want; my being obliged to hide the ring you gave me from father's eyes; that's the sort of thing, Mr Gabriel Pendle.'

'I know it is a painful position, dearest, but — '

'Painful position!' echoed the girl, contemptuously. 'Oh, I don't care two straws about the painful position. It's the danger I'm thinking about.'

'Danger! What do you mean? Danger from whom?'

'From Mrs Pansey; from Mr Cargrim. She guesses a lot and he knows more than is good for either you or I. I don't want to lose my character.'

'Bell! no one dare say a word against your character.'

'I should think not,' retorted Miss Mosk, firing up. 'I'd have the law on them if they did. I can look after myself, I hope, and there's no man I know likely to get the better of me. I don't say I'm an aristocrat, Gabriel, but I'm an honest girl, and as good a lady as any of them. I'll make you a first-class wife in spite of my bringing up.'

Gabriel kissed her. 'My darling Bell, you are the sweetest and cleverest woman in the world. You know how I adore you.'

Bell knew very well, for she was sharp enough to distinguish between genuine and spurious affection. Strange as it may appear, the refined and educated young clergyman was deeply in love with this handsome, bold woman of the people. Some lovers of flowers prefer full-blown roses, ripe and red, to the most exquisite buds.

Gabriel's tastes were the same, and he admired the florid beauty of Bell with all the ardour of his young and impetuous heart. He was blind to her liking for incongruous colours in dress: he was deaf to her bold expressions and defects in grammar. What lured him was her ripe, rich, exuberant beauty; what charmed him was the flash of her white teeth and the brilliancy of her eyes when she smiled; what dominated him was her strong will and practical way of looking on worldly affairs. Opposite natures are often attracted to one another by the very fact that they are so undeniably unlike, and the very characteristics in Bell which pleased Gabriel were those which he lacked himself.

Undoubtedly he loved her, but, it may be asked, did she love him? and that is the more difficult question to answer. Candidly speaking, Bell had an affection for Gabriel. She liked his good looks, his refined voice; his very weakness of character was not unpleasing to her. But she did not love him sufficiently to marry him for himself alone. What she wished to marry was the gentleman, the clergyman, the son of the Bishop of Beorminster, and unless Gabriel could give her all the pleasures and delights attendant on his worldly position, she was not prepared to become Mrs Gabriel Pendle. It was to make this clear to him, to clinch the bargain, to show that she was willing to barter her milkmaid beauty and strong common sense for his position and possible money, that she had come to see him. Not being bemused with love, Bell Mosk was thoroughly practical, and so spoke very much to the point. Never was there so prosaic an interview.

'Well, it just comes to this,' she said determinedly, 'I'm not going to be kept in the background serving out beer any longer. If I am worth marrying I am worth acknowledging, and that's just what you've got to do, Gabriel.'

'But my father!' faltered Gabriel, nervously, for he saw in a flash the difficulties of his position.

'What about your father? He can't eat me, can he?'

'He can cut me off with a shilling, my dear. And that's just what he will do if he knows I'm engaged to you. Surely, Bell, with your strong common sense, you can see that for yourself!'

'Of course I see it,' retorted Bell, sharply,

for the speech was not flattering to her vanity; 'all the same, something must be done.'

'We must wait.'

'I'm sick of waiting.'

Gabriel rose to his feet and began to pace to and fro. 'You cannot desire our marriage more than I do,' he said fondly. 'I wish to make you my wife in as public a manner as possible. But you know I have only a small income as a curate, and you would not wish us to begin life on a pittance.'

'I should think not. I've had enough of cutting and contriving. But how do you intend to get enough for us to marry on?'

'My father has promised me the rectorship of Heathcroft. The present incumbent is old and cannot possibly live long.'

'I believe he'll live on just to spite us,' grumbled Bell. 'How much is the living worth?'

'Six hundred a year; there is also the rectory, you know.'

'Well, I daresay we can manage on that, Gabriel. Perhaps, after all, it will be best to wait, but I don't like it.'

'Neither do I, my dear. If you like, I'll tell my father and marry you to-morrow.'

'Then you would lose Heathcroft.'

'It's extremely probable I would,' replied Gabriel, dryly.

'In that case we'll wait,' said Bell, springing up briskly. 'I don't suppose that old man is immortal, and I'm willing to stick to you for another twelve months.'

'Bell! I thought you loved me sufficiently to accept any position.'

'I do love you, Gabriel, but I'm not a fool, and I'm not cut out for a poor man's wife. I've had quite enough of being a poor man's daughter. When poverty comes in at the door, love flies out of the window. That's as true as true. No! we'll wait till the old rector dies, but if he lasts longer than twelve months, I'll lose heart and have to look about me for another husband in my own rank of life.'

'Bell,' said Gabriel, in a pained voice, 'you are cruel!'

'Rubbish!' replied the practical barmaid, 'I'm sensible. Now, come and see mother.'

13

A Stormy Night

Having given Gabriel plainly to understand the terms upon which she was prepared to continue their secret engagement, Bell kissed him once or twice to soften the rigour of her speech. Then she intimated that she would return alone to The Derby Winner, and that Gabriel could follow after a reasonable interval of time had elapsed. She also explained the meaning of these precautions.

'If the old cats of the town saw you and I walking along on Sunday night,' said she, at the door of the vestry, 'they would screech out that we were keeping company, and in any case would couple our names together. If they did, father would make it so warm for me that I should have to tell the truth, and then — well,' added Miss Mosk, with a brilliant smile, 'you know his temper and my temper.'

'You are sure it is quite safe for you to go home alone?' said Gabriel, who was infected with the upper-class prejudice that every unmarried girl should be provided with a chaperon.

'Safe!' echoed the dauntless Bell, in a tone

of supreme contempt. 'My dear Gabriel, I'd be safe in the middle of Timbuctoo!'

'There are many of these rough harvest labourers about here, you know.'

'I'll slap their faces if they speak to me. I'd like to see them try it, that's all. And now, good-bye for the present, dear. I must get home as soon as possible, for there is a storm coming, and I don't want to get my Sunday-go-to-meeting clothes spoilt.'

When she slipped off like a white ghost into the gathering darkness, Gabriel remained at the door and looked up to the fast-clouding sky. It was now about nine o'clock, and the night was hot and thundery, and so airless that it was difficult to breathe. Overhead, masses of black cloud, heavy with storm, hung low down over the town, and the earth, panting and worn out with the heat, waited thirstily for the cool drench of the rain. Evidently a witch-tempest was brewing in the halls of heaven on no small scale, and Gabriel wished that it would break at once to relieve the strain from which nature seemed to suffer. Whether it was the fatigue of his day's labour, or the late interview with Bell which depressed him, he did not know, but he felt singularly pessimistic and his mind was filled with premonitions of ill. Like most people with highly-strung natures, Gabriel was easily affected by atmospheric influence, so no doubt the palpable electricity in the dry, hot air depressed his nerves, but whether this was the cause of his restlessness he could not say. He felt anxious and melancholy, and was worried by a sense of coming ill, though what such ill might be, or from what quarter it would come, he knew not. While thus gloomily contemplative, the great bell of the cathedral boomed out nine deep strokes, and the hollow sound breaking in on his reflections made him wake up, shake off his dismal thoughts, and sent him inside to attend to his work. Yet the memory of those forebodings occurred to him often in after days, and read by the light of after events, he was unable to decide whether the expectation of evil, so strongly forced upon him then, was due to natural or supernatural causes. At present he ascribed his anxieties to the disturbed state of the atmosphere.

In the meantime, Bell, who was a healthy young woman, with no nerves to be affected by the atmosphere, walked swiftly homeward along the airless streets. There were few people on their feet, for the night was too close for exercise, and the majority of the inhabitants sat in chairs before their doors, weary and out of temper. Nature and her creatures were waiting for the windows of the firmament to be opened, for the air to be cleansed, for life to be renewed. Bell met none of the harvesters and was not molested in any way. Had she been spoken to, or hustled, there is no doubt she would have been as good as her word and have slapped her assailant's face. Fortunately, there was no need for her to proceed to such extremes.

At the door of The Derby Winner she was rather surprised to find Miss Whichello waiting for her. The little old lady wore her poke bonnet and old-fashioned black silk cloak, and appeared anxious and nervous, and altogether unlike her usual cheery self. Bell liked Miss Whichello as much as she disliked Mrs Pansey, therefore she greeted her with unfeigned pleasure, although she could not help expressing her surprise that the visitor was in that quarter of the town so late at night. Miss Whichello produced a parcel from under her voluminous cloak and offered it as an explanation of her presence.

'This is a pot of calf's-foot jelly for your mother, Miss Mosk,' she said. 'Mr Cargrim came to luncheon at my house to-day, and he told me how ill your mother is. I was informed that she was asleep, so, not wishing to disturb her, I waited until you returned.'

'It is very kind of you to take so much trouble, Miss Whichello,' said Bell, gratefully receiving the jelly. 'I hope you have not been waiting long.'

'Only ten minutes; your servant told me that you would return soon.'

'I have been to church and stopped after service to talk to some friends, Miss Whichello. Won't you come in for a few minutes? I'll see if my mother is awake.'

'Thank you, I'll come in for a time, but do not waken your mother on my account. Sleep is always the best medicine in case of sickness. I hope Mrs Mosk is careful of her diet.'

'Well, she eats very little.'

'That is wise; very little food, but that little nourishing and frequently administered. Give her a cup of beef-tea two or three times in the night, my dear, and you'll find it will sustain the body wonderfully.'

'I'll remember to do so,' replied Bell, gravely, although she had no intention of remaining awake all night to heat beef-tea and dose her mother with it, especially as the invalid was not ill enough for such extreme measures. But she was so touched by Miss Whichello's kindness that she would not have offended her, by scouting her prescription, for the world.

By this time Miss Whichello was seated in a little private parlour off the bar, illuminated by an oil-lamp. This Bell turned up, and then she noticed that her visitor looked anxious and ill at ease. Once or twice she attempted to speak, but closed her mouth again. Bell wondered if Mrs Pansey had been at work coupling her name with that of Gabriel's, and whether Miss Whichello had come down to relieve her conscience by warning her against seeing too much of the curate. But, as she knew very well, Miss Whichello was too nervous and too much of a lady to give her opinion on questions unasked, and therefore, banishing the defiant look which had begun to harden her face, she waited to hear if it was any other reason than bestowing the jelly which had brought the little old spinster to so disreputable a quarter of the town at so untoward an hour. Finally Miss Whichello's real reason for calling came out by degrees, and in true feminine fashion she approached the main point by side issues.

'Is your father in, Miss Mosk?' she asked, clasping and unclasping her hands feverishly on her lap.

'No, Miss Whichello. He rode over this afternoon to Southberry on business, and we do not expect him back till to-morrow morning. Poor father!' sighed Bell, 'he went away in anything but good spirits, for he is terribly worried over money matters.'

'The payment of his rent is troubling him, perhaps!'

'Yes, Miss Whichello. This is an expensive hotel, and the rent is high. We find it so difficult to make the place pay that we are behindhand with the rent. Sir Harry Brace, our landlord, has been very kind in waiting, but we can't expect him to stand out of his money much longer. I'm afraid in the end we'll have to give up The Derby Winner. But it is no good my worrying you about our troubles,' concluded Bell, in a more vivacious tone; 'what do you wish to see father about, Miss Whichello? Anything that I can do?'

'Well, my dear, it's this way,' said the old lady, nervously. 'You know that I have a much larger income than I need, and that I am always ready to help the deserving.'

'I know, Miss Whichello! You give help where Mrs Pansey only gives advice. I know who is most thought of; that I do!'

'Mrs Pansey has her own methods of dispensing charity, Miss Mosk.'

'Tracts and interference,' muttered Bell, under her breath; 'meddlesome old tabby that she is.'

'Mr Cargrim was at my house to-day, as I told you,' pursued Miss Whichello, not having heard this remark, 'and he mentioned a man called Jentham as a poor creature in need of help.'

'He's a poor creature, I daresay,' said Miss

Mosk, tossing her head, 'for he owes father more money than he can pay, although he does say that he'll settle his bill next week. But he's a bad lot.'

'A bad lot, Miss Mosk?'

'As bad as they make 'em, Miss Whichello. Don't you give him a penny, for he'll only waste it on drink.'

'Does he drink to excess?'

'I should think so; he finishes a bottle of brandy every day.'

'Oh, Miss Mosk, how very dreadful!' cried Miss Whichello, quite in the style of Daisy Norsham. 'Why is he staying in Beorminster?'

'I don't know, but it's for no good, you may be sure. If he isn't here he's hob-nobbing with those gipsy wretches who have a camp on Southberry Common. Mother Jael and he are always together.'

'Can you describe him?' asked Miss Whichello, with some hesitation.

'He is tall and thin, with a dark, wicked-looking face, and he has a nasty scar on the right cheek, slanting across it to the mouth. But the funny thing is, that with all his rags and drunkenness there is something of the gentleman about him. I don't like him, yet I can't dislike him. He's attractive in his own way from his very wickedness. But I'm sure,' finished Bell, with a vigorous nod, 'that he's a black-hearted Nero. He has done a deal of damage in his time both to men and women; I'm as sure of that as I sit here, though I can give no reason for saying so.'

Miss Whichello listened to this graphic description in silence. She was very pale, and held her handkerchief to her mouth with one trembling hand; the other beat nervously on her lap, and it was only by a strong effort of will that she managed to conquer her emotion.

'I daresay you are right,' she observed, in a tremulous voice. 'Indeed, I might have expected as much, for last night he frightened my niece and her maid on the high road. I thought it would be best to give him money and send him away, so that so evil a man should not remain here to be a source of danger to the town.'

'Give him money!' cried Miss Mosk. 'I'd give him the cat-o'-nine tails if I had my way. Don't you trouble about him, Miss Whichello; he's no good.'

'But if I could see him I might soften his heart,' pleaded the old lady, very much in earnest.

'Soften a brick-bat,' rejoined Bell; 'you'd have just as much success with one as with the other. Besides, you can't see him, Miss Whichello — at all events, not to-night — for he's on the common with his nasty gipsies, and won't be back till the morning. I wish he'd stay away altogether, I do.'

'In that case I shall not trouble about him,' said the old lady, rising; 'on some future occasion I may see him. But you need not say I was asking for him, Miss Mosk.'

'I won't say a word; he'd only come worrying round your house if he thought you wanted to give him money.'

'Oh, he mustn't do that; he mustn't come there!' cried Miss Whichello, alarmed.

'He won't, for I'll hold my tongue. You can rest easy on that score, Miss Whichello. But my advice is, don't pick him up out of the mire; he'll only fall back into it again.'

'You have a bad opinion of him, Miss Mosk.'

'The very worst,' replied Bell, conducting her guest to the door; 'he's a gaol-bird and a scallywag, and all that's bad. Well, good-night, Miss Whichello, and thank you for the jelly.'

'There is no need for thanks, Miss Mosk. Good-night!' and the old lady tripped up the street, keeping in the middle of it, lest any robber should spring out on her from the shadow of the houses.

The storm was coming nearer, and soon would break directly over the town, for flashes of lightning were weaving fiery patterns against the black clouds, and every now and then a hoarse growl of thunder went grinding across the sky. Anxious to escape the coming downfall, Miss Whichello climbed up the street towards the cathedral as quickly and steadily as her old legs could carry her. Just as she emerged into the close, a shadow blacker than the blackness of the night glided past her. A zigzag of lightning cut the sky at the moment and revealed the face of Mr Cargrim, who in his turn recognised the old lady in the bluish glare.

'Miss Whichello!' he exclaimed; 'what a surprise!'

'You may well say that, Mr Cargrim,' replied the old lady, with a nervous movement, for the sound of his voice and the sudden view of his face startled her not a little. 'It is not often I am out at this hour, but I have been taking some jelly to Mrs Mosk.'

'You are a good Samaritan, Miss Whichello. I hope she is better?'

'I think so, but I did not see her, as she is asleep. I spoke with her daughter, however.'

'I trust you were not molested by that ruffian Jentham, who stays at The Derby Winner,' said Cargrim, with hypocritical anxiety.

'Oh, no! he is away on Southberry Heath

with his gipsy friends, I believe — at least, Miss Mosk told me so. Good-night, Mr Cargrim,' she added, evidently not anxious to prolong the conversation. 'I wish to get under shelter before the storm breaks.'

'Let me see you to your door at least.'

Miss Whichello rejected this officious offer by dryly remarking that she had accomplished the worst part of her journey, and bidding the chaplain 'Good-night,' tripped across the square to her own Jenny Wren nest. Cargrim looked after her with a doubtful look as she vanished into the darkness, then, turning on his heel, walked swiftly down the street towards Eastgate. He had as much aversion to getting wet as a cat, and put his best foot foremost so as to reach the palace before the rain came on. Besides, it was ten o'clock — a late hour for a respectable parson to be abroad.

'She's been trying to see Jentham,' thought Mr Cargrim, recalling Miss Whichello's nervous hesitation. 'I wonder what she knows about him. The man is a mystery, and is in Beorminster for no good purpose. Miss Whichello and the bishop both know that purpose, I'm certain. Well! well! two secrets are better than one, and if I gain a knowledge of them both, I may inhabit Heathcroft Rectory sooner than I expect.'

Cargrim's meditations were here cut short by the falling of heavy drops of rain, and he put all his mind into his muscles to travel the faster. Indeed, he almost ran through the new town, and was soon out on the country road which conducted to the palace. But, in spite of all his speed, the rain caught him, for with an incessant play of lightning and a constant roll of thunder came a regular tropical downpour. The rain descended in one solid mass, flooding the ground and beating flat the crops. Cargrim was drenched to the skin, and by the time he slipped through the small iron gate near the big ones, into the episcopalian park, he looked like a lean water-rat. Being in a bad temper from his shower bath, he was almost as venomous as that animal, and raced up the avenue in his sodden clothing, shivering and dripping. Suddenly he heard the quick trot of a horse, and guessing that the bishop was returning, he stood aside in the shadow of the trees to let his superior pass by. Like the chaplain, Dr Pendle was streaming with water, and his horse's hoofs plashed up the sodden ground as though he were crossing a marsh. By the livid glare of the lightnings which shot streaks of blue fire through the descending deluge, Cargrim caught a glimpse of the bishop's face. It was deathly pale, and bore a look of mingled horror and terror. Another moment and he had passed into the blackness of the drenching rain, leaving Cargrim marvelling at the torture of the mind which could produce so terrible an expression.

'It is the face of Cain,' whispered Cargrim to himself. 'What can his secret be?'

14

'Rumour Full of Tongues'

It is almost impossible to learn the genesis of a rumour. It may be started by a look, a word, a gesture, and it spreads with such marvellous rapidity that by the time public curiosity is fully aroused, no one can trace the original source, so many and winding are the channels through which it has flowed. Yet there are exceptions to this general rule, especially in criminal cases, where, for the safety of the public, it is absolutely necessary to get to the bottom of the matter. Therefore, the rumour which pervaded Beorminster on Monday morning was soon traced by the police to a carter from Southberry. This man mentioned to a friend that, when crossing the Heath during the early morning, he had come across the body of a man. The rumour — weak in its genesis — stated first that a man had been hurt, later on that he had been wounded; by noon it was announced that he was dead, and finally the actual truth came out that the man had been murdered. The police authorities saw the carter and were conducted by him to the corpse, which, after examination, they brought to the dead-house in Beorminster. Then all doubt came to an end, and it was officially declared during the afternoon that Jentham, the military vagabond lately resident at The Derby Winner, had been shot through the heart. But even rumour, prolific as it is in invention, could not suggest who had murdered the man.

So unusual an event in the quiet cathedral city caused the greatest excitement, and the streets were filled with people talking over the matter. Amateur detectives, swilling beer in public-houses, gave their opinions about the crime, and the more beer they drank, the wilder and more impossible became their theories. Some suggested that the gipsies camped on Southberry Heath, who were continually fighting amongst themselves, had killed the miserable creature; others, asserting that the scamp was desperately poor, hinted at suicide induced by sheer despair; but the most generally accepted opinion was that Jentham had been killed in some drunken frolic by one or more Irish harvesters. The Beorminster reporters visited the police station and endeavoured to learn what Inspector Tinkler thought. He had seen the body, he had viewed the spot where it had been found, he had examined the carter,

Giles Crake, so he was the man most likely to give satisfactory answers to the questions as to who had killed the man, and why he had been shot. But Inspector Tinkler was the most wary of officials, and pending the inquest and the verdict of twelve good men and true, he declined to commit himself to an opinion. The result of this reticence was that the reporters had to fall back on their inventive faculties, and next morning published three theories, side by side, concerning the murder, so that the *Beorminster Chronicle* containing these suppositions proved to be as interesting as a police novel, and quite as unreliable. But it amused its readers and sold largely, therefore proprietor and editor were quite satisfied that fiction was as good as fact to tickle the long ears of a credulous public.

As the dead man had lodged at The Derby Winner, and many people had known him there, quite a sensation was caused by the report of his untimely end. From morning till night the public-house was thronged with customers, thirsting both for news and beer. Nevertheless, although business was so brisk, Mosk was by no means in a good temper. He had returned early that morning from Southberry, and had been one of the first to hear about the matter. When he heard who had been killed, he regarded the committal of the crime quite in a personal light, for the dead man owed him money, and his death had discharged the debt in a way of which Mr Mosk did not approve. He frequently referred to his loss during the day, when congratulated by unthinking customers on the excellent trade the assassination had brought about.

'For, as I allays ses,' remarked one wiseacre, 'it's an ill wind as don't blow good to somebody.'

'Yah!' growled Mosk, in his beery voice, 'it's about as broad as it's long so far as I'm concerned. I've lost a couple of quid through Jentham goin' and gettin' shot, and it will take a good many tankards of bitter at thru'p'nce to make that up.'

'Oo d'y' think shot 'im, Mr Mosk?'

'Arsk me sum'thin' easier, carn't you? I don't know nothin' about the cove, I don't; he comes 'ere two, three weeks ago, and leaves owin' me money. Where he comes from, or who he is, or what he's bin doin' to get shot I know no more nor you do. All I does know,' finished Mosk, emphatically, 'is as I've lost two bloomin' quid, an' that's a lot to a poor man like me.'

'Well, father, it's no good making a fuss over it,' cried Bell, who overheard his grumbling. 'If Jentham hadn't been shot, we wouldn't be doing so well. For my part, I'm sorry for the poor soul.'

'Poor blackguard, you mean!'

'No, I don't. I don't call any corpse a blackguard. If he was one, I daresay he's being punished enough now without our calling him names. He wasn't the kind of man I fancied, but there's no denying he was attractive in his own wicked way.'

'Ah!' said a dirty-looking man, who was more than suspected of being a welcher, 'couldn't he tell slap-up yarns about H'injins an' 'eathens as bows down to stocks and stones. Oh, no! not he — '

'He could lie like a one-year-old, if that's what y' mean,' said Mosk.

'Bloomin' fine lyin', any'ow,' retorted the critic. 'I'd git orf the turf if I cud spit 'em out that style; mek m' fortin', I would, on th' paipers.'

'Y've bin chucked orf the turf often enough as it is,' replied the landlord, sourly, whereat, to give the conversation a less personal application, the dirty welcher remarked that he would drain another bitter.

'I suppose you'll be as drunk as a pig by night,' said Bell, taking the order. 'Jentham was bad, but he wasn't a swine like you.'

'Garn! 'e got drunk, didn't he? Oh, no! You bet he didn't.'

'He got drunk like a gentleman, at all

events. None of your sauce, Black, or I'll have you chucked. You know me by this time, I hope.'

In fact, as several of the customers remarked, Miss Bell was in a fine temper that morning, and her tongue raged round like a prairie fire. This bad humour was ascribed by the public to the extra work entailed on her by the sensation caused by the murder, but the true cause lay with Gabriel. He had promised faithfully, on the previous night, to come round and see Mrs Mosk, but, to Bell's anger, had failed to put in an appearance — the first time he had done such a thing. As Miss Mosk's object was always to have an ostensible reason for seeing Gabriel in order to protect her character, she was not at all pleased that he had not turned her excuse for calling on him into an actual fact. It is true that Gabriel presented himself late in the afternoon and requested to see the invalid, but instead of taking him up to the sickroom, Bell whirled the curate into a small back parlour and closed the door, in order, as she remarked, 'to have it out with him.'

'Now, then,' said she, planting her back against the door, 'what do you mean by treating me like a bit of dirt?'

'You mean that I did not come round last night, Bell?'

'Yes, I do. I told mother you would visit her. I said to Jacob Jarper as I'd come to ask you to see mother, and you go and make me out a liar by not turning up. What do you mean?'

'I was ill and couldn't keep my promise,' said Gabriel, shortly.

'Ill!' said Bell, looking him up and down; 'well, you do look ill. You've been washed and wrung out till you're limp as a rag. White in the face, black under the eyes! What have you been doing with yourself, I'd like to know. You were all right when I left you last night.'

'The weather affected my nerves,' explained Gabriel, with a weary sigh, passing his thin hand across his anxious face. 'I felt that it was impossible for me to sit in a close room and talk to a sick woman, so I went round to the stables where I keep my horse, and took him out in order to get a breath of fresh air.'

'What! You rode out at that late hour, in all that storm?'

'The storm came on later. I went out almost immediately after you left, and got back at half-past ten. It wasn't so very late.'

'Well, of all mad things!' said Bell, grimly. 'It's easy seen, Mr Gabriel Pendle, how badly you want a wife at your elbow. Where did you go?'

'I rode out on to Southberry Heath,'

replied Gabriel, with some hesitation.

'Lord ha' mercy! Where Jentham's corpse was found?'

The curate shuddered. 'I didn't see any corpse,' he said, painfully and slowly. 'Instead of keeping to the high road, I struck out cross-country. It was only this morning that I heard of the unfortunate man's untimely end.'

'You didn't meet anyone likely to have laid him out?'

'No! I met no one. I felt too ill to notice passers-by, but the ride did me good, and I feel much better this morning.'

'You don't look better,' said Bell, with another searching glance. 'One would think you had killed the man yourself!'

'Bell!' protested Gabriel, almost in an hysterical tone, for his nerves were not yet under control, and the crude speeches of the girl made him wince.

'Well! well! I'm only joking. I know you wouldn't hurt a fly. But you do look ill, that's a fact. Let me get you some brandy.'

'No, thank you, brandy would only make me worse. Let me go up and see your mother.'

'I sha'n't! You're not fit to see anyone. Go home and lie down till your nerves get right. You can see me after five if you like, for I'm going to the dead-house to have a look at Jentham's body.'

'What! to see the corpse of that unhappy man,' cried Gabriel, shrinking away.

'Why not?' answered Bell, coolly, for she had that peculiar love of looking on dead bodies characteristic of the lower classes. 'I want to see how they killed him.'

'How who killed him?'

'The person as did it, silly. Though I don't know who could have shot him unless it was that old cat of a Mrs Pansey. Well, I can't stay here talking all day, and father will be wondering what I'm up to. You go home and lie down, Gabriel.'

'Not just now. I must walk up to the palace.'

'Hum! The bishop will be in a fine way about this murder. It's years since anyone got killed here. I hope they'll catch the wretch as shot Jentham, though I can't say I liked him myself.'

'I hope they will catch him,' replied Gabriel, mechanically. 'Good-day, Miss Mosk! I shall call and see your mother to-morrow.'

'Good-day, Mr Pendle, and thank you, oh, so much!'

This particular form of farewell was intended for the ears of Mr Mosk and the general public, but it failed in its object so far as the especial person it was intended to impress was concerned. When the black-clothed form of Gabriel vanished, Mr Mosk handed over the business of the bar to an active pot-boy, and conducted his daughter back to the little parlour. Bell saw from his lowering brow that her father was suspicious of her lengthened interview with the curate, and was bent upon causing trouble. However, she was not the kind of girl to be daunted by black looks, and, moreover, was conscious that her father would be rather pleased than otherwise to hear that she was honourably engaged to the son of Bishop Pendle, so she sat down calmly enough at his gruff command, and awaited the coming storm. If driven into a corner, she intended to tell the truth, therefore she faced her father with the greatest coolness.

'What d'y mean by it?' cried Mosk, bursting into angry words as soon as the door was closed; 'what d'y mean, you hussy?'

'Now, look here, father,' said Bell, quickly, 'you keep a civil tongue in your head or I won't use mine. I'm not a hussy, and you have no right to call me one.'

'No right! Ain't I your lawfully begotten father?'

'Yes, you are, worse luck! I'd have had a duke for my father if I'd been asked what I wanted.'

'Wouldn't a bishop content you?' sneered Mosk, with a scowl on his pimply face.

'You're talking of Mr Pendle, are you?' said Bell, wilfully misunderstanding the insinuation.

'Yes, I am, you jade! and I won't have it. I tell you I won't!'

'Won't have what, father? Give it a name.'

'Why, this carrying on with that parson chap. Not as I've a word to say against Mr Pendle, because he's worth a dozen of the Cargrim lot, but he's gentry and you're not!'

'What's that got to do with it?' demanded Bell, with supreme contempt.

'This much,' raved Mosk, clenching his fist, 'that I won't have you running after him. D'y hear?'

'I hear; there is no need for you to rage the house down, father. I'm not running after Mr Pendle; he's running after me.'

'That's just as bad. You'll lose your character.'

Bell fired up, and bounced to her feet. 'Who dares to say a word against my character?' she asked, panting and red.

'Old Jarper, for one. He said you went to see Mr Pendle last night.'

'So I did.'

'Oh, you did, did you? and here you've bin talking alone with him this morning for the last hour. What d'y mean by disgracing me?'

'Disgracing you!' scoffed Bell. 'Your character needs a lot of disgracing, doesn't it? Now, be sensible, father,' she added, advancing towards him, 'and I'll tell you the truth. I didn't intend to, but as you are so unreasonable I may as well set your mind at rest.'

'What are you driving at?' growled Mosk, struck by her placid manner.

'Well, to put the thing into a nutshell, Mr Pendle is going to marry me.'

'Marry you! Get along!'

'I don't see why you should doubt my word,' cried Bell, with an angry flush. 'I'm engaged to him as honourably as any young lady could be. He has written me lots of letters promising to make me his wife, he has given me a ring, and we're only waiting till he's appointed to be rector of Heathcroft to marry.'

'Well, I'm d—d,' observed Mr Mosk, slowly. 'Is this true?'

'I'll show you the ring and letters if you like,' said Bell, tartly, 'but I don't see why you should be so surprised. I'm good enough for him, I hope?'

'You're good-lookin', I dessay, Bell, but he's gentry.'

'I'm going to be gentry too, and I'll hold my own with the best of them. As Bishop Pendle's daughter-in-law, I'll scratch the eyes out of any of 'em as doesn't give me my place.'

Mosk drew a long breath. 'Bishop Pendle's

daughter-in-law,' he repeated, looking at his daughter with admiration. 'My stars! you are a clever girl, Bell.'

'I'm clever enough to get what I want, father, so long as you don't put your foot into it. Hold your tongue until I tell you when to speak. If the bishop knew of this now, he'd cut Gabriel off with a shilling.'

'Oh, he would, would he?' said Mosk, in so strange a tone that Bell looked at him with some wonder.

'Of course he would,' said she, quietly; 'but when Gabriel is rector of Heathcroft it won't matter. We'll then have money enough to do without his consent.'

'Give me a kiss, my girl,' cried Mosk, clasping her to his breast. 'You're a credit to me, that you are. Oh, curse it! Bell, think of old Mother Pansey!'

Father and daughter looked at one another and burst out laughing.

15

The Gipsy Ring

Almost at the very time Mosk was congratulating his daughter on the conquest of the curate, Captain Pendle was paying a visit to the Jenny Wren nest. He had only succeeded in obtaining a Saturday to Monday leave from his colonel, who did not approve of young officers being too long or too often absent from their duties, and was rejoining his regiment that very evening. As soon as he could get away from the palace he had left his portmanteau at the station and had come up to the Cathedral Close to see Mab. Much to his gratification he found her alone in the quaint old drawing-room, and blessed the Providence which had sent him thither at so propitious an hour.

'Aunty is lying down,' explained Mab, who looked rather worried and pale; 'she has been so upset over this horrid murder.'

'Egad! it has upset everyone,' said George, throwing himself into a chair. 'My father is so annoyed at such a thing happening in his diocese that he has retreated to his library and shut himself up. I could hardly get him to say good-bye. Though, upon my word,' added George, waxing warm, 'I don't see that the death of a wretched tramp is of such moment; yet it seems to have annoyed everyone.'

'Including yourself,' said Mab, remarking how worried her lover looked, and how far from being his pleasant, natural self.

'Yes, my dearest, including myself. When the bishop is annoyed my mother fidgets over him until she makes herself ill. Knowing this, he is usually careful not to let her see him when he is out of sorts, but to-day he was not so discreet, and the consequence is that my mother has an attack of nerves, and is lying on her sofa bathed in tears, with Lucy in attendance. Of course, all this has upset me in my turn.'

'Well, George, I suppose it is natural that the bishop should be put out, for such a terrible crime has not been committed here for years. Indeed, the *Chronicle* of last week was remarking how free from crime this place was.'

'And naturally the gods gave them the lie by arranging a first-class murder straight away,' said George, with a shrug. 'But why everybody should be in such a state I can't see. The palace is like an undertaker's establishment when business is dull. The only person who seems at all cheerful is that fellow Cargrim.'

'He ought to be annoyed for the bishop's sake.'

'Faith, then, he isn't, Mab. He's going about rubbing his hands and grinning like a Cheshire cat. I think the sight of him irritated me more than the mourners. I'm glad to go back to my work.'

'Are you glad to leave me?'

'No, you dear goose,' said he, taking her hand affectionately; 'that is the bitter drop in my cup. However, I have brought you something to draw us closer together. There!'

'Oh, George!' cried Mab, looking in ecstasy at the ring he had slipped on her finger, 'what a lovely, lovely ring, and what a queer one! — three turquoise stones set in a braid of silver. I never saw so unique a pattern.'

'I daresay not. It's not the kind of ring you'll come across every day, and precious hard work I had to get it.'

'Did you buy it in Beorminster?' asked Miss Arden, putting her head on one side to admire the peculiar setting of the blue stones.

'No; I bought it from Mother Jael.'

'From Mother Jael! — that old gipsy fortune-teller?'

'Precisely; from that very identical old Witch of Endor. I saw it on her lean paw when I was last in Beorminster, and she came hovering round to tell my fortune. The queer look of it took my fancy, and I determined to secure it for our engagement ring. However, the old lady wasn't to be bribed into parting with it, but last night I rode out to the camp on Southberry Common and succeeded in getting it off her. She is a regular Jew at a bargain, and haggled for an hour before she would let me have it. Ultimately I gave her the price she asked, and there it is on your pretty hand.'

'How sweet of you, George, to take so much trouble! I shall value the ring greatly for your sake.'

'And for your own too, I hope. It is a lucky ring, and came from the East, Mother Jael said, in the old, old days. It looks rather Egyptian, so perhaps Cleopatra wore it when she went to meet Anthony!'

'Such nonsense! but it is a dear, lovely ring, and I'll wear it always.'

'I think I deserve a kiss from you for my trouble,' said George, drawing her lovely, glowing face towards him. 'There, darling; the next ring I place on your finger will be a plain golden one, not from the East, but from an honest Beorminster jeweller.'

'But, George' — Mab laid her head on his breast — 'I am not sure if I ought to accept it, really. Your father does not know of our engagement.'

'I intend to tell him when I next visit Beorminster, my love. Indeed, but that he takes this wretched murder so much to heart I would have told him to-day. Still, you need not scruple to wear it, dearest, for your aunt and my mother are both agreed that you will make me the sweetest of wives.'

'Aunty is always urging me to ask you to tell your father.'

'Then you can inform her that I'll do so next — why, here *is* your aunt, my dear.'

'Aunty!' cried Mab, as Miss Whichello, like a little white ghost, moved into the room. 'I thought your head was so bad.'

'It is better now, my dear,' replied the old lady, who really looked very ill. 'How do you do, Captain Pendle?'

'Hadn't you better call me George, Miss Whichello?'

'No, I hadn't, my dear man; at least, not until your engagement with Mab is an accomplished fact.'

'But it is an accomplished fact now, aunty,' said Mab, showing the ring. 'Here is the visible sign of our engagement.'

'A strange ring, but very charming,' pronounced Miss Whichello, examining the jewel. 'But does the bishop know?'

'I intend to tell him when I come back next week,' said George, promptly. 'At present he is too upset with this murder to pay much attention to my love affairs.'

'Upset with this murder!' cried the little lady, dropping into a chair. 'I don't wonder at it. I am quite ill with the news.'

'I'm sure I don't see why, aunty. This Jentham tramp wasn't a relative, you know.'

Miss Whichello shuddered, and, if possible, turned paler. 'He was a human being, Mab,' she said, in a low voice, 'and it is terrible to think that the poor wretch, however evil he may have been, should have come to so miserable an end. Is it known who shot him, Captain Pendle?'

'No; there are all sorts of rumours, of course, but none of them very reliable. It's a pity, too,' added George, reflectively, 'for if I had only been a little earlier in leaving Mother Jael I might have heard the shot and captured the murderer.'

'What do you mean, Captain Pendle?' cried Miss Whichello, with a start.

'Why, didn't I tell you? No, of course I didn't; it was Mab I told.'

'What did you tell her?' questioned the old lady, with some impatience.

'That I was on Southberry Heath last night.'

'What were you doing there?'

'Seeing after that gipsy ring for Mab,' explained George, pulling his moustache. 'I bought it of Mother Jael, and had to ride out to the camp to make the bargain. As I am going back into harness to-day, there wasn't much time to lose, so I went off last night after dinner, between eight and nine o'clock, and the old jade kept me so long fixing up the business that I didn't reach home until eleven. By Jove! I got a jolly ducking; looked like an insane river god dripping with wet.'

'Did you see anything of the murder, Captain Pendle?'

'No; didn't even hear the shot, though that wasn't to be wondered at, considering the row made by rain and thunder.'

'Where was the body found?'

'Somewhere in a ditch near the high road, I believe. At all events, it wasn't in the way, or my gee would have tumbled across it.'

Miss Whichello reflected. 'The bishop was over at Southberry yesterday, was he not?' she asked.

'Yes, at a confirmation service. He rode back across the common, and reached the palace just before I did — about half an hour or so.'

'Did he hear or see anything?'

'Not to my knowledge; but the truth is, I haven't had an opportunity of asking questions. He is so annoyed at the disgrace to the diocese by the committal of this crime that he's quite beside himself. I was just telling Mab about it when you came in. Six o'clock!' cried Captain George, starting up as the chimes rang out. 'I must be off. If I'm late at barracks my colonel will parade me to-morrow, and go down my throat, spurs, boots and all.'

'Wait a moment, Captain Pendle, and I'll come with you.'

'But your headache, aunty?' remonstrated Mab.

'My dear, a walk in the fresh air will do me good. I shall go with Captain Pendle to the station. Make your adieux, young people, while I put on my bonnet and cloak.'

When Miss Whichello left the room, Mab, who had been admiring her ring during the foregoing conversation, was so impressed with its quaint beauty that she again thanked George for having given it to her. This piece of politeness led to an exhibition of tenderness on the part of the departing lover, and during the dragon's absence this foolish young couple talked the charming nonsense which people in their condition particularly affect. Realism is a very good thing in its own way, but to set down an actual love conversation would be carrying it to excess. Only the exaggerated exaltation of mind attendant on love-making can enable lovers to endure the transcendentalism with which they bore one another. And then the look which makes an arrow of the most trifling phrase, the caress which gives the merest glance a most eloquent meaning — how can prosaic pen and ink and paper report these fittingly? The sympathetic reader must guess what George and Mab said to one another. He must fancy how they said it, and he or she must see in his or her mind's eye how young and beautiful and glowing they looked when Miss Whichello, as the prose of their poetry, walked into the room. The dear old lady smiled approvingly when she saw their bright faces, for she too had lived in Arcady, although the envious gods had turned her out of it long since.

'Now, Captain Pendle, when you have done talking nonsense with that child I'm ready.'

'Do call me George, Miss Whichello,' entreated the captain.

'No, sir; not until your father gives this engagement his episcopalian blessing. No nonsense. Come along.'

But Miss Whichello's bark was worse than her bite, for she discreetly left the room, so that the love-birds could take a tender leave of each other, and Captain Pendle found her standing on the steps outside with a broad smile on her face.

'You are sure you have not forgotten your gloves, Captain Pendle?' she asked smilingly.

'No,' replied George, innocently, 'I have them with me.'

'Oh!' exclaimed Miss Whichello, marching down the steps like a toy soldier, 'in my youth young men in your condition *always* forgot their gloves.'

'By Jove! I have left something behind me, though.'

'Your heart, probably. Never mind, it is in safe keeping. None of your tricks, sir. Come, come!' and Miss Whichello marched the captain off with a twinkle in her bright eyes. The little old lady was one of those loved by the gods, for she would undoubtedly die young in heart.

Still, as she walked with Captain Pendle to the station in the gathering darkness, she looked worried and white. George could not see her face in the dusk, and moreover was too much taken up with his late charming interview to notice his companion's preoccupation. In spite of her sympathy, Miss Whichello grew weary of a monologue on the part of George, in which the name of 'Mab' occurred fifty times and more. She was glad when the train steamed off with this too-happy lover, and promised to deliver all kinds of unnecessary messages to the girl George had left behind him.

'But let them be happy while they can,' murmured Miss Whichello, as she tripped back through the town. 'Poor souls, if they only knew what I know.'

As Miss Whichello had the meaning of this enigmatic speech in her mind, she did not think it was necessary to put it into words, but, silent and pensive, walked along the crowded pavement. Shortly she turned down a side street which led to the police-station, and there paused in a quiet corner to pin a veil round her head — a veil so thick that her features could hardly be distinguished through it. The poor lady adopted this as a kind of disguise, forgetting that her old-fashioned poke bonnet and quaint silk cloak were as well known to the inhabitants of Beorminster as the cathedral itself. That early-century garb was as familiar to the rascality of the slums as to the richer citizens; even the police knew it well, for they had often seen its charitable wearer by the bedsides of dying paupers. It thus happened that, when Miss Whichello presented herself at the police-station to Inspector Tinkler, he knew her at once, in spite of her foolish little veil. Moreover, in greeting her he pronounced her name.

'Hush, hush, Mr Inspector,' whispered Miss Whichello, with a mysterious glance around. 'I do not wish it to be known that I called here.'

'You can depend upon my discretion, Miss Whichello, ma'am,' said the inspector, who was a bluff and tyrannical ex-sergeant. 'And what can I do for you?'

Miss Whichello looked round again. 'I wish, Mr Inspector,' said she, in a very small voice, 'to be taken by you to the dead-house.'

'To the dead-house, Miss Whichello, ma'am!' said the iron Tinkler, hardly able to conceal his astonishment, although it was against his disciplinarian ideas to show emotion.

'There is a dead man in there, Mr Inspector, whom I knew under very different circumstances more than twenty years ago.'

'Answers to the name of Jentham, perhaps?' suggested Mr Inspector.

'Yes, he called himself Jentham, I believe. I — I — I wish to see his body;' and the little old lady looked anxiously into Tinkler's purple face.

'Miss Whichello, ma'am,' said the ex-sergeant with an official air, 'this request requires reflection. Do you know the party in question?'

'I knew him, as I told you, more than twenty years ago. He was then a very talented violinist, and I heard him play frequently in London.'

'What was his name, Miss Whichello, ma'am?'

'His name then, Mr Inspector, was Amaru!'
'A stage name I take it to be, ma'am!'
'Yes! a stage name.'
'What was his real name?'
'I can't say,' replied Miss Whichello, in a hesitating voice. 'I knew him only as Amaru.'
'Humph! here he called himself Jentham. Do you know anything about this murder, Miss Whichello, ma'am?' and the inspector fixed a blood-shot grey eye on the thick veil.
'No! no! I know nothing about the murder!' cried Miss Whichello in earnest tones. 'I heard that this man Jentham looked like a gipsy and was marked with a scar on the right cheek. From that description I thought that he might be Amaru, and I wish to see his body to be certain that I am right.'
'Well, Miss Whichello, ma'am,' said the stern Tinkler, after some deliberation, 'your request is out of the usual course of things; but knowing you as a good and charitable lady, and thinking you may throw some light on this mysterious crime — why, I'll show you the corpse with pleasure.'
'One moment,' said the old lady, laying a detaining hand on the inspector's blue cloth sleeve. 'I must tell you that I can throw no light on the subject; if I could I would. I simply desire to see the body of this man and to satisfy myself that he is Amaru.'

'Very good, Miss Whichello, ma'am; you shall see it.'

'And you'll not mention that I came here, Mr Inspector.'

'I give you my word, ma'am — the word of a soldier. This way, Miss Whichello, this way.'

Following the rigid figure of the inspector, the little old lady was conducted by him to a small building of galvanised tin in the rear of the police-station. Several idlers were hanging about, amongst them being Miss Bell Mosk, who was trying to persuade a handsome young policeman to gratify her morbid curiosity. Her eyes opened to their widest width when she recognised Miss Whichello's silk cloak and poke bonnet, and saw them vanish into the dead-house.

'Well I never!' said Miss Mosk. 'I never thought she'd be fond of corpses at her time of life, seeing as she'll soon be one herself.'

The little old lady and the inspector remained within for five or six minutes. When they came out the tears were falling fast beneath Miss Whichello's veil.

'Is that the man?' asked Tinkler, in a low voice.

'Yes!' replied Miss Whichello; 'that is the man I knew as Amaru.'

16

The Zeal of Inspector Tinkler

The strange affair of Jentham's murder continued to occupy the attention of the Beorminster public throughout the week; and on the day when the inquest was held, popular excitement rose to fever heat. Inspector Tinkler, feeling that the County expected him to do great things worthy of his reputation as a zealous officer, worked his hardest to gather evidence likely to elucidate the mystery of the death; but in spite of the most strenuous exertions, his efforts resulted in total failure. The collected details proved to be of the most meagre description, and when the coroner sat on the body nothing transpired to reveal the name, or even indicate the identity of the assassin who had provided him with a body to sit on. It really seemed as though the Southberry murder would end in being relegated to the list of undiscovered crimes.

'For I can't work miracles,' explained the indignant Tinkler, when reproached with this result, 'and somehow the case has got out of hand. The motive for the shooting can't be got at; the pistol used ain't to be picked up, search how you may; and as for the murdering villain who fired it, if he ain't down below where he ought to be, I'll take my oath as a soldier he ain't above ground. Take it how you will, this case is a corker and no mistake.'

It had certainly occurred to Tinkler's bothered mind that Miss Whichello should be called as a witness, if only to prove that at one time the dead man had occupied a better position in the world, but after a short interview with her he had abandoned this idea. Miss Whichello declared that she could throw no light on the affair, and that she had lost sight of the quondam violinist for over thirty years. Her recognition of him as Amaru had been entirely due to the description of his gipsy looks and the noticeable cicatrice on his face; and she pointed out to Tinkler that she had not seen the so-called Jentham till after his death; moreover, it was unlikely that events which had occurred thirty years before could have resulted in the man's violent death at the present time; and Miss Whichello insisted that she knew nothing of the creature's later circumstances or acquaintances. Being thus ignorant, it was not to be expected that her evidence would be of any value, so at her earnest request Tinkler held his tongue, and forebore to summon her as a witness. Miss Whichello was greatly relieved in her own mind when the inspector came to this conclusion, but she did not let Tinkler see her relief.

From Mosk, the officer had learned that the vagabond who called himself Jentham had appeared at The Derby Winner some three weeks previous to the time of his death. He had given no information as to where he had last rested, but, so far as Mosk knew, had dropped down from the sky. Certainly his conversation when he was intoxicated showed that he had travelled a great deal, and that his past was concerned with robbery, and bloodshed, and lawlessness; but the man had talked generally as any traveller might, had refrained from mentioning names, and altogether had spoken so loosely that nothing likely to lead to a tangible result could be gathered from his rambling discourses. He had paid his board and lodging for the first week, but thereafter had lived on credit, and at the time of his death had owed Mosk over two pounds, principally for strong drink. Usually he slept at The Derby Winner and loafed about the streets all day, but at times he went over to the gipsy camp near Southberry and fraternised with the Romany.

This was the gist of Mosk's information, but he added, as an afterthought, that Jentham had promised to pay him when certain monies which he expected came into his possession.

'Who was going to pay him this money?' asked Tinkler, pricking up his ears.

'Carn't y'arsk me somethin' easier?' growled Mosk; 'how should I know? He said he was goin' to get the dibs, but who from, or where from, I dunno', for he held his tongue so far.'

'There was no money in the pockets of the clothes worn by the body,' said Tinkler, musingly.

'I dessay not, Mr Inspector. I don't b'lieve the cove was expecting any money, I don't. 'Twas all moonshine — his talk, to make me trust him for bed and grub, and a blamed fool I've bin doin' so,' grumbled Mosk.

'The pockets were turned inside out, though.'

'Oh, they was, was they, Mr Inspector? Well, that does look queer. But if there was any light-fingered business to be done, I dessay them gipsies hev somethin' to do with it.'

'Did the man go to the gipsy camp on Sunday night?'

'Bell ses he did,' replied Mr Mosk, 'but I went over to Southberry in the arternoon about a little 'oss as I'm sweet on, so I don't know what he did, save by 'earsay.'

Bell, on being questioned by the inspector,

declared that Jentham had loitered about the hotel the greater part of Sunday, but had taken his departure about five o'clock. He did not say that he was going to the camp, but as he often paid a visit to it, she presumed that he had gone there during that evening. 'Especially as you found his corpse on the common, Mr Tinkler,' said Bell, 'no doubt the poor wretch was coming back from them gipsies.'

'Humph! it's not a bad idea,' said Tinkler, scratching his well-shaven chin. 'Strikes me as I'll go and look up Mother Jael.'

The result of an interview with that iniquitous old beldame proved that Jentham had certainly been the guest of the gipsies on Sunday evening but had returned to Beorminster shortly after nine o'clock. He had stated that he was going back to The Derby Winner, and as it was his custom to come and go when he pleased, the Romany had not taken much notice of his departure. A vagrant like Jentham was quite independent of time.

'He was one of your lot, I suppose?' said Mr Inspector, taking a few notes in his pocket-book — a secretive little article which shut with a patent clasp.

'Yes, dearie, yes! Lord bless 'ee,' mumbled Mother Jael, blinking her cunning eyes, 'he was one of the gentle Romany sure enough.'

'Was he with you long, granny?'

'Three week, lovey, jus' three week. He cum to Beorminster and got weary like of you Gentiles, so he made hisself comforbal with us.'

'Blackguards to blackguards, and birds of a feather,' murmured Tinkler; then asked if Jentham had told Mother Jael anything about himself.

'He!' screeched the old hag, 'he niver tol' me a word. He cum an' he go'd; but he kep his red rag to himself, he did. *Duvel!* he was a cunning one that Jentham.'

'Was his name Jentham, mother; or was it something else?'

'He called hisself so, dearie, but I niver knowed one of that gentle Romany as had a Gentile name. We sticks to our own mos'ly. Job! I shud think so.'

'Are you sure he was a gipsy?'

'Course I am, my noble Gorgio! He could patter the calo jib with the best of 'um. He know'd lots wot the Gentiles don' know, an' he had the eagle beak an' the peaked eye. Oh, tiny Jesus was a Romany chal, or may I die for it!'

'Do you know who killed him?' asked Tinkler, abruptly.

'No, lovey. 'Tweren't one of us, tho' you puts allays the wust on our backs. Job! dog do niver eat dog, as I knows, dearie.'

'He left your camp at nine o'clock?'

'Thereabouts, my lamb; jes' arter nine!'

'Was he sober or drunk?'

'Betwix' an' between, lovey; he cud walk straight an' talk straight, an' look arter his blessed life.'

'Humph! seems as though he couldn't,' said Mr Inspector, dryly.

'*Duvel!* that's a true sayin',' said Mother Jael, with a nod, 'but I don' know wot cum to him, dearie.'

At the inquest Mother Jael was called as a witness, and told the jury much the same story as she had related to Tinkler, with further details as to the movements of the gipsies on that night. She declared that none of the tribe had left the camp; that Jentham had gone away alone, comparatively sober; and that she did not hear of his murder until late the next day. In spite of examination and cross-examination, Mother Jael could give no evidence as to Jentham's real name, or about his past, or why he was lingering at Beorminster. 'He cum'd an' he go'd,' said Mother Jael, with the air of an oracle, and that was the extent of her information, delivered in a croaking, shuffling, unconvincing manner.

The carter, Giles Crake, who had found

the body, was a stupid yokel whose knowledge was entirely limited to his immediate surroundings. Perched on his cart, he had seen the body lying in a ditch half full of water, on the other side of an earthen mound, which extended along the side of the main road. The spot where he discovered it was near Beorminster, and about five miles from the gipsy camp. The man had been shot through the heart; his pockets had been emptied and turned inside out; and evidently after the murder the robber had dragged the body over the mound into the ditch. Giles had not touched the corpse, being fearful of getting into trouble, but had come on at once to Beorminster to inform the police of his discovery.

It was Dr Graham who had examined the body when first discovered, and according to his evidence the man had been shot through the heart shortly before ten o'clock on Sunday night. The pistol had been fired so close that the clothing of the deceased over the heart was scorched and blackened with the powder of the cartridge. 'And from this fact,' added Graham, with one of his shrewd glances, 'I gather that the murderer must have been known to Jentham!'

'How is that, doctor?' asked one of the jury.

'Because he must have held him in talk

while contemplating the crime, sir. The murderer and his victim must almost have been breast to breast, and while the attention of the latter was distracted in some way, the assassin must have shot him at close quarters.'

'This is all theory, Dr Graham,' said the coroner, who was a rival practitioner.

'It seems to me that the whole case rests on theory,' retorted Graham, and shrugged his shoulders.

Before the evidence concerning the matter closed, Inspector Tinkler explained how difficult it had been to collect even the few details which the jury had heard. He stated also that although the strictest search had been made in the vicinity of the crime, the weapon with which it had been committed could not be found. As the shooting had been done during a downfall of rain, the assassin's and his victim's footmarks were visible in the soft clay of the roadway; also there were the marks of horses' hoofs, so it was probable that the murderer had been mounted. If this were so, neither gipsies nor harvesters could have killed the wretched man, as neither the one lot nor the other possessed horses and —

'The gipsies have horses to draw their caravans!' interrupted a sharp-looking juryman.

'To draw their caravans I admit,' said the

undaunted Tinkler, 'but not to ride on. Besides, I would remind you, Mr Jobson, as Mother Jael declares, that none of her crowd left the camp on that night.'

'Oh, she'd declare anything,' muttered Jobson, who had no great opinion of Tinkler's brains. 'Have the footmarks in the road been measured?'

'No, they haven't, Mr Jobson!'

'Then they should have, Mr Inspector; you can tell a lot from a footmark, as I've heard. It's what the French call the Bertillon system of identification, that's what it is.'

'I don't need to go to France to learn my business,' said Tinkler, tartly, 'and if I did get the measurements of them footmarks, how am I to know which is which — Jentham's or his murderer's? and how can I go round the whole of Beorminster to see whose feet fit 'em? I ask you that, Mr Jobson, sir.'

At this point, judging that the discussion had gone far enough, the coroner intervened and said that Mr Inspector had done his best to unravel a very difficult case. That he had not succeeded was the fault of the case and not of Mr Inspector, and for his part, he thought that the thanks of the Beorminster citizens were due to the efforts of so zealous and intelligent an officer as Tinkler. This sapient speech reduced the recalcitrant

Jobson to silence, but he still held to his opinion that the over-confident Tinkler had bungled the matter, and in this view he was silently but heartily supported by shrewd Dr Graham, who privately considered that Mr Inspector Tinkler was little better than an ass. However, he did not give vent to this offensive opinion.

The summing-up of the coroner called for little remark. He was a worthy country doctor, with as much brains as would cover a sixpence, and the case was beyond him in every way. His remarks to the jury — equally stupid, with the exception of Jobson — were to the effect that it was evidently impossible to find out who had killed Jentham, that the man was a quarrelsome vagabond who probably had many enemies; that no doubt while crossing the common in a drunken humour he had met with someone as bad as himself, and had come to high words with him; and that the unknown man, being armed, had no doubt shot the deceased in a fit of rage. 'He robbed the body, I daresay, gentlemen,' concluded the coroner, 'and then threw it into the ditch to conceal the evidence of his crime. As we don't know the man, and are never likely to know him, I can only suggest that you should find a verdict in accordance with the evidence supplied to you by the zeal of Inspector Tinkler. Man has done all he can to find out this Cain, but his efforts have been vain, so we must leave the punishment of the murderer to God; and as Holy Scripture says that 'murder will out,' I have no doubt that some day the criminal will be brought to justice.'

After this wise speech it was not surprising that the jury brought in a verdict, 'That the deceased Jentham met with a violent death at the hands of some person or persons unknown,' that being the kind of verdict which juries without brains — as in the present instance — generally give. Having thus settled the matter to their own bovine satisfaction, the jury went away after having been thanked for their zeal by the coroner. That gentleman was great on zeal.

'Hum! Hum! Hum!' said Dr Graham to himself, 'there's too much zeal altogether. I wonder what M. de Talleyrand would have thought of these cabbages and their zeal. Well, Mr Inspector,' he added aloud, 'so you've finished off the matter nicely.'

'We have done our best, Dr Graham, sir.'

'And you don't know who killed the man?'

'No, sir, I don't; and what's more, I don't believe anybody ever will know.'

'Humph, that's your opinion, is it? Do you read much, Mr Inspector?'

'A novel at times, sir. I'm fond of a good novel.'

'Then let me recommend to your attention the works of a French author, by name Gaboriau. There's a man in them called Lecoq, who would have found out the truth, Mr Inspector.'

'Fiction, Dr Graham, sir! Fiction.'

'True enough, Mr Inspector, but most fiction is founded on fact.'

'Well, sir,' said Tinkler, with a superior wise smile, 'I should like to see our case in the hands of your Mr Lecoq.'

'So should I, Mr Inspector, or in the hands of Sherlock Holmes. Bless me, Tinkler, they'd do almost as much as you have done. It is a pity that you are not a character in fiction, Tinkler.'

'Why, sir? Why, may I ask?'

'Because your author might have touched you up in weak parts, and have gifted you with some brains. Good-day, Mr Inspector.'

While Graham walked away chuckling at his banter of this red-tape official, the official himself stood gasping like a fish out of the water, and trying to realise the insult levelled at his dignity. Jobson — a small man — sidled round to the front of him and made a comment on the situation.

'It all comes of your not measuring them

footmarks,' said Jobson. 'In detective novels the clever fellows always do that, but you'd never be put into a book, not you!'

'You'll be put into jail,' cried the outraged inspector.

'It's more than Jentham's murderer will if you've got the catching of him,' said Jobson, and walked off.

17

A Clerical Detective

All this time Mr Michael Cargrim had not been idle. On hearing of the murder, his thoughts had immediately centred themselves on the bishop. To say that the chaplain was shocked is to express his feelings much too mildly; he was horrified! thunderstruck! terrified! in fact, there was no word in the English tongue strong enough to explain his superlative state of mind. It was characteristic of the man's malignant nature that he was fully prepared to believe in Dr Pendle's guilt without hearing any evidence for or against this opinion. He was aware that Jentham had been cognisant of some weighty secret concerning the bishop's past, for the concealing of which he was to have been bribed, and when the report of the murder reached the chaplain's ears, he quite believed that in place of paying the sum agreed upon, Dr Pendle had settled accounts with the blackmailer by shooting him. Cargrim took this extreme view of the matter for two reasons; firstly, because he had gathered from the bishop's movements, and Jentham's talk of Tom Tiddler's ground, that a meeting on Southberry Heath had been arranged between the pair; secondly, because no money was found on the dead body, which would have been the case had the bribe been paid. To the circumstantial evidence that the turned-out pockets pointed to robbery, Mr Cargrim, at the moment, strangely enough, paid no attention.

In considering the case, Cargrim's wish was very much the father to the thought, for he desired to believe in the bishop's guilt, as the knowledge of it would give him a great deal of power over his ecclesiastical superior. If he could only collect sufficient evidence to convict Dr Pendle of murdering Jentham, and could show him the links in the chain of circumstances by which he arrived at such a conclusion, he had little doubt but that the bishop, to induce him to hide the crime, would become his abject slave. To gain such an immense power, and use it for the furtherance of his own interests, Cargrim was quite prepared to compound a possible felony; so the last case of the bishop would be worse than the first. Instead of being in Jentham's power he would be in Cargrim's; and in place of taking the form of money, the blackmail would assume that of influence. So Mr Cargrim argued the case out; and so he determined to shape his plans: yet he had a certain hesitancy in taking the first step. He had, as he firmly believed, a knowledge that Dr Pendle was a murderer; yet although the possession of such a secret gave him unlimited power, he was afraid to use it, for its mere exercise in the present lack of material evidence to prove its truth was a ticklish job. Cargrim felt like a man gripping a comet by its tail, and doubtful whether to hold on or let go. However, this uncertain state of things could be remedied by a strict examination into the circumstances of the case; therefore Cargrim set his mind to searching them out. He had been present at the inquest, but none of the witnesses brought forward by the bungling Tinkler had made any statement likely to implicate the bishop. Evidently no suspicion connecting Dr Pendle with Jentham existed in the minds of police or public. Cargrim could have set such a rumour afloat by a mere hint that the dead man and the bishop's strange visitor on the night of the reception had been one and the same; but he did not think it judicious to do this. He wanted the bishop's secret to be his alone, and the more spotless was Dr Pendle's public character, the more anxious he would be to retain it by becoming Cargrim's slave in order that the chaplain might be silent regarding his guilt. But to obtain such an advantage it was necessary for Cargrim to acquaint himself with the way in which Dr Pendle had committed the crime. And this, as he was obliged to work by stealth, was no easy task.

After some cogitation the wily chaplain concluded that it would be best to hear the general opinion of the Beorminster gossips in order to pick up any stray scraps of information likely to be of use to him. Afterwards he intended to call on Mr Inspector Tinkler and hear officially the more immediate details of the case. By what he heard from the police and the social prattlers, Cargrim hoped to be guided in constructing his case against Dr Pendle. Then there was the bishop's London journey; the bishop's cheque-book with its missing butt; the bishop's journey to and from Southberry on the day and night when the murder had been committed; all these facts would go far to implicate him in the matter. Also Cargrim desired to find the missing pistol, and the papers which had evidently been taken from the corpse. This last idea was purely theoretical, as was Cargrim's fancy that Jentham's power over Dr Pendle had to do with certain papers. He argued from the fact that the pockets of the dead man's clothes had been turned inside out. Cargrim did not believe that the bishop had paid the blackmail, therefore the pockets could not have been searched for the money; the more so, as no possible robber could have known that Jentham would be possessed of a sum worth committing murder for on that night. On the other hand, if Jentham had possessed papers which inculpated the bishop in any crime, it was probable that, after shooting him, the assassin had searched for, and had obtained, the papers to which he attached so much value. It was the bishop who had turned the pockets inside out, and, as Cargrim decided, for the above reason. Certainly, from a commonsense point of view, Cargrim's theory, knowing what he did know, was feasible enough.

Having thus arrived at a point where it was necessary to transmute thought into action, Mr Cargrim assumed his best clerical uniform, his tallest and whitest jam-pot collar, and drew on a pair of delicate lavender gloves. Spotless and neat and eminently sanctimonious, the chaplain took his demure way towards Mrs Pansey's residence, as he judged very rightly that she would be the most likely person to afford him possible information. The archdeacon's widow lived on the outskirts of Beorminster, in a gloomy old barrack of a mansion, surrounded by a large garden, which in its turn was girdled by a high red brick wall with broken glass bottles on the top, as though Mrs Pansey dwelt in a gaol, and was on no account to be allowed out. Had such a thing been possible, the whole of Beorminster humanity, rich and poor, would willingly have subscribed large sums to build the wall higher, and to add spikes to the glass bottles. Anything to keep Mrs Pansey in her gaol, and prevent her issuing forth as a social scourge.

Into the gaol Mr Cargrim was admitted with certain solemnity by a sour-faced footman whose milk of human kindness had turned acid in the thunderstorms of Mrs Pansey's spite. This engaging Cerberus conducted the chaplain into a large and sepulchral drawing-room in which the good lady and Miss Norsham were partaking of afternoon tea. Mrs Pansey wore her customary skirts of solemn black, and looked more gloomy than ever; but Daisy, the elderly sylph, brightened the room with a dress of white muslin adorned with many little bows of white ribbon, so that — sartorially speaking — she was very young, and very virginal, and quite angelical in looks. Both ladies were pleased to see their visitor and received him warmly in their several ways;

that is, Mrs Pansey groaned and Daisy giggled.

'Oh, how very nice of you to call, dear Mr Cargrim,' said the sylph. 'Mrs Pansey and I are positively dying to hear all about this very dreadful inquest. Tea?'

'Thank you; no sugar. Ah!' sighed Mr Cargrim, taking his cup, 'it is a terrible thing to think that an inquest should be held in Beorminster on the slaughtered body of a human being. Bread and butter! thank you!'

'It's a judgment,' declared Mrs Pansey, and devoured a buttery little square of toast with another groan louder than the first.

'Oh, do tell me who killed the poor thing, Mr Cargrim,' gushed Daisy, childishly.

'No one knows, Miss Norsham. The jury brought in a verdict of wilful murder against some person or persons unknown. You must excuse me if I speak too technically, but those are the precise words of the verdict.'

'And very silly words they are!' pronounced the hostess, *ex cathedra*; 'but what can you expect from a parcel of trading fools?'

'But, Mrs Pansey, no one knows who killed this man.'

'They should find out, Mr Cargrim.'

'They have tried to do so and have failed!'

'That shows that what I say is true. Police and jury are fools,' said Mrs Pansey, with the triumphant air of one clinching an argument.

'Oh, dear, it is so very strange!' said the fair Daisy. 'I wonder really what could have been the motive for the murder?'

'As the pockets were turned inside out,' said Mr Cargrim, 'it is believed that robbery was the motive.'

'Rubbish!' said Mrs Pansey, shaking her skirts; 'there is a deal more in this crime than meets the eye.'

'I believe general opinion is agreed upon that point,' said the chaplain, dryly.

'What is Miss Whichello's opinion?' demanded the archdeacon's widow. Cargrim could not suppress a start. It was strange that Mrs Pansey should allude to Miss Whichello, when he also had his suspicions regarding her knowledge of the dead man.

'I don't see what she has to do with it,' he said quietly, with the intention of arriving at Mrs Pansey's meaning.

'Ah! no more can anyone else, Mr Cargrim. But I know! I know!'

'Know what? dear Mrs Pansey. Oh, really! you are not going to say that poor Miss Whichello fired that horrid pistol.'

'I don't say anything, Daisy, as I don't want to figure in a libel action; but I should like to know why Miss Whichello went to the dead-house to see the body.'

'Did she go there? are you sure?' exclaimed the chaplain, much surprised.

'I can believe my own eyes, can't I!' snapped Mrs Pansey. 'I saw her myself, for I was down near the police-station the other evening on one of my visits to the poor. There, while returning home by the dead-house, I saw that hussy of a Bell Mosk making eyes at a policeman, and I recognised Miss Whichello for all her veil.'

'Did she wear a veil?'

'I should think so; and a very thick one. But if she wants to do underhand things she should change her bonnet and cloak. I knew them! don't tell me!'

Certainly, Miss Whichello's actions seemed suspicious; and, anxious to learn their meaning from the lady herself, Cargrim mentally determined to visit the Jenny Wren house after leaving Mrs Pansey, instead of calling on Miss Tancred, as he had intended. However, he was in no hurry; and, asking Daisy for a second cup of tea to prolong his stay, went on drawing out his hostess.

'How very strange!' said he, in allusion to Miss Whichello. 'I wonder why she went to view so terrible a sight as that man's body.'

'Ah!' replied Mrs Pansey, with a shake of her turban, 'we all want to know that. But I'll find her out; that I will.'

'But, dear Mrs Pansey, you don't think sweet Miss Whichello has anything to do with this very dreadful murder?'

'I accuse no one, Daisy. I simply think!'

'What do you think?' questioned Cargrim, rather sharply.

'I think — what I think,' was Mrs Pansey's enigmatic response; and she shut her mouth hard. Honestly speaking, the artful old lady was as puzzled by Miss Whichello's visit to the dead-house as her hearers, and she could bring no very tangible accusation against her, but Mrs Pansey well knew the art of spreading scandal, and was quite satisfied that her significant silence — about nothing — would end in creating something against Miss Whichello. When she saw Cargrim look at Daisy, and Daisy look back to Cargrim, and remembered that their tongues were only a degree less venomous than her own, she was quite satisfied that a seed had been sown likely to produce a very fertile crop of baseless talk. The prospect cheered her greatly, for Mrs Pansey hated Miss Whichello as much as a certain personage she quoted on occasions is said to hate holy water.

'You are quite an Ear of Dionysius,' said the chaplain, with a complimentary smirk; 'everything seems to come to you.'

'I make it my business to know what is

going on, Mr Cargrim,' replied the lady, much gratified, 'in order to stem the torrent of infidelity, debauchery, lying and flattery which rolls through this city.'

'Oh, dear me! how strange it is that the dear bishop saw nothing of this frightful murder,' exclaimed Daisy, who had been reflecting. 'He rode back from Southberry late on Sunday night, I hear.'

'His lordship saw nothing, I am sure,' said Cargrim, hastily, for it was not his design to incriminate Dr Pendle; 'if he had, he would have mentioned it to me. And you know, Miss Norsham, there was quite a tempest on that night, so even if his lordship had passed near the scene of the murder, he could not have heard the shot of the assassin or the cry of the victim. The rain and thunder would in all human probability have drowned both.'

'Besides which his lordship is neither sharp-eared nor observant,' said Mrs Pansey, spitefully; 'a man less fitted to be a bishop doesn't live.'

'Oh, dear Mrs Pansey! you are too hard on him.'

'Rubbish! don't tell me! What about his sons, Mr Cargrim? Did they hear anything?'

'I don't quite follow you, Mrs Pansey.'

'Bless the man, I'm talking English, I hope. Both George and Gabriel Pendle were on

Southberry Heath on Sunday night.'

'Are you sure!' cried the chaplain, doubtful if he heard aright.

'Of course I am sure,' snorted the lady. 'Would I speak so positively if I wasn't? No, indeed. I got the news from my page-boy.'

'Really! from that sweet little Cyril!'

'Yes, from that worthless scamp Cyril! Cyril,' repeated Mrs Pansey, with a snort, 'the idea of a pauper like Mrs Jennings giving her brat such a fine name. Well, it was Cyril's night out on Sunday, and he did not come home till late, and then made his appearance very wet and dirty. He told me that he had been on Southberry Heath and had been almost knocked into a ditch by Mr Pendle galloping past. I asked him which Mr Pendle had been out riding on Sunday, and he declared that he had seen them both — George about eight o'clock when he was on the Heath, and Gabriel shortly after nine, as he was coming home. I gave the wretched boy a good scolding, no supper, and a psalm to commit to memory!'

'George and Gabriel Pendle riding on Southberry Heath on that night,' said the chaplain, thoughtfully; 'it is very strange.'

'Strange!' almost shouted Mrs Pansey, 'it's worse than strange — it's Sabbath-breaking — and their father riding also. No wonder the mystery of iniquity doth work, when those high in the land break the fourth commandment; are you going, Mr Cargrim?'

'Yes! I am sorry to leave such charming company, but I have an engagement. Good-bye, Miss Norsham; your tea was worthy of the fair hands which made it. Good-bye, Mrs Pansey. Let us hope that the authorities will discover and punish this unknown Cain.'

'Cain or Jezebel,' said Mrs Pansey, darkly, 'it's one or the other of them.'

Whether the good lady meant to indicate Miss Whichello by the second name, Mr Cargrim did not stay to inquire, as he was in a hurry to see her himself and find out why she had visited the dead-house. He therefore bowed and smiled himself out of Mrs Pansey's gaol, and walked as rapidly as he was able to the little house in the shadow of the cathedral towers. Here he found Miss Whichello all alone, as Mab had gone out to tea with some friends. The little lady welcomed him warmly, quite ignorant of what a viper she was inviting to warm itself on her hearth, and visitor and hostess were soon chattering amicably on the most friendly of terms.

Gradually Cargrim brought round the conversation to Mrs Pansey and mentioned that he had been paying her a visit.

'I hope you enjoyed yourself, I'm sure, Mr Cargrim,' said Miss Whichello, good-humouredly, 'but it gives me no pleasure to visit Mrs Pansey.'

'Well, do you know, Miss Whichello, I find her rather amusing. She is a very observant lady, and converses wittily about what she observes.'

'She talks scandal, if that is what you mean.'

'I am afraid that word is rather harsh, Miss Whichello.'

'It may be, sir, but it is rather appropriate — to Mrs Pansey! Well! and who was she talking about to-day?'

'About several people, my dear lady; yourself amongst the number.'

'Indeed!' Miss Whichello drew her little body up stiffly. 'And had she anything unpleasant to say about me?'

'Oh, not at all. She only remarked that she saw you visiting the dead-house last week.'

Miss Whichello let fall her cup with a crash, and turned pale. 'How does she know that?' was her sharp question.

'She saw you,' repeated the chaplain; 'and in spite of your veil she recognised you by your cloak and bonnet.'

'I am greatly obliged to Mrs Pansey for the interest she takes in my business,' said Miss Whichello, in her most stately manner. 'I did visit the Beorminster dead-house. There!'

18

The Chaplain on the Warpath

Miss Whichello's frank admission that she had visited the dead-house rather disconcerted Mr Cargrim. From the circumstance of the veil, he had presumed that she wished her errand there to be unknown, in which case her conduct would have appeared highly suspicious, since she was supposed to know nothing about Jentham or Jentham's murder. But her ready acknowledgment of the fact apparently showed that she had nothing to conceal. Cargrim, for all his acuteness, did not guess that of two evils Miss Whichello had chosen the least. In truth, she did not wish her visit to the dead-house to be known, but as Mrs Pansey was cognisant of it, she judged it wiser to neutralise any possible harm that that lady could do by admitting the original statement to be a true one. This honesty would take the wind out of Mrs Pansey's sails, and prevent her from distorting an admitted fact into a fiction of hinted wickedness. Furthermore, Miss Whichello was prepared to give Cargrim a sufficient reason for her visit, so that he might not invent one. Only by so open a course could she keep the secret of her thirty-year-old acquaintance with the dead man. As a rule, the little old lady hated subterfuge, but in this case her only chance of safety lay in beating Pansey, Cargrim and Company with their own weapons. And who can say that she was acting wrongly?

'Yes, Mr Cargrim,' she repeated, looking him directly in the face, 'Mrs Pansey is right. I was at the dead-house and I went to see the corpse of the man Jentham. I suppose you — and Mrs Pansey — wonder why I did so?'

'Oh, my dear lady!' remonstrated the embarrassed chaplain, 'by no means; such knowledge is none of our business — that is, none of *my* business.'

'You have made it your business, however!' observed Miss Whichello, dryly, 'else you would scarcely have informed me of Mrs Pansey's unwarrantable remarks on my private affairs. Well, Mr Cargrim, I suppose you know that this tramp attacked my niece on the high road.'

'Yes, Miss Whichello, I know that.'

'Very good; as I considered that the man was a dangerous character I thought that he should be compelled to leave Beorminster; so I went to The Derby Winner on the night that you met me, in order to — '

'To see Mrs Mosk!' interrupted Cargrim, softly, hoping to entrap her.

'In order to see Mrs Mosk, and in order to see Jentham. I intended to tell him that if he did not leave Beorminster at once that I should inform the police of his attack on Miss Arden. Also, as I was willing to give him a chance of reforming his conduct, I intended to supply him with a small sum for his immediate departure. On that night, however, I did not see him, as he had gone over to the gipsy camp. When I heard that he was dead I could scarcely believe it, so, to set my mind at rest, and to satisfy myself that Mab would be in no further danger from his insolence when she walked abroad, I visited the dead-house and saw his body. That, Mr Cargrim, was the sole reason for my visit; and as it concerned myself alone, I wore a veil so as not to provoke remark. It seems that I was wrong, since Mrs Pansey has been discussing me. However, I hope you will set her mind at rest by telling her what I have told you.'

'Really, my dear Miss Whichello, you are very severe; I assure you all this explanation is needless.'

'Not while Mrs Pansey has so venomous a tongue, Mr Cargrim. She is quite capable of twisting my innocent desire to assure myself that Mab was safe from this man into some extraordinary statement without a word of truth in it. I shouldn't be surprised if Mrs Pansey had hinted to you that I had killed this creature.'

As this was precisely what the archdeacon's widow had done, Cargrim felt horribly uncomfortable under the scorn of Miss Whichello's justifiable indignation. He grew red, and smiled feebly, and murmured weak apologies; all of which Miss Whichello saw and heard with supreme contempt. Mr Cargrim, by his late tittle-tattling conversation, had fallen in her good opinion; and she was not going to let him off without a sharp rebuke for his unfounded chatter. Cutting short his murmurs, she proceeded to nip in the bud any further reports he or Mrs Pansey might spread in connection with the murder, by explaining much more than was needful.

'And if Mrs Pansey should hear that Captain Pendle was on Southberry Heath on Sunday night,' she continued, 'I trust that she will not accuse him of shooting the man, although as I know, and you know also, Mr Cargrim, she is quite capable of doing so.'

'Was Captain Pendle on Southberry Heath?' asked Cargrim, who was already acquainted with this fact, although he did not think it necessary to tell Miss Whichello so.

'You don't say so?'

'Yes, he was! He rode over to the gipsy camp to purchase an engagement ring for Miss Arden from Mother Jael. That ring is now on her finger.'

'So Miss Arden is engaged to Captain Pendle,' cried Cargrim, in a gushing manner. 'I congratulate you, and her, and him.'

'Thank you, Mr Cargrim,' said Miss Whichello, stiffly.

'I suppose Captain Pendle saw nothing of Jentham at the gipsy camp?'

'No! he never saw the man at all that evening.'

'Did he hear the shot fired?'

'Of course he did not!' cried Miss Whichello, wrathfully. 'How could he hear with the noise of the storm? You might as well ask if the bishop did; he was on Southberry Heath on that night.'

'Oh, yes, but he heard nothing, dear lady; he told me so.'

'You seem to be very interested in this murder, Mr Cargrim,' said the little lady, with a keen look.

'Naturally, everyone in Beorminster is interested in it. I hope the criminal will be captured.'

'I hope so too; do you know who he is?'

'I? my dear lady, how should I know?'

'I thought Mrs Pansey might have told you!' said Miss Whichello, coolly. 'She knows all that goes on, and a good deal that doesn't. But you can tell her that both I and Captain Pendle are innocent, although I *did* visit the dead-house, and although he *was* on Southberry Heath when the crime was committed.'

'You are very severe, dear lady!' said Cargrim, rising to take his leave, for he was anxious to extricate himself from his very uncomfortable and undignified position.

'Solomon was even more severe, Mr Cargrim. He said, 'Burning lips and a wicked heart are like a potsherd covered with silver dross.' I fancy there were Mrs Panseys in those days, Mr Cargrim.'

In the face of this choice proverb Mr Cargrim beat a hasty retreat. Altogether Miss Whichello was too much for him; and for once in his life he was at a loss how to gloss over his defeat. Not until he was in Tinkler's office did he recover his feeling of superiority. With a man — especially with a social inferior — he felt that he could deal; but who can contend with a woman's tongue? It is her sword and shield; her mouth is her bow; her words are the arrows; and the man who hopes to withstand such an armoury of deadly weapons is a superfine idiot. Cargrim, not being one, had run away; but in his rage at being compelled to take flight, he almost exceeded Mrs Pansey in hating the cause of it. Miss Whichello had certainly gained a victory, but she had also made an enemy.

'So the inquest is over, Mr Inspector,' said the ruffled Cargrim, smoothing his plumes.

'Over and done with, sir; and the corpse is now six feet under earth.'

'A sad end, Mr Inspector, and a sad life. To be a wanderer on the face of the earth; to be violently removed when sinning; to be buried at the expense of an alien parish; what a fate for a baptised Christian.'

'Don't you take on so, Mr Cargrim, sir!' said Tinkler, grimly. 'There was precious little religion about Jentham, and he was buried in a much better fashion than he deserved, and not by the parish either.'

Cargrim looked up suddenly. 'Who paid for his funeral then?'

'A charitable la — person, sir, whose name I am not at liberty to tell anyone, at her own request.'

'At her own request,' said the chaplain, noting Tinkler's slips and putting two and two together with wondrous rapidity. 'Ah, Miss Whichello is indeed a good lady.'

'Did you — do you know — are you aware that Miss Whichello buried him, sir?'

stammered the inspector, considerably astonished.

'I have just come from her house,' replied Cargrim, answering the question in the affirmative by implication.

'Well, she asked me not to tell anyone, sir; but as she told you, I s'pose I can say as she buried that corpse with a good deal of expense.'

'It is not to be wondered at, seeing that she took an interest in the wretched creature,' said Cargrim, delicately feeling his way. 'I trust that the sight of his body in the dead-house didn't shock her nerves.'

'Did she tell you she visited the dead-house?' asked Tinkler, his eyes growing larger at the extent of the chaplain's information.

'Of course she did,' replied Cargrim, and this was truer than most of his remarks.

Tinkler brought down a heavy fist with a bang on his desk. 'Then I'm blest, Mr Cargrim, sir, if I can understand what she meant by asking me to hold my tongue.'

'Ah, Mr Inspector, the good lady is one of those rare spirits who 'do good by stealth and blush to find it fame.''

'Seems a kind of silly to go on like that, sir!'

'We are not all rare spirits, Tinkler.'

'I don't know what the world would be if we were, Mr Cargrim, sir. But Miss Whichello seemed so anxious that I should hold my tongue about the visit and the burial that I can't make out why she talked about them to you or to anybody.'

'I cannot myself fathom her reason for such unnecessary secrecy, Mr Inspector; unless it is that she wishes the murderer to be discovered.'

'Well, she can't spot him,' said Tinkler, emphatically, 'for all she knows about Jentham is thirty years old.'

Cargrim could scarcely suppress a start at this unexpected information. So Miss Whichello did know something about the dead man after all; and doubtless her connection with Jentham had to do with the secret of the bishop. Cargrim felt that he was on the eve of an important discovery; for Tinkler, thinking that Miss Whichello had made a confidant of the chaplain, babbled on innocently, without guessing that his attentive listener was making a base use of him. The shrug of the shoulders with which Cargrim commented on his last remark made Tinkler talk further.

'Besides!' said he, expansively, 'what does Miss Whichello know? Only that the man was a violinist thirty years ago, and that he called himself Amaru. Those details don't throw any light on the murder, Mr Cargrim, sir.'

The chaplain mentally noted the former

name and former profession of Jentham and shook his head. 'Such information is utterly useless,' he said gravely, 'and the people with whom Amaru *alias* Jentham associated then are doubtless all dead by this time.'

'Well, Miss Whichello didn't mention any of his friends, sir, but I daresay it wouldn't be much use if she did. Beyond the man's former name and business as a fiddler she told me nothing. I suppose, sir, she didn't tell you anything likely to help us?'

'No! I don't think the past can help the present, Mr Tinkler. But what is your candid opinion about this case?'

'I think it is a mystery, Mr Cargrim, sir, and is likely to remain one.'

'You don't anticipate that the murderer will be found?'

'No!' replied Mr Inspector, gruffly. 'I don't.'

'Cannot Mosk, with whom Jentham was lodging, enlighten you?'

Tinkler shook his head. 'Mosk said that Jentham owed him money, and promised to pay him this week; but that I believe was all moonshine.'

'But Jentham might have expected to receive money, Mr Inspector?'

'Not he, Mr Cargrim, sir. He knew no one here who would lend or give him a farthing.

He had no money on him when his corpse was found!'

'Yet the body had been robbed!'

'Oh, yes, the body was robbed sure enough, for we found the pockets turned inside out. But the murderer only took the rubbish a vagabond was likely to have on him.'

'Were any papers taken, do you think, Mr Inspector?'

'Papers!' echoed Tinkler, scratching his head. 'What papers?'

'Well!' said Cargrim, shirking a true explanation, 'papers likely to reveal his real name and the reason of his haunting Beorminster.'

'I don't think there could have been any papers, Mr Cargrim, sir. If there had been, we'd ha' found 'em. The murderer wouldn't have taken rubbish like that.'

'But why was the man killed?' persisted the chaplain.

'He was killed in a row,' said Tinkler, decisively, 'that's my theory. Mother Jael says that he was half seas over when he left the camp, so I daresay he met some labourer who quarrelled with him and used his pistol.'

'But is it likely that a labourer would have a pistol?'

'Why not? Those harvesters don't trust one

another, and it's just as likely as not that one of them would keep a pistol to protect his property from the other.'

'Was search made for the pistol?'

'Yes, it was, and no pistol was found. I tell you what, Mr Cargrim,' said Tinkler, rising in rigid military fashion, 'it's my opinion that there is too much tall talk about this case. Jentham was shot in a drunken row, and the murderer has cleared out of the district. That is the whole explanation of the matter.'

'I daresay you are right, Mr Inspector,' sighed Cargrim, putting on his hat. 'We are all apt to elevate the commonplace into the romantic.'

'Or make a mountain out of a mole hill, which is plain English,' said Tinkler. 'Good-day, Mr Cargrim.'

'Good-day, Tinkler, and many thanks for your lucid statement of the case. I have no doubt that his lordship, the bishop, will take your very sensible view of the matter.'

As it was now late, Mr Cargrim returned to the palace, not ill pleased with his afternoon's work. He had learned that Miss Whichello had visited the dead-house, that she had known the dead man as a violinist under the name of Amaru, and had buried him for old acquaintance sake at her own expense. Also he had been informed that Captain Pendle and his brother Gabriel had been on Southberry Heath on the very night, and about the very time, when the man had been shot; so, with all these materials, Mr Cargrim hoped sooner or later to build up a very pretty case against the bishop. If Miss Whichello was mixed up with the matter, so much the better. At this moment Mr Cargrim's meditation was broken in upon by the voice of Dr Graham.

'You are the very man I want, Cargrim. The bishop has written asking me to call tonight and see him. Just tell him that I am engaged this evening, but that I will attend on him to-morrow morning at ten o'clock.'

'Oh! ho!' soliloquised Cargrim, when the doctor, evidently in a great hurry, went off, 'so his lordship wants to see Dr Graham. I wonder what that is for?'

19

The Bishop's Request

Whatever Dr Pendle may have thought of the Southberry murder, he kept his opinion very much to himself. It is true that he expressed himself horrified at the occurrence of so barbarous a crime in his diocese, that he spoke pityingly of the wretched victim, that he was interested in hearing the result of the inquest, but in each case he was guarded in his remarks. At first, on hearing of the crime, his face had betrayed — at all events, to Cargrim's jealous scrutiny — an expression of relief, but shortly afterwards — on second thoughts, as one might say — there came into his eyes a look of apprehension. That look which seemed to expect the drawing near of evil days never left them again, and daily his face grew thinner and whiter, his manner more restless and ill at ease. He seemed as uncomfortable as was Damocles under the hair-suspended sword.

Other people besides the chaplain noticed the change, but, unlike Cargrim, they did not ascribe it to a consciousness of guilt, but to ill health. Mrs Pendle, who was extremely fond of her husband, and was well informed with regard to the newest treatment and the latest fashionable medicine, insisted that the bishop suffered from nerves brought on by overwork, and plaintively suggested that he should take the cure for them at some German Bad. But the bishop, sturdy old Briton that he was, insisted that so long as he could keep on his feet there was no necessity for his women-folk to make a fuss over him, and declared that it was merely the change in the weather which caused him — as he phrased it — to feel a trifle out of sorts.

'It is hot one day and cold the next, my dear,' he said in answer to his wife's remonstrances, 'as if the clerk of the weather didn't know his own mind. How can you expect the liver of a fat, lazy old man like me not to respond to these sudden changes of temperature?'

'Fat, bishop!' cried Mrs Pendle, in vexed tones. 'You are not fat; you have a fine figure for a man of your age. And as to lazy, there is no one in the Church who works harder than you do. No one can deny that.'

'You flatter me, my love!'

'You under-rate yourself, my dear. But if it *is* liver, why not try Woodhall Spa? I believe the treatment there is very drastic and beneficial. Why not go there, bishop? I'm sure a holiday would do you no harm.'

'I haven't time for a holiday, Amy. My liver must get well as best it can while I go about my daily duties — that is if it *is* my liver.'

'I don't believe it is,' remarked Mrs Pendle; 'it is nerves, my dear, nothing else. You hardly eat anything, you start at your own shadow, and at times you are too irritable for words. Go to Droitwich for those unruly nerves of yours, and try brine baths.'

'I rather think you should go to Nauheim for that weak heart of yours, my love,' replied Dr Pendle, arranging his wife's pillows; 'in fact, I want you and Lucy to go there next month.'

'Indeed, bishop, I shall do no such thing! You are not fit to look after yourself.'

'Then Graham shall look after me.'

'Dr Graham!' echoed Mrs Pendle, with contempt. 'He is old-fashioned, and quite ignorant of the new medicines. No, bishop, you must go to Droitwich.'

'And you, my dear, to Nauheim!'

At this point matters came to an issue between them, for Mrs Pendle, who like most people possessed a fund of what may be called nervous obstinacy, positively refused to leave England. On his side, the bishop insisted more eagerly than was his custom that Mrs Pendle should undergo the Schott treatment at Nauheim. For some time the argument was maintained with equal determination on both sides, until Mrs Pendle concluded it by bursting into tears and protesting that her husband did not understand her in the least. Whereupon, as the only way to soothe her, the bishop admitted that he was in the wrong and apologised.

All the same, he was determined that his wife should go abroad, and thinking she might yield to professional persuasions, he sent for Dr Graham. By Cargrim a message was brought that the doctor would be with the bishop next morning, so Pendle, not to provoke further argument, said nothing more on the subject to his wife. But here Lucy came on the scene, and seemed equally as averse as her mother to Continental travel. She immediately entered her protest against the proposed journey.

'Mamma is better now than ever she was,' said Lucy, 'and if she goes to Nauheim the treatment will only weaken her.'

'It will strengthen her in the long run, Lucy. I hear wonderful accounts of the Nauheim cures.'

'Oh, papa, every Bad says that it cures more patients than any other, just as every Bad advertises that its waters have so much per cent more salt or sodium or iodine, or whatever they call it, than the rest. Besides, if you really think mamma should try this cure she can have it at Bath or in London. They say it is just as good in either place as at Nauheim.'

'I think not, Lucy; and I wish you and your mother to go abroad for a month or two. My mind is made up on the subject.'

'Why, papa,' cried Lucy, playfully, 'one would think you wanted to get rid of us.'

The bishop winced and turned a shade paler. 'You are talking at random, my dear,' he said gravely; 'if it were not for your mother's good I should not deprive myself of your society.'

'Poor mother!' sighed Lucy, and 'poor Harry,' she added as an afterthought.

'There need be no 'poor Harry' about the matter,' said Dr Pendle, rather sharply. 'If that is what is troubling you, I daresay Harry will be glad to escort you and your mother over to Germany.'

Lucy became a rosy red with pleasure. 'Do you really think Harry will like to come?' she asked in a fluttering voice.

'He is no true lover if he doesn't,' replied her father, with a wan smile. 'Now, run away, my love, I am busy. To-morrow we shall settle the question of your going.'

When to-morrow came, Cargrim, all on fire with curiosity, tried his hardest to stay in the library when Dr Graham came; but as the bishop wished his interview to be private, he intimated the fact pretty plainly to his obsequious chaplain. In fact, he spoke so sharply that Cargrim felt distinctly aggrieved; and but for the trained control he kept of his temper, might have said something to show Dr Pendle the suspicions he entertained. However, the time was not yet ripe for him to place all his cards on the table, for he had not yet conceived a plausible case against the bishop. He was on the point of pronouncing the name 'Amaru' to see if it would startle Dr Pendle, but remembering his former failures when he had introduced the name of 'Jentham' to the bishop's notice, he was wise enough to hold his tongue. It would not do to arouse Dr Pendle's suspicions until he could accuse him plainly of murdering the man, and could produce evidence to substantiate his accusation. The evidence Cargrim wished to obtain was that of the cheque butt and the pistol, but as yet he did not see his way how to become possessed of either. Pending doing so, he hid himself in the grass like the snake he was, ready to strike his unsuspecting benefactor when he could do so with safety and effect.

In accordance with his resolution on this point, Mr Cargrim was meek and truckling while he was with the bishop, and when Dr Graham was announced he sidled out of the library with a bland smile. Dr Graham gave him a curt nod in response to his gracious greeting, and closed the door himself before he advanced to meet the bishop. Nay, more, so violent was his dislike to good Mr Cargrim, that he made a few remarks about that apostle before coming to the object of his visit.

'If you were a student of Lavater, bishop,' said he, rubbing his hands, 'you would not tolerate that Jesuitical Rodin near you for one moment.'

'Jesuitical Rodin, doctor! I do not understand.'

'Ah, that comes of not reading French novels, my lord!'

'I do not approve of the moral tone of French fiction,' said the bishop, stiffly.

'Few of our English Pharisees do,' replied Graham, dryly; 'not that I rank you among the hypocrites, bishop, so do not take my remark in too literal a sense.'

'I am not so thin-skinned or self-conscious as to do so, Graham. But your meaning of a Jesuitical Rodin?'

'It is explained in *The Wandering Jew* of Eugene Sue, bishop. You should read that novel if only to arrive by analogy at the true character of your chaplain. Rodin is one of the personages in the book, and Rodin,' said the doctor decisively, 'is Cargrim!'

'You are severe, doctor. Michael is an estimable young man.'

'Michael and the Dragon!' said Graham, playing upon the name. 'Humph! he is more like the latter than the former. Mr Michael Cargrim is the young serpent as Satan is the old one.'

'I always understood that you considered Satan a myth, doctor!'

'So I do; so he is; a bogey of the Middle and Classical Ages constructed out of Pluto and Pan. But he serves excellently well for an illustration of your pet parson.'

'Cargrim is not a pet of mine,' rejoined the bishop, coldly, 'and I do not say that he is a perfect character. Still, he is not bad enough to be compared to Satan. You speak too hurriedly, doctor, and, if you will pardon my saying so, too irreligiously.'

'I beg your pardon, I forgot that I was addressing a bishop. But as to that young man, he is a bad and dangerous character.'

'Doctor, doctor,' protested the bishop, raising a deprecating hand.

'Yes, he is,' insisted Graham; 'his goodness and meekness are all on the surface! I am convinced that he is a kind of human mole who works underground, and makes mischief in secret ways. If you have a cupboard with a skeleton, bishop, take care Mr Cargrim doesn't steal the key.'

Graham spoke with some meaning, for since the illness of Dr Pendle after Jentham's visit, he had suspected that the bishop was worried in his mind, and that he possessed a secret which was wearing him out. Had he known that the strange visitor was one and the same with the murdered man, he might have spoken still more to the point; but the doctor was ignorant of this and consequently conceived the bishop's secret to be much more harmless than it really was. However, his words touched his host nearly, for Dr Pendle started and grew nervous, and looked so haggard and worried that Graham continued his speech without giving him time to make a remark.

'However, I did not come here to discuss Cargrim,' he said cheerfully, 'but because you sent for me. It is about time,' said Graham, grimly, surveying the bishop's wasted face and embarrassed manner. 'You are looking about as ill as a man can look. What is the matter with you?'

'Nothing is the matter with me. I am in my usual health.'

'You look it,' said the doctor, ironically. 'Good Lord, man!' with sudden wrath, 'why in the name of the Thirty-Nine Articles can't you tell me the truth?'

'The truth?' echoed the bishop, faintly.

'Yes, my lord, I said the truth, and I mean the truth. If you are not wrong in body you are in mind. A man doesn't lose flesh, and colour, and appetite, and self-control for nothing. You want me to cure you. Well, I can't, unless you show me the root of your trouble.'

'I am worried over a private affair,' confessed Pendle, driven into a corner.

'Something wrong?' asked Graham, raising his eyebrows.

'Yes, something is very wrong.'

'Can't it be put right?'

'I fear not,' said the bishop, in hopeless tones. 'It is one of those things beyond the power of mortal man to put right.'

'Your trouble must be serious,' said Graham, with a grave face.

'It is very serious. You can't help me. I can't help myself. I must endure my sorrow as best I may. After all, God strengthens the back for the burden.'

'Oh, Lord!' groaned Graham to himself, 'that make-the-best-of-it-view seems to be the gist of Christianity. What the deuce is the good of laying a too-weighty burden on any back, when you've got to strengthen it to bear it? Well, bishop,' he added aloud, 'I have no right to ask for a glimpse of your skeleton. But can I help you in any way?'

'Yes,' cried the bishop, eagerly. 'I sent for you to request your aid. You can help me, Graham, and very materially.'

'I'm willing to do so. What shall I do?'

'Send my wife and daughter over to Nauheim on the pretext that Mrs Pendle requires the baths, and keep them there for two months.'

Dr Graham looked puzzled, for he could by no means conceive the meaning of so odd a request. In common with other people, he was accustomed to consider Bishop and Mrs Pendle a model couple, who would be as miserable as two separated love-birds if parted. Yet here was the husband asking his aid to send away the wife on what he admitted was a transparent pretext. For the moment he was nonplussed.

'Pardon me, bishop,' he said delicately, 'but have you had words with your wife?'

'No! no! God forbid, Graham. She is as good and tender as she always is: as dear to me as she ever was. But I wish her to go away for a time, and I desire Lucy to accompany her. Yesterday I suggested that they should take a trip to Nauheim, but both of them seemed unwilling to go. Yet they must go!' cried the bishop, vehemently; 'and you must help me in my trouble by insisting upon their immediate departure.'

Graham was more perplexed than ever. 'Has your secret trouble anything to do with Mrs Pendle?' he demanded, hardly knowing what to say.

'It has everything to do with her!'

'Does she know that it has?'

'No, she knows nothing — not even that I am keeping a secret from her; doctor,' said Pendle, rising. 'If I could tell you my trouble I would, but I cannot; I dare not! If you help me, you must do so with implicit confidence in me, knowing that I am acting for the best.'

'Well, bishop, you place me rather in a cleft stick,' said the doctor, looking at the agitated face of the man with his shrewd little eyes. 'I don't like acting in the dark. One should always look before he leaps, you know.'

'But, good heavens, man! I am not asking you to do anything wrong. My request is a perfectly reasonable one. I want my wife and daughter to leave England for a time, and you can induce them to take the journey.'

'Well,' said Graham, calmly, 'I shall do so.'

'Thank you, Graham. It is good of you to

accede to my request.'

'I wouldn't do it for everyone,' said Graham, sharply. 'And although I do not like being shut out from your confidence, I know you well enough to trust you thoroughly. A couple of months at Nauheim may do your wife good, and — as you tell me — will relieve your mind.'

'It will certainly relieve my mind,' said the bishop, very emphatically.

'Very good, my lord. I'll do my very best to persuade Mrs Pendle and your daughter to undertake the journey.'

'Of course,' said Pendle, anxiously, 'you won't tell them all I have told you! I do not wish to explain myself too minutely to them.'

'I am not quite so indiscreet as you think, my lord,' replied Graham, with some dryness. 'Your wife shall leave Beorminster for Nauheim thinking that your desire for her departure is entirely on account of her health.'

'Thank you again, doctor!' and the bishop held out his hand.

'Come,' said Graham to himself as he took it, 'this secret can't be anything very dreadful if he gives me his hand. My lord!' he added aloud, 'I shall see Mrs Pendle at once. But before closing this conversation I would give you a warning.'

'A warning!' stammered the bishop, starting back.

'A very necessary warning,' said the doctor, solemnly. 'If you have a secret, beware of Cargrim.'

20

Mother Jael

Doctor Graham was not the man to fail in carrying through successfully any scheme he undertook, and what he had promised the bishop he duly fulfilled. After a rather lengthy interview with Mrs Pendle and her daughter, he succeeded in arousing their interest in Nauheim and its baths: so much so, that before he left the palace they were as eager to go as formerly they had been to stay. This seeming miracle was accomplished mainly by a skilful appeal to Mrs Pendle's love for experimenting with new medical discoveries in connection with her health. She had never tried the Schott treatment for heart dilation, and indeed had heard very little about it; but when fully informed on the subject, her interest in it was soon awakened. She soon came to look on the carbolic spring of Nauheim as the true fountain of youth, and was sanguine that by bathing for a few weeks in its life-giving waters she would return to Beorminster hale and hearty, and full of vitality. If ever Hope told a flattering tale, she did to Mrs Pendle through the lips of cunning Dr Graham.

'I thought you knew nothing about new medicines or treatments,' she observed graciously; 'or, if you did, that you were too conservative to prescribe them. I see I was wrong.'

'You were decidedly wrong, Mrs Pendle. It is only a fool who ceases to acquire knowledge and benefit by it. I am not a cabbage although I do live in a vegetable garden.'

Lucy's consent was gained through the glowing description of the benefit her mother would receive from the Nauheim waters, and the opportune arrival of Sir Harry Brace contributed to the wished-for result. The ardent lover immediately declared his willingness to escort Lucy to the world's end. Wherever Lucy was, the Garden of Eden blossomed; and while Mrs Pendle was being pickled and massaged and put to bed for recuperative slumbers, he hoped to have his future wife all to himself. In her sweet company even the dull little German watering-place would prove a Paradise. Cupid is the sole miracle-worker in these days of scepticism.

'It is all right, bishop!' said the victorious doctor. 'The ladies will be off, with Brace in attendance, as soon as they can pack up a waggon load of feminine frippery.'

'I am sincerely glad to hear it,' said Dr Pendle, and heaved a sigh of relief which made Graham wag his head and put in a word of advice.

'You must take a trip yourself, my lord,' he said decisively; 'nothing like change for mental worry. Go to Bath, or Putney, or Jericho, bishop; travel is your anodyne.'

'I cannot leave Beorminster just now, Graham. When I can I shall take your advice.'

The doctor shrugged his shoulders and walked towards the door. There he paused and looked back at the unhappy face of the bishop. A thought struck him and he returned.

'Pendle,' he said gently, 'I am your oldest friend and one who honours and respects you above all men. Why not tell me your trouble and let me help you? I shall keep your secret, whatever it may be.'

'I have no fears on that score, Graham. If I could trust anyone I should trust you; but I cannot tell you what is in my mind. No useful result would come of such candour, for only the One above can help me out of my difficulties.'

'Is it money worries, bishop?'

'No, my worldly affairs are most prosperous.'

'It is not this murder that is troubling you, I suppose?'

The bishop became as pale as the paper on the desk before him, and convulsively clutched the arms of his chair. 'The — the murder!' he stammered, 'the murder, Graham. Why should that trouble me?'

'Cargrim told me that you were greatly upset that such a thing should have occurred in your diocese.'

'I am annoyed about it,' replied Pendle, in a low voice, 'but it is not the untimely death of that unhappy man which worries me.'

'Then I give it up,' said the doctor, with another shrug.

'Graham!'

'Yes, what is it?'

'Do you think that there is any chance of the murderer of this man being discovered?'

'If the case had been handled by a London detective while the clues were fresh I daresay there might have been a chance,' replied the doctor. 'But that mutton-headed Tinkler has made such a muddle of the affair that I am certain the murderer will never be captured.'

'Has anything new been discovered since the inquest?'

'Nothing. So far as I know, Tinkler is satisfied and the matter is at an end. Whosoever killed Jentham has only his own conscience to fear.'

'And God!' said the bishop, softly.

'I always understood that what you Churchmen call conscience was the still small voice of the Deity,' replied Graham, drily; 'there is no use in being tautological, bishop. Well, good-day, my lord.'

'Good-day, doctor, and many, many thanks for your kindly help.'

'Not at all. I only wish that you would let me help you to some purpose by treating me as your friend and unburdening your mind. There is one great truth that you should become a convert to, bishop.'

'Ay, ay, what is that?' said Pendle, listlessly.

'That medical men are the father-confessors of Protestantism. Good-day!'

Outside the library Cargrim was idling about, in the hope of picking up some crumbs of information, when Graham took his departure. But the little doctor, who was not in the best of tempers for another conversation, shot past the chaplain like a bolt from the bow; and by the time Cargrim recovered from such brusque treatment was half-way down the avenue, fuming and fretting at his inability to understand the attitude of Bishop Pendle. Dr Graham loved a secret as a magpie does a piece of stolen money, and he was simply frantic to find out what vexed his friend; the more so as he believed that he could help him to bear his trouble by sympathy, and perhaps by advice do away with it altogether. He could not even make a guess at the bishop's hidden trouble, and ran over all known crimes in his mind, from murder to arson, without coming to any conclusion. Yet something extraordinary must be the matter to move so easy-going, healthy a man as Dr Pendle.

'I know more of his life than most people,' thought Graham, as he trotted briskly along, 'and there is nothing in it that I can see to upset him so. He hasn't forged, or coined, or murdered, or sold himself to Pluto-Pan Satan so far as I know; and he is too clear-headed and sane to have a monomania about a non-existent trouble. Dear, dear,' the doctor shook his head sadly, 'I shall never understand human nature; there is always an abyss below an abyss, and the firmest seeming ground is usually quagmire when you come to step on it. George Pendle is a riddle which would puzzle the Sphinx. Hum! hum! another fabulous beast. Well, well, I can only wait and watch until I discover the truth, and then — well, what then? — why, nothing!' And Graham, having talked himself into a *cul-de-sac* of thought, shook his head furiously and strove to dismiss the matter from his too inquisitive mind. But not all his philosophy and will could accomplish the impossible. 'We are a finite lot of fools,' said he, 'and when we think we know most we know least. How that nameless Unseen Power must smile at our attempts to scale the stars,' by which remark it will be seen that Dr Graham was not the atheist Beorminster believed him to be. And here may end his speculations for the present.

Shortly, Mrs Pendle and Lucy began to pack a vast number of boxes with garments needful and ornamental, and sufficient in quantity to last them for at least twelve months. It is true that they intended to remain away only eight weeks, but the preparations for departure were worthy of the starting out of a crusade. They must take this; they could certainly not leave that; warm dresses were needed for possible cold weather; cool frocks were requisite for probable hot days; they must have smart dresses as they would no doubt go out a great deal; and three or four tea-gowns each, as they might stay indoors altogether. In short, their stock of millinery would have clothed at least half-a-dozen women, although both ladies protested plaintively that they had absolutely nothing to wear, and that it would be necessary to go shopping in London for a few days, if only to make themselves look presentable. Harry Brace, the thoughtless bachelor, was struck dumb when he saw the immense quantity of luggage which went off in and on a bus to the railway station in the charge of a nurse and a lady's-maid.

'Oh, Lord!' said he, aghast, 'are we starting out on an African expedition, Lucy?'

'Well, I'm sure, Harry, mamma and I are only taking what is absolutely necessary. Other women would take twice as much.'

'Wait until you and Lucy leave for your honeymoon, Brace,' said the bishop, with a smile at his prospective son-in-law's long face. 'She will be one of the other women then.'

'In that case,' said Harry, a trifle grimly, 'Lucy will have to decide if I am to go as a bridegroom or a luggage agent.'

Of course all Beorminster knew that Mrs Pendle was going to Nauheim for the treatment; and of course all Beorminster — that is, the feminine portion of it — came to take tender farewells of the travellers. Every day up to the moment of departure Mrs Pendle's drawing-room was crowded with ladies all relating their experiences of English and Continental travelling. Lucy took leave of at least a dozen dear friends; and from the way in which Mrs Pendle was lamented over, and blessed, and warned, and advised by the wives of the inferior clergy, one would have thought that her destination was the moon, and that she would never get back again. Altogether the palace was no home for a quiet prelate in those days.

At the last moment Mrs Pendle found that she would be wretched if her bishop did not accompany her some way on the journey; so Dr Pendle went with the travellers to London, and spent a pleasant day or so, being hurried about from shop to shop. If he had not been the most angelic bishop in England he would have revolted; but as he was anxious that his wife should have no cause of complaint, he exhausted himself with the utmost amiability. But the longest lane has a turning, and the day came when Mrs Pendle and Lucy, attended by the dazed Harry, left for Nauheim *via* Queenborough, Flushing and Cologne. Mrs Pendle declared, as the train moved away, that she was thoroughly exhausted, which statement the bishop quite believed. His wonder was that she and Lucy were not dead and buried.

On returning to the empty palace, Bishop Pendle settled himself down for a long rest. Remembering Graham's hint, he saw as little of Cargrim as was compatible with the relationship of business. The chaplain noted that he was being avoided, and guessing that someone had placed Dr Pendle on his guard against him, became more secretive and watchful than ever. But in spite of all his spying he met with little success, for although the bishop still continued weary-eyed and worried-looking, he went about his work with more zest than usual. Indeed, he attended so closely to the duties of his position that Cargrim fancied he was trying to forget his wickedness by distracting his mind. But, as usual, the chaplain had no tangible reason for this belief.

And about this time, when most industrious, the bishop began to be haunted, not by a ghost, which would have been bearable as ghosts appear usually only in the nighttime, but by a queer little old woman in a red cloak, who supported herself with a crutch and looked like a wicked fairy. This, as the bishop ascertained by a casual question, was Mother Jael, the gipsy friend of Jentham, and the knowledge of her identity did not make him the easier in his mind. He could not conceive what she meant by her constant attendance on him; and but that he believed in the wisdom of letting sleeping dogs lie, he would have resented her pertinacity. The sight of her became almost insupportable.

Whether Mother Jael intended to terrify the bishop or not it is hard to say, but the way in which she followed him tormented him beyond measure. When he left the palace she was there on the road; when he preached in the cathedral she lurked among the congregation; when he strolled about Beorminster she watched him round corners, but she never approached him, she never spoke to him, and frequently vanished as mysteriously and unexpectedly as she appeared. Wherever he went, wherever he looked, that crimson cloak was sure to meet his eye. Mother Jael was old and bent and witch-like, with elf locks of white hair and a yellow, wrinkled face; but her eyes burned like two fiery stars under her frosted brows, and with these she stared hard at Bishop Pendle, until he felt almost mesmerised by the intensity of her gaze. She became a perfect nightmare to the man, much the same as the little old woman of the coffer was to Abudah, the merchant in the fantastic eastern tale; but, unlike that pertinacious beldam, she apparently had no message to deliver. She only stared and stared with her glittering, evil eyes, until the bishop — his nerves not being under control with this constant persecution — almost fancied that the powers of darkness had leagued themselves against him, and had sent this hell-hag to haunt and torment him.

Several times he strove to speak to her, for he thought that even the proverb of sleeping dogs might be acted upon too literally; but Mother Jael always managed to shuffle out of the way. She appeared to have the power of disintegrating her body, for where she disappeared to on these occasions the bishop never could find out. One minute he would see her in her red cloak, leaning on her crutch and staring at him steadily, but let him take one step in her direction and she would vanish like a ghost. No wonder the bishop's nerves began to give way; the constant sight of that silent figure with its menacing gaze would have driven many a man out of his mind, but Dr Pendle resisted the panic which seized him at times, and strove to face the apparition — for Mother Jael's flittings deserved such a name — with control and calmness. But the effort was beyond his strength at times.

As the weeks went by, Cargrim also began to notice the persecution of Mother Jael, and connecting her with Jentham and Jentham with the bishop, he began to wonder if she knew the truth about the murder. It was not improbable, he thought, that she might be possessed of more important knowledge than she had imparted to the police, and a single word from her might bring home the crime to the bishop. If he was innocent, why did she haunt him? But again, if he was guilty, why did she avoid him? To gain an answer to this riddle, Cargrim attempted when possible to seize the elusive phantom of Mother Jael, but three or four times she managed to vanish in her witch-like way. At length one day when she was watching the bishop talking to the dean at the northern door of the cathedral, Cargrim came softly behind her and seized her arm. Mother Jael turned with a squeak like a trapped rabbit.

'Why do you watch the bishop?' asked Cargrim, sharply.

'Bless ye, lovey, I don't watch 'im,' whined Mother Jael, cringing.

'Nonsense, I've seen you look at him several times.'

'There ain't no harm in that, my lamb. They do say as a cat kin look at a queen; and why not a pore gipsy at a noble bishop? I say, dearie,' she added, in a hoarse whisper, 'what's his first name?'

'The bishop's first name? George. Why do you want to know?'

'George!' pondered Mother Jael, taking no notice of the question, 'I allays though' the sojir was George!'

'He is George too, called after his father. Answer me! Why do you want to know the bishop's name? and why do you watch him?'

'Ah, my noble Gorgio, that's tellings!'

'No doubt, so just tell it to me.'

'Lord, lovey! the likes of you don't want to know what the likes of me thinks.'

Cargrim lost his temper at these evasions. 'You are a bad character, Mother Jael. I shall warn the police about you.'

'Oh, tiny Jesius, hear him! I ain't done nothing wrong. I'm a pore old gipsy; strike me dead if I ain't.'

'If you tell me something,' said Cargrim, changing his tactics, 'you shall have this,' and he produced a coin.

Mother Jael eyed the bright half-sovereign he held between finger and thumb, and her old eyes glistened. 'Yes, dearie, yes! What is it?'

'Tell me the truth about the murder,' whispered Cargrim, with a glance in the direction of the bishop.

Mother Jael gave a shrill screech, grabbed the half-sovereign, and shuffled away so rapidly that she was round the corner before Cargrim could recover from his surprise. At once he followed, but in spite of all his search he could not find the old hag. Yet she had her eye on him.

'George! and George!' said Mother Jael, who was watching him from an odd angle of the wall into which she had squeezed herself, 'I wonder which of 'em did it?'

21

Mrs Pansey's Festival

Once a year the archdeacon's widow discharged her social obligations by throwing open the gaol in which she dwelt. Her festival, to which all that Beorminster could boast of in the way of society was invited, usually took the form of an out-of-door party, as Mrs Pansey found that she could receive more people, and trouble herself less about their entertainment, by filling her grounds than by crushing them into the rather small reception-rooms of her house. Besides, the gardens were really charming, and the wide-spreading green of the lawns, surrounded by ample flower-beds, now brilliant with rainbow blossoms, looked most picturesque when thronged with well-dressed, well-bred, well-pleased guests. Nearly all the invitations had been accepted; firstly, because Mrs Pansey made things unpleasant afterwards for such defiant spirits as stayed away; secondly, for the very attractive reason that the meat and drink provided by the hostess were of the best. Thus Mrs Pansey's entertainments were usually the most successful of the

Beorminster season.

On this auspicious occasion the clerk of the weather had granted the hostess an especially fine day. Sunshine filled the cloudless arch of the blue sky; the air was warm, but tempered by a softly-blowing breeze; and the guests, to do honour at once to Mrs Pansey and the delightful weather, wore their most becoming and coolest costumes. Pretty girls laughed in the sunshine; matrons gossiped beneath the rustling trees; and the sober black coats of the clerical element subdued the too-vivid tints of the feminine frippery. The scene was animated and full of colour and movement, so that even Mrs Pansey's grim countenance expanded into an unusual smile when greeting fresh arrivals. At intervals a band played lively dance music; there was croquet and lawn-tennis for the young; iced coffee and scandal for the old. Altogether, the company, being mostly youthful and unthinking, was enjoying itself immensely, as the chatter and laughter, and smiling and bowing amply testified.

'Altogether, I may regard it as a distinct success,' said Mrs Pansey, as, attired in her most Hamlet-like weeds, she received her guests under the shade of a many-coloured Japanese umbrella. 'And the gardens really look nice.'

'The gardens of Paradise!' observed the complimentary Cargrim, who was smirking at the elbow of his hostess.

'Don't distort Holy Writ, if — you — please!' snapped Mrs Pansey, who still reserved the right of being disagreeable even at her own entertainment; 'but if you do call this the Garden of Eden, I daresay there are plenty of serpents about.'

'And many Adams and Eves!' said Dr Graham, surveying the company with his usual cynicism; 'but I don't see Lilith, Mrs Pansey.'

'Lilith, doctor! what an improper name!'

'And what an improper person, my dear lady. Lilith was the other wife of Father Adam.'

'How dare you, Dr Graham! the first man a bigamist! Ridiculous! Profane! Only one rib was taken out of Adam!'

'Lilith wasn't manufactured out of a rib, Mrs Pansey. The devil created her to deceive Adam. At least, so the Rabbinists tell us!'

'Oh, those Jewish creatures!' said the lady, with a sniff. 'I don't think much of their opinion. What do Jews know about the Bible?'

'As much as authors generally know about their own books, I suppose,' said Graham, drily.

'We are becoming theological,' observed

Cargrim, smoothly.

'Not to say blasphemous,' growled Mrs Pansey; 'at least, the doctor is, like all sceptics of his infidel profession. Remember Ananias and his lies, sir.'

'I shall rather remember Eve and her curiosity,' laughed Graham, 'and to follow so good an example let me inquire what yonder very pretty tent contains, Mrs Pansey?'

'That is a piece of Daisy's foolishness, doctor. It contains a gipsy, whom she induced me to hire for some fortune-telling rubbish.'

'Oh, how sweet! how jolly!' cried a mixed chorus of young voices. 'A real gipsy, Mrs Pansey?' and the good lady was besieged with questions.

'She is cunning and dirty enough to be genuine, my dears. Some of you may know her. Mother Jael!'

'Aroint thee, witch!' cried Dr Graham, 'that old beldam; oh, she can 'pen dukherin' to some purpose. I have heard of her; so have the police.'

'What language is that?' asked Miss Whichello, who came up at this moment with a smile and a word for all; 'it sounds like swearing.'

'I'd like to see anyone swear here,' said Mrs Pansey, grimly.

'Set your mind at rest, dear lady, I was

speaking Romany — the black language — the calo jib which the gipsies brought from the East when they came to plunder the hencoops of Europe.'

'Do you mean to tell me that those creatures have a language of their own?' asked Miss Whichello, disbelievingly.

'Why not? I daresay their ancestors made bricks on the plain of Shinar, and were lucky enough to gain a language without the trouble of learning it.'

'You allude to the Tower of Babel, sir!' said Mrs Pansey, with a scowl.

'Rather to the Tower of Fable, dear lady, since the whole story is a myth.'

Not caring to hear this duel of words, and rather surprised to learn that Mother Jael was present, Cargrim slipped away at the first opportunity to ponder over the information and consider what use he could make of it. So the old woman still followed the bishop? — had followed him even into society, and had made herself Mrs Pansey's professional fortune-teller so that she might still continue to vex the eyes of her victim with the sight of her eternal red cloak. Dr Pendle was at that very moment walking amongst the guests, with his youngest son by his side, and appeared to be more cheerful and more like his former self than he had been for some time. Apparently he was as yet ignorant that Mother Jael was in his immediate vicinity; but Cargrim determined that he should be warned of her presence as speedily as possible, and be lured into having an interview with her so that his scheming chaplain might see what would come of the meeting. Also Cargrim resolved to see the old gipsy himself and renew the conversation which she had broken off when she had thieved his gold. In one way or another he foresaw that it would be absolutely necessary to force the woman into making some definite statement either inculpating or exonerating the bishop in respect of Jentham's death. Therefore, having come to this conclusion, Cargrim strolled watchfully through the merry crowd. It was his purpose to inform Dr Pendle that Mother Jael was telling fortunes in the gaily-striped tent, and his determination to bring — if possible — the prelate into contact with the old hag. From such a meeting artful Mr Cargrim hoped to gather some useful information from the conversation and behaviour of the pair.

Unfortunately Cargrim was impeded in the execution of this scheme from the fact of his remarkable popularity. He could not take two steps without being addressed by one or more of his lady admirers; and although he saw the bishop no great distance away, he could not reach him by reason of the detaining sirens. As gracefully as possible he eluded their snares, but when confronted by Daisy Norsham hanging on the arm of Dean Alder, he almost gave up hope of reaching his goal. There was but little chance of escape from Daisy and her small talk. Moreover, she was rather bored by the instructive conversation of the ancient parson, and wanted to attach herself to some younger and more frivolous man. Cupid in cap and gown and spectacles is a decidedly prosy divinity.

'Oh, dear Mr Cargrim!' cried the gushing Daisy, 'is it really you? Oh, how very sweet of you to come to-day! And what is the very latest news of poor, dear Mrs Pendle?'

'I believe the Nauheim baths are doing her a great deal of good, Miss Norsham. If you will excuse — '

'Nauheim!' croaked the dean, with a dry cough, 'is unknown to me save as a geographical expression, but the town of Baden-Baden, formally called Aurelia Aquensis, was much frequented by the Romans on account of its salubrious and health-giving springs. I may also instance Aachen, vulgarly termed Aix-la-Chapelle, but known to the Latins as Aquisgranum or — '

'How interesting!' interrupted Daisy, cutting short this stream of information. 'You do seem to know everything, Mr Dean. The only German watering-place I have been to is Wiesbaden, where the doctors made me get up at five o'clock to drink the waters. And fancy, Mr Cargrim, a band played at the Kochbrunnen at seven in the morning. Did you ever hear anything so horrid?'

'Music at so early an hour would be trying, Miss Norsham!'

'Aqua Mattiacæ was the Roman appellation of Wiesbaden,' murmured Dr Alder, twiddling his eye-glass. 'I hear on good medical authority that the waters are most beneficial to renovate health and arrest decay. I should advise his lordship, the bishop, to visit the springs, for of late I have noticed that he appears to be sadly out of sorts.'

'He is looking much better to-day,' observed the chaplain, with a glance at the bishop, who was now conversing with Miss Whichello.

'Oh, the poor, dear bishop should have his fortune told by Mother Jael.'

'That would hardly be in keeping with his exalted position, Miss Norsham.'

'Oh, really, I don't see that it is so very dreadful,' cried Daisy, with one of her silvery peals of artificial laughter, 'and it's only fun. Mother Jael might tell him if he was going to be ill or not, you know, and he could take medicine if he was. Besides, she does tell the truth; oh, really, it's too awful what she knew about me. But I'm glad to say she prophesied a lovely future.'

'Marriage and money, I presume.'

'Well, you are clever, Mr Cargrim; that is just the fortune she told me. How did you guess? I'm to meet my future husband here; he is to be rich and adore me, and I'm to be very, very happy.'

'I am sure so charming a young lady deserves to be,' said Cargrim, bowing.

'*Siderum regina bicornis audi, Luna puellas*,' quoted Mr Dean, with a side glance at the radiant Daisy; and if that confident lady had understood Latin, she would have judged from this satirical quotation that Dr Alder was not so subjugated by her charms as to contemplate matrimony. But being ignorant, she was — in accordance with the proverb — blissful, and babbled on with a never-failing stream of small talk, which was at times momentarily obstructed by the heavy masses of information cast into it by the dean.

Leaving this would-be May and wary old December to their unequal flirtation, Cargrim again attempted to reach the bishop, but was captured by Miss Tancred, much to his disgust. She entertained him with a long and minute account of her rheumatic pains and the means by which she hoped to cure them. Held thus as firmly as the wedding guest was by the Ancient Mariner, Cargrim lost the chance of hearing a very interesting conversation between Miss Whichello and the bishop; but, from the clouded brow of Dr Pendle, he saw that something was wrong, and chafed at his enforced detention. Nevertheless, Miss Tancred kept him beside her until she exhausted her trickle of small talk. It took all Cargrim's tact and politeness and Christianity to endure patiently her gabble.

'Yes, bishop,' Miss Whichello was saying, with some annoyance, 'your son has admired my niece for some considerable time. Lately they became engaged, but I refused to give my consent until your sanction and approval had been obtained.'

'George has said nothing to me on the subject,' replied Dr Pendle, in a vexed tone. 'Yet he should certainly have done so before speaking to your niece.'

'No doubt! but unfortunately young men's heads do not always guide their hearts. Still, Captain Pendle promised me to tell you all during his present visit to Beorminster. And, of course, both Mrs Pendle and your daughter Lucy know of his love for Mab.'

'It would appear that I am the sole person ignorant of the engagement, Miss Whichello.'

'It was not with my consent that you were kept in ignorance, bishop. But I really do not see why you should discourage the match. You can see for yourself that they make a handsome pair.'

Dr Pendle cast an angry look towards the end of the lawn, where George and Mab were talking earnestly together.

'I don't deny their physical suitability,' he said severely, 'but more than good looks are needed to make a happy marriage.'

'Am I to understand that you disapprove of my niece?' cried the little old lady, drawing herself up.

'By no means; by no means; how can you think me so wanting in courtesy? But I must confess that I desire my son to make a good match.'

'You should rather wish him to get a good wife,' retorted Miss Whichello, who was becoming annoyed. 'But if it is fortune you desire, I can set your mind at rest on that point. Mab will inherit my money when I die; and should she marry Captain Pendle during my lifetime, I shall allow the young couple a thousand a year.'

'A thousand a year, Miss Whichello!'

'Yes! and more if necessary. Let me tell you, bishop, I am much better off than people think.'

The bishop, rather nonplussed, looked down at his neat boots and very becoming gaiters. 'I am not so worldly-minded as you infer, Miss Whichello,' said he, mildly; 'and did George desire to marry a poor girl, I have enough money of my own to humour his whim. But if his heart is set on making Miss Arden his wife, I should like — if you will pardon my candour — to know more about the young lady.'

'Mab is the best and most charming girl in the world,' said the little Jennie Wren, pale, and a trifle nervous.

'I can see that for myself. You misunderstand me, Miss Whichello, so I must speak more explicitly. Who is Miss Arden?'

'She is my niece,' replied Miss Whichello, with trembling dignity. 'The only child of my poor sister, who died when Mab was an infant in arms.'

'Quite so!' assented the bishop, with a nod. 'I have always understood such to be the case. But — er — Mr Arden?'

'Mr Arden!' faltered the old lady, turning her face from the company, that its pallor and anxiety might not be seen.

'Her father! is he alive?'

'No!' cried Miss Whichello, shaking her head. 'He died long, long ago.'

'Who was he?'

'A — a — a gentleman! — a gentleman of independent fortune.'

Dr Pendle bit his nether lip and looked embarrassed. 'Miss Whichello,' he said at length, in a hesitating tone, 'your niece is a charming young lady, and, so far as she herself is concerned, is quite fit to become the wife of my son George.'

'I should think so indeed!' cried the little lady, with buckram civility.

'But,' continued the bishop, with emphasis, 'I have heard rumours about her parentage which do not satisfy me. Whether these are true or not is best known to yourself, Miss Whichello; but before consenting to the engagement you speak of, I should like to be fully informed on the point.'

'To what rumours does your lordship refer?' asked Miss Whichello, very pale-faced, but very quiet.

'This is neither the time nor place to inform you,' said the bishop, hastily; 'I see Mr Cargrim advancing. On another occasion, Miss Whichello, we shall talk about the matter.'

As the chaplain, with three or four young ladies, including Miss Norsham, was bearing down on the bishop, Miss Whichello recognised the justice of his speech, and not feeling equal to talk frivolity, she hastily retreated and ran into the house to fight down her emotion. What the poor little woman felt was known only to herself; but she foresaw that the course of true love, so far as it concerned George and Mab, was not likely to run smooth. Still, she put a brave face on it and hoped for the best.

In the meantime, Bishop Pendle was enveloped in a whirl of petticoats, as Cargrim's Amazonian escort, prompted by the chaplain, was insisting that he should have his fortune told by Mother Jael. The bishop looked perturbed on hearing that his red-cloaked phantom was so close at hand, but he managed to keep his countenance, and laughingly refused to comply with the demand of the ladies.

'Think of what the newspapers would say,' he urged, 'if a bishop were to consult this Witch of Endor.'

'Oh, but really, it is only a joke!'

'A dignitary of the Church shouldn't joke, Miss Norsham.'

'Why not, your lordship?' put in Cargrim, amiably. 'I have heard that Richelieu played with a kitten.'

'I am not Richelieu,' replied Dr Pendle, drily, 'nor is Mother Jael a kitten.'

'It's for a charity, bishop,' said Daisy, imploringly. 'I pay Mother Jael for the day, and give the rest to Mrs Pansey's Home for servants out of work.'

'Oh, for a charity,' repeated Dr Pendle, smiling; 'that puts quite a different complexion on the question. What do you say, Mr Cargrim?'

'I don't think that your lordship can refuse the prayer of these charming young ladies,' replied the chaplain, obsequiously.

Now, the bishop really wished to see Mother Jael in order to learn why she haunted him so persistently; and as she had always vanished heretofore, he thought that the present would be a very good time to catch her. He therefore humoured the joke of fortune-telling for his own satisfaction, and explained as much to the expectant company.

'Well, well, young ladies,' said he, good-naturedly, 'I suppose I must consent to be victimised if only to further the charitable purposes of Mrs Pansey. Where dwells the sybil?'

'In this tent! This way, your lordship!'

Dr Pendle advanced towards the gaily-striped tent, smiling broadly, and with a playful shake of the head at the laughing nymphs around, he invaded the privacy of Mother Jael. With a sigh of relief at having accomplished his purpose, Cargrim let fall the flap which he had held up for the bishop's entry, and turned away, rubbing his hands. His aim was attained. It now remained to be seen what would come of the meeting between bishop and gipsy.

22

Mr Mosk is Indiscreet

While the bishop was conversing with Miss Whichello about the engagement of George and Mab, the young people themselves were discussing the self-same subject with much ardour. Captain Pendle had placed two chairs near a quick-set hedge, beyond the hearing of other guests, and on these he and Mab were seated as closely as was possible without attracting the eyes of onlookers. Their attitude and actions were guarded and indifferent for the misleading of the company, but their conversation, not being likely to be overheard, was confidential and lover-like enough. No spectator from casual observation could have guessed their secret.

'You must tell your father about our engagement at once,' said Mab, with decision. 'He should have known of it before I consented to wear this ring.'

'I'll tell him to-morrow, dearest, although I am sorry that Lucy and the mater are not here to support me.'

'But you don't think that he will object to me, George?'

'I — should — think — not!' replied Captain Pendle, smiling at the very idea; 'object to have the prettiest daughter-in-law in the county. You don't know what an eye for beauty the bishop has.'

'If you are so sure of his consent I wonder you did not tell him before,' pouted Mab. 'Aunty has been very angry at my keeping our engagement secret.'

'Darling, you know it isn't a secret. We told Cargrim, and when he is aware of it the whole town is. I didn't want to tell my father until I was sure you would marry me.'

'You have been sure of that for a long time.'

'In a sort of way,' asserted Captain Pendle; 'but I was not absolutely certain until I placed a ring on that pretty hand. Now I'll tell my father, get his episcopalian benediction, and wire the news to Lucy and the mater. We shall be married in spring. Miss Whichello will be the bridesmaid, and all will be hay and sunshine.'

'What nonsense you talk, George!'

'I'd do more than talk nonsense if the eyes of Europe were not on us. Mother Jael is telling fortunes in that tent, my fairy queen, so let us go in and question her about the future. Besides,' added George, with an insinuating smile, 'I don't suppose she would mind if I gave you one kiss.'

Mab laughed and shook her head. 'You will have to dispense with both kiss and fortune for the present,' said she, 'for your father has this moment gone into the tent.'

'What! is Saul also among the prophets?' cried George, with uplifted eyebrows. 'Won't there be a shine in the tents of Shem when it is published abroad that Bishop Pendle has patronised the Witch of Endor. I wonder what he wants to know. Surely the scroll of his fortune is made up.'

'George,' said Mab, gravely, 'your father has been much worried lately.'

'About what?' By whom?'

'I don't know, but he looks worried.'

'Oh, he is fidgeting because my mother is away; he always fusses about her health like a hen with one chick.'

'Be more respectful, my dear,' corrected Mab, demurely.

'I'll be anything you like, sweet prude, if you'll only fly with me far from this madding crowd. Hang it! here is someone coming to disturb us.'

'It is your brother.'

'So it is. Hullo, Gabriel, why that solemn brow?'

'I have just heard bad news,' said Gabriel,

pausing before them. 'Old Mr Leigh is dying.'

'What! the rector of Heathcroft? I don't call that bad news, old boy, seeing that his death gives you your step.'

'George!' cried Mab and Gabriel in a breath, 'how can you?'

'Well, Leigh is old and ripe enough to die, isn't he?' said the incorrigible George. 'Remember what the old Scotch sexton said to the weeping mourners, 'What are ye greeting aboot? If ye dinna bring them at eighty, when wull ye bring them?' My Scotch accent is bad,' added Captain Pendle, 'but the story itself is a thing of beauty.'

'I want to tell my father the news,' said Gabriel, indignantly turning away from George's wink. 'Where is he?'

'With moth — Oh, there he is,' cried Mab, as the bishop issued from the sibyl's tent. 'Oh, George, how ill he looks!'

'By Jove, yes! He is as pale as a ghost. Come and see what is wrong, Gabriel. Excuse me a moment, Mab.'

The two brothers walked forward, but before they could reach their father he was already taking his leave and shaking hands with Mrs Pansey. His face was white, his eyes were anxious, and it was only by sheer force of will that he could excuse himself to his hostess in his ordinary voice.

'I am afraid the sun has been too much for me, Mrs Pansey,' he said in his usual sauve tones, 'and the close atmosphere of that tent is rather trying. I regret being obliged to leave so charming a scene, but I feel sure you will excuse me.'

'Certainly, bishop,' said Mrs Pansey, graciously enough, 'but won't you have a glass of sherry or — '

'Nothing, thank you; nothing. Good-bye, Mrs Pansey; your *fête* has been most successful. Ah, Gabriel,' catching sight of his youngest son, 'will you be so good as to come with me?'

'Are you ill, sir?' asked George, with solicitude.

'No, no! a little out of sorts, perhaps. The sun, merely the sun;' and waving his hand in a hurried manner, Dr Pendle withdrew as quickly as his dignity permitted, leaning on Gabriel's arm. The curate's face was as colourless as that of his father, and he seemed equally as nervous in manner. Captain Pendle returned to Mab in a state of bewilderment, for which there was surely sufficient cause.

'I never saw the bishop so put out before,' said he with a puzzled look. 'Old Mother Jael must have prophesied blue ruin and murder.'

Murder! The ominous word struck on the ears of Cargrim, who was passing at the moment, and he smiled cruelly as he heard the half-joking tone in which it was spoken. Captain George Pendle little thought that the chaplain took his jesting speech in earnest, and was more convinced than ever that the bishop had killed Jentham, and had just been warned by Mother Jael that she knew the truth. This then, as Cargrim considered, was her reason for haunting the bishop in his incomings and outgoings.

Of course it was impossible that the bishop's agitation could have escaped the attention of the assembled guests, and many remarks were made as to its probable cause. His sudden illness at his own reception was recalled, and, taken in conjunction with this seizure, it was observed that Dr Pendle was working too hard, that his constitution was breaking up and that he sadly needed a rest. The opinion on this last point was unanimous.

'For I will say,' remarked Mrs Pansey, who was an adept at damning with faint praise, 'that the bishop works as hard as his capacity of brain will let him.'

'And that is a great deal,' said Dr Graham, tartly. 'Bishop Pendle is one of the cleverest men in England.'

'That is right, doctor,' replied the undaunted Mrs Pansey. 'Always speak well of your patients.'

Altogether, so high stood the bishop's

reputation as a transparently honest man that no one suspected anything was wrong save Graham and Mr Cargrim. The former remembered Dr Pendle's unacknowledged secret, and wondered if the gipsy was in possession of it, while the latter was satisfied that the bishop had been driven away by the fears roused by Mother Jael's communication, whatever that might be. But the general opinion was that too much work and too much sun had occasioned the bishop's illness, and it was spoken of very lightly as a mere temporary ailment soon to be set right by complete change and complete rest. Thus Dr Pendle's reputation of the past stood him in good stead, and saved his character thoroughly in the present.

'Now,' said Cargrim to himself, 'I know for certain that Mother Jael is aware of the truth, also that the truth implicates the bishop in Jentham's death. I shall just go in and question her at once. She can't escape from that tent so easily as she vanished the other day.'

But Cargrim quite underrated Mother Jael's power of making herself scarce, for when he entered the tent he found it tenanted only by Daisy Norsham, who was looking in some bewilderment at an empty chair. The cunning old gipsy had once more melted into thin air.

'Where is she?' demanded Cargrim, regretting that his clerical garb prevented him from using appropriate language.

'Oh, really, dear Mr Cargrim, I don't know. After the dear bishop came out so upset with the heat, we all ran to look after him, so I suppose Mother Jael felt the heat also, and left while our backs were turned. It is really very vexing,' sighed Daisy, 'for lots of girls are simply dying to have their fortunes told. And, oh!' making a sudden discovery, 'how very, very dreadful!'

'What is it?' asked the chaplain, staring at her tragic face.

'That wicked old woman has taken all the money. Oh, poor Mrs Pansey's home!'

'She has no doubt run off with the money,' said Cargrim, in what was for him a savage tone. 'I must question the servants about her departure. Miss Norsham, I am afraid that your beautiful nature has been imposed upon by this deceitful vagrant.'

Whether this was so or not, one thing was clear: that Mother Jael had gone off with a considerable amount of loose silver in her pocket. The servants knew nothing of her departure, so there was no doubt that the old crone, used to dodging and hiding, had slipped out of the garden by some back way, while the guests had been commiserating the bishop's slight illness. As Cargrim wanted to see the gipsy at once, and hoped to force her into confessing the truth by threatening to have her arrested with the stolen money in her pocket, he followed on her trail while it was yet fresh. Certainly Mother Jael had left no particular track by which she could be traced, but Cargrim, knowing something of her habits, judged that she would either strike across Southberry Heath to the tents of her tribe or take refuge for the time being at The Derby Winner. It was more probable that she would go to the hotel than run the risk of being arrested in the gipsy camp, so Cargrim, adopting this argument, took his way down to Eastgate. He hoped to run Mother Jael to earth in the tap-room of the hotel.

On arriving at The Derby Winner, he walked straight into the bar, and found it presided over by a grinning pot-boy. A noise of singing and shouting came from the little parlour at the back, and when the chaplain asked for Mr Mosk, he was informed by the smiling Ganymede that 'th' guv'nor was injiyin' of hisself, and goin' on like one o'clock.'

'Dear! dear!' said the scandalised chaplain, 'am I to understand that your master has taken more than is good for him?'

'Yuss; he's jist drunk up to jollyness, sir.'

'And Miss Mosk?'

'She's a-tryin' to git 'im t' bed, is young missus, an' old missus is cryin' upstairs.'

'I shall certainly speak about this to the authorities,' said Cargrim, in an angry tone. 'You are sober enough to answer my questions, I hope?'

'Yuss, sir; I'm strite,' growled the pot-boy, pulling his forelock.

'Then tell me if that gipsy woman, Mother Jael, is here?'

'No, sir, sh' ain't. I ain't set eyes on 'er for I do'no how long.'

The man spoke earnestly enough, and was evidently telling the truth. Much disappointed to find that the old crone was not in the neighbourhood, the chaplain was about to depart when he heard Mosk begin to sing in a husky voice, and also became aware that Bell, as he judged from the raised tones of her voice, was scolding her father thoroughly. His sense of duty got the better of his anxiety to find Mother Jael, and feeling that his presence was required, he passed swiftly to the back of the house, and threw open the door of the parlour with fine clerical indignation.

'What is all this noise, Mosk?' he cried sharply. 'Do you wish to lose your license?'

Mosk, who was seated in an arm-chair, smiling and singing, with a very red face, was struck dumb by the chaplain's sudden entrance and sharp rebuke. Bell, flushed and angered, was also astonished to see Mr Cargrim, but hailed his arrival with joy as likely to have some moral influence on her riotous father. Personally she detested Cargrim, but she respected his cloth, and was glad to see him wield the thunders of his clerical position.

'That is right, Mr Cargrim!' she cried with flashing eyes. 'Tell him he ought to be ashamed of drinking and singing with mother so ill upstairs.'

'I don't mean t'do any 'arm,' said Mosk, rising sheepishly, for the shock of Cargrim's appearance sobered him a good deal. 'I wos jus' havin' a glass to celebrate a joyful day.'

'Cannot you take your glass without becoming intoxicated?' said Cargrim, in disgust. 'I tell you what, Mosk, if you go on in this way, I shall make it my business to warn Sir Harry Brace against you.'

'I told you how t'would be, father,' put in Bell, reproachfully.

'You onnatural child, goin' agin your parent,' growled Mr Mosk. 'Wasn't I drinking to your health, 'cause the old 'un at Heathcroft wos passin' to his long 'ome? Tell me that!'

'What do you mean, Mosk?' asked the chaplain, starting.

'Nothing, sir,' interposed Bell, hurriedly.

'Father don't know what he is sayin'.'

'Yes, I do,' contradicted her father, sulkily. 'Old Mr Leigh, th' pass'n of Heathcroft, is dying, and when he dies you'll live at Heathcroft with — '

'Father! father! hold your tongue!'

'With my son-in-law Gabriel!'

'Your — son-in-law,' gasped Cargrim, recoiling. 'Is — is your daughter the wife of young Mr Pendle?'

'No, I am not, Mr Cargrim,' cried Bell, nervously. 'It's father's nonsense.'

'It's Bible truth, savin' your presence,' said Mosk, striking the table. 'Young Mr Pendle is engaged to marry you, ain't he? and he's goin' to hev the livin' of Heathcroft, ain't he? and old Leigh's a-dyin' fast, ain't he?'

'Go on, father, you've done it now,' said Bell, resignedly, and sat down.

Cargrim was almost too surprised to speak. The rector of Heathcroft — dying; Gabriel engaged to marry this common woman. He looked from one to the other in amazement; at the triumphant Mosk, and the blushing girl.

'Is this true, Miss Mosk?' he asked doubtfully.

'Yes! I am engaged to marry Gabriel Pendle,' cried Bell, with a toss of her head. 'You can tell the whole town so if you like.

Neither he nor I will contradict you.'

'It's as true as true!' growled Mosk. 'My daughter's going to be a lady.'

'I congratulate you both,' said Cargrim, gravely. 'This will be a surprise to the bishop,' and feeling himself unequal to the situation, he made his escape.

'Well, father,' said Bell, 'this is a pretty kettle of fish, this is!'

23

In the Library

Certainly there was little enough to admire in Mr Cargrim's character, still he was not altogether a bad man. In common with his fellow-creatures he also had his good qualities, but these were somewhat rusty for want of use. As Mrs Rawdon Crawley, *née* Sharp, remarked, most people can be good on five thousand a year; and if Cargrim had been high-placed and wealthy he would no doubt have developed his better instincts for lack of reasons to make use of his worser. But being only a poor curate, he had a long ladder to climb, which he thought could be ascended more rapidly by kicking down all those who impeded his progress, and by holding on to the skirts of those who were a few rungs higher. Therefore he was not very nice in his distinction between good and evil, and did not mind by what means he succeeded, so long as he was successful. He knew very well that he was not a favourite with the bishop, and that Dr Pendle would not give him more of the Levitical loaves and fishes than he could help; but as the holder of the Beorminster See was the sole dispenser of these viands with whom Cargrim was acquainted, it behoved him at all risks to compel the bestowal of gifts which were not likely to be given of free will. Therefore, Cargrim plotted, and planned, and schemed to learn the bishop's secret and set him under his thumb.

But with all the will in the world this schemer was not clever enough to deal with the evidence he had accumulated. The bishop had had an understanding with Jentham; he had attempted to secure his silence, as was proved by the torn-out butt of the cheque-book; he had — as Cargrim suspected — killed the blackmailer to bury his secret in the grave, and he had been warned by Mother Jael that she knew of his wicked act. This was the evidence, but Cargrim did not know how to place it ship-shape, in order to prove to Bishop Pendle that he had him in his power. It needed a trained mind to grapple with these confused facts, to follow out clues, to arrange details, and Cargrim recognised that it was needful to hire a helper. With this idea he resolved to visit London and there engage the services of a private inquiry agent; and as there was no time to be lost, he decided to ask the bishop for leave of absence on that very night. There is nothing so excellent as prompt attention to business, even when it consists of the dirtiest kind.

Nevertheless, to allow his better nature some small opportunity of exercise, Cargrim determined to afford the bishop one chance of escape. The visit to The Derby Winner had given him at once a weapon and a piece of information. The rector of Heathcroft was dying, so in the nature of things it was probable that the living would soon be vacant. From various hints, Cargrim was aware that the bishop destined this snug post for his younger son. But Gabriel Pendle was engaged to marry Bell Mosk, and when the bishop was informed of that fact, Cargrim had little doubt but that he would refuse to consecrate his son to the living. Then, failing Gabriel, the chaplain hoped that Dr Pendle might give it to him, and if he did so, Mr Cargrim was quite willing to let bygones be bygones. He would not search out the bishop's secret — at all events for the present — although, if Dean Alder died, he might make a later use of his knowledge to get himself elected to the vacant post. However, the immediate business in hand was to secure Heathcroft Rectory at the expense of Gabriel; so Mr Cargrim walked rapidly to the palace, with the intention of informing the bishop without delay of the young man's disgraceful conduct. Only at the conclusion of the interview could he determine his future course. If, angered at Gabriel, the bishop gave him the living, he would let the bishop settle his account with his conscience, but if Dr Pendle refused, he would then go up to London and hire a bloodhound to follow the trail of Dr Pendle's crime even to his very doorstep. In thus giving his patron an alternative, Cargrim thought himself a very virtuous person indeed. Yet, so far as he knew, he might be compounding a felony; but that knowledge did not trouble him in the least.

With this pretty little scheme in his head, the chaplain entered the library in which Dr Pendle was usually to be found, and sure enough the bishop was there, sitting all alone and looking as wretched as a man could. His face was grey and drawn — he had aged so markedly since Mrs Pendle's garden-party that Mr Cargrim was quite shocked — and he started nervously when his chaplain glided into the room. A nerve-storm, consequent on his interview with Mother Jael, had exhausted the bishop's vitality, and he seemed hardly able to lift his head. The utter prostration of the man would have appealed to anyone save Cargrim, but that astute young parson had an end to gain and was not to be turned from it by any display of mental misery. He put his victim on the rack, and tortured him as delicately and scientifically as any Inquisition of the good old days when Mother Church, anticipating the saying of the French Revolution, said to the backsliders of her flock, 'Be my child, lest I kill thee.' So Cargrim, like a modern Torquemada, racked the soul instead of the body, and devoted himself very earnestly to this congenial talk.

'I beg your pardon, my lord,' said he, making a feint of retiring, 'I did not know that your lordship was engaged.'

'I am not engaged,' replied the bishop, seemingly glad to escape from his own sad thoughts; 'come in, come in. You have left Mrs Pansey's *fête* rather early.'

'But not so early as you, sir,' said the chaplain, taking a chair where he could command an uninterrupted view of the bishop's face. 'I fear you are not well, my lord.'

'No, Cargrim, I am not well. In spite of my desire to continue my duties, I am afraid that I shall be forced to take a holiday for my health's sake.'

'Your lordship cannot do better than join Mrs Pendle at Nauheim.'

'I was thinking of doing so,' said the bishop, glancing at a letter at his elbow, 'especially as Sir Harry Brace is coming back on business to Beorminster. I do not wish my wife to be alone in her present uncertain state of health. As to my own, I'm afraid no springs will cure it; my disease is of the mind, not of the body.'

'Ah!' sighed Cargrim, sagely, 'the very worst kind of disease. May I ask what you are troubled about in your mind?'

'About many things, Cargrim, many things. Amongst them the fact of this disgraceful murder. It is a reflection on the diocese that the criminal is not caught and punished.'

'Does your lordship wish the assassin to be captured?' asked the chaplain, in his softest tone, and with much apparent simplicity.

Dr Pendle raised his head and darted a keen look at his questioner. 'Of course I do,' he answered sharply, 'and I am much annoyed that our local police have not been clever enough to hunt him down. Have you heard whether any more evidence has been found?'

'None likely to indicate the assassin, my lord. But I believe that the police have gathered some information about the victim's past.'

The bishop's hand clenched itself so tightly that the knuckles whitened. 'About Jentham!' he muttered in a low voice, and not looking at the chaplain; 'ay, ay, what about him?'

'It seems, my lord,' said Cargrim, watchful of his companion's face, 'that thirty years ago the man was a violinist in London and his professional name was Amaru.'

'A violinist! Amaru!' repeated Dr Pendle, and looked so relieved that Cargrim saw he had not received the answer he expected. 'A professional name you say?'

'Yes, your lordship,' replied the chaplain, trying hard to conceal his disappointment. 'No doubt the man's real name was Jentham.'

'No doubt,' assented the bishop, indifferently, 'although I daresay so notorious a vagrant must have possessed at least half a dozen names.'

It was on the tip of Cargrim's tongue to ask by what name Jentham had been known to his superior, but restrained by the knowledge of his incapacity to follow up the question, he was wise enough not to put it. Also, as he wished to come to an understanding with the bishop on the subject of the Heathcroft living, he turned the conversation in that direction by remarking that Mr Leigh was reported as dying.

'So Gabriel informed me,' said Dr Pendle, with a nod. 'I am truly sorry to hear it. Mr Leigh has been rector of Heathcroft parish for many years.'

'For twenty-five years, your lordship; but latterly he has been rather lax in his rule. What is needed in Heathcroft is a young and earnest man with a capacity for organisation, one who by words and deeds may be able to move the sluggish souls of the parishioners, who can contrive and direct and guide.'

'You describe an ideal rector, Cargrim,' remarked Dr Pendle, rather dryly, 'a kind of bishop in embryo; but where is such a paragon to be found?'

The chaplain coloured and looked conscious. 'I do not describe myself as a paragon,' said he, in a low voice; 'nevertheless, should your lordship think fit to present me with the Heathcroft cure of souls, I should strive to approach in some degree the ideal I have described.'

The bishop was no stranger to Cargrim's ambition, as it was not the first time that the chaplain had hinted that he would make a good rector of Heathcroft, therefore he did not feel surprised at being approached so crudely on the subject. With a testy gesture he pushed back his chair and looked rather frowningly on the presumptuous parson. But Cargrim was too sure of his ability to deal with the bishop to be daunted by looks, and with his sleek head on one side and a suave smile on his pale lips, he waited for the thunders from the episcopalian throne. However, the bishop was just as diplomatic as his chaplain, and too wise to give way to the temper he felt at so downright a request, approached the matter in an outwardly mild spirit.

'Heathcroft is a large parish,' said his lordship, meditatively.

'And therefore needs a hard-working young rector,' replied Cargrim. 'I am, of course, aware of my own deficiencies, but these may be remedied by prayer and by a humble spirit.'

'Mr Cargrim,' said the bishop, with a smile, 'do you remember the rather heterodox story of the farmer's comment on prayer being offered up for rain? 'What is the use of praying for rain,' said he, 'when the wind is in this quarter?' I am inclined,' added Dr Pendle, looking very intently at Cargrim, 'to agree with the farmer.'

'Does that mean that your lordship will not give me the living?'

'We will come to that later, Mr Cargrim. At present I mean that no prayers will remedy our deficiencies unless the desire to do so begins in our own breasts.'

'Will your lordship indicate the particular deficiencies I should remedy?' asked the chaplain, outwardly calm, but inwardly raging.

'I think, Mr Cargrim,' said the bishop,

gently, 'that your ambition is apt to take precedence of your religious feelings, else you would hardly adopt so extreme a course as to ask me so bluntly for a living. If I deemed it advisable that you should be rector of Heathcroft, I should bestow it on you without the necessity of your asking me to give it to you; but to be plain with you, Mr Cargrim, I have other designs when the living becomes vacant.'

'In that case, we need say no more, your lordship.'

'Pardon me, you must permit me to say this much,' said Dr Pendle, in his most stately manner, 'that I desire you to continue in your present position until you have more experience in diocesan work. It is not every young man, Mr Cargrim, who has so excellent an opportunity of acquainting himself with the internal management of the Catholic Church. Your father was a dear friend of mine,' continued the bishop, with emotion, 'and in my younger days I owed him much. For his sake, and for your own, I wish to help you as much as I can, but you must permit me to be the best judge of when and how to advance your interests. These ambitions of yours, Michael, which I have observed on several occasions, are dangerous to your better qualities. A clergyman of our

Church is a man, and — being a priest — something more than a man; therefore it behoves him to be humble and religious and intent upon his immediate work for the glory of God. Should he rise, it must be by such qualities that he attains a higher post in the Church; but should he remain all his days in a humble position, he can die content, knowing he has thought not of himself but of his God. Believe me, my dear young friend, I speak from experience, and it is better for you to leave your future in my hands.'

These sentiments, being the antithesis to those of Cargrim, were of course extremely unpalatable to one of his nature. He knew that he was more ambitious than religious; but it was galling to think that Dr Pendle should have been clever enough to gauge his character so truly. His mask of humility and deference had been torn off, and he was better known to the bishop than was at all agreeable to his cunning nature. He saw that so far as the Heathcroft living was concerned he would never obtain it as a free gift from Dr Pendle, therefore it only remained to adopt the worser course, and force the prelate to accede to his request. Having thus decided, Mr Cargrim, with great self-control, smoothed his face to a meek smile, and even displayed a little emotion in order to show the bishop how touched he was by the kindly speech which had crushed his ambition.

'I am quite content to leave my future in your hands,' he said, with all possible suavity, 'and indeed, my lord, I know that you are my best — my only friend. The deficiency to which you allude shall be conquered by me if possible, and I trust that shortly I shall merit your lordship's more unreserved approbation.'

'Why,' said the bishop, shaking him heartily by the hand, 'that is a very worthy speech, Michael, and I shall bear it in mind. We are still friends, I trust, in spite of what I consider it was my duty to say.'

'Certainly we are friends, sir; I am honoured by the interest you take in me. And now, my lord,' added Cargrim, with a sweet smile, 'may I prefer a little request which was in my mind when I came to see you?'

'Of course! of course, Michael; what is it?'

'I have some business to transact in London, my lord; and I should like, with your permission, to be absent from my duties for a few days.'

'With pleasure,' assented the bishop; 'go when you like, Cargrim. I am only too pleased that you should ask me for a holiday.'

'Many thanks, your lordship,' said Cargrim, rising. 'Then I shall leave the palace to-morrow morning, and will return towards the end of the week. As there is nothing of particular importance to attend to, I trust your lordship will be able to dispense with my services during my few days' absence without trouble to yourself.'

'Set your mind at rest, Cargrim; you can take your holiday.'

'I again thank your lordship. It only remains for me to say that if — as I have heard — your lordship intends to make Mr Gabriel rector of Heathcroft, I trust he will be as earnest and devout there as he has been in Beorminster.'

'I have not yet decided how to fill up the vacancy,' said the bishop, coldly, 'and let me remind you, Mr Cargrim, that as yet the present rector of Heathcroft still holds the living.'

'I do but anticipate the inevitable, my lord,' said Cargrim, preparing to drive his sting into the bishop, 'and certainly, the sooner Mr Gabriel is advanced to the living the better it will be for his matrimonial prospects.'

Dr Pendle stared. 'I don't understand you!' he said stiffly.

'What!' Mr Cargrim threw up his hands in astonishment. 'Has not Mr Gabriel informed your lordship of his engagement?'

'Engagement!' echoed the bishop, half

rising, 'do you mean to tell me that Gabriel is engaged, and without my knowledge!'

'Oh, your lordship! — I thought you knew — most indiscreet of me,' murmured Cargrim, in pretended confusion.

'To whom is my son engaged?' asked the bishop, sharply.

'To — to — really, I feel most embarrassed,' said the chaplain. 'I should not have taken — '

'Answer at once, sir,' cried Dr Pendle, irritably. 'To whom is my son Gabriel engaged? I insist upon knowing.'

'In that case, I must tell your lordship that Mr Gabriel is engaged to marry Miss Bell Mosk!'

The bishop bounded out of his chair. 'Bell Mosk! the daughter of the landlord of The Derby Winner?'

'Yes, your lordship.'

'The — the — the — barmaid! My son! — oh, it is — it is impossible!'

'I had it from the lips of the young lady herself,' said Cargrim, delighted at the bishop's annoyance. 'Certainly Miss Mosk is hardly fitted to be the wife of a future rector — still, she is a handsome — '

'Stop, sir!' cried the bishop, imperiously, 'don't dare to couple my son's name with that of — of — of a barmaid. I cannot — I will not — I dare not believe it!'

'Nevertheless, it is true!'

'Impossible! incredible! the boy must be mad!'

'He is in love, which is much the same thing,' said Cargrim, with more boldness than he usually displayed before Dr Pendle; 'but to assure yourself of its truth, let me suggest that your lordship should question Mr Gabriel yourself. I believe he is in the palace.'

'Thank you, Mr Cargrim,' said the bishop, recovering from his first surprise. 'I thank you for the information, but I am afraid you have been misled. My son would never choose a wife out of a bar.'

'It is to be hoped he will see the folly of doing so, my lord,' replied the chaplain, backing towards the door, 'and now I shall take my leave, assuring your lordship that I should never have spoken of Mr Gabriel's engagement had I not believed that you were informed on the point.'

The bishop made no reply, but sank into a chair, looking the picture of misery. After a glance at him, Cargrim left the room, rubbing his hands. 'I think I have given you a very good Roland for your Oliver, my lord!' he murmured.

24

The Bishop Asserts Himself

On being left alone, the bishop sat motionless in his chair for some considerable time. The information conveyed by Cargrim struck at his pride, but in his heart he knew well that he had as little right to be proud as to resent the blow. Casting a look over the past, he saw that Dr Graham had been right in his reference to the Ring of Polycrates, for although he was outwardly still prosperous and high-placed, shame had come upon him, and evil was about to befall. From the moment of Jentham's secret visit a blight had fallen on his fortunes, a curse had come upon his house, and in a thousand hidden ways he had been tortured, although for no fault of his own. There was his secret which he did not dare even to think of; there was the enforced absence of his wife and daughter, whom he had been compelled to send away; there was the hidden enmity of Cargrim, which he did not know how to baffle; and now there was the shame of Gabriel's engagement to a barmaid; of George's choice of a wife, who, if rumour could be believed, was the daughter of a scoundrel. With these ills heaped upon his head, the bishop did not know how he could ever raise it again.

Still, all these woes were locked up in his own breast, and to the world he was yet the popular, prosperous Bishop of Beorminster. This impression and position he was resolved to maintain at all costs, therefore, to put an end to his last trouble, he concluded to speak seriously to his sons on the subject of unequal marriages. A pressure of the electric button summoned the servant, who was instructed to request Captain Pendle and Mr Gabriel to see their father at once in the library. It would seem as though they almost expected the message, for in a few minutes they were both in the room; George, with his usual jaunty, confident air, but Gabriel with an anxious look. Yet neither of the young men guessed why the bishop had sent for them; least of all George, who never dreamed for a moment that his father would oppose his engagement with Mab Arden.

'Sit down, both of you,' said Dr Pendle, in grave tones, 'I have something serious to say,' and the bishop took up an imposing position on the hearthrug. The two sons looked at one another.

'There is no bad news from Nauheim, I

hope, sir?' said George, quite ignorant of the meaning of this exordium.

'No. Lucy's last letter about your mother was very cheerful indeed. I wish to speak seriously to both of you. As you are the elder, George, I shall begin with you; Gabriel, I shall reason with later.'

'Reason with me,' wondered the curate. 'Have I been doing anything which requires me to be reasoned with?' and he gave a half smile, never thinking how soon his jest would be turned into bitter earnest.

'I think a word in season will do you no harm,' answered his father, austerely, 'but I shall address myself to George first.'

'I am all attention, sir,' said the captain, rather weary of this solemnity. 'What have I done?'

'You have concealed from me the fact of your engagement to Miss Arden.'

'Oh!' cried George, smiling, 'so Miss Whichello has been speaking!'

'Yes, she spoke to me to-day, and told me that you had formally engaged yourself to her niece without my knowledge or sanction. May I inquire your reason for so singular a course?'

'Is it singular, sir?' asked George, in a half-joking tone. 'I always understood that it was first necessary to obtain the lady's consent before making the matter public. I asked Mab to be my wife when I last visited Beorminster, and I intended to tell you of it this time, but I find that Miss Whichello has saved me the trouble. However, now that you know the truth, sir,' said Captain Pendle, with his sunny smile, 'may I ask for your approval and blessing?'

'You may ask,' said the bishop, coldly, 'but you shall have neither.'

'Father!' The answer was so unexpected that George jumped up from his chair with a cry of surprise, and even Gabriel, who was in the secret of his brother's love for Mab, looked astonished and pained.

'I do not approve of the engagement,' went on the bishop, imperturbably.

'You — do — not — approve — of — Mab!' said Captain Pendle, slowly, and his face became pale with anger.

'I said nothing about the lady,' corrected the bishop, haughtily; 'you will be pleased, sir, to take my words as I speak them. I do not approve of the engagement.'

'On what grounds?' asked George, quietly enough.

'I know nothing about Miss Arden's parents.'

'She is the daughter of Miss Whichello's sister.'

'I am aware of that, but what about her father?'

'Her father!' repeated George, rather perplexed. 'I never inquired about her father; I do not know anything about him.'

'Indeed!' said the bishop, 'it is just as well that you do not.'

Captain Pendle looked disturbed. 'Is there anything wrong with him?' he asked nervously. 'I thought he was dead and buried ages ago.'

'I believe he is dead; but from all accounts he was a scoundrel.'

'From whose account, bishop?'

'Mrs Pansey's for one.'

'Father!' cried Gabriel, 'surely you know that Mrs Pansey's gossip is most unreliable.'

'Not in this instance,' replied the bishop, promptly. 'Mrs Pansey told me some twenty-six years ago, when Miss Whichello brought her niece to this city, that the child's father was little better than a gaol-bird.'

'Did she know him?' asked George, sharply.

'That I cannot say, but she assured me that she spoke the truth. I paid no attention to her talk, nor did I question Miss Whichello on the subject. In those days it had no interest for me, but now that I find my son desires to marry the girl, I must refuse my consent until I learn all about her birth and parentage.'

'Miss Whichello will tell us about that!' said George, hopefully.

'Let us trust that Miss Whichello dare tell us.'

'Dare, sir!' cried Captain Pendle, gnawing his moustache.

'I used the word advisedly, George. If what Mrs Pansey asserts is true, Miss Whichello will feel a natural reluctance to confess the truth about Miss Arden's father.'

'Admitting as much,' urged Gabriel, seeing that George kept silent, 'surely you will not visit the sins of the father on the innocent child?'

'It is scriptural law, my son.'

'It is not the law of Christ,' replied the curate.

'Law or no law!' said Captain Pendle, determinedly, 'I shall not give Mab up. Her father may have been a Nero for all I care. I marry his daughter all the same; she is a good, pure, sweet woman.'

'I admit that she is all that,' said the bishop, 'and I do not want you to give her up without due inquiry into the matter of which I speak. But it is my desire that you should return to your regiment until the affair can be sifted.'

'Who should sift it but I?' inquired George, hotly.

'If you place it in my hands all will — I

trust — be well, my son. I shall see Miss Whichello and Mrs Pansey and learn the truth.'

'And if the truth be as cruel as you suspect?'

'In that case,' said the bishop, slowly, 'I shall consider the matter; you must not think that I wish you to break off your engagement altogether, George, but I desire you to suspend it, so to speak. For the reasons I have stated, I disapprove of your marrying Miss Arden, but it may be that, should I be informed fully about her father, I may change my mind. In the meantime, I wish you to rejoin your regiment and remain with it until I send for you.'

'And if I refuse?'

'In that case,' said the bishop, sternly, 'I shall refuse my consent altogether. Should you refuse to acknowledge my authority I shall treat you as a stranger. But I have been a good father to you, George, and I trust that you will see fit to obey me.'

'I am not a child,' said Captain Pendle, sullenly.

'You are a man of the world,' replied his father, skilfully, 'and as such must see that I am speaking for your own good. I ask merely for delay, so that the truth may be known before you engage yourself irrevocably to this young lady.'

'I look upon my engagement as irrevocable! I have asked Mab to be my wife, I have given her a ring, I have won her heart; I should be a mean hound,' cried George, lashing himself into a rage, 'if I gave her up for the lying gossip of an old she-devil like Mrs Pansey.'

'Your language is not decorous, sir.'

'I — I beg your pardon, father, but don't be too hard on me.'

'Your own good sense should tell you that I am not hard on you.'

'Indeed,' put in Gabriel, 'I think that my father has reason on his side, George.'

'You are not in love,' growled the captain, unconvinced.

A pale smile flitted over Gabriel's lips, not unnoticed by the bishop, but as he purposed speaking to him later, he made no remark on it at the moment.

'What do you wish me to do, sir?' asked George, after a pause.

'I have told you,' rejoined the bishop, mildly. 'I desire you to rejoin your regiment and not come back to Beorminster until I send for you.'

'Do you object to my seeing Mab before I go?'

'By no means; see both Miss Arden and Miss Whichello if you like, and tell them both that it is by my desire you go away.'

'Well, sir,' said Captain Pendle, slowly, 'I am willing to obey you and return to my work, but I refuse to give up Mab,' and not trusting himself to speak further, lest he should lose his temper altogether, he abruptly left the room. The bishop saw him retire with a sigh and shook his head. Immediately afterwards he addressed himself to Gabriel, who, with some apprehension, was waiting for him to speak.

'Gabriel,' said Dr Pendle, picking up a letter, 'Harry has written to me from Nauheim, saying that he is compelled to return home on business. As I do not wish your mother and Lucy to be alone, it is my desire that you should join them — at once!'

The curate was rather amazed at the peremptory tone of this speech, but hastened to assure his father that he was quite willing to go. The reason given for the journey seemed to him a sufficient one, and he had no suspicion that his father's real motive was to separate him from Bell. The bishop saw that this was the case, and forthwith came to the principal point of the interview.

'Do you know why I wish you to go abroad?' he asked sharply.

'To join my mother and Lucy — you told me so.'

'That is one reason, Gabriel; but there is

another and more important one.'

A remembrance of his secret engagement turned the curate's face crimson; but he faltered out that he did not understand what his father meant.

'I think you understand well enough,' said Dr Pendle, sternly. 'I allude to your disgraceful conduct in connection with that woman at The Derby Winner.'

'If you allude to my engagement to Miss Mosk, sir,' cried Gabriel, with spirit, 'there is no need to use the word disgraceful. My conduct towards that young lady has been honourable throughout.'

'And what about your conduct towards your father?' asked the bishop.

Gabriel hung his head. 'I intended to tell you,' he stammered, 'when — '

'When you could summon up courage to do so,' interrupted Dr Pendle, in cutting tones. 'Unfortunately, your candour was not equal to your capability for deception, so I was obliged to learn the truth from a stranger.'

'Cargrim!' cried Gabriel, his instinct telling him the name of his betrayer.

'Yes, from Mr Cargrim. He heard the truth from the lips of this girl herself. She informed him that she was engaged to marry you — you, my son.'

'It is true!' said Gabriel, in a low voice. 'I

wish to make her my wife.'

'Make her your wife!' cried Dr Pendle, angrily; 'this common girl — this — this barmaid — this — '

'I shall not listen to Bell being called names even by you, father,' said Gabriel, proudly. 'She is a good girl, a respectable girl — a beautiful girl!'

'And a barmaid,' said the bishop, dryly. 'I congratulate you on the daughter-in-law you have selected for your mother!'

Gabriel winced. Much as he loved Bell, the idea of her being in the society of his delicate, refined mother was not a pleasant one. He could not conceal from himself that although the jewel he wished to pick out of the gutter might shine brilliantly there, it might not glitter so much when translated to a higher sphere and placed beside more polished gems. Therefore, he could find no answer to his father's speech, and wisely kept silence.

'Certainly, my sons are a comfort to me!' continued the bishop, sarcastically. 'I have brought them up in what I judged to be a wise and judicious manner, but it seems I am mistaken, since the first use they make of their training is to deceive the father who has never deceived them.'

'I admit that I have behaved badly, father.'

'No one can deny that, sir. The question is,

do you intend to continue behaving badly?'

'I love Bell dearly — very dearly!'

The bishop groaned and sat down helplessly in his chair. 'It is incredible,' he said. 'How can you, with your refined tastes and up-bringing, love this — this — ? Well, I shall not call her names. No doubt Miss Mosk is well enough in her way, but she is not a proper wife for my son.'

'Our hearts are not always under control, father.'

'They should be, Gabriel. The head should always guide the heart; that is only common sense. Besides, you are too young to know your own mind. This girl is handsome and scheming, and has infatuated you in your innocence. I should be a bad father to you if I did not rescue you from her wiles. To do so, it is my intention that you shall go abroad for a time.'

'I am willing to go abroad, father, but I shall never, never forget Bell!'

'You speak with all the confidence of a young man in love for the first time, Gabriel. I am glad that you are still sufficiently obedient to obey me. Of course, you know that I cannot consent to your making this girl your wife.'

'I thought that you might be angry,' faltered Gabriel.

'I am more hurt than angry,' replied the

bishop. 'Have you given this young woman a promise of marriage?'

'Yes, father; I gave her an engagement ring.'

'I congratulate you, sir, on your methodical behaviour. However, it is no use arguing with one so infatuated as you are. All I can do is to test your affection by parting you from Miss Mosk. When you return from Nauheim we shall speak further on the subject.'

'When do you wish me to go, father?' asked Gabriel, rising submissively.

'To-morrow,' said the bishop, coldly. 'You can leave me now.'

'I am sorry — '

'Sorry!' cried Dr Pendle, with a frown. 'What is the use of words without deeds? Both you and George have given me a sore heart this day. I thought that I could trust my sons; I find that I cannot. If — But it is useless to talk further. I shall see what absence can do in both cases. Now leave me, if you please.'

The bishop turned to his desk and busied himself with some papers, while Gabriel, after a moment's hesitation, left the room with a deep sigh. Dr Pendle, finding himself alone, leaned back in his chair and groaned aloud.

'I have averted the danger for the time being,' he said sadly, 'but the future — ah, me! what of the future?'

25

Mr Baltic, Missionary

About this time there appeared in Beorminster an elderly, weather-beaten man, with a persuasive tongue and the quick, alert eye of a fowl. He looked like a sailor, and as such was an object of curiosity to inland folk; but he called himself a missionary, saying that he had laboured these many years in the Lord's vineyard of the South Seas, and had returned to England for a sight of white faces and a smack of civilisation. This hybrid individual was named Ben Baltic, and had the hoarse voice of a mariner accustomed to out-roar storms, but his conversation was free from nautical oaths, and remarkably entertaining by reason of his adventurous life. He could not be said to be obtrusively religious, yet he gave everyone the impression of being a good and earnest worker, and one who practised what he preached, for he neither smoked nor gambled nor drank strong waters. Yet there was nothing Pharisaic about his speech or bearing.

In a pilot suit of rough blue cloth, with a

red bandanna handkerchief and a wide-brimmed hat of Panama straw, Mr Baltic took up his residence at The Derby Winner, and, rolling about Beorminster in the true style of Jack ashore, speedily made friends with people high and low. The low he became acquainted with on his own account, as a word and a smile in his good-humoured way was sufficient to establish at least a temporary friendship; but he owed his familiarity with the 'high' to the good offices of Mr Cargrim. That gentleman returned from his holiday with much apparent satisfaction, and declared himself greatly benefited by the change. Shortly after his resumption of his duties, he received a visit from Baltic the missionary, who presented him with a letter of introduction from a prominent London vicar. From this epistle the chaplain learned that Baltic was a rough diamond with a gift of untutored eloquence, that he desired to rest for a week or two in Beorminster, and that any little attention shown to him would be grateful to the writer. It said much for Mr Cargrim's goodwill and charity that, on learning all this, he at once opened his arms and heart to the missionary-mariner. He declared his willingness to make Baltic's stay as pleasant as he could, but was shocked to learn that the new-comer had taken up his abode at The Derby Winner. His feelings extended even so far as remonstrance.

'For,' said Cargrim, shaking his head, 'I assure you, Mr Baltic, that the place is anything but respectable.'

'And for such reason I stay there, sir. If you want to do good begin with the worst; that's my motto. The Christian heathen can't be worse than the Pagan heathen, I take it, Mr Cargrim.'

'I don't know so much about that,' sighed Cargrim. 'Refined vice is always the most terrible. Witness the iniquities of Babylon and Rome.'

'There ain't much refinement about that blackguard public,' answered the missionary, without the shadow of a smile, 'and if I can stop all the swearing and drinking and shuffling of the devil's picture-books which goes on there, I'll be busy at the Lord's work, I reckon.'

From this position Baltic refused to budge, so in the end Cargrim left off trying to dissuade him, and the conversation became of a more confidential character. Evidently the man's qualities were not over-praised in the letter of introduction, for, on meeting him once or twice and knowing him better, Cargrim found occasion to present him to the bishop. Baltic's descriptions of his South Sea labours fascinated Dr Pendle by their colour and wildness, and he suggested that the missionary should deliver a discourse of the same quality to the public. A hall was hired; the lecture was advertised as being under the patronage of the bishop, and so many tickets were sold that the building was crowded with the best Beorminster society, led by Mrs Pansey. The missionary, after introducing himself as a plain and unlettered man, launched out into a wonderfully vigorous and picturesque description of those Islands of Paradise which bloom like gardens amid the blue waters of the Pacific Ocean. He described the fecundity and luxuriance of Nature, drew word-portraits of the mild, brown-skinned Polynesians, wept over their enthralment by a debased system of idolatry, and painted the blessings which would befall them when converted to the gentle religion of Christ. Baltic had the gift of enchaining his hearers, and the audience hung upon his speech with breathless attention. The natural genius of the man poured forth in burning words and eloquent apostrophes. The subject was picturesque, the language was inspiriting, the man a born orator, and, when the audience dispersed, everyone, from the bishop downward, agreed that Beorminster was entertaining an untutored Demosthenes. Dr Pendle sighed as he thought of the many dull sermons he had been compelled to endure, and wondered why the majority of his educated clergy should fall so far behind the untaught, unconsecrated, rough-mannered missionary.

From the time of that lecture, Ben Baltic, for all his lowly birth and uncouth ways, became the lion of Beorminster. He was invited by Mrs Pansey to afternoon tea; he was in request at garden-parties; he gave lectures in surrounding parishes, and, on the whole, created an undeniable sensation in the sober cathedral city. Baltic observed much and said little; his eyes were alert, his tongue was discreet, and, even when borne on the highest tide of popularity, he lost none of his modesty and good humour. He still continued to dwell at The Derby Winner, where his influence was salutary, for the customers there drank less and swore less when he was known to be present. Certainly, such reformation did not please Mr Mosk over-much, and he frequently grumbled that it was hard a man should have his trade spoilt by a psalm-singing missionary, but a wholesome fear of Cargrim's threat to inform Sir Harry checked him from asking Baltic to leave. Moreover, the man was greatly liked by Mrs Mosk on account of his religious spirit, and approved of by Bell from the order he kept in the hotel. Therefore Mosk, being in the minority, could only stand on one side and grumble, which he did with true English zeal.

It was while Baltic was thus exciting Beorminster that Sir Harry Brace came back. Gabriel, in pursuance of his father's wish, had gone over to Nauheim after a short interview with Bell, in which he had told her of his father's opposition to the match. Bell was cast down, but did not despair, as she thought that the bishop might soften towards Gabriel during his absence; so she sent him abroad with a promise that she would remain true to him until he returned. When the curate joined Mrs Pendle and Lucy, Sir Harry, with much regret, had to relinquish his pre-nuptial honeymoon, and returned to Beorminster in the lowest of spirits. The bishop did not tell him about Gabriel's infatuation for Bell, nor did he explain that George had engaged himself secretly to Mab Arden, so Harry was quite in the dark as regards the domestic dissensions, and, ascribing the bishop's gloom to the absence of his family, visited him frequently in order to cheer him up. But the dark hour was on Bishop Pendle, and notwithstanding the harping of this David, the evil spirit would not depart.

'What is the matter with the bishop?' asked

Harry one evening of Cargrim. 'He is as glum as an owl.'

'I do not know what ails him,' replied the chaplain, who, for reasons of his own, was resolved to hold his tongue, 'unless it is that he has been working too hard of late.'

'It isn't that, Cargrim; all the years I have known him he has never been so down-in-the-mouth before. I fancy he has something on his mind.'

'If you think so, Sir Harry, why not ask him?'

Brace shook his head. 'That would never do!' he answered. 'The bishop doesn't like to be asked questions. I wish I could see him livelier; is there nothing you can suggest to cheer him up?'

'Baltic might deliver another lecture on the South Seas!' said Cargrim, blandly. 'His lordship was pleased with the last one.'

'Baltic!' repeated Sir Harry, giving a meditative twist to his black moustache, 'that missionary fellow. I was going to ask you something about him!'

Cargrim looked surprised and slightly nervous. 'Beyond that he is a missionary, and is down here for his health's sake, I know nothing about him,' he said hastily.

'You introduced him to the bishop, didn't you?'

‘Yes. He brought a letter of introduction to me from the Vicar of St Ann’s in Kensington, but his biography was not given me.’

‘He’s been in the South Seas, hasn’t he?’

‘I believe that his labours lay amongst the natives of the islands!’

‘Well, I know him!’ said Brace, with a nod.

‘You know him!’ repeated the chaplain, anxiously.

‘Yes. Met him five years ago in Samoa; he was more of a beach-comber than a missionary in those days. Ben Baltic he calls himself, doesn’t he? I thought so! It’s the same man.’

‘He is a very worthy person, Sir Harry!’

‘So you say. I suppose people improve when they get older, but he wasn’t a saint when I knew him. He racketed about a good deal. Humph! perhaps he repented when I saved his life.’

‘Did you save his life?’

‘Well, yes. Baltic was raising Cain in some drunken row along with a set of Kanakas, and one of ’em got him under to slip a knife into him. I caught the scoundrel a clip on the jaw and sent him flying. There wasn’t much fight in old Ben when I straightened him out after that. So he’s turned devil-dodger. I must have a look at him in his new capacity.’

‘Whatever he has been,’ said Cargrim, who

appeared uneasy during the recital of this little story, 'I am sure that he has repented of his past errors and is now quite sincere in his religious convictions.'

'I'll judge of that for myself, if you don't mind,' drawled the baronet, with a twinkle in his dark eyes, and nodding to Cargrim, he strolled off, leaving that gentleman very uncomfortable. Sir Harry saw that he was so, and wondered why any story affecting Baltic should render the chaplain uneasy. He received an explanation some days later from the missionary himself.

Brace possessed a handsome family seat, embosomed in a leafy park, some five miles from the city. At present it was undergoing alterations and repairs, so that it might be a more perfect residence when the future Lady Brace crossed its threshold as a bride. Consequently the greater part of the house was in confusion, and given over to painters, plasterers, and such-like upsetting people. Harry, however, had decided to live in his own particular rooms, so that he might see that everything was carried out in accordance with Lucy's wish, and the wing he inhabited was in fairly good order. Still, Sir Harry being a bachelor, and extremely untidy, his den, as he called it, was in a state of pleasing muddle, which oftentimes drew forth rebukes from

Lucy. She was resolved to train her Harry into better ways when she had the wifely right to correct him, but, as she frequently remarked, it would be the thirteenth labour of Hercules to cleanse this modern Augean stable.

Harry himself, with male obstinacy, always asserted that the room was tidy enough, and that he hated to live in a prim apartment. He said that he could lay his hand on anything he wanted, and that the seeming confusion was perfect order to him. Lucy gave up arguing on these grounds, but privately determined that when the honeymoon was over she would have a grand 'clarin up' time like Dinah in *Uncle Tom's Cabin*. In the meanwhile, Harry continued to dwell amongst his confused household gods, like Marius amid the ruins of Carthage.

And after all, the 'den,' if untidy, was a very pleasant apartment, decorated extensively with evidences of Harry's athletic tastes. There were boxing-gloves, fencing-foils, dumb-bells, and other aids to muscular exertion; silver cups won at college sports were ranged on the mantelpiece; on one wall hung a selection of savage weapons which Harry had brought from Africa and the South Seas; on the other, a hunting trophy of whip, spurs, cap and fox's brush was arranged; and pictures of celebrated horses and famous jockeys were placed here, there and everywhere. The writing-table, pushed up close to the window, was littered with papers, and letters and plans, and before this Harry was seated one morning writing a letter to Lucy, when the servant informed him that Mr Baltic was waiting without. Harry gave orders for his instant admittance, as he was curious to see again the sinner turned saint, and anxious to learn what tide from the far South Seas had stranded him in respectable, unromantic Beorminster.

When the visitor entered with his burly figure and bright, observant eyes, Harry gave him a friendly nod, but knowing more about Baltic than the rest of Beorminster, did not offer him his hand. From his height of six feet, he looked down on the thick-set little missionary, and telling him to be seated, made him welcome in a sufficiently genial fashion, nevertheless with a certain reserve. He was not quite certain if Baltic's conversion was genuine, and if he found proof of hypocrisy, was prepared to fall foul of him forthwith. Sir Harry was not particularly religious, but he was honest, and hated cant with all his soul.

'Well, Ben!' said he, looking sharply at his visitor's solemn red face, 'who would have thought of seeing you in these latitudes?'

'We never know what is before us, sir,'

replied Baltic, in his deep, rough voice. 'It was no more in my mind that I should meet you under your own fig-tree than it was that I should receive a call through you!'

'Receive a call, man! What do you mean?' asked Harry, negligently. 'By the way, will you have a cigar?'

'No thank you, sir. I don't smoke now.'

'A whisky and soda, then?'

'I have given up strong waters, sir.'

'Here is repentance indeed!' observed the baronet, with some sarcasm. 'You have changed since the Samoan days, Baltic!'

'Thanks be to Christ, sir, I have,' said the man, reverently, 'and my call was through you, sir. When you saved my life I resolved to lead a new one, and I sought out Mr Eva, the missionary, who gave me hope of being a better man. I listened to his preaching, Sir Harry, I read the Gospels, I wrestled with my sinful self, and after a long fight I was made strong. My doubts were set at rest, my sins were washed in the Blood of the Lamb, and since He took me into His holy keeping, I have striven to be worthy of His great love.'

Baltic spoke so simply, and with such nobility, that Brace could not but believe that he was in earnest. There was no spurious affectation, no cant about the man; his words were grave, his manner was earnest, and his speech came from the fulness of his heart. If there had been a false note, a false look, Harry would have detected both, and great would have been his disgust and wrath. But the dignity of the speech, the simplicity of the description, impressed him with a belief that Baltic was speaking truly. The man was a rough sailor, and therefore not cunning enough to feign an emotion he did not feel, so, almost against his will, Brace was obliged to believe that he saw before him a Saul converted into a Paul. The change of Pagan Ben into Christian Baltic was little else than miraculous.

'And are you now a missionary?' said Brace, after a reflective pause.

'No, Sir Harry,' answered the man, calmly, and with dignity, 'I am a private inquiry agent!'

26

The Amazement of Sir Harry Brace

'A private inquiry agent!' Sir Harry jumped up from his chair with an angry look, and a sharp ejaculation, neither of which disturbed his visitor. With his red bandanna handkerchief spread on his knees, and his straw hat resting on the handkerchief, Baltic looked at his flushed host calmly and solemnly without moving a muscle, or even winking an eye. Brace did not know whether to treat the ex-sailor as a madman or as an impudent impostor. The situation was almost embarrassing.

'What do you mean, sir,' he asked angrily, 'by coming to me with a cock-and-bull story about your conversion, and then telling me that you are a private inquiry agent, which is little less than a spy?'

'Is it impossible for such a one to be a Christian, Sir Harry?'

'I should think so. One who earns his living by sneaking can scarcely act up to the ethics of the Gospels.'

'I don't earn my living by sneaking,' replied

Baltic, coolly. 'If I did, I shouldn't explain my business to you as I have done — as I am doing. My work is honourable enough, sir, for I am ranged against evil-doers, and it is my duty to bring their works to naught. There is no need for me to defend my profession to anyone but you, Sir Harry, as no one but yourself, and perhaps two other people, know what I really am.'

'They shall know it,' spoke Sir Harry, hastily. 'All Beorminster shall know of it. We don't care for wolves in sheep's clothing here.'

'Better be sure that I am a wolf before you talk rashly,' said Baltic, in no wise disturbed. 'I came here to speak to you openly, because you saved my life, and that debt I wish to square. And let me tell you, sir, that it isn't Christianity, or even justice, to hear one side of the question and not the other.'

Harry looked puzzled. 'You are an enigma to me, Baltic.'

'I am here to explain myself, sir. As your hand dashed aside the knife of that Kanaka you have a claim on my confidence. You'll be a sad man and a glad man when you hear my story, sir.'

Harry resumed his seat, shrugged his shoulders, and took a leisurely look at his self-possessed visitor. 'Sad and glad are contradictory terms, my friend,' said he, carelessly. 'I would rather you explained riddles than propounded them.'

'Sir Harry! Sir Harry! it is the riddle of man's life upon this earth that I am trying to explain.'

'You have set yourself a hard task, Baltic, for so far as I can see, there is no reading of that riddle.'

'Save by the light of the Gospel, sir, which makes all things plain.'

'Baltic,' said Brace, bluntly, 'there is that about you which would make me sorry to find you a Pharisee or a hypocrite. Therefore, if you please, we will stop religion and allegory, and come to plain matter-of-fact. When I knew you in Samoa, you were a sailor without a ship.'

'Add a castaway and a child of the devil, sir, and you will describe me as I was then,' burst out Baltic, in his deep voice. 'Hear me, Sir Harry, and gauge me as I should be gauged. I was, as you know, a drunken, godless, swearing dog, in the grip of Satan as fuel for hell; but when you saved my worthless life I saw that it behoved me, as it does all men, to repent. I sought out a missionary, who heard my story and set my feet in the right path. I listened to his preaching, I read the Good Book, and so learned how I could be saved. The missionary made me his fellow-labourer in the islands, and I strove to bring the poor heathen to the foot of the cross. For three years I laboured there, until it was borne in upon me that I was called upon by the Spirit to labour in the greater vineyard of London. Therefore, I came to England and looked round to see what task was fittest for my hand. On every side I saw evil prosper. The wicked, as I noted, flourished like a green bay tree; so, to bring them to repentance and punishment, I became a private inquiry agent.'

'Humph! that is a novel kind of missionary enterprise, Baltic.'

'It is a righteous one, Sir Harry. I search out iniquities; I snare the wicked man in his own nets; I make void the devices of his evil heart. If I cannot prevent crimes, I can at least punish them by bringing their doers within the grip of the law. Then when punished by man, they repent and turn to God, and thereby are saved through their own lusts.'

'Not in many cases, I am afraid. So you regard yourself as a kind of scourge for the wicked?'

'Yes! When I state that I am a missionary, I regard myself as one who works in a new way.'

'A kind of *fin-de-siècle* apostle, in fact,' said Brace, dryly. 'But isn't the term 'missionary' rather a misnomer?'

'No!' replied Baltic, earnestly. 'I do my work in a different way, that is all. I baffle the wicked, and by showing them the futility of sin, induce them to lead a new life. I make them fall, only to aid them to rise; for when all is lost, their hearts soften.'

'You give them a kind of Hobson's choice, I see,' commented Sir Harry, who was puzzled by the man's conception of his work, but saw that he spoke in all seriousness. 'Well, Baltic, it is a queer way of calling sinners to repentance, and I can't understand it myself.'

'My method of conversion is certainly open to misconstruction, sir. That is why I term myself rather a missionary than a private inquiry agent.'

'I see; you don't wish to scare your promising flock of criminals. Does anyone here know that you are a private inquiry agent?'

'Mr Cargrim does,' said the ex-sailor, calmly, 'and one other.'

Harry leaned forward with an incredulous look. 'Cargrim knows,' he said in utter amazement. 'I should think he would be the last man to approve of your ideas, with his narrow views and clerical red-tapism.'

'Perhaps, so, sir; but in this case my views

happen to fall in with his own. I came to see you, Sir Harry, in order to ease my mind on that point.'

'In order to ease your mind!' repeated Brace, with a keen look. 'Go on.'

'Sir Harry, I speak to you in confidence about Mr Cargrim. I do not like that man, sir.'

'You belong to the majority, then, Baltic. Few people like Cargrim, or trust him. But what is he to you?'

'My employer. Yes, sir, you may well look astonished. Mr Cargrim asked me down to Beorminster for a certain purpose.'

'Connected with his self-aggrandisement, no doubt.'

'That I cannot tell you, Sir Harry, as Mr Cargrim has not told me his motive for engaging me in my business capacity. All I know is that he wishes me to discover who killed a man called Jentham.'

'The deuce!' Harry jumped up with an excited look. 'Why is he taking the trouble to do that?'

'I can't say, sir, unless it is that he dislikes Bishop Pendle!'

'Dislikes Bishop Pendle, man! And what has all this to do with the murder of Jentham?'

'Sir,' said Baltic, with a cautious glance around, and sinking his voice to a whisper,

'Mr Cargrim suspects Dr Pendle of the crime.'

'What!!!' Sir Harry turned the colour of chalk, and sprang back until he almost touched the wall. 'You hound!' said he, speaking with unnatural calmness, 'do you dare to sit there and tell me that you have come here to watch the bishop?'

'Yes, Sir Harry,' was Baltic's stolid rejoinder, 'and calling me names won't do away with the fact.'

'Does Cargrim believe that the bishop killed this man?'

'Yes, sir, he does, and wishes me to bring the crime home to him.'

'Curse you!' roared Harry, striding across the room, and towering over the unmoved Baltic, 'I'll wring your neck, sir, if you dare to hint at such a thing.'

'I am merely stating facts, Sir Harry — facts,' he added pointedly, 'which I wish you to know.'

'For what purpose?'

'That you may assist me.'

'To hunt down the bishop, I suppose,' said Sir Harry, quivering with rage.

'No, sir, to save the bishop from Mr Cargrim.'

'Then you do not believe that the bishop is guilty.'

'Sir,' said Baltic, with dignity, 'in London

and in Beorminster I have collected certain evidence which, on the face of it, incriminates the bishop. But since knowing Dr Pendle I have been observant of his looks and demeanour, and — after much thought — I have come to the conclusion that he is innocent of this crime which Mr Cargrim lays to his charge. It is because of this belief that I tell you my mind and seek your assistance. We must work together, sir, and discover the real criminal so as to baffle Mr Cargrim.'

'Cargrim, Cargrim,' repeated Brace, angrily, 'he is a bad lot.'

'That is what I say, Sir Harry. He is one who spreads a snare, and I wish him to be taken in it himself.'

'Yet Cargrim is your employer, and pays you,' sneered Sir Harry.

'You are wrong,' replied Baltic, quietly. 'I do not take payment for my work.'

'How do you live then? You were not independent when I knew you.'

'That is true, Sir Harry, but when I arrived in England I found that my father was dead, and had left me sufficient to live upon. Therefore I take no fee for my work, but labour to punish the wicked, for religion's sake.'

Brace muttered something about the heat, and wiped his forehead as he resumed his seat. The peculiar views held by Baltic perplexed him greatly, and he could not reconcile the man's desire to capture criminals with his belief in a religion, the keynote of which is, 'God is love.' Evidently Baltic wished to convert sinners by playing on their fears rather than by appealing to their religious feelings, although it was certainly true that those rascals with whom he had to deal probably had no elements of belief whatsoever in their seared minds.

But be this as it may, Baltic's mission was both novel and strange, and might in some degree prove successful from its very originality. Torquemada burned bodies to save souls, but this man exposed vices, so that those who committed them, being banned by the law, and made outcasts from civilisation, should find no friend but the Deity. Harry was not clever enough to understand the ethics of this conception, therefore he abandoned any attempt to do so, and treating Baltic purely as an ordinary detective, addressed himself to the task of arriving at the evidence which was said to inculpate Dr Pendle in the murder of Jentham. The ex-sailor accepted the common ground of argument, and in his turn abandoned theology for the business of everyday life. Common sense was needed to expose and abase and overturn those criminals whose talents enabled them to conceal their wickedness; proselytism could follow in due course. There was the germ of a new sect in Baltic's conception of Christianity as a terrorising religion.

'Let me hear your evidence against the bishop,' said Sir Harry, calm and business-like.

Baltic complied with this request and gave the outlines of the case in barren detail. 'Sir,' said he, gravely, 'some weeks ago, while there was a reception at the palace, this man Jentham called to see the bishop and evidently attempted to blackmail him on account of some secret. Afterwards Jentham, not being able to pay for his board and lodging at The Derby Winner, promised Mosk, the landlord, that he would discharge his bill shortly, as he expected the next week to receive much money. From whom he did not say, but while drunk he boasted that Southberry Heath was Tom Tiddler's ground, on which he could pick up gold and silver. In the meantime, Bishop Pendle went up to London and drew out of the Ophir Bank a sum of two hundred pounds, in twenty ten-pound notes. With this money he returned to Beorminster and kept an appointment, on the common, with Jentham, when returning on Sunday night from Southberry. Whether he paid him the blackmail I cannot say; whether he killed the man no one can declare honestly; but it is undoubtedly true that, the next morning, Jentham, whom the bishop regarded as his enemy, was found dead. These, sir, are the bare facts of the case, and, as you can see, they certainly appear to inculpate Dr Pendle in the crime.'

This calm and pitiless statement chilled Sir Harry's blood. Although he could not bring himself to believe that the bishop was guilty, yet he saw plainly enough that the evidence tended, almost beyond all doubt, to incriminate the prelate. Yet there might be flaws even in so complete an indictment, and Harry, seeking for them, began eagerly to question Baltic.

'Who told you all this?' he demanded with some apprehension.

'Mr Cargrim told me some parts, and I found out others for myself, sir.'

'Does Cargrim know the nature of Dr Pendle's secret?'

'Not that I know of, Sir Harry.'

'Is he certain that there is one?'

'Quite certain,' replied Baltic, emphatically; 'if only on account of Jentham's boast about being able to get money, and the fact that Bishop Pendle went up to London to procure the blackmail.'

'How does he know — how does anyone know that the bishop did so?'

'Because a butt was torn out of Dr Pendle's London cheque-book,' said Baltic, 'and I made inquiries at the Ophir Bank, which resulted in my discovery that a cheque for two hundred had been drawn on the day the bishop was in town.'

'Come now, Baltic, it is not likely that any bank would give you that information without a warrant; but I don't suppose you dared to procure one against his lordship.'

'Sir,' said Baltic, rolling up his red handkerchief, 'I had not sufficient evidence to procure a warrant, also I am not in the service of the Government, nevertheless, I have my own ways of procuring information, which I decline to explain. These served me so well in this instance that I know Bishop Pendle drew a cheque for two hundred pounds, and moreover, I have the numbers of the notes. If the money was paid to Jentham, and afterwards was taken from his dead body by the assassin, I hope to trace these notes; in which case I may capture the murderer.'

'In your character of a private inquiry agent?'

'No, Sir Harry, I cannot take that much upon myself. I mentioned that one other person knew of my profession; that person is Inspector Tinkler.'

'Man!' cried Brace, with a start, 'you have not dared to accuse the bishop to Tinkler!'

'Oh, no, sir!' rejoined the ex-sailor,

composedly. 'All I have done is to tell Tinkler that I wish to hunt down the murderer of Jentham, and to induce him to obtain for me a warrant of arrest against Mother Jael.'

'Mother Jael, the gipsy hag! You don't suspect her, surely!'

'Not of the murder; but I suspect her of knowing the truth. Tinkler got me a warrant on the ground of her being concerned in the crime — say, as an accessory after the fact. To-morrow, Sir Harry, I ride over to the gipsy camp, and then with this warrant I intend to frighten Mother Jael into confessing what she knows.'

Harry smiled grimly. 'If you get the truth out of her you will be a clever man, Baltic. Does the bishop know that you suspect him?'

'I don't suspect him, sir,' replied Baltic, rising, 'and the bishop knows nothing, as he believes that I am a missionary.'

'Well, you are, in your own peculiar way.'

'Thank you, Sir Harry. Only you and Mr Cargrim and Mr Tinkler are aware of the truth, and I tell you all this, sir, as I neither approve of, nor believe in, Mr Cargrim. I am certain that Dr Pendle is innocent; Mr Cargrim is equally certain that he is guilty; so I am working to prove the truth, and that,' concluded the solemn Baltic, 'will not be what Mr Cargrim desires.'

'Good God! the man must hate the bishop.'

'Bating your taking the name of God in vain, sir, I believe he does.'

'Well, Baltic, I am greatly obliged to you for your confidence, and feel thankful that you are on our side. You can command my services in any way you like, but keep me posted up in all you do.'

'Sir!' said Baltic, gravely, shaking hands with his host, 'you can look upon me as your friend and well-wisher.'

27

What Mother Jael Knew

Now, when Baltic and his grizzled head had vanished, Sir Harry must needs betake himself to Dr Graham for the easing of his mind. The doctor had known the young man since he was a little lad, and on more than one occasion had given him that practical kind of advice which results from experience; therefore, when Harry was perplexed over matters too deep for him — as he was now — he invariably sought counsel of his old friend. In the present instance — for his own sake, for the sake of Lucy and Lucy's father — he told Graham the whole story of Bishop Pendle's presumed guilt; of Baltic's mission to disprove it; and of Cargrim's underhanded doings. Graham listened to the details in silence, and contented himself with a grim smile or two when Cargrim's treachery was touched upon. When in possession of the facts, he commented firstly on the behaviour of the chaplain.

'I always thought that the fellow was a cur!' said he, contemptuously, 'and now I am certain of it.'

'Curs bite, sir,' said Brace, sententiously, 'and we must muzzle this one else there will be the devil to pay.'

'No doubt, when Cargrim receives his wages. Well, lad, and what do you propose doing?'

'I came to ask your advice, doctor!'

'Here it is, then. Hold your tongue and do nothing.'

'What! and leave that hound to plot against the bishop?'

'A cleverer head than yours is counter-plotting him, Brace,' warned the doctor. 'While Cargrim, having faith in Baltic, leaves the matter of the murder in his hands, there can be no open scandal.'

Harry stared, and moodily tugged at his moustache. 'I never thought to hear you hint that the bishop was guilty,' he grumbled.

'And I,' retorted Graham, 'never thought to hear a man of your sense make so silly a speech. The bishop is innocent; I'll stake my life on that. Nevertheless, he has a secret, and if there is a scandal about this murder, the secret — whatever it is — may become public property.'

'Humph! that is to be avoided certainly. But the secret can be nothing harmful.'

'If it were not,' replied Graham, drily, 'Pendle would not take such pains to conceal it. People don't pay two hundred pounds for nothing harmful, my lad.'

'Do you believe that the money was paid?'

'Yes, on Southberry Heath, shortly before the murder. And what is more,' added Graham, warmly, 'I believe that the assassin knew that Jentham had received the money, and shot him to obtain it.'

'If that is so,' argued Harry, 'the assassin would no doubt wish to take the benefit of his crime and use the money. If he did, the numbers of the notes being known, they would be traced, whereas — '

'Whereas Baltic, who got the numbers from the bank, has not yet had time to trace them. Wait, Brace, wait! Time, in this matter, may work wonders.'

'But, doctor, do you trust Baltic?'

'Yes, my friend, I always trust fanatics in their own particular line of monomania. Besides, for all his religious craze, Baltic appears to be a shrewd man; also he is a silent one, so if anyone can carry the matter through judiciously, he is the person.'

'What about Cargrim?'

'Leave him alone, lad; with sufficient rope he'll surely hang himself.'

'Shouldn't the bishop be warned, doctor?'

'I think not. If we watch Cargrim and trust Baltic we shall be able to protect Pendle from the consequences of his folly.'

'Folly! What folly?'

'The folly of having a secret. Only women should have secrets, for they alone know how to keep them.'

'Everyone is of the opposite opinion,' said Brace, with a grin.

'And, as usual, everyone is wrong,' retorted Graham. 'Do you think I have been a doctor all these years and don't know the sex? — that is, so far as a man may know them. You take my word for it, Brace, that a woman knows how to hold her tongue. It is a popular fallacy to suppose that she doesn't. You try and get a secret out of a woman which she thinks is worth keeping, and see how you'll fare. She will laugh, and talk and lie, and tell you everything — except what you want to know. What strength is to a man, cunning is to a woman. They are the potters, we are the clay, and — and — and my discourse is as discursive as that of Praed's vicar,' finished the doctor, with a dry chuckle.

'It has led us a long way from the main point,' agreed Harry, 'and that is — what is Dr Pendle's secret?'

Graham shook his head and shrugged his shoulders. 'You ask more than I can tell you,' he said sadly. 'Whatever it is, Pendle intends to keep it to himself. All we can do is to trust Baltic.'

'Well, doctor,' said Harry, taking a reluctant leave, for he wished to thresh out the matter into absolute chaff, 'you know best, so I shall follow your advice.'

'I am glad of that,' was Graham's reply. 'My time is too valuable to be wasted.'

While this conversation was taking place, Baltic was walking briskly across the brown heath, in the full blaze of the noonday. A merciless sun flamed like a furnace in the cloudless sky; and over the vast expanse of dry burnt herbage lay a veil of misty, tremulous heat. Every pool of water flashed like a mirror in the sun-rays; the drone of myriad insects rose from the ground; the lark's clear music rained down from the sky; and the ex-sailor, trudging along the white and dusty highway, almost persuaded himself that he was back in some tropical land, less gorgeous, but quite as sultry, as the one he had left. The day was fitter for mid-June rather than late September.

Baltic made so much concession to the unusual weather as to drape his red handkerchief over his head and place his Panama hat on top of it; but he still wore the thick pilot suit, buttoned up tightly, and stepped out smartly, as though he were a salamander impervious to heat. With his long arms swinging by his side, his steady, grey eyes observant of all around him, he rolled on, in true nautical style, towards the gipsy camp. This was not hard to discover, for it lay only a mile or so from Southberry Junction, some little distance off the main road. The missionary saw a huddle of caravans, a few straying horses, a cluster of tawny, half-clad children rioting in the sunshine; and knowing that this was his port of call, he stepped off the road on to the grass, and made directly for the encampment. He had a warrant for Mother Jael's arrest in his pocket, but save himself there was no one to execute it, and it might be difficult to take the old woman in charge when she was — so to speak — safe in the heart of her kingdom. However, Baltic regarded the warrant only as a means to an end, and did not intend to use it, other than as a bogey to terrify Mother Jael into confession. He trusted more to his religiosity and persuasive capabilities than to the power of the law. Nevertheless, being practical as well as sentimental, he was glad to have the warrant in case of need; for it was possible that a heathenish witch like Mother Jael might fear man more than God. Finally, Baltic had some experience of casting religious pearls before pagan swine, and therefore was discreet in his use of spiritual remedies.

Dogs barked and children screeched when Baltic stepped into the circle formed by caravans and tents; and several swart, sinewy, gipsy men darted threatening glances at him as an intrusive stranger. There burned a fire near one of the caravans, over which was slung a kettle, swinging from a tripod of iron, and this was filled with some savoury stew, which sent forth appetising odours. A dark, handsome girl, with golden earrings, and a yellow handkerchief twisted picturesquely round her black hair, was the cook, and she turned to face Baltic with a scowl when he inquired for Mother Jael. Evidently the Gentiles were no favourites in the camp of these outcasts, for the men lounging about murmured, the women tittered and sneered, and the very children spat out evil words in the Romany language. But Baltic, used to black skins and black looks, was not daunted by this inhospitable reception, and in grave tones repeated his inquiry for the sibyl.

'Who are you, *juggel-mush*[1]?' asked a sinister-looking Hercules.

'I am one who wishes to see Mother Jael,' replied Baltic, in his deep voice.

'*Arromali*[2]!' sneered the Cleopatra-like

---

[1] *Juggel-mush*: a dog-man

[2] *Arromali*: truly

cook. 'She has more to do than to see every cheating, choring Gentile.'

'Give me money, my royal master,' croaked a frightful cripple. 'My own little purse is empty.'

'Oh, what a handsome Gorgio!' whined a hag, interspersing her speech with curses. '(May evil befall him!) Good luck for gold, dearie. (I spit on your corpse, Gentile!) Charity! Charity!'

A girl seated on the steps of a caravan cracked her fingers, and spitting three times for the evil eye, burst into a song: —

'With my kissings and caressings
I can gain gold from the Gentiles;
But to evil change my blessings.'

All this clatter and clamour of harsh voices, mouthing the wild gipsies' jargon, had no effect on Baltic. Seeing that he could gain nothing from the mocking crowd, he pushed back one or two, who seemed disposed to be affectionate with a view to robbing his pockets, and shouted loudly, 'Mother Jael! Mother Jael!' till the place rang with his roaring.

Before the gipsies could recover from their astonishment at this sudden change of front, a dishevelled grey head was poked out from one of the black tents, and a thin high voice piped, 'Dearie! lovey! Mother Jael be here!'

'I thought I would bring you out of your burrow,' said Baltic, grimly, as he strode towards her; 'in with you again, old Witch of Endor, and let me follow.'

'*Hindity-mush*[1]!' growled one or two, but the appearance of Mother Jael, and a few words from her, sent the whole gang back to their idling and working; while Baltic, quite undisturbed, dropped on all fours and crawled into the black tent, at the tail of the hag. She croaked out a welcome to her visitor, and squatting on a tumbled mattress, leered at him like a foul old toad. Baltic sat down near the opening of the tent, so as to get as much fresh air as possible, and also to watch Mother Jael's face by the glimmer of light which crept in. Spreading his handsome handkerchief on his knee, according to custom, and placing his hat thereon, he looked straightly at the old hag, and spoke slowly.

'Do you know why I am here, old woman?' he demanded.

'Yes, dearie, yes! Ain't it yer forting as y' wan's tole? Oh, my pretty one, you asks ole mother for a fair future! I knows! I knows!'

'You know wrong then!' retorted Baltic, coolly. 'I am one who has no dealings with

[1] *Hindity-mush*: a dirty creature

witches and familiar spirits. I ask you to tell me, not my fortune — which lies in the hand of the Almighty — but the name of the man who murdered the creature Jentham.'

Mother Jael made an odd whistling sound, and her cunning old face became as expressionless as a mask. In a second, save for her wicked black eyes, which smouldered like two sparks of fire under her drooping lids, she became a picture of stupidity and senility. 'Bless 'ee, my pretty master, I knows nought; all I knows I told the Gentiles yonder,' and the hag pointed a crooked finger in the direction of Beorminster.

'Mother of the witches, you lie!' cried Baltic, in very good Romany.

The eyes of Mother Jael blazed up like torches at the sound of the familiar tongue, and she eyed the weather-beaten face of Baltic with an amazement too genuine to be feigned. '*Duvel!*' said she, in a high key of astonishment, 'who is this Gorgio who patters with the gab of a gentle Romany?'

'I am a brother of the tribe, my sister.'

'No gipsy, though,' said the hag, in the black language. 'You have not the glossy eye of the true Roman.'

'No Roman am I, my sister, save by adoption. As a lad I left the Gentiles' roof for the merry tent of Egypt, and for many years I called Lovels and Stanleys my blood-brothers.'

'Then why come you with a double face, little child?' croaked the beldam, who knew that Baltic was speaking the truth from his knowledge of the gipsy tongue. 'As a Gentile I would speak no word, but my brother you are, and as my brother you shall know.'

'Know who killed Jentham!' said Baltic, hastily.

'Of a truth, brother. But call him not Jentham, for he was of Pharaoh's blood.'

'A gipsy, mother, or only a Romany rye?'

'Of the old blood, of the true blood, of our religion verily, my brother. One of the Lovels he was, who left our merry life to eat with Gorgios and fiddle gold out of their pockets.'

'He called himself Amaru then, did he not?' said Baltic, who had heard this much from Cargrim, to whom it had filtered from Miss Whichello through Tinkler.

'It is so, brother. Amaru he called himself, and Jentham and Creagth, and a dozen other names when cheating and choring the Gentiles. But a Bosvile he was born, and a Bosvile he died.'

'That is just it!' said Baltic, in English, for he grew weary of using the gipsy language, in which, from disuse, he was no great proficient. 'How did he die?'

'He was shot, lovey,' replied Mother Jael, relapsing also into the vulgar tongue; 'shot, dearie, on this blessed common.'

'Who shot him?'

'Job! my noble rye, I can't say. Jentham, he come 'ere to patter the calo jib and drink with us. He said as he had to see some Gentile on that night! La! la! la!' she piped thinly, 'an evil night for him!'

'On Sunday night — the night he was killed?'

'Yes, pretty one. The Gorgio was to give him money for somethin' he knowed.'

'Who was the Gorgio?'

'I don' know, lovey! I don' know!'

'What was the secret, then?' asked Baltic, casting round for information.

'Bless 'ee, my tiny! Jentham nivir tole me. An' I was curis to know, my dove, so when he walks away half-seas over I goes too. I follows, lovey, I follow, but I nivir did cotch him up, fur rain and storm comed mos' dreful.'

'Did you not see him on that night, then?'

'Sight of my eyes, I sawr 'im dead. I 'eard a shot, and I run, and run, dearie, fur I know'd as 'e 'ad no pistol; but I los' m'way, my royal rye, and it was ony when th' storm rolled off as I foun' 'im. He was lyin' in a ditch. Such was his grave,' continued Mother Jael, speaking in her own tongue, 'water and grass and storm-clouds above, brother. I was afraid to touch him, afraid to wait, as these Gentiles might think I had slain the man. I got back into the road, I did, and there I picked up this, which I brought to the camp with me. But I never showed it to the police, brother, for I feared the Gentile jails.'

This proved to be a neat little silver-mounted pistol which Mother Jael fished out from the interior of the mattress. Baltic balanced it in his hand, and believing, as was surely natural, that Jentham had been killed with this weapon, he examined it carefully.

'G. P.,' said he, reading the initials graven on the silver shield of the butt.

'Ah!' chuckled Mother Jael, hugging herself. 'George Pendle that is, lovey. But which of 'em, my tender dove — the father or the son?'

'Humph!' remarked Baltic, meditatively, 'they are both called George.'

'But they ain't both called murderer, my brother. George Pendle shot that Bosvile sure enough, an' ef y'arsk me, dearie, it was the son — the captain — the sodger. Ah, that it was!'

28

The Return of Gabriel

'My dear Daisy, I am sorry you are going away, as it has been a great pleasure for me to have you in my house. I hope you will visit me again next year, and then you may be more fortunate.'

Mrs Pansey made this amiable little speech — which nevertheless, like a scorpion, had a sting in its tail — to Miss Norsham on the platform of the Beorminster railway station. After a stay of two months, the town mouse was departing as she had come — a single young woman; and Mrs Pansey's last word was meant to remind her of failure. Daisy was quick enough to guess this, but, displeased at the taunt, chose to understand it in another and more gracious sense, so as to disconcert her spiteful friend.

'Fortunate! Oh, dear Mrs Pansey, I have been very fortunate this time. Really, you have been most kind; you have given me everything I wanted.'

'Excepting a husband, my dear,' rejoined the archdeacon's widow, determined that there should be no misunderstanding this time.

'Ah! it was out of your power to give me a husband,' murmured Daisy, wincing.

'Quite true, my dear; just as it was out of your power to gain one for yourself. Still, I am sorry that Dr Alder did not propose.'

'Indeed!' Daisy tossed her head. 'I should certainly have refused him had he done so. A woman may not marry her grandfather.'

'A woman may not, but a woman would, rather than remain single,' snapped Mrs Pansey, with considerable spite.

Miss Norsham carefully inserted a corner of a foolish little handkerchief into one eye. 'Oh, dear, I do call it nasty of you to speak to me so,' said she, tearfully. 'You needn't think, like all men do, that every woman wants to be married. I'm sure I don't.'

The old lady smiled grimly at this appalling lie, but thinking that she had been a little hard on her departing guest, hastened to apologise. 'I'm sure you don't, dear, and very sensible it is of you to say so. Judging from my own experience with the archdeacon, I should certainly advise no one to marry.'

'You are wise after the event,' muttered Daisy, with some anger, 'but here is my train, Mrs Pansey, thank you!' and she slipped into a first-class carriage, looking decidedly cross and very defiant. To fail in husband-hunting was bad enough, but to be taunted with the failure was unbearable. Daisy no longer wondered that Mrs Pansey was hated in Beorminster; her own feelings at the moment urged her to thrust the good lady under the wheels of the engine.

'Well, dear, I'll say good-bye,' said Mrs Pansey, screwing her grim face into an amiable smile. 'Be sure you give my love to your mother, dear,' and the two kissed with that show of affection to be seen existing between ladies who do not love one another over much.

'Horrid old cat!' said Daisy to herself, as she waved her handkerchief from the now moving train.

'Dear me! how I dislike that girl,' soliloquised Mrs Pansey, shaking her reticule at the departing Daisy. 'Well! well! no one can say that I have not done my duty by her,' and much pleased with herself, the good lady stalked majestically out of the station, on the lookout to seize upon and worry any of her friends who might be in the vicinity. For his sins Providence sent Gabriel into her clutches, and Mrs Pansey was transfixed with astonishment at the sight of him issuing from the station.

'Mr Pendle!' she said, placing herself

directly in his way, 'I thought you were at Nauheim. What is wrong? Is your mother ill? Is she coming back? Are you in trouble?'

Gabriel could not answer all, or even one of these questions on the instant, for the sudden appearance and speech of the Beorminster busybody had taken him by surprise. He looked haggard and white, and there were dark circles under his eyes, as though he suffered from want of sleep. Still, the journey from Nauheim might account for his weary looks, and would have done so to anyone less suspicious than Mrs Pansey; but that good lady scented a mystery, and wanted an explanation. This, Gabriel, with less than his usual courtesy, declined to furnish. However, to give her some food for her mind, he answered her questions categorically.

'I have just returned from Nauheim, Mrs Pansey,' he said hurriedly. 'There is nothing wrong, so far as I am aware. My mother is much better, and is benefiting greatly by the baths. She is coming back within the month, and I am not in trouble. Is there anything else you wish to know?'

'Yes, Mr Pendle, there is,' said Mrs Pansey, in no wise abashed. 'Why do you look so ill?'

'I am not ill, but I have had a long sea-passage, a weary railway journey, and I feel hot, and dirty, and worn out. Naturally, under the circumstances, I don't look the picture of health.'

'Humph! trips abroad don't do *you* much good.'

Gabriel bowed, and turned away to direct the porter to place his portmanteau in a fly. Offended by his silence, Mrs Pansey shook out her skirts and tossed her sable plumes. 'You have not brought back French politeness, young man,' said Mrs Pansey, acridly.

'I have been in Germany,' retorted Gabriel, as though that fact accounted for his lack of courtesy. 'Good-bye for the present, Mrs Pansey; I'll apologise for my shortcomings when I recover from my journey.'

'Oh, you will, will you?' growled the archdeacon's widow, as Gabriel lifted his hat and drove off; 'you'll do more than apologise, young man, you'll explain. Hoity-toity! here's brazen assurance,' and Mrs Pansey, with her Roman beak in the air, marched off, wondering in her own curious mind what could be the reason of Gabriel's sudden return.

Her curiosity would have been gratified had she been present in Dr Graham's consulting-room an hour later; for after Gabriel had bathed and brushed up at his lodgings, he paid an immediate visit to the little doctor. Graham happened to be at home, as he had not yet set out on his round of professional visits, and he was as much astonished as Mrs Pansey when the curate made his appearance. Also, like Mrs Pansey, he was struck by the young man's worn looks.

'What! Gabriel,' he cried, when the curate entered, 'this is an unexpected pleasure. You look ill, lad!'

'I am ill,' replied Gabriel, dropping into a chair with an air of fatigue. 'I feel very much worried, and I have come to ask for your advice.'

'Very pleased to give it to you, my boy, but why not consult the bishop?'

'My father is the last man in the world I would consult, doctor.'

'That is a strange speech, Gabriel,' said Graham, with a keen look.

'It is the prelude to a stranger story! I have come to confide in you because you have known me all my life, doctor, and because you are the most intimate friend my father has.'

'Have you been getting into trouble?'

'No. My story concerns my father more than it does me.'

'Concerns your father!' repeated the doctor, with a sudden recollection of the bishop's secret. 'Are you sure that I am the proper person to consult?'

'I am certain of it. I know — I know — well, what I do know is something I have not the courage to speak to my father about. For God's sake, doctor, let me tell you my suspicions and hear your advice.'

'Your suspicions!' said Graham, starting from his chair, with a chill in his blood. 'About — about — that — that murder?'

'God forbid, doctor. No! not about the murder, but about the man who was murdered.'

'Jentham?'

'Yes, about the man who called himself Jentham. Are you sure we are quite private here, doctor?'

Graham nodded, and walking to the door turned the key. Then he came back to his seat and fixed his eyes on the perturbed face of the young man. 'Does your father know that you are back?' he asked.

'No one knows that I am here save Mrs Pansey.'

'Then it won't be a secret long,' said Graham, drily; 'that old magpie is as good as the town crier. You left your mother well?'

'Quite well; and Lucy also. I made an excuse to come back.'

'Then your mother and sister do not know what you are about to tell me?'

Gabriel made a gesture of horror. 'God

forbid!' said he again, then clasped his hands over his white face and burst into half-hysterical speech. 'Oh, the horror of it, the horror of it!' he wailed. 'If what I know is true, then all our lives are ruined.'

'Is it so very terrible, my boy?'

'So terrible that I dare not question my father! I must tell you, for only you can advise and help us all. Doctor! doctor! the very thought drives me mad — indeed, I feel half mad already.'

'You are worn out, Gabriel. Wait one moment.'

The doctor saw that his visitor's nerves were overstrained, and that, unless the tension were relaxed, he would probably end in having a fit of hysteria. The poor young fellow, born of a weakly mother, was neurotic in the extreme, and had in him a feminine strain, which made him unequal to facing trouble or anxiety. Even as he sat there, shaking and white-faced, the nerve-storm came on, and racked and knotted and tortured every fibre of his being, until a burst of tears came to his relief, and almost in a swoon he lay back limply in his chair. Graham mixed him a strong dose of valerian, felt his pulse, and made him lie down on the sofa. Also, he darkened the room, and placed a wet handkerchief on the curate's forehead.

Gabriel closed his eyes, and lay on the couch as still as any corpse, while the doctor, who knew what he suffered, watched him with infinite pity.

'Poor lad!' he murmured, holding Gabriel's hand in his firm, warm clasp. 'Nature is indeed a harsh stepmother to you. With your nerves, the pin-prickles of life are so many dagger-thrusts. Do you feel better now?' he asked, as Gabriel opened his eyes with a languid sigh.

'Much better and more composed,' replied the wan curate, sitting up. 'You have given me a magical drug.'

'You may well call it that. This particular preparation of valerian is nepenthe for the nerves. But you are not quite recovered yet; the swell remains after the storm, you know. Why not postpone your story?'

'I cannot! I dare not!' said Gabriel, earnestly. 'I must ease my mind by telling it to you. Doctor, do you know that the visitor who made my father ill on the night of the reception was Jentham?'

'No, my boy, I did not know that. Who told you?'

'John, our old servant, who admitted him. He told me about Jentham just before I went to Nauheim.'

'Did Jentham give his name?'

'No, but John, like many other people, saw

the body in the dead-house. He there recognised Jentham by his gipsy looks and the scar on his face. Well, doctor, I wondered what the man could have said to so upset the bishop, but of course I did not dare to ask him. By the time I got to Germany the episode passed out of my mind.'

'And what recalled it?'

'Something my mother said. We were in the Kurgarten listening to the band when a Heidelberg student, with his face all seamed and slashed, walked past us.'

'I know; students in Germany are proud of those duelling scars. Well, Gabriel, and what then?'

The curate quivered all over, and instead of replying directly, asked what seemed to be an irrelevant question. 'Did you know that my mother was a widow when my father married her?' he demanded in low tones.

'Of course I did,' replied Graham, cheerily. 'I was practising in Marylebone then, and your father was vicar of St Benedict's. Why, I was at his wedding, Gabriel, and very pretty your mother looked. She was a Mrs Krant, whose husband had been killed while serving as a volunteer in the Franco-Prussian War!'

'Did you ever see her husband?'

'No; she did not come to Marylebone until he had left her. The rascal deserted the poor young thing and went abroad to fight. But why do you ask all these questions? They cannot but be painful.'

'Because the sight of that student's face recalled her first husband to my mother. She said that Krant had a long scar on the right cheek. I immediately thought of Jentham.'

'Good God!' cried Graham, pushing back his chair. 'What do you mean, lad?'

'Wait! wait!' said Gabriel, feverishly. 'I asked my mother to describe the features of her first husband. Not suspecting my reason for asking, she did so. Krant, she said, was tall, lean, swart and black-eyed, with a scar on the right cheek running from the ear to the mouth. Doctor!' cried Gabriel, clutching Graham's hand, 'that is the very portrait of the man Jentham.'

'Gabriel!' whispered the little doctor, hoarsely, 'do you mean to say — '

'I mean to say that Krant did not die, that Jentham was Krant, and that when he called on my father he appeared as one from the dead. He is dead now, but he was alive when my mother became my father's wife.'

'Impossible! Impossible!' repeated Graham, who was ashy pale, and shaken out of his ordinary self. 'Krant died — died at Sedan. Your father went over and saw his grave!'

'He did not see the corpse, though. I tell

you I am right, doctor. Krant did not die. My mother is not my father's wife, and we — we — George, Lucy and myself are in the eyes of the law — nobody's children.' The curate uttered these last words almost in a shriek, and fell back on the couch, covering his face with two trembling hands.

Graham sat staring straight before him with an expression of absolute horror on his withered brown face. He recalled Pendle's sudden illness after Jentham had paid that fatal visit; his refusal to confess the real cause of his attack; his admission that he had a secret which he did not dare to reveal even to his oldest friend, and his strange act in sending away his wife and daughter to Nauheim. All these things gave colour to Gabriel's supposition that Jentham was Krant returned from the dead; but after all it was a supposition merely, and quite unsupported by fact.

'There is no proof of it,' said Graham, hoarsely; 'no proof.'

'Ask my father for the proof,' murmured Gabriel. 'I dare not!'

The doctor could understand that speech very well, and now saw the reason why Gabriel had chosen to speak to him rather than to the bishop. It might be true, after all, this frightful fact, he thought, and as in a flash he saw ruin, disaster, shame, terror following in the train of its becoming known. This, then, was the bishop's secret, and Graham in his quick way decided that at all costs it must be preserved, if only for the sake of Mrs Pendle and her children. The first step towards attaining this end was to see the bishop and hear confirmation or denial from his own lips. Once Graham knew all the facts he fancied that he might in some way — at present he knew not how — help his wretched friend. With characteristic promptitude he decided on the spot how to act.

'Gabriel,' he said, bending over the unhappy young man, 'I shall see your father about this at once. I cannot, I dare not believe it to be true, unless with his own lips he confirms the identity of Krant with Jentham. You wait here until I return, and sleep if you can.'

'Sleep!' groaned Gabriel. 'Oh, God! shall I ever sleep again?'

'My friend,' said the little doctor, solemnly, 'you have no right to doubt your father's honour until you hear what he has to say. Jentham may not be Krant as you suspect. It may be a chance likeness — a — '

Gabriel shook his head. 'You can't argue away what I know to be true,' he muttered, looking at the floor with dry, wild eyes. 'See my father and tell him what I have told you. He will not be able to deny his shame and the disgrace of his children.'

'That we shall see,' said Graham, with a cheerfulness he was far from feeling. 'I shall see him at once. Gabriel, my boy, hope for the best!'

Again the curate shook his head, and with a groan flung himself down on the couch with his face to the wall. Seeing that words were vain, the doctor threw one glance of pity on his prostrate form, and with a sigh passed out of the room.

29

The Confession of Bishop Pendle

Mr Cargrim was very much out of temper, and Baltic was the cause of his unchristian state of mind. As the employer of the so-called missionary and actual inquiry agent, the chaplain expected to be informed of every fresh discovery, but with this view Baltic did not concur. In his solemn way he informed Cargrim that he preferred keeping his information and methods and suspicions to himself until he was sure of capturing the actual criminal. When the man was lodged in Beorminster Jail — when his complicity in the crime was proved beyond all doubt — then Baltic promised to write out, for the edification of his employer, a detailed account of the steps taken to bring about so satisfactory a result. And from this stern determination all Cargrim's arguments failed to move him.

This state of things was the more vexatious as Cargrim knew that the ex-sailor had seen Mother Jael, and shrewdly suspected that he had obtained from the beldam valuable information likely to incriminate the bishop. Whether his newly-found evidence did so or not, Baltic gravely declined to say, and Cargrim was furious at being left in ignorance. He was particularly anxious that Dr Pendle's guilt should be proved without loss of time, as Mr Leigh of Heathcroft was sinking rapidly, and on any day a new rector might be needed for that very desirable parish. Certainly Cargrim, as he fondly imagined, had thwarted Gabriel's candidature by revealing the young man's love for Bell Mosk to the bishop. Still, even if Gabriel were not nominated, Dr Pendle had plainly informed Cargrim that he need not expect the appointment, so the chaplain foresaw that unless he obtained power over the bishop before Leigh's death, the benefice would be given to some stranger. It was no wonder, then, that he resented the silence of Baltic and felt enraged at his own impotence. He almost regretted having sought the assistance of a man who appeared more likely to be a hindrance than a help. For once, Cargrim's scheming brain could devise no remedy.

Lurking about the library as usual, Mr Cargrim was much astonished to receive a visit from Dr Graham. Of course, the visit was to the bishop, but Cargrim, being alone in the library, came forward in his silky, obsequious way to receive the new-comer, and politely asked what he could do for him.

'You can inform the bishop that I wish to see him, if you please,' said Graham, with a perfectly expressionless face.

'His lordship is at present taking a short rest,' replied Cargrim, blandly, 'but anything I can do — '

'You can do nothing, Mr Cargrim. I wish for a private interview with Dr Pendle.'

'Your business must be important.'

'It is,' retorted Graham, abruptly; 'so important that I must see the bishop at once.'

'Oh, certainly, doctor. I am sorry to see that you do not look well.'

'Thank you; I am as well as can be expected.'

'Really! considering what, Dr Graham?'

'Considering the way I am kept waiting here, Mr Cargrim,' after which pointed speech there was nothing left for the defeated chaplain but to retreat as gracefully as he could. Yet Cargrim might have known, from past experience, that a duel of words with sharp-tongued Dr Graham could only end in his discomfiture. But in spite of all his cunning he usually burnt his fingers at a twice-touched flame.

Extremely curious to know the reason of Graham's unexpected visit and haggard looks, Cargrim, having informed the bishop that the doctor was waiting for him, attempted to make a third in the interview by gliding in behind his superior. Graham, however, was too sharp for him, and after a few words with the bishop, intimated to the chaplain that his presence was not necessary. So Cargrim, like the Peri at the Gates of Paradise, was forced to lurk as near the library door as he dared, and he strained his ears in vain to overhear what the pair were talking about. Had he known that the revelation of Bishop Pendle's secret formed the gist of the interview, he would have been even more enraged than he was. But, for the time being, Fate was against the wily chaplain, and, in the end, he was compelled to betake himself to a solitary and sulky walk, during which his reflections concerning Graham and Baltic were the reverse of amiable. As a defeated sneak, Mr Cargrim was not a credit to his cloth.

Dr Pendle had the bewildered air of a man suddenly roused from sleep, and was inclined to be peevish with Graham for calling at so untoward a time. Yet it was five o'clock in the afternoon, which was scarcely a suitable hour for slumber, as the doctor bluntly remarked.

'I was not asleep,' said the bishop, settling himself at his writing-table. 'I simply lay down for half an hour or so.'

'Worn out with worry, I suppose?'

'Yes,' Dr Pendle sighed; 'my burden is almost greater than I can bear.'

'I quite agree with you,' replied Graham, 'therefore I have come to help you to bear it.'

'That is impossible. To do so, you must know the truth, and — God help me! — I dare not tell it even to you.'

'There is no need for you to do so, Pendle. I know your secret.'

The bishop twisted his chair round with a rapid movement and stared at the sympathetic face of Graham with an expression of blended terror and amazement. Hardly could his tongue frame itself to speech.

'You — know — my — secret!' stuttered Pendle, with pale lips.

'Yes, I know that Krant did not die at Sedan as we supposed. I know that he returned to life — to Beorminster — to you, under the name of Jentham! Hold up, man! don't give way,' for the bishop, with a heavy sigh, had fallen forward on his desk, and, with his grey head buried in his arms, lay there silent and broken down in an agony of doubt, and fear and shame.

'Play the man, George Pendle,' said Graham, who knew that the father was more virile than the son, and therefore needed the tonic of words rather than the soothing anodyne of medicine. 'If you believe in what you preach, if you are a true servant of your God, call upon religion, upon your Deity, for help to bear your troubles. Stand up manfully, my friend, and face the worst!'

'Alas! alas! many waters have gone over me, Graham.'

'Can you expect anything else if you permit yourself to sink without an effort?' said the doctor, rather cynically; 'but if you cannot gain strength from Christianity, then be a Stoic, and independent of supernatural aid.'

The bishop lifted his head and suddenly rose to his full height, until he towered above the little doctor. His pale face took upon itself a calmer expression, and stretching out his arm, he rolled forth a text from the Psalms in his deepest voice, in his most stately manner: 'In God is my salvation and my glory, the rock of my strength, and my refuge is in God.'

'Good!' said Graham, with a satisfied nod; 'that is the proper spirit in which to meet trouble. And now, Pendle, with your leave, we will approach the subject with more particularity.'

'It will be as well,' replied the bishop, and he spoke collectedly and gravely, with no trace of his late excitement. When he most needed it, strength had come to him from above; and he was able to discuss the sore matter of his domestic troubles with courage and with judgment.

'How did you learn my secret, Graham?' he asked, after a pause.

'Indirectly from Gabriel.'

'Gabriel,' said the bishop, trembling, 'is at Nauheim!'

'You are mistaken, Pendle. He returned to Beorminster this morning, and as he was afraid to speak to you on the subject of Jentham, he came to ask my advice. The poor lad is broken down and ill, and is now lying in my consulting-room until I return.'

'How did Gabriel learn the truth?' asked Pendle, with a look of pain.

'From something his mother said.'

The bishop, in spite of his enforced calmness, groaned aloud. 'Does she know of it?' he murmured, while drops of perspiration beaded his forehead and betrayed his inward agony. 'Could not that shame be spared me?'

'Do not be hasty, Pendle, your wife knows nothing.'

'Thank God!' said the bishop, fervently; then added, almost immediately, 'You say my wife. Alas! alas! that I dare not call her so.'

'It is true, then?' asked Graham, becoming very pale.

'Perfectly true. Krant was not killed. Krant returned here under the name of Jentham. My wife is not my wife! My children are illegitimate; they have no name; outcasts they are. Oh, the shame! Oh, the disgrace!' and Dr Pendle groaned aloud.

Graham sympathised with the man's distress, which was surely natural under the terrible calamity which had befallen him and his. George Pendle was a priest, a prelate, but he was also a son of Adam, and liable, like all mortals, the strongest as the weakest, to moments of doubt, of fear, of trembling, of utter dismay. Had the evil come upon him alone, he might have borne it with more patience, but when it parted him from his dearly-loved wife, when it made outcasts of the children he was so proud of, who can wonder that he should feel inclined to cry with Job, 'Is it good unto Thee that Thou should'st oppress!' Nevertheless, like Job, the bishop held fast his integrity.

Yet that he might have some comfort in his affliction, that one pang might be spared to him, Graham assured him that Mrs Pendle was ignorant of the truth, and related in full the story of how Gabriel had come to connect Jentham with Krant. Pendle listened in silence, and inwardly thanked God that at least so much mercy had been vouchsafed him. Then in his turn he made a confidant of his old friend, recalled the early days of his courtship and marriage, spoke of the long interval of peace and quiet happiness which he and his wife had enjoyed, and ended with a detailed account of the disguised Krant's visit and threats, and the anguish his re-appearance had caused.

'You remember, Graham!' he said, with wonderful self-control, 'how almost thirty years ago I was the Vicar of St Benedict's in Marylebone, and how you, my old college friend, practised medicine in the same parish.'

'I remember, Pendle; there is no need for you to make your heart ache by recalling the past.'

'I must, my friend,' said the bishop, firmly, 'in order that you may fully understand my position. As you know, my dear wife — for I still must call her so — came to reside there under her married name of Mrs Krant. She was poor and unhappy, and when I called upon her, as the vicar of the parish, she told me her miserable story. How she had left her home and family for the sake of that wretch who had attracted her weak, girlish affections by his physical beauty and fascinating manners; how he treated her ill, spent the most of her money, and finally left her, within a year of the marriage, with just enough remaining out of her fortune to save her from starvation. She told me that Krant had gone to Paris, and was serving as a volunteer in the French army, while she, broken down and unhappy, had come to my parish to give herself to God and labour amongst the poor.'

'She was a charming woman! She is so now!' said Graham, with a sigh. 'I do not wonder that you loved her.'

'Loved, sir! Why speak in the past tense? I love her still. I shall always love that sweet companion of these many happy years. From the time I saw her in those poor London lodgings I loved her with all the strength of my manhood. But you know that, being already married, she could not be my wife. Then, shortly after the surrender of Sedan, that letter came to tell her that her husband was dead, and dying, had asked her pardon for his wicked ways. Alas! alas! that letter was false!'

'We both of us believed it to be genuine at the time, Pendle, and you went over to France after the war to see the man's grave.'

'I did, and I saw the grave — saw it with its tombstone, in a little Alsace graveyard, with the name Stephen Krant painted thereon in black German letters. I never doubted but that he lay below, and I looked far and wide for the man, Leon Durand, who had written that letter at the request of his dying comrade. I ask you, Graham, who would have disbelieved the evidence of letter and tombstone?'

'No one, certainly!' replied Graham, gravely; 'but it was a pity that you could not find Leon Durand, so as to put the matter beyond all doubt.'

'Find him!' echoed the bishop, passionately. 'No one on earth could have found the man. He did not exist.'

'Then who wrote the letter?'

'Krant himself, as he told me in this very room, the wicked plotter!'

'But his handwriting; would not his wife have — '

'No!' cried Pendle, rising and pacing to and fro, greatly agitated, 'the man disguised his hand so that his wife should not recognise it. He did not wish to be bound to her, but to wander far and wide, and live his own sinful life. That was why he sent the forged letter to make Amy believe that he was dead. And she did believe, the more especially after I returned to tell how I had seen his grave. I thought also that he was dead. So did you, Graham.'

'Certainly,' assented Graham, 'there was no reason to doubt the fact. Who would have believed that Krant was such a scoundrel?'

'I called him that when he came to see me here,' said Dr Pendle, with a passionate gesture. 'Old man and priest as I am, I could have killed him as he sat in yonder chair, smiling at my misery, and taunting me with my position.'

'How did he find out that you had married Mrs Krant?'

'By going back to the Marylebone parish. He had been wandering all over the face of the earth, like the Cain he was; but meeting with no good fortune, he came back to England to find out Amy, and, I suppose, rob her of the little money he had permitted her to keep. He knew of her address in Marylebone, as she had told him where she was going before he deserted her.'

'But how did he learn about the marriage?' asked Graham, again.

'I cannot tell; but he knew that his wife, after his desertion, devoted herself to good works, so no doubt he went to the church and asked about her. The old verger who saw us married is still alive, so I suppose he told Krant that Amy was my wife, and that I was the Bishop of Beorminster. But, however he learned the truth, he found his way here, and when I came into this room during the reception I found him waiting for me.'

'How did you recognise a man you had not seen?'

'By a portrait Amy had shown me, and by the description she gave me of his gipsy looks and the scar on his cheek. He had not altered at all, and I beheld before me the same wicked face I had seen in the portrait. I was confused at first, as I knew the face but not the name. When he told me that he was Stephen Krant, that my wife was really his wife, that my children had no name, I — I — oh, God!' cried Pendle, covering his face with his hands, 'it was terrible! terrible!'

'My poor friend!'

The bishop threw himself into a chair. 'After close on thirty years,' he moaned, 'think of it, Graham — the shame, the horror! Oh, God!'

30

Blackmail

For some moments Graham did not speak, but looked with pity on the grief-shaken frame and bowed shoulders of his sorely-tried friend. Indeed, the position of the man was such that he did not see what comfort he could administer, and so, very wisely, held his peace. However, when the bishop, growing more composed, remained still silent, he could not forbear offering him a trifle of consolation.

'Don't grieve so, Pendle!' he said, laying his hand on the other's shoulder; 'it is not your fault that you are in this position.'

The bishop sighed, and murmured with a shake of his head, '*Omnis qui facit peccatum, servus est peccati!*'

'But you have not done sin!' cried Graham, dissenting from the text. 'You! your wife! myself! everyone thought that Krant was dead and buried. The man fled, and lied, and forged, to gain his freedom — to shake off the marriage bonds which galled him. He was the sinner, not you, my poor innocent friend!'

'True enough, doctor, but I am the sufferer. Had God in His mercy not sustained me in my hour of trial, I do not know how I should have borne my misery, weak, erring mortal that I am.'

'That speech is one befitting your age and office,' said the doctor, gravely, 'and I quite approve of it. All the same, there is another religious saying — I don't know if it can be called a text — 'God helps those who help themselves.' You will do well, Pendle, to lay that to heart.'

'How can I help myself?' said the bishop, hopelessly. 'The man is dead now, without doubt; but he was alive when I married his supposed widow, therefore the ceremony is null and void. There is no getting behind that fact.'

'Have you consulted a lawyer on your position?'

'No. The law cannot sanction a union — at least in my eyes — which I know to be against the tenets of the Church. So far as I know, if a husband deserts his wife, and is not heard of for seven years, she can marry again after that period without being liable to prosecution as a bigamist, but in any case the second ceremony is not legal.'

'Mrs Krant became your wife before the expiration of seven years, I know,' said

Graham, wrinkling his brow.

'Certainly. And therefore she is — in the eyes of the law — a bigamist' — the bishop shuddered — 'although, God knows, she fully believed her husband to be dead. But the religious point of view is the one I take, doctor; as a Churchman, I cannot live with a woman whom I know is not my wife. It was for that reason that I sent her away!'

'But you cannot keep her away for ever, bishop! — at all events, unless you explain the position to her.'

'I dare not do that in her present state of health; the shock would kill her. No, Graham, I see that sooner or later she must know, but I wished for her absence that I might gain time to consider my terrible position. I have considered it in every way — but, God help me! I can see no hope — no escape. Alas! alas! I am sorely, sorely tried.'

Graham reflected. 'Are you perfectly certain that Jentham and Krant are one and the same man?' he asked doubtfully.

'I am certain of it,' replied Pendle, decisively. 'I could not be deceived in the dark gipsy face, in the peculiar cicatrice on the right cheek. And he knew all about my wife, Graham — about her family, her maiden name, the amount of her fortune, her taking up parish work in Marylebone. Above all, he showed me the certificate of his marriage, and a number of letters written to him by Amy, reproaching him with his cruel desertion. Oh, there can be no doubt that this Jentham is — or rather was — Stephen Krant.'

'It would seem so!' sighed Graham, heavily. 'Evidently there is no hope of proving him to be an impostor in the face of such evidence.

'He came to extort money, I suppose?'

'Need you ask!' said the bishop, bitterly. 'Yes, his sole object was blackmail; he was content to let things remain as they are, provided his silence was purchased at his own price. He told me that if I paid him two hundred pounds he would hand over certificate and letters and disappear, never to trouble me again.'

'I doubt if such a blackguard would keep his word, Pendle. Moreover, although novelists and dramatists attach such a value to marriage certificates, they are really not worth the paper they are written on — save, perhaps, as immediate evidence. The register of the church in which the ceremony took place is the important document, and that can neither be handed over nor destroyed. Krant was giving you withered leaves for your good gold, Pendle. Still, Needs must when Sir Urian drives, so I suppose you agreed to the bribe.'

The bishop's grey head drooped on his breast, his eyes sought the carpet, and he looked like a man overwhelmed with shame. 'Yes,' he replied, in low tones of pain, 'I had not the courage to face the consequences. Indeed, what else could I do? I could not have the man denounce my marriage as a false one, force himself into the presence of my delicate wife, and tell my children that they are nameless. The shock would have killed Amy; it would have broken my children's hearts; it would have shamed me in my high position before the eyes of all England. I was innocent; I am innocent. Yes, but the fact remained, as it remains now, that I am not married to Amy, that my children are not entitled to bear my name. I ask you, Graham — I ask you, what else could I do than pay the money in the face of such shame and disgrace?'

'There is no need to excuse yourself to me, Pendle. I do not blame you in the least.'

'But I blame myself — in part,' replied the bishop, sadly. 'As an honest man I knew that my marriage was illegal; as a priest I was bound to put away the woman who was not — who is not my wife. But think of the shame to her, of the disgrace to my innocent children. I could not do it, Graham, I could not do it. Satan came to me in such a guise that I yielded to his tempting without a struggle. I agreed to buy Jentham's silence at his own price; and as I did not wish him to come here again, lest Amy should see him, I made an appointment to meet him on Southberry Heath on Sunday night, and there pay him his two hundred pounds blackmail.'

'Did you speak with him on the spot where his corpse was afterwards found?' asked Graham, in a low voice, not daring to look at his friend.

'No,' answered the bishop, simply, not suspecting that the doctor hinted at the murder; 'I met him at the crossroads.'

'You had the money with you, I suppose?'

'I had the money in notes of tens. As I was unwilling to draw so large a sum from the Beorminster Bank, lest my doing so should provoke comment, I made a special journey to London and obtained the money there.'

'I think you were over-careful, bishop.'

'Graham, I tell you I was overcome with fear, not so much for myself as for those dear to me. You know how the most secret things become known in this city; and I dreaded lest my action should become public property, and should be connected in some way with Jentham. Why, I even tore the butt of the cheque I drew out of the book, lest any record should remain likely to excite suspicion. I took the most elaborate precautions to guard against discoveries.'

'And rather unnecessary ones,' rejoined Graham, dryly. 'Well, and you met the scamp?'

'I did, on Sunday night — that Sunday I was at Southberry holding a confirmation service, and as I rode back, shortly after eight in the evening, I met Jentham, by appointment, at the crossroads. It was a stormy and wet night, Graham, and I half thought that he would not come to the rendezvous, but he was there, sure enough, and in no very good temper at his wetting, I did not get off my horse, but handed down the packet of notes, and asked him for the certificate and letters.'

'Which, no doubt, he declined to part with at the last moment.'

'You are right,' said the bishop, mournfully; 'he declared that he would keep the certificate until he received another hundred pounds.'

'The scoundrel! What did you say?'

'What could I say but 'Yes'? I was in the man's power. At any cost, if I wanted to save myself and those dear to me, I had to secure the written evidence he possessed. I told him that I had not the extra money with me, but that if he met me in the same place a week later he should have it. I then rode away downcast and wretched. The next day,' concluded the bishop, quietly, 'I heard that my enemy was dead.'

'Murdered,' said Graham, explicitly.

'Murdered, as you say,' rejoined Pendle, tremulously; 'and oh, my friend, I fear that the Cain who slew him now has the certificate in his possession, and holds my secret. What I have suffered with that knowledge, God alone knows. Every day, every hour, I have been expecting a call from the assassin.'

'The deuce you have!' said the doctor, surprised into unbecoming language.

'Yes; he may come and blackmail me also, Graham!'

'Not when he runs the risk of being hanged, my friend.'

'But you forget,' said the bishop, with a sigh. 'He may trust to his knowledge of my secret to force me to conceal his sin.'

'Would you be coerced in that way?'

Dr Pendle threw back his noble head, and, looking intently at his friend, replied in a firm and unfaltering tone. 'No,' said he, gravely. 'Even at the cost of my secret becoming known, I should have the man arrested.'

'Well,' said Graham, with a shrug, 'you are

more of a hero than I am, bishop. The cost of exposing the wretch seems too great.'

'Graham! Graham! I must do what is right at all hazards.'

'Fiat justitia ruat cœlum!' muttered the doctor. 'There is a morsel of dictionary Latin for you. The heavens above your family will certainly fall if you speak out.'

The bishop winced and whitened. 'It is a heavy burden, Graham, a heavy, heavy burden, but God will give me strength to bear it. He will save me according to His mercy.'

The little doctor looked meditatively at his boots. He wished to tell Pendle that the chaplain suspected him of the murder, and that Baltic, the missionary, had been brought to Beorminster to prove such suspicions, but at the present moment he did not see how he could conveniently introduce the information. Moreover, the bishop seemed to be so utterly unconscious that anyone could accuse him of the crime, that Graham shrank from being the busybody to enlighten him. Yet it was necessary that he should be informed, if only that he might be placed on his guard against the machinations of Cargrim. Of course, the doctor never for one moment thought of his respected friend as the author of a deed of violence, and quite believed his account of the meeting with Jentham. The bishop's simple way of relating the episode would have convinced any liberal-minded man of his innocence and rectitude. His accents, and looks, and candour, all carried conviction.

Finally Graham hit upon a method of leading up to the subject of Cargrim's treachery, by referring to the old gipsy and her fortune-telling at Mrs Pansey's garden-party. 'What does Mother Jael know of your secret?' he asked with some hesitation.

'Nothing!' replied the bishop, promptly; 'it is impossible that she can know anything, unless' — here he paused — 'unless she is aware of who killed Jentham, and has seen the certificate and letters!'

'Do you think she knows who murdered the man?'

'I — cannot — say. At that garden-party I went into the tent to humour some ladies who wished me to have my fortune told.'

'I saw you go in, bishop; and you came out looking disturbed.'

'No wonder, Graham; for Mother Jael, under the pretence of reading my hand, hinted at my secret. I fancied, from what she said, that she knew what it was; and I accused her of having gained the information from Jentham's assassin. However, she would not speak plainly, but warned me of coming trouble, and talked about blood and the grave, until I really believe she fancied I had killed the man. I could make nothing of her, so I left the tent considerably discomposed, as you may guess. I intended to see her on another occasion, but as yet I have not done so.'

'Is it your belief that the woman knows your secret?' asked Graham.

'No. On consideration, I concluded that she knew a little, but not much — at all events, not sufficient to hurt me in any way. Krant — that is Jentham — was of gipsy blood, and I fancied that he had seen Mother Jael, and perhaps, in his boastful way, had hinted at his power over me. Still, I am quite certain that, for his own sake, he did not reveal my secret. And after all, Graham, the allusions of Mother Jael were vague and unsatisfactory, although they disturbed me sufficiently to make me anxious for the moment.'

'Well, bishop, I agree with you. Mother Jael cannot know much or she would have spoken plainer. So far as she is concerned, I fancy your secret is pretty safe; but,' added Graham, with a glance at the door, 'what about Cargrim?'

'He knows nothing, Graham.'

'Perhaps not, but he suspects much.'

'Suspects!' echoed the bishop, in scared tones. 'What can he suspect?'

'That you killed Jentham,' said Graham, quietly.

Dr Pendle looked incredulously at his friend. 'I — I — murder — I kill — what — Cargrim — says,' he stammered; then asked him with a sharp rush of speech, 'Is the man mad?'

'No; but he is a scoundrel, as I told you. Listen, bishop,' and in his rapid way Graham reported to Dr Pendle all that Harry Brace had told him regarding Cargrim and his schemes.

The bishop listened in incredulous silence; but, almost against his will, he was obliged to believe in Graham's story. That a man whom he trusted, whom he had treated with such kindness, should have dug this pit for him to fall into, was almost beyond belief; and when the truth of the accusation was forced upon him, he hardly knew what to say about so great a traitor. But he made up his mind to one thing. 'I shall dismiss him at once!' he said determinedly.

'No, bishop. It is unwise to drive a rat into a corner; and Cargrim may prove himself dangerous if sharply treated. Better tolerate his presence until Baltic discovers the real criminal.'

'I don't like the position,' said the bishop, frowning.

'No man would. However, it is better to temporise than to risk all and lose all. Better let him remain, Pendle.'

'Very well, Graham, I shall take your advice.'

'Good!' Graham rose to depart. 'And Gabriel?' he asked, with his hand on the door.

'Send him to me, doctor. I must speak to him.'

'You won't scold him for seeing me first, I hope.'

'Scold him,' said the bishop, with a melancholy smile. 'Alas, my friend, the situation is too serious for scolding!'

31

Mr Baltic on the Trail

What took place at the interview between Gabriel and his father, Dr Graham never knew; and indeed never sought to know. He was a discreet man even for a doctor, and meddled with no one's business, unless — as in the present instance — forced to do so. But even then his discretion showed itself; for after advising the bishop to tolerate the presence of Cargrim until Baltic had solved the riddle he was set to guess, and after sending Gabriel to the palace, he abstained from further inquiries and discussions in connection with murder and secret. He had every faith in Baltic, and quite believed that in time the missionary would lay his hand on the actual murderer. When this was accomplished, and Cargrim's attempt to gain illegal power over Pendle was thwarted; then — all chance of a public scandal being at an end — would be the moment to consider how the bishop should act in reference to his false marriage. Certainly there was the possible danger that the criminal might learn the secret from the certificate and papers, and might reveal it when captured; but Graham thought it best to ignore this difficulty until it should actually arise. For, after all, such a contingency might not occur.

'The certificate of marriage between Krant and his wife will reveal nothing to a man unacquainted with Mrs Pendle's previous name; and without such knowledge he cannot know that she married the bishop while her first husband was alive. Certainly she might have mentioned Pendle's name in the letters, but she would not write of him as a lover or as a possible husband; therefore, unless the assassin knows something of the story, which is improbable, and unless he can connect the name of Mrs Krant with Mrs Pendle — which on the face of it is impossible — I do not see how he is to learn the truth. He may guess, or he may know for certain, that Jentham received the two hundred pounds from the bishop, but he cannot guess that the price was paid for certificate and letters, especially as he found them on the body, and knows that they were not handed over for the money. No; on the whole, I think Pendle is mistaken; in my opinion there is no danger to be feared from the assassin, whomsoever he may be.'

In this way Graham argued with himself,

and shortly came to the comfortable conclusion that Dr Pendle's secret would never become a public scandal. Now that Jentham, *alias* Krant, was dead, the secret was known to three people only — namely, to the bishop, to himself, and to Gabriel. If none of the three betrayed it — and they had the strongest reason for silence — no one else would, or could. The question of the murder was the immediate matter for consideration; and once Dr Pendle's innocence was proved by the capture of the real assassin, Cargrim could be dismissed in well-merited disgrace. With all the will in the world he could not then harm the bishop, seeing that he was ignorant of the dead man's relation to Mrs Pendle. Other danger there was none; of that the little doctor was absolutely assured.

Perhaps the bishop argued in this way also; or it may be he found a certain amount of relief in sharing his troubles with Gabriel and Graham; but he certainly appeared more cheerful and less worried than formerly, and even tolerated the society of Cargrim with equanimity, although he detested playing a part so foreign to his frank and honourable nature. However, he saw the necessity of masking his dislike until the sting of this domestic viper could be rendered innocuous, and was sufficiently gracious on such occasions as he came into contact with him. Gabriel was less called upon to be courteous to the schemer, as, having come to a complete understanding with his father, he rarely visited the palace; but when he did so his demeanour towards Mr Cargrim was much the same as of yore. For the good of their domestic peace, both father and son concealed their real feelings, and succeeded as creditably as was possible with men of their honourable natures. But they were not cunning enough — or perhaps sufficiently guarded — to deceive the artful chaplain. Evil himself, he was always on the alert to see evil in others.

'I wonder what all this means,' he ruminated one day after vainly attempting to learn why Gabriel had returned so unexpectedly to Beorminster. 'The bishop seems unnecessarily polite, and young Pendle appears to be careful how he speaks. They surely can't suspect me of knowing about the murder. Perhaps Baltic has been talking; I'll just give him a word of warning.'

This he did, and was promptly told by the ex-sailor not to advise on points of which he was ignorant. 'I know my business, sir, none better,' observed Baltic, in his solemn way, 'and there are few men who are more aware of the value of a silent tongue.'

'You may be an admirable detective, as you say,' retorted Cargrim, nettled by the rebuke, 'but I have only your word for it; and you will permit me to observe that I have not yet seen a proof of your capabilities.'

'All in good time, Mr Cargrim. More haste less speed, sir. I fancy I am on the right track at last.'

'Can you guess who killed the man?' asked the chaplain, eagerly waiting for the bishop's name to be pronounced.

'I never guess, sir. I theorise from external evidence, and then try, with such brains as God has given me, to prove my theories.'

'You have gained some evidence, then?'

'If I have, Mr Cargrim, you'll hear it when I place the murderer in the dock. It is foolish to show half-finished work.'

'But if the mur — '

'Hold hard, sir!' interrupted Baltic, raising his head. 'I'll so far depart from my rule as to tell you one thing — whosoever killed Jentham, it was not Bishop Pendle.'

Cargrim grew red and angry. 'I tell you it was!' he almost shouted, although this conversation took place in a quiet corner near the cathedral, and thereby required prudent speech and demeanour. 'Didn't Dr Pendle meet Jentham on the common?'

'We presume so, sir, but as yet we have no

proof of the meeting.'

'At least you know that he paid Jentham two hundred pounds.'

'Perhaps he did; maybe he didn't,' returned Baltic, quietly. 'He certainly drew out that amount from the Ophir Bank, but, not having traced the notes, I can't say if he paid it to the man.'

'But I am sure he did,' insisted Cargrim, still angry.

'In that case, sir, why ask me for my opinion?' replied the imperturbable Baltic.

If Mr Cargrim had not been a clergyman, he would have sworn at the complacent demeanour of the agent, and even as it was he felt inclined to risk a relieving oath or two. But knowing Baltic's religious temperament, he was wise enough not to lay himself open to further rebuke; so he turned the matter off with a laugh, and observed that no doubt Mr Baltic knew his own business best.

'I think I can safely say so, sir,' rejoined Baltic, gravely. 'By the way, did you not tell me that Captain George Pendle was on the common when the murder took place?'

'Yes, George was there, and so was Gabriel. Mrs Pansey's page saw them both.'

'And where is Captain Pendle now, sir?'

'At Wincaster with his regiment; but the bishop has sent for him to come to

Beorminster, so I expect he will be here within the week.'

'I am glad of that, Mr Cargrim, as I wish to ask Captain Pendle a few questions.'

'Do you suspect him?'

'I can't rightly say, sir,' answered Baltic, wiping his face with the red bandanna. 'Later on I may form an opinion. Mr Gabriel Pendle comes to The Derby Winner sometimes, I see.'

'Yes; he is in love with the barmaid there.'

Baltic looked up sharply. 'Mosk's daughter, sir?'

'The same. He wants to marry Bell Mosk.'

'Does — he — indeed?' drawled the agent, flicking his thumb nail against his teeth. 'Well, Mr Cargrim, he might do worse. There is a lot of good in that young woman, sir. Mr Gabriel Pendle has lately returned from abroad, I hear.'

'Yes, from Nauheim.'

'That is in Germany, I take it, sir. Did he travel on a Cook's ticket, do you know?'

'I believe he did.'

'Oh! humph! I'll say good-bye, then, Mr Cargrim, for the present. I shall see you when I return from London.'

'Are you going to ask about Gabriel's ticket at Cook's?'

'There's no telling, sir. I may look in.'

'Do you think that Gab — '

'I think nothing as yet, Mr Cargrim; when I do, I'll tell you my thoughts. Good-day, sir! God bless you!' And Baltic, with a satisfied expression on his face, rolled away in a nautical manner.

'God bless me indeed!' muttered Cargrim, in much displeasure, for neither the speech nor the manner of the man pleased him. 'Ugh! I wish Baltic would stick to either religion or business. At present he is a kind of moral hermaphrodite, good for neither one thing nor another. I wonder if he suspects the bishop or his two sons? I don't believe Dr Pendle is innocent; but if he is, either George or Gabriel is guilty. Well, if that is so, I'll still be able to make the bishop give me Heathcroft. He will rather do that than see one of his sons hanged and the name disgraced. Still, I hope Baltic will bring home the crime to his lordship.'

With this amiable wish, Mr Cargrim quickened his pace to catch up with Miss Whichello, whom he saw tripping across the square towards the Jenny Wren house. The little old lady looked rosy and complacent, at peace with herself and the whole of Beorminster. Nevertheless, her expression changed when she saw Mr Cargrim sliding gracefully towards her, and she received him with marked coldness. As yet she had not forgiven him for his unauthorised interference on behalf of Mrs Pansey. Cargrim was quick to observe her buckram civility, but diplomatically took no notice of its frigidity. On the contrary, he was more gushing and more expansive than ever.

'A happy meeting, my dear lady,' he said, with a beaming glance. 'Had I not met you, I should have called to see you as the bearer of good news.'

'Really!' replied Miss Whichello, drily. 'That will be a relief from hearing bad news, Mr Cargrim. I have had sufficient trouble of late.'

'Ah!' sighed the chaplain, falling into his professional drawl, 'how true is the saying of Job, 'Man is born — ''

'I don't want to hear about Job,' interrupted Miss Whichello, crossly. 'He is the greatest bore of all the patriarchs.'

'Job, dear lady, was not a patriarch.'

'Nevertheless, he is a bore, Mr Cargrim. What is your good news?'

'Captain Pendle is coming to Beorminster this week, Miss Whichello.'

'Oh,' said the little old lady, with a satirical smile, 'you are a day after the fair, Mr Cargrim. I heard that news this morning.'

'Indeed! But the bishop only sent for

Captain Pendle yesterday.'

'Quite so; and Miss Arden received a telegram from Captain Pendle this morning.'

'Ah! Miss Whichello, young love! young love!'

The little lady could have shaken Cargrim for the smirk with which he made this remark. However, she restrained her very natural impulse, and merely remarked — rather irrelevantly, it must be confessed — that if two young and handsome people in love with one another were not happy in their first blush of passion they never would be.

'No doubt, dear lady. I only trust that such happiness may last. But there is no sky without a cloud.'

'And there is no bee without a sting, and no rose without a thorn. I know all those consoling proverbs, Mr Cargrim, but they don't apply to my turtle-doves.'

Cargrim rubbed his hands softly together. 'Long may you continue to think so, my dear lady,' said he, with a sad look.

'What do you mean, sir?' asked Miss Whichello, sharply.

'I mean that it is as well to be prepared for the worst,' said Cargrim, in his blandest manner. 'The course of true love — but you are weary of such trite sayings. Good-day, Miss Whichello!' He raised his hat and turned away. 'One last proverb — Joy in the morning means grief at night.'

When Mr Cargrim walked away briskly after delivering this Parthian shaft, Miss Whichello stood looking after him with an expression of nervous worry on her rosy face. She had her own reasons to apprehend trouble in connection with the engagement, and although these were unknown to the chaplain, his chance arrow had hit the mark. The thoughts of the little old lady at once reverted to the conversation with the bishop at the garden-party.

'Mrs Pansey again,' thought Miss Whichello, resuming her walk at a slower pace. 'I shall have to call on her, and appeal either to her fears or her charity, otherwise she may cause trouble.'

In the meantime, Mr Baltic, proceeding in his grave way towards Eastgate, had fallen in with Gabriel coming from The Derby Winner. As yet the two had never met, and save the name, young Pendle knew nothing about the ex-sailor. Nevertheless, when face to face with him, he recognised the man at once as a private inquiry agent whom he had once spoken to in Whitechapel. The knowledge of his father's secret, of Jentham's murder and of this stranger's profession mingled confusedly in Gabriel's head, and his heart knocked at his ribs for very fear.

'I met you in London some years ago,' he said nervously.

'Yes, Mr Pendle; but then I did not know your name, nor did you know mine.'

'How did you recognise me?' asked Gabriel.

'I have a good memory for faces, sir,' returned Baltic, 'but, as a matter of fact, Sir Harry Brace pointed you out to me.'

'Sir Har — oh, then you are Baltic!'

'At your service, Mr Pendle. I am down here on business.'

'I know all about it,' replied Gabriel, recovering his nerve with the knowledge of the man's name and inclination to side with the bishop.

'Indeed, sir! And who told you about it?'

'Sir Harry told Dr Graham, who informed my father, who spoke to me.'

'Oh!' Baltic looked seriously at the curate's pale face. 'Then the bishop knows that I am an inquiry agent.'

'He does, Mr Baltic. And, to tell you the truth, he is not at all pleased that you presented yourself in our city as a missionary.'

'I am a missionary,' answered the ex-sailor, quietly. 'I explained as much to Sir Harry, but it would seem that he has told the worst and kept back the best.'

'I don't understand,' said the curate, much bewildered.

'Sir, it would take too long for me to explain why I call myself a missionary, but you can rest assured that I am not sailing under false colours. As it is, you know me as an agent; and you know also my purpose in coming here.'

'Yes! I know that you are investigating the mur — '

'We are in the street, sir,' interrupted Baltic, with a glance at passers-by; 'it is as well to be discreet. One moment.' He led Gabriel into a quiet alley, comparatively free from listeners. 'This is a rather rough sort of neighbourhood, sir.'

'Rough certainly, but not dangerous,' replied Gabriel, puzzled by the remark.

'Don't you carry a pistol, Mr Pendle?'

'No! Why should I?'

'Why indeed? If the Gospel is not a protection enough, no earthly arms will prevail. Your name is Gabriel, I think, sir.'

'Yes! Gabriel Pendle; but I don't see — '

'I'm coming to an explanation, sir. G. P.,' mused Baltic — 'same initials as those of your father and brother, eh, Mr Pendle?'

'Certainly. Both the bishop and my brother are named George.'

'G. P. all three,' said Baltic, with a nod. 'Do

you travel abroad with a Cook's ticket, sir?'

'Usually! Why do you — '

'A through ticket to — say Nauheim — is about three pounds, I believe?'

'I paid that for mine, Mr Baltic. May I ask why you question me in this manner?' demanded Gabriel, irritably.

Baltic tapped Gabriel's chest three times with his forefinger. 'For your own safety, Mr Pendle. Good-day, sir!'

32

The Initials

As has before been stated, Dr Graham had another conversation with his persecuted friend, in which he advised him to tolerate the presence of Cargrim until Baltic captured the actual criminal. It was also at this second interview that the bishop asked Graham if he should tell George the truth. This question the little doctor answered promptly in the negative.

'For what is the use of telling him?' said he, argumentatively; 'doing so will make you uncomfortable and George very unhappy.'

'But George must learn the truth sooner or later.'

'I don't see that it is necessary to inform him of it at all,' retorted Graham, obstinately, 'and at all events you need not explain until forced to do so. One thing at a time, bishop. At present your task is to baffle Cargrim and kick the scoundrel out of the house when the murderer is found. Then we can discuss the matter of the marriage with Mrs Pendle.'

'Graham!' — the bishop's utterance of the

name was like a cry of pain — 'I cannot — I dare not tell Amy!'

'You must, Pendle, since she is the principal person concerned in the matter. You know how Gabriel learned the truth from her casual description of her first husband. Well, when Mrs Pendle returns to Beorminster, she may — I don't say that she will, mind you — but she may speak of Krant again, since, so far as she is concerned, there is no need for her to keep the fact of her first marriage secret.'

'Except that she may not wish to recall unhappy days,' put in the bishop, softly. 'Indeed, I wonder that Amy could bring herself to speak of Krant to her son and mine.'

'Women, my friend, do and say things at which they wonder themselves,' said the misogynist, cynically; 'probably Mrs Pendle acted on the impulse of the moment and regretted it immediately the words were out of her mouth. Still, she may describe Krant again when she comes back, and her listener may be as clever as Gabriel was in putting two and two together, and connecting your wife's first husband with Krant. Should such a thing occur — and it might occur — your secret would become the common property of this scandalmongering place, and your last condition would be worse than your first. Also,' continued Graham, with the air of a person clinching an argument, 'if you and Mrs Pendle are to part, my poor friend, she must be told the reason for such separation.'

'Part!' echoed the bishop, indignantly. 'My dear Amy and I shall never part, doctor. I wonder that you can suggest such a thing. Now that Krant is dead beyond all doubt, I shall marry his widow at once.'

'Quite so, and quite right,' assented Graham, emphatically; 'but in that case, as you can see for yourself, you must tell her that the first marriage is null and void, so as to account for the necessity of the second ceremony.' The doctor paused and reflected. 'Old scatterbrain that I am,' said he, with a shrug, 'I quite forgot that way out of the difficulty. A second marriage! Of course! and there is your riddle solved.'

'No doubt, so far as Amy and I are concerned,' said Pendle, gloomily, 'but so late a ceremony will not make my children legitimate. In England, marriage is not a retrospective act.'

'They manage these things better in France,' opined Graham, in the manner of Sterne; 'there a man can legitimise his children born out of wedlock if he so chooses. There was a talk of modifying the English Act in the same way; but, of course, the very nice people with nasty ideas shrieked out in their usual pig-headed style about legalised immorality. However,' pursued the doctor, in a more cheerful tone, 'I do not see that you need worry yourself on that point, bishop. You can depend upon Gabriel and me holding our tongues; you need not tell Lucy or George, and when you marry your wife for the second time, all things can go on as before. 'What the eye does not see, the heart does not grieve at,' you know.'

'But my eye sees, and my heart grieves,' groaned the bishop.

'Pish! don't make an inquisition of your conscience, Pendle. You have done no wrong; like greatness, evil has been thrust upon you.'

'I am certainly an innocent sinner, Graham.'

'Of course you are; but now that we have found the remedy, that is all over and done with. Wait till Jentham's murderer is found, then turn Cargrim out of doors, marry Mrs Krant in some out-of-the-way parish, and make a fresh will in favour of your children. There you are, bishop! Don't worry any more about the matter.'

'You don't think that I should tell Brace that — ?'

'I certainly don't think that you should disgrace your daughter in the eyes of her future husband,' retorted the doctor, hotly; 'marry your wife and hold your tongue. Even the Recording Angel can take no note of so obviously just a course.'

'I think you are right, Graham,' said the bishop, shaking his friend's hand with an expression of relief. 'In justice to my children, I must be silent. I shall act as you suggest.'

'Then that being so, you are a man again,' said Graham, jocularly, 'and now you can send for George to pay you a visit.'

'Do you think there is any necessity, Graham? The sight of him — '

'Will do you good, Pendle. Don't martyrise yourself and look on your children as so many visible evidences of sin. Bosh! I tell you, bosh!' cried the doctor, vigorously if ungallantly. 'Send for George, send for Mrs Pendle and Lucy, and throw all these morbid ideas to the wind. If you do not,' added Graham, raising a threatening finger, 'I shall write out a certificate for the transfer of the cleverest bishop in England to a lunatic asylum.'

'Well, well, I won't risk that,' said the bishop, smiling. 'George shall come back at once.'

'And all will be gas and gaiters, to quote the immortal Boz. Good-day, bishop! I have prescribed your medicine; see that you take it.'

'You are a tonic in yourself, Graham.'

'All men of sense are, Pendle. They are the salt of the earth, the oxygen in the moral atmosphere. If it wasn't for my common sense, bishop,' said the doctor, with a twinkle, 'I believe I should be weak enough to come and hear you preach.'

Dr Pendle laughed. 'I am afraid the age of miracles is past, my friend. As a bishop, I should reprove you, but — '

'But, as a good, sensible fellow, you'll take my advice. Well, well, bishop, I have had more obstinate patients than my college chum. Good-day, good-day,' and the little doctor skipped out of the library with a gay look and a merry nod, leaving the bishop relieved and smiling, and devoutly thankful for the solution of his life's riddle. At that moment the noble verse of the Psalmist was in his mind and upon his lips — 'God is our refuge and our strength: a very present help in trouble.' Bishop Pendle was proving the truth of that text.

So the exiled lover was permitted to return to Beorminster, and very pleased he was to find himself once more in the vicinity of his beloved. After congratulating the bishop on his recovered cheerfulness and placidity, George brought forward the name of Mab, and was pleased to find that his father was by no means so opposed to the match as formerly. Dr Pendle admitted again that Mab was a singularly charming young lady, and that his son might do worse than marry her. Late events had humbled the bishop's pride considerably; and the knowledge that George was nameless, induced him to consider Miss Arden more favourably as a wife for the young man. She was at least a lady, and not a barmaid like Bell Mosk; so the painful fact of Gabriel setting his heart so low made George's superior choice quite a brilliant match in comparison. On these grounds, the bishop intimated to Captain Pendle that, on consideration, he was disposed to overlook the rumours about Miss Arden's disreputable father and accept her as a daughter-in-law. It was with this joyful news that George, glowing and eager, as a lover should be, made his appearance the next morning at the Jenny Wren house.

'Thank God the bishop is reasonable,' cried Miss Whichello, when George explained the new position. 'I knew that Mab would gain his heart in the end.'

'She gained mine in the beginning,' said Captain George, fondly, 'and that, after all, is the principal thing.'

'What! your own heart, egotist! Does mine then count for nothing?'

'Oh!' said George, slipping his arm round her waist, 'if we begin on that subject, my litany will be as long as the Athanasian Creed, and quite as devout.'

'Captain Pendle!' exclaimed Miss Whichello, scandalised both by embrace and speech — both rather trying to a religious spinster.

'Miss Whichello,' mimicked the gay lover, 'am I not to be received into the family under the name of George?'

'That depends on your behaviour, Captain Pendle. But I am both pleased and relieved that the bishop consents to the marriage.'

'Aunty!' cried Mab, reddening a trifle, 'don't talk as though it were a favour. I do not look upon myself as worthless, by any means.'

'Worthless!' echoed George, gaily; 'then is gold mere dross, and diamonds but pebbles. You are the beauty of the universe, my darling, and I your lowest slave.' He threw himself at her feet. 'Set your pretty foot on my neck, my queen!'

'Captain Pendle,' said Miss Whichello, striving to stifle a laugh, 'if you don't get up and behave properly I shall leave the room.'

'If you do, aunty, he will get worse,' smiled Mab, ruffling what the barber had left of her lover's hair. 'Get up at once, you — you mad Romeo.'

George rose obediently, and dusted his

knees. 'Juliet, I obey,' said he, tragically; 'but no, you are not Juliet of the garden; you are Cleopatra! Semiramis! the most imperious and queenly of women. Where did you get your rich Eastern beauty from, Mab? What are you, an Arabian princess, doing in our cold grey West? You are like some dark-browed queen! A daughter of Bohemia! A Romany sorceress!'

Mab laughed, but Miss Whichello heaved a quick, impatient sigh, as though these Eastern comparisons annoyed her. George was unconsciously making remarks which cut her to the heart; and almost unable to control her feelings, she muttered some excuse and glided hastily from the room. With the inherent selfishness of love, neither George nor Mab paid any attention to her emotion or departure, but whispered and smiled and caressed one another, well pleased at their sweet solitude. George spent one golden hour in paradise, then unwillingly tore himself away. Only Shakespeare could have done justice to the passion of their parting. Kisses and sighs, last looks, final handclasps, and then George in the sunshine of the square, with Mab waving her handkerchief from the open casement. But, alas! workaday prose always succeeds Arcadian rhyme, and with the sinking sun dies the glory of the day.

With his mind hanging betwixt a mental heaven and earth, after the similitude of Mahomet's coffin, George walked slowly down the street, until he was brought like a shot eagle to the ground by a touch on the shoulder. Now, as there is nothing more annoying than such a bailiff's salute, George wheeled round with some vigorous language on the tip of his tongue, but did not use it when he found himself facing Sir Harry Brace.

'Oh, it's you!' said Captain Pendle, lamely. 'Well, with your experience, you should know better than to pull up a fellow unawares.'

'You talk in riddles, my good George,' said Harry, staring, as well he might, at this not very coherent speech.

'I have just left Miss Arden,' explained George, quite unabashed, for he did not care if the whole world knew of his love.

'Oh, I beg your pardon, I understand,' replied Brace, with a broad smile; 'but you must excuse me, old chap. I am — I am out of practice lately, you see. 'My love she is in Germanee,' as the old song says. I wish to speak with you.'

'All right. Where shall we go?'

'To the club. I must see you privately.'

The Beorminster Club was just a short distance down the street, so George followed

Harry into its hospitable portals and finally accepted a comfortable chair in the smoking-room, which, luckily for the purpose of Brace, was empty at that hour. The two young men each ordered a cool hock-and-soda and lighted two very excellent cigarettes which came out of the pocket of extravagant George. Then they began to talk, and Harry opened the conversation with a question.

'George,' he said, with a serious look on his usually merry face, 'were you on Southberry Heath on the night that poor devil was murdered?'

'Oh, yes,' replied Captain Pendle, with some wonder at the question. 'I rode over to the gipsy camp to buy a particular ring from Mother Jael.'

'For Miss Arden, I suppose?'

'Yes; I wished for a necromantic symbol of our engagement.'

'Did you hear or see anything of the murder?'

'Good Lord, no!' cried the startled George, sitting up straight. 'I should have been at the inquest had I seen the act, or even heard the shot.'

'Did you carry a pistol with you on that night?'

'As I wasn't riding through Central Africa, I did not. What is the meaning of these mysterious questions?'

Brace answered this query by slipping his hand into his breast-pocket and producing therefrom a neat little pistol, toy-like, but deadly enough in the hand of a good marksman. 'Is this yours?' he asked, holding it out for Captain Pendle's inspection.

'Certainly it is,' said George, handling the weapon; 'here are my initials on the butt. Where did you get this?'

'It was found by Mother Jael near the spot where Jentham was murdered.'

Captain Pendle clapped down the pistol on the table with an ejaculation of amazement. 'Was he shot with this, Harry?'

'Without doubt!' replied Brace, gravely. 'Therefore, as it is your property, I wish to know how it came to be used for that purpose.'

'Great Scott, Brace! you don't think that I killed the blackguard?'

'I think nothing so ridiculous,' protested Sir Harry, testily.

'You talk as if you did, though,' retorted George, smartly. 'I thrashed that Jentham beast for insulting Mab, but I didn't shoot him.'

'But the pistol is yours.'

'I admit that, but — Good Lord!' cried Captain Pendle, starting to his feet.

'What now?' asked Brace, turning pale and cold on the instant.

'Gabriel! Gabriel! I — I gave this pistol to him.'

'You gave this pistol to Gabriel? When? Where?'

'In London,' explained George, rapidly. 'When he was in Whitechapel I knew that he went among a lot of roughs and thieves, so I insisted that he should carry this pistol for his protection. He was unwilling to do so at first, but in the end I persuaded him to slip it into his pocket. I have not seen it from that day to this.'

'And it was found near Jentham's corpse,' said Brace, with a groan.

The two young men looked at one another in horrified silence, the same thoughts in the mind of each. The pistol had been in the possession of Gabriel; and Gabriel on the night of the murder had been in the vicinity of the crime.

'It — it is impossible,' whispered George, almost inaudibly, 'Gabriel can explain.'

'Gabriel *must* explain,' said Brace, firmly; 'it is a matter of life and death!'

33

Mr Baltic Explains Himself

It was Miss Whichello, who, on the statement of Mrs Pansey as reported by Mr Cargrim, had told George of his brother's presence on Southberry Heath at the time of Jentham's murder. She had casually mentioned the fact during an idle conversation; but never for one moment had she dreamed of connecting Gabriel with so atrocious a crime. Nor indeed did Captain Pendle, until the fact was rudely and unexpectedly brought home to him by the production of the pistol. Nevertheless, despite this material evidence, he vehemently refused to credit that so gentle a being as Gabriel had slain a fellow-creature deliberately and in cold blood, particularly as on the face of it no reason could be assigned for so hazardous an act. The curate, in his loyal brother's opinion, was neither a vindictive fool nor an aimless murderer.

With this latter opinion Sir Harry very heartily agreed. He had the highest respect for Gabriel as a man and a priest, and could not believe that he had wantonly committed a brutal crime, so repulsive to his benign nature, so contrary to the purity and teachings of his life. He was quite satisfied that the young man both could, and would, explain how the pistol had passed out of his possession; but he did not seek the explanation himself. Baltic, previous to his departure for London, had made Brace promise to question Captain Pendle about the pistol, and report to him the result of such conversation. Now that the pistol was proved to have been in the keeping of Gabriel, the baronet knew very well that Baltic would prefer to question so important a witness himself. Therefore, while waiting for the agent's return, he not only himself refrained from seeing Gabriel, but persuaded George not to do so.

'Your questions will only do more harm than good!' expostulated Brace, 'as you have neither the trained capacity nor the experience to examine into the matter. Baltic returns to-morrow, and as I have every faith in his judgment and discretion, it will be much better to let him handle it.'

'Who is this Baltic you talk of so much?' asked the captain, impatiently.

'He is a private inquiry agent who is trying to discover the man who killed Jentham.'

'On behalf of Tinkler, I suppose?'

'He is working with Tinkler in the matter,' replied Brace, evasively, for he did not want to inform George, the rash and fiery, of his father's peril and Cargrim's treachery.

'Baltic is a London detective, no doubt?'

'Yes, his brains are more equal than Tinkler's to the task of solving the riddle.'

'He won't arrest Gabriel, I hope,' said George, anxiously.

'Not unless he is absolutely certain that Gabriel committed the crime; and I am satisfied that he will never arrive at that certainty.'

'I — should — think — not,' cried Captain Pendle, with disdain. 'Gabriel, poor boy, would not kill a fly, let alone a man. Still, these legal bloodhounds are coarse and unscrupulous.'

'Baltic is not, George. He is quite a new type of detective, and works rather from a religious than a judicial point of view.'

'I never heard of a religious detective before,' remarked George, scornfully.

'Nor I; it is a new departure, and I am not sure but that it is a good one, incongruous as it may seem.'

'Is the man a hypocrite?'

'By no means. He is thoroughly in earnest. Here, in public, he calls himself a missionary.'

'Oh! oh! the wolf in the skin of a sheep!'

'Not at all. The man is — well, it is no use my explaining, as you will see him shortly, and then can judge for yourself. But if you will take my advice, George, you will let Baltic figure the matter out on his own slate, as the Americans say. Don't mention his name or actual business to anyone. Believe me, I know what I am talking about.'

'Very well,' grumbled George, convinced by Harry's earnestness, but by no means pleased to be condemned to an interval of ignorance and inactivity. 'I shall hold my tongue and close my eyes. But you agree with me that Gabriel did not kill the brute?'

'Of course! From the first I never had any doubts on that score.'

Here for the time being the conversation ended, and George went his way to play the part of a careless onlooker. But for his promise, he would have warned Gabriel of the danger which threatened him, and probably have complicated matters by premature anger. Luckily for all things, his faith in Brace's good sense was strong enough to deter him from so rash and headlong a course; therefore, at home and abroad, he assumed a gaiety he did not feel. So here in the episcopalian palace of Beorminster were three people, each one masking his real feelings in intercourse with the others.

The bishop, his son and his scheming chaplain were actors in a comedy of life which — in the opinion of the last — might easily end up as a tragedy. No wonder their behaviour was constrained, no wonder they avoided one another. They were as men living over a powder magazine which the least spark would explode with thunderous noise and damaging effect.

Baltic was the *deus ex machinâ* to strike the spark for ignition, but he seemed in no hurry to do so. Punctual to his promise he returned to Beorminster, and heard Sir Harry's report about the pistol with grave attention. Without venturing an opinion for or against the curate, he asked Sir Harry to preserve a strict silence until such time as he gave him leave to speak, and afterwards took his way to Gabriel's lodgings in the lower part of the town. There he was fortunate enough to find young Pendle within doors, and after a lengthy interview with him on matters connected with the crime, he again sought the baronet. A detailed explanation to that gentleman resulted in a visit of both to Sir Harry's bank, and an interesting conversation with its manager. When Brace and Baltic finally found themselves on the pavement, the face of the first wore an expression of exultation, while the latter, in his reticent way, looked soberly satisfied. Both had every reason for these signs of triumph, for they had touched the highest pinnacle of success.

'I suppose there can be no doubt about it, Baltic?'

'None whatever, Sir Harry. Every link in the chain of evidence is complete.'

'You are a wonderful man, Baltic; you have scored off that fool of a Tinkler in a very neat way.'

'The inspector is no fool in his own sphere, sir,' reproved the serious ex-sailor, 'but this case happened to be beyond it.'

'And beyond him also,' chuckled the baronet.

'There is no denying that, Sir Harry. However, the man is useful in his own place, and having done my part, I shall now ask him to do his.'

'What is his task, eh?'

'To procure a warrant on my evidence. The man must be arrested this afternoon.'

'And then, Baltic?'

'Then, sir,' said the man, solemnly, 'I shall be no longer an agent, but a missionary; and in my own poor way I shall strive to bring him to repentance.'

'After bringing him to the gallows. A queer way of inducing good, Baltic.'

'Whoso loseth all gaineth all,' quoted

Baltic, in all earnestness; 'my mission is not to destroy souls but to save them.'

'Humph! you destroy the material part for the salvation of the spiritual. A man called Torquemada conducted his religious crusade in the same way some hundreds of years ago, and has been cursed for his system by humanity ever since. Your morality — or rather I should say your religiosity — is beyond me, Baltic.'

'*Magnas veritas et praevalebit!*' misquoted Baltic, solemnly, and, touching his hat roughly, turned away to finish the work he felt himself called upon by his religious convictions to execute.

Harry looked after him with a satirical smile. 'You filched that morsel of dog Latin out of the end of the English dictionary, my friend,' he thought, 'and your untutored mind does not apply it with particular relevancy. But I see that, like all fanatics, you distort texts and sayings into fitting your own peculiar views. Well, well, the ends you aim at are right enough, no doubt, but your method of reaching them is as queer a one as ever came under my notice. Go your ways, Torquemada Baltic, there are the germs of a mighty intolerant sect in your kind of teaching, I fear,' and in his turn Sir Harry went about his own affairs.

Inspector Tinkler, more purple-faced and important than ever, sat in his private office, twirling his thumbs and nodding his head for lack of business on which to employ his mighty mind. The afternoon, by some freak of the sun which had to do with his solar majesty's unusual spotty complexion, was exceptionally hot for a late September day, and the heat made Mr Inspector drowsy and indolent. He might have fallen into the condition of an official sleeping beauty, but that a sharp knock at the door roused him sufficiently to bid the knocker enter, whereupon a well-fed policeman presented himself with the information — delivered in a sleepy, beefy voice — that Mr Baltic wished to see Mr Tinkler. The name acted like a douche of iced water on the inspector, and he sharply ordered the visitor to be admitted at once. In another minute Baltic was in the office, saluting the head of the Beorminster police in his usual grave style.

'Ha, Mr Baltic, sir!' rasped out Tinkler, in his parade voice, 'I am glad to see you. There is a seat, and here am I; both at your service.'

'Thank you, Mr Inspector,' said Baltic, and, taking a seat, carefully covered his knees with the red bandanna, and adjusted his straw hat on top of it according to custom.

'Well, sir, well,' grunted Mr Inspector,

pompously, 'and how does your little affair get on?'

'It has got on so far, sir, that I have come to ask you for a warrant of arrest.'

'By George! eh! what! Have you found him?' roared Tinkler, starting back with an incredulous look.

'I have discovered the man who murdered Jentham! Yes.'

'Good!' snapped Tinkler, trying to conceal his amazement by a reversion to his abrupt military manner. 'His name?'

'I'll tell you that when I have related my evidence incriminating him. It is as well to be orderly, Mr Inspector.'

'Certainly, Mr Baltic, sir. Order is at the base of all discipline.'

'I should rather say that discipline is the basis of order,' returned Baltic, with a dry smile; 'however, we can discuss that question later. At present I shall detail my evidence against' — Mr Inspector leaned eagerly forward — 'against the man who killed Jentham.' Mr Inspector threw himself back with a disappointed snort.

' 'Tention!' threw out Tinkler, and arranged pen and ink and paper to take notes. 'Now, Mr Baltic, sir!'

'My knowledge of the man Jentham,' droned Baltic, in his monotonous voice, 'begins at the moment I was informed by Mr Cargrim that he called at the palace to see Bishop Pendle a few days before he met with his violent end. It would appear — although of this I am not absolutely certain — that the bishop knew Jentham when he occupied a more respectable position and answered to another name!'

'Memorandum,' wrote down Tinkler, 'to inquire if his lordship can supply information regarding the past of the so-called Jentham.'

'The bishop,' continued the narrator, with a covert smile at Tinkler's unnecessary scribbling, 'was apparently sorry to see an old friend in a homeless and penniless condition, for to help him on in the world he gave him the sum of two hundred pounds.'

'That,' declared Tinkler, throwing down his pen, 'is charity gone mad — if' — he emphasised the word — 'if, mark me, it is true.'

'If it were not true I should not state it,' rejoined Baltic, gravely. 'As a Christian I have a great regard for the truth. Bishop Pendle drew that sum out of his London account in twenty ten-pound notes. I have the numbers of those notes, and I traced several to the possession of the assassin, who must have taken them from the corpse. On these grounds, Mr Inspector, I assert that Dr

Pendle gave Jentham two hundred pounds.' Tinkler again took up his pen. 'Memo,' he set down, 'to ask his lordship if he helped the so-called Jentham with money. If so, how much?'

'As you know,' resumed Baltic, with deliberation, 'Jentham was shot through the heart, but the pistol could not be found. It is now in my possession, and I obtained it from Mother Jael!'

'What! did she kill the poor devil?'

'I have already said that the murderer is a man, Mr Inspector. Mother Jael knows nothing about the crime, save that she heard the shot and afterwards picked up the pistol near the corpse. I obtained it from her with considerable ease!'

'By threatening her with the warrant I gave you, no doubt.'

Baltic shook his head. 'I made no mention of the warrant, nor did I produce it,' he replied, 'but I happen to know something of the Romany tongue, and be what the Spaniards call *affeciado* to the gipsies. When Mother Jael was convinced that I was a brother of tent and road, she gave me the pistol without ado. It is best to work by kindness, Mr Inspector.'

'We can't all be gipsies, Mr Baltic, sir. Proceed! What about the pistol?'

'The pistol,' continued Baltic, passing over the envious sneer, 'had a silver plate on the butt, inscribed with the letters 'G.P.' I did not know if the weapon belonged to Bishop George Pendle, Captain George Pendle, or to Mr Gabriel Pendle.'

Inspector Tinkler looked up aghast. 'By Jupiter! sir, you don't mean to tell me that you suspected the bishop? Damme, Mr Baltic, how dare you?'

Now the missionary was not going to confide in this official thick-head regarding Cargrim's suspicions of the bishop, which had led him to connect the pistol with the prelate; so he evaded the difficulty by explaining that as the lent money was a link between the bishop and Jentham, and the initials on the pistol were those of his lordship, he naturally fancied that the weapon belonged to Dr Pendle, 'although I will not go so far as to say that I suspected him,' finished Baltic, smoothly.

'I should think not!' growled Tinkler, wrathfully. 'Bishops don't murder tramps in England, whatever they may do in the South Seas!' and he made a third note, 'Memo. — To ask his lordship if he lost a pistol.'

'As Captain George Pendle is a soldier, Mr Inspector, I fancied — on the testimony of the initials — that the pistol might belong to him. On putting the question to him, it appeared that the weapon was his property — '

'The devil!'

'But that he had lent it to Mr Gabriel Pendle to protect himself from roughs when that young gentleman was a curate in Whitechapel, London.'

'Well, I'm — d— blessed!' ejaculated Tinkler, with staring eyes; 'so Mr Gabriel killed Jentham!'

'Don't jump to conclusions, Mr Inspector. Gabriel Pendle is innocent. I never thought that he was guilty, but I fancied that he might supply links in the chain of evidence to trace the real murderer. Of course, you know that Mr Gabriel lately went to Germany?'

'Yes, I know that.'

'Very good! As the initials 'G. P.' also stood for Gabriel Pendle, I was not at all sure but what the pistol might be his. For the moment I assumed that it was, that he had shot Jentham, and that the stolen money had been used by him.'

'But you hadn't the shadow of a proof, Mr Baltic.'

'I had the pistol with the initials,' retorted the missionary, 'but, as I said, I never suspected Mr Gabriel. I only assumed his guilt for the moment to enable me to trace the actual criminal. To make a long story short,

Mr Inspector, I went up to London and called at Cook's office. There I discovered that Mr Gabriel had paid for his ticket with a ten-pound note. That note,' added Baltic, impressively, 'was one of those given by the bishop to Jentham and stolen by the assassin from the body of his victim. I knew it by the number.'

Tinkler thumped the desk with his hand in a state of uncontrolled excitement. 'Then Mr Gabriel must be guilty,' he declared in his most stentorian voice.

'Hush, if you please,' said Baltic, with a glance at the door. 'There is no need to let your subordinates know what is not true.'

'What is not true, sir?'

'Precisely. I questioned Mr Gabriel on my return, and learned that he had changed a twenty-pound note at The Derby Winner prior to his departure for Germany. Mosk, the landlord, gave him the ten I traced to Cook's and two fives. Hush, please! Mr Gabriel also told me that he had lent the pistol to Mosk to protect himself from tramps when riding to and from Southberry, so — '

'I see! I see!' roared Tinkler, purple with excitement. 'Mosk is the guilty man!'

'Quite so,' rejoined Baltic, unmoved. 'You have hit upon the right man at last.'

'So Bill Mosk shot Jentham. Oh, Lord! Damme! Why?'

'Don't swear, Mr Inspector, and I'll tell you. Mosk committed the murder to get the two hundred pounds. I suspected Mosk almost from the beginning. The man was almost always drunk and frequently in tears. I found out while at The Derby Winner that he could not pay his rent shortly before Jentham's murder. After the crime I learned from Sir Harry Brace, the landlord, that Mosk had paid his rent. When Mr Gabriel told me about the lending of the pistol and the changing of the note, I went to Sir Harry's bank, and there, Mr Inspector, I discovered that the bank-notes with which he paid his rent were those given by the bishop to Jentham. On that evidence, on the evidence of the pistol, on the evidence that Mosk was absent at Southberry on the night of the murder, I ask you to obtain a warrant and arrest the man this afternoon.'

'I shall see a magistrate about it at once,' fussed Tinkler, tearing up his now useless memoranda. 'Bill Mosk! Damme! Bill Mosk! I never should have thought a drunken hound like him would have the pluck to do it. Hang me if I did!'

'I don't call it pluck to shoot an unarmed man, Mr Inspector. It is rather the act of a coward.'

'Coward or not, he must swing for it,'

growled Tinkler. 'Mr Baltic, sir, I am proud of you. You have done what I could not do myself. Take my hand and my thanks, sir. Become a detective, sir, and learn our trade. When you know our business you will do wonders, sir, wonders!'

In the same patronising way a rush-light might have congratulated the sun on his illuminating powers and have advised him to become — a penny candle.

34

The Wages of Sin

While the wickedness and fate of Mosk were being discussed and settled in Inspector Tinkler's office, Bishop Pendle was meditating on a very important subject, important both to his domestic circle and to the wider claims of his exalted position. This was none other than a consideration of Gabriel's engagement to the hotelkeeper's daughter, and an argument with himself as to whether or no he should consent to so obvious a *mésalliance*. The bishop was essentially a fair dealer, and not the man to do things by halves, therefore it occurred to him that, as he had consented to George's marriage with Mab, he was bound in all honour to deliberate on the position of his youngest son with regard to Miss Mosk. To use a homely but forcible proverb, it was scarcely just to make beef of one and mutton of the other, the more especially as Gabriel had behaved extremely well in relation to his knowledge of his parents' painful position and his own nameless condition. Some sons so placed would have regarded themselves as absolved from all filial ties, but Gabriel, with true honour and true affection, never dreamed of acting in so heartless a manner; on the contrary, he clung the closer to his unhappy father, and gave him, as formerly, both obedience and filial love. Such honourable conduct, such tender kindness, deserved to be rewarded, and, as the bishop determined, rewarded it should be in the only way left to him.

Having arrived at this liberal conclusion, Dr Pendle decided to make himself personally known to Bell and see with his own eyes the reported beauty which had captivated Gabriel. Also, he wished to judge for himself as to the girl's clever mind and modesty and common sense, all of which natural gifts Gabriel had represented her as possessing in no ordinary degree. Therefore, on the very afternoon when trouble was brewing against Mosk in the Beorminster Police Office, the bishop of the See took his way to The Derby Winner. The sight of Dr Pendle in the narrow streets of the old town fluttered the slatternly dwellers therein not a little, and the majority of the women whisked indoors in mortal terror, lest they should be reproved *ex cathedra* for their untidy looks and unswept doorsteps. It was like the descent of an Olympian god, and awestruck mortals fled swift-footed from the glory of his presence. To use a vigorous American phrase, they made themselves scarce.

The good bishop was amused and rather amazed by this universal scattering, for it was his wish to be loved rather than feared. He was in a decidedly benign frame of mind, as on that very morning he had received a letter from his wife stating that she was coming home within a few days, much benefited by the Nauheim baths. This latter piece of intelligence particularly pleased the bishop, as he judged thereby that his wife would be better able to endure the news of her first husband's untimely reappearance. Dr Pendle was anxious that she should know all at once, so that he could marry her again as speedily as possible, and thereby put an end to an uncomfortable and dangerous state of things. Thus reflecting and thus deciding, the bishop descended the stony street in his usual stately manner, and even patted the heads of one or two stray urchins, who smiled in his face with all the confidence of childhood. Afterwards, the mothers of those especial children were offensively proud at this episcopal blessing, and had 'words' with less fortunate mothers in consequence. Out of such slight events can dissensions arise.

As Dr Pendle neared The Derby Winner he was unlucky enough to encounter Mrs

Pansey, who was that afternoon harassing the neighbourhood with one of her parochial visitations. She carried a black bag stuffed with bundles of badly-printed, badly-written tracts, and was distributing this dry fodder as food for Christian souls, along with a quantity of advice and reproof. The men swore, the women wept, the children scrambled out of the way when Mrs Pansey swooped down like a black vulture; and when the bishop chanced upon her he looked round as though he wished to follow the grateful example of the vanishing population. But Mrs Pansey gave him no chance. She blocked the way, spread out her hands to signify pleasure, and, without greeting the bishop, bellowed out in pretty loud tones, 'At last! at last! and not before you are needed, Dr Pendle.'

'Am I needed?' asked the mystified bishop, mildly.

'The Derby Winner!' was all that Mrs Pansey vouchsafed in the way of an explanation, and cast a glance over her shoulder at the public-house.

'The Derby Winner,' repeated Dr Pendle, reddening, as he wondered if this busybody guessed his errand. 'I am now on my way there.'

'I am glad to hear it, bishop!' said Mrs Pansey, with a toss of her plumed bonnet.

'How often have I asked you to personally examine into the drinking and gambling and loose pleasures which make it a Jericho of sin?'

'Yes, yes, I remember you said something about it when you were at the palace.'

'Said something about it, my lord; I said everything about it, but now that you will see it for yourself, I trust you will ask Sir Harry Brace to shut it up.'

'Dear, dear!' said the bishop, nervously, 'that is an extreme measure.'

'An extreme necessity, rather,' retorted Mrs Pansey, wagging an admonitory finger; 'do not compound with shameless sin, bishop. The house is a regular upas tree. It makes the men drunkards' — Mrs Pansey raised her voice so that the whole neighbourhood might hear — 'the women sluts' — there was an angry murmur from the houses at this term — 'and the children — the children — ' Mrs Pansey seized a passing brat. 'Look at this — this image of the Creator,' and she offered the now weeping child as an illustration.

Before Dr Pendle could say a word, the door of a near house was flung violently open, and a blowzy, red-faced young woman pounced out, all on fire for a fight. She tore the small sinner from the grasp of Mrs Pansey, and began to scold vigorously. 'Ho indeed, mum! ho indeed! and would you be pleased to repeat what you're a-talkin' of behind ladies' backs?'

'Mrs Trumbly! the bishop, woman!'

'No more a woman than yourself, mum; and beggin' his lordship's parding, I 'opes as he'll tell widders as ain't bin mothers not to poke their stuck-up noses into what they knows nothing of.'

By this time a crowd was collecting, and evinced lively signs of pleasure at the prospect of seeing the Bishop of Beorminster as umpire in a street row. But the bishop had heard quite enough of the affray, and without mincing matters fled as quickly as his dignity would permit towards the friendly shelter of The Derby Winner, leaving Mesdames Pansey and Trumbly in the thick of a wordy war. The first-named lady held her own for some considerable time, until routed by her antagonist's superior knowledge of Billingsgate. Then it appeared very plainly that for once she had met with her match, and she hastily abandoned the field, pursued by a storm of highly-coloured abuse from the irate Mrs Trumbly. It was many a long day before Mrs Pansey ventured into that neighbourhood again; and she ever afterwards referred to it in terms which a rigid Calvinist usually applies to Papal Rome. As for Mrs Trumbly herself, the archdeacon's widow said the whole Commination Service over *her* with heartfelt and prayerful earnestness.

Bell flushed and whitened, and stammered and trembled, when she beheld the imposing figure of the bishop standing in the dark, narrow passage. To her he was a far-removed deity throned upon inaccessible heights, awesome and powerful, to be propitiated with humbleness and prayer; and the mere sight of him in her immediate neighbourhood brought her heart into her mouth. For once she lost her nonchalant demeanour, her free and easy speech, and stood nervously silent before him with hanging head and reddened cheeks. Fortunately for her she was dressed that day in a quiet and well-fitting frock of blue serge, and wore less than her usual number of jingling brassy ornaments. The bishop, who had an eye for a comely figure and a pretty face, approved of her looks; but he was clever enough to see that, however painted and shaped, she was made of very common clay, and would never be able to take her place amongst the porcelain maidens to whom Gabriel was accustomed. Still she seemed modest and shy as a maid should be, and Dr Pendle looked on her kindly and encouragingly.

'You are Miss Mosk, are you not?' he

asked, raising his hat.

'Yes, my — my lord,' faltered Bell, not daring to raise her eyes above the bishop's gaiters. 'I am Bell Mosk.'

'In that case I should like some conversation with you. Can you take me to a more private place?'

'The little parlour, my lord; this way, please,' and Bell, reassured by her visitor's kindly manner, conducted him into her father's private snuggery at the back of the bar. Here she placed a chair for the bishop, and waited anxiously to hear if he came to scold or praise. Dr Pendle came to the point at once.

'I presume you know who I am, Miss Mosk?' he said quietly.

'Oh, yes, sir; the Bishop of Beorminster.'

'Quite so; but I am here less as the bishop than as Gabriel's father.'

'Yes,' whispered Bell, and stole a frightened look at the speaker's face.

'There is no need to be alarmed,' said Dr Pendle, encouragingly. 'I do not come here to scold you.'

'I hope not, my lord!' said Miss Mosk, recovering herself a trifle, 'as I have done nothing to be scolded for. If I am in love with Gabriel, and he with me, 'tis only human nature, and as such can't be run down.'

'That entirely depends upon the point of view which is taken,' observed the bishop, mildly. 'For instance, I have a right to be annoyed that my son should engage himself to you without consulting me.'

Bell produced a foolish little lace handkerchief. 'Of course, I know I ain't a lady, sir,' said she, tearfully. 'But I do love Gabriel, and I'm sure I'll do my best to make him happy.'

'I do not doubt that, Miss Mosk; but are you sure that you are wise in marrying out of your sphere?'

'King Cophetua loved a beggar maid, my lord; and the Lord of Burleigh married a village girl,' said Bell, who knew her Tennyson, 'and I'm sure I'm as good as both lots.'

'Certainly,' assented the bishop, dryly; 'but if I remember rightly, the Lord of Burleigh's bride sank under her burden of honours.'

Bell tossed her head in spite of the bishop's presence. 'Oh, she had no backbone, not a bit. I've got heaps more sense than she had. But you mustn't think I want to run after gentlemen, sir. I have had plenty of offers; and I can get more if I want to. Gabriel has only to say the word and the engagement is off.'

'Indeed, I think that would be the wiser course,' replied the bishop, who wondered more and more what Gabriel could see in this commonplace beauty attractive to his refined nature, 'but I know that my son loves you dearly, and I wish to see him happy.'

'I hope you don't think I want to make him miserable, sir,' cried Bell, her colour and temper rising.

'No! no! Miss Mosk. But a matter like this requires reflection and consideration.'

'We have reflected, my lord. Gabriel and me's going to marry.'

'Indeed!' will you not ask my consent?'

'I ask it now, sir! I'm sure,' said Bell, again becoming tearful, 'this ain't my idea of love-making, to be badgered into saying I'm not good enough for him. If he's a man let him marry me, if he's a worm he needn't. I've no call to go begging. No, indeed!'

The bishop began to feel somewhat embarrassed, for Miss Mosk applied every word to herself in so personal a way, that whatever he said constituted a ground of offence, and he scarcely knew upon what lines to conduct so delicate a conversation. Also the girl was crying, and her tears made Dr Pendle fear that he was exercising his superiority in a brutal manner. Fortunately the conversation was brought abruptly to an end, for while the bishop was casting about how to resume it, the door opened softly and

Mr Mosk presented himself.

'Father!' cried Bell, in anything but pleased tones.

'My gal!' replied Mosk, with husky tenderness — 'and in tears. What 'ave you bin sayin' to her, sir?' he added, with a ferocious glance at Pendle.

'Hush, father! 'tis his lordship, the bishop.'

'I know'd the bishop's looks afore you was born, my gal,' said Mosk, playfully, 'and it's proud I am to see 'im under m' umble roof. Lor'! 'ere's a 'appy family meeting.'

'I think,' said the bishop, with a glance at Mosk to assure himself that the man was sober — 'I think, Miss Mosk, that it is advisable your father and myself should have a few words in private.'

'I don't want father to interfere — ' began Bell, when her parent gripped her arm, and cutting her short with a scowl conducted her to the door.

'Don't you git m' back up,' he whispered savagely, 'or you'll be cussedly sorry for yerself an' everyone else. Go to yer mother.'

'But, father, I — '

'Go to yer mother, I tell y',' growled the man, whereupon Bell, seeing that her father was in a soberly brutal state, which was much more dangerous than his usual drunken condition, hastily left the room, and closed the door after her. 'An' now, m' lord,' continued Mosk, returning to the bishop, 'jus' look at me.'

Dr Pendle did so, but it was not a pretty object he contemplated, for the man was untidy, unwashed and frowsy in looks. He was red-eyed and white-faced, but perfectly sober, although there was every appearance about him of having only lately recovered from a prolonged debauch. Consequently his temper was morose and uncertain, and the bishop, having a respect for the dignity of his position and cloth, felt uneasy at the prospect of a quarrel with this degraded creature. But Dr Pendle's spirit was not one to fail him in such an emergency, and he surveyed Mr Caliban in a cool and leisurely manner.

'I'm a father, I am!' continued Mosk, defiantly, 'an' as good a father as you. My gal's goin' to marry your son. Now, m' lord, what have you to say to that?'

'Moderate your tone, my man,' said the bishop, imperiously; 'a conversation conducted in this manner can hardly be productive of good results either to yourself or to your daughter.'

'I don' mean any 'arm!' replied Mosk, rather cowed, 'but I mean to 'ave m' rights, I do.'

'Your rights? What do you mean?'

'M' rights as a father,' explained the man, sulkily. 'Your son's bin runnin' arter m' gal, and lowerin' of her good name.'

'Hold your tongue, sir. Mr Pendle's intentions with regard to Miss Mosk are most honourable.'

'They'd better be,' threatened the other, 'or I'll know how to make 'em so. Ah, that I shall.'

'You talk idly, man,' said the bishop, coldly.

'I talk wot'll do, m' lord. Who's yer son, anyhow? My gal's as good as he, an' a sight better. She's born on the right side of the blanket, she is. There now!'

A qualm as of deadly sickness seized Dr Pendle, and he started from his chair with a pale face and a startled eye.

'What do you — you — you mean, man?' he asked again.

Mosk laughed scornfully, and lugging a packet of papers out of his pocket flung it on the table. 'That's what I mean,' said he; 'certif'cate! letters! story! Yer wife ain't yer wife; Gabriel's only Gabriel an' not Pendle at all!'

'Certificate! letters!' gasped the bishop, snatching them up. 'You got these from Jentham.'

'That I did; he left them with me afore he went out to meet you.'

'You — you murderer!'

'Murderer! Halloa!' cried Mosk, recoiling, pale and startled.

'Murderer!' repeated Dr Pendle. 'Jentham showed these to me on the common; you must have taken them from his dead body. You are the man who shot him.'

'It's a lie,' whispered Mosk, with pale lips, shrinking back, 'an' if I did, you daren't tell. I know your secret.'

'Secret or not, you shall suffer for your crime,' cried the bishop, with a stride towards the door.

'Stand back! It's a lie! I'm desperate. I didn't kill — Hark!'

There was a noise outside which terrified the guilty conscience of the murderer. He did not know that the officers of justice were at the door, nor did the bishop, but the unexpected sound turned their blood to water, and made their hearts, the innocent and the guilty, knock at their ribs. A sharp knock came at the door.

'Help!' cried the bishop. 'The murderer!' and he sprang forward to throw himself on the shaking, shambling wretch. Mosk eluded him, but uttered a squeaking cry like the shriek of a hunted hare in the jaws of the greyhound. The next instant the room seemed to swarm with men, and the bishop as in a dream heard the merciless formula of the law pronounced by Tinkler, —

'In the name of the Queen I arrest you, William Mosk, on a charge of murder.'

35

The Honour of Gabriel

Great as had been the popular excitement over Jentham's death, it was almost mild compared with that which swept through Beorminster when his murderer was discovered and arrested. No one had ever thought of connecting Mosk with the crime; and even on his seizure by warrant many declined to believe in his guilt. Nevertheless, when the man was brought before the magistrates, the evidence adduced against him by Baltic was so strong and clear and irrefutable that, without a dissenting word from the Bench, the prisoner was committed to stand his trial at the ensuing assizes. Mosk made no defence; he did not even offer a remark; but, accepting his fate with sullen apathy, sunk into a lethargic, unobservant state, out of which nothing and no person could arouse him. His brain appeared to have been stunned by the suddenness of his calamity.

Many people expressed surprise that Bishop Pendle should have been present when the man was arrested, and some blamed him for having even gone to The Derby Winner. A disreputable pot-house, they whispered, was not the neighbourhood in which a spiritual lord should be found. But Mrs Pansey, for once on the side of right, soon put a stop to such talk by informing one and all that the bishop had visited the hotel at her request in order to satisfy himself that the reports and scandals about it were true. That Mosk should have been arrested while Dr Pendle was making his inquiries was a pure coincidence, and it was greatly to the bishop's credit that he had helped to secure the murderer. In fact, Mrs Pansey was not very sure but what he had taken the wretch in charge with his own august hands.

And the bishop himself? He was glad that Mrs Pansey, to foster her own vanity, had put this complexion on his visit to the hotel, as it did away with any need of a true but uncomfortable explanation. Also he had carried home with him the packet tossed on the table by Mosk, therefore, so far as actual proof was concerned, his secret was still his own. But the murderer knew it, for not only were the certificate and letters in the bundle, but there was also a sheet of memoranda set down by Krant, *alias* Jentham, which proved clearly that the so-called Mrs Pendle was really his wife.

'If I destroy these papers,' thought the

bishop, 'all immediate evidence likely to reveal the truth will be done away with. But Mosk knows that Amy is not my wife; that my marriage is illegal, that my children are nameless; out of revenge for my share in his arrest, he may tell someone the story and reveal the name of the church wherein Amy was married to Krant. Then the register there will disclose my secret to anyone curious enough to search the books. What shall I do? What can I do? I dare not visit Mosk. I dare not ask Graham to see him. There is nothing to be done but to hope for the best. If this miserable man speaks out, I shall be ruined.'

Dr Pendle quite expected ruin, for he had no hope that a coarse and cruel criminal would be honourable enough to hold his tongue. But this belief, although natural enough, showed how the bishop misjudged the man. From the moment of his arrest, Mosk spoke no ill of Dr Pendle; he hinted at no secret, and to all appearances was quite determined to carry it with him to the scaffold. On the third day of his arrest, however, he roused himself from his sullen silence, and asked that young Mr Pendle might be sent for. The governor of the prison, anticipating a confession to be made in due form to a priest, hastily sent for Gabriel. The young man obeyed the summons at once, for, his father having informed him of Mosk's acquaintance with the secret, he was most anxious to learn from the man himself whether he intended to talk or keep silent. It was with a beating heart that Gabriel was ushered into the prison cell.

By special permission the interview was allowed to be private, for Mosk positively refused to speak in the presence of a third person. He was sitting on his bed when the parson entered, but looked up with a gleam of joy in his blood-shot eyes when he was left alone with the young man.

' 'Tis good of you to come and see a poor devil, Mr Pendle,' he said in a grateful voice. 'Y'll be no loser by yer kin'ness, I can tell y'.'

'To whom should a priest come, save to those who need him?'

'Oh, stow that!' growled Mosk, in a tone of disgust; 'if I want religion I can get more than enough from that Baltic cove. He's never done preachin' and prayin' as if I were a bloomin' 'eathen. No, Mr Pendle, it ain't as a priest as I asked y' t' see me, but as a man — as a gentleman!' His voice broke. 'It's about my poor gal,' he whispered.

'About Bell,' faltered Gabriel, nervously clasping his hands together.

'Yes! I s'pose, sir, you won't think of marryin' her now?'

'Mosk! Mosk! who am I that I should visit your sins on her innocent head?'

'Hold 'ard!' cried Mosk, his face lighting up; 'does that Bible speech mean as y' are goin' to behave honourable?'

'How else did you expect me to behave? Mosk!' said Gabriel, laying a slim hand on the man's knee, 'after your arrest I went to The Derby Winner. It is shut up, and I was unable to enter, as Bell refused to see me. The shock of your evil deed has made your wife so ill that her life is despaired of. Bell is by her bedside night and day, so this is no time for me to talk of marriage. But I give you my word of honour, that in spite of the disgrace you have brought upon her, Bell shall be my wife.'

Mosk burst out crying like a child. 'God bless you, Mr Pendle!' he sobbed, catching at Gabriel's hand. 'You have lifted a weight off my heart. I don't care if I do swing now; I daresay I deserve to swing, but as long as she's all right! — my poor gal! It's a sore disgrace to her. And Susan, too. Susan's dyin', y' say! Well, it's my fault; but if I've sinned I've got to pay a long price for it.'

'Alas! alas! the wages of sin is death.'

'I don't want religion, I tell 'ee,' said Mosk, drying his eyes; 'I've lived bad and I'll die bad.'

'Mosk! Mosk! even at the eleventh hour — '

'That's all right, Mr Pendle; I know all about th' 'leventh hour, and repentance and the rest of th' rot. Stow it, sir, and listen. You'll keep true to my gal?'

'On the honour of a gentleman. I love her; she is as dear to me now as she ever was.'

'That's wot I expected y' to say, sir. Y' allays wos a gentleman. Now you 'ark, Mr Pendle; I knows all about that mar — '

'Don't speak of it!' interrupted Gabriel, with a shudder.

'I ain't goin' to, sir. His lor'ship 'ave the papers I took from him as I did for; so no one but yerself an' yer father knows about 'em. I sha'n't breathe a word about that Krant marriage to a single, solitary soul, and when I dies the secret will die with me. You're actin' square by my poor gal, sir, so I'm agoin' to act square by you. It ain't for me to cover with shame the name as you're goin' to give my Bell.'

'Thank you!' gasped Gabriel, whose emotion at this promise was so great that he could hardly speak, 'thank you!'

'I don' need no thanks, sir; you're square, an' I'm square. So now as I've got that orf m' mind you'd better go. I ain't fit company for the likes of you.'

'Let me say a prayer, Mosk?'

'No, sir; it's too late to pray for me.'

Gabriel raised his hand solemnly. 'As Christ liveth, it is not too late. Though your sins be as — '

'Goo'bye,' interrupted Mosk, and throwing himself on his bed, he turned his face to the wall. Not another word of confession or repentance could Gabriel get him to speak. Nevertheless, the clergyman knelt down on the chill stones and implored God's pardon for this stubborn sinner, whose heart was hardened against the divine grace. Mosk gave no sign of hearing the supplication; but when Gabriel was passing out of the cell, he suddenly rushed forward and kissed his hand. 'God, in His mercy, pity and pardon you, Mosk,' said Gabriel, and left the wretched man with his frozen heart shivering under the black, black shadow of the gallows.

It was with a sense of relief that the curate found himself once more in the sunshine. As he walked swiftly along towards the palace, to carry the good news to his father, he thanked God in his heart that the shadow of impending disaster had passed away. The incriminating papers were in the right hands; their secret was known only to himself, to Graham, and to the bishop. When the truth was told to his mother, and her position had been rectified by a second marriage, Gabriel felt that all would be safe. Cargrim knew nothing of the truth, and therefore could do nothing. With the discovery of the actual criminal all his wicked plans had come to naught; and it only remained for the man he had wronged so deeply to take from him the position of trust which he had so dishonourably abused. As for Gabriel himself, he determined to marry Bell Mosk, as he had promised her miserable father, and to sail with his wife for the mission fields of the South Seas. There they could begin a new life, and, happy in one another's love, would forget the past in assiduous labours amongst the heathen. Baltic knew the South Seas; Baltic could advise and direct how they should begin to labour in that vineyard of the Lord; and Baltic could start them on a new career for the glory of God and the sowing of the good seed. With thoughts like these, Gabriel walked along, wrapped in almost apocalyptic visions, and saw with inspired gaze the past sorrows of himself and Bell fade and vanish in the glory of a God-guided, God-provided future. It was not the career he had shadowed forth for himself; but he resigned his ambitions for Bell's sake, and aided by love overcame his preference for civilised ease. *Vincit, qui se vincit*.

While Gabriel was thus battling, and thus

overcoming, Baltic was seated beside Mosk, striving to bring him to a due sense of his wickedness and weakness, and need of God's forgiveness. He had prayed, and reproved, and persuaded, and besought, many times before; but had hitherto been baffled by the cynicism and stubborn nature of the man. One less enthusiastic than Baltic would have been discouraged, but, braced by fanaticism, the man was resolved to conquer this adversary of Christ and win back an erring soul from the ranks of Satan's evil host. With his well-worn Bible on his knee, he expounded text after text, amplified the message of redemption and pardon, and, with all the eloquence religion had taught his tongue, urged Mosk to plead for mercy from the God he had so deeply offended. But all in vain.

'Wot's th' use of livin' bad all these years, and then turnin' good for five minutes?' growled Mosk, contemptuously. 'There ain't no sense in it.'

'Think of the penitent thief, my brother. He was in the same position as you now are, yet he was promised paradise by God's own Son!'

Mosk shrugged his shoulders. 'It's easy enough promisin', I daresay; but 'ow do I know, or do you know as the promise 'ull be kept?'

'Believe and you shall be saved.'

'I can't believe what you say.'

'Not what I say, poor sinner, but what Christ says.'

There was no possible answer to this last remark, so Mosk launched out on another topic. 'I like yer cheek, I do,' he growled; 'it's you that have got me into this mess, and now you wants me to take up with your preaching.'

'I want to save your soul, man!'

'You'd much better have saved my life. If you'd left me alone I wouldn't have bin caught.'

'Then you would have gone on living in a state of sin. So long as you were safe from the punishment of man you would not have turned to God. Now you must. He is your only friend.'

'It's more nor you are. I don't call it friendship to bring a man to the gallows!'

'I do — when he has committed a crime,' said Baltic, gravely. 'You must suffer and repent, or God will not forgive you. You are Cain, for you have slain your brother.'

'You've got to prove that,' growled Mosk, cunningly; 'look, Mr Baltic, jus' drop religion for a bit, and tell me 'ow you know as I killed that cove.'

Baltic closed his Bible, and looked mildly at the prisoner. 'The evidence against you is perfectly clear, Mosk,' said he, deliberately. 'I traced the notes stolen from the dead man to your possession. You paid your rent to Sir Harry Brace with the fruits of your sin.'

'Yes, I did!' said Mosk, sullenly. 'I know it ain't no good sayin' as I didn't kill Jentham, for you're one too many for me. But wot business had he to go talkin' of hundreds of pounds to a poor chap like me as 'adn't one copper to rub agin the other? If he'd held his tongue I'd 'ave known nothin', and he'd 'ave bin alive now for you to try your 'and on in the religious way. Jentham was a bad 'un, if you like.'

'We are all sinners, Mosk.'

'Some of us are wuss than others. With the 'ception of murderin' Jentham and priggin' his cash, I ain't done nothin' to no one as I knows of. Look here, Mr Baltic, I've done one bit of business to-day with the parson, and now I'm goin' to do another bit with you. 'Ave you pen and paper?'

'Yes!' Baltic produced his pocket-book and a stylographic pen. 'Are you going to confess?'

'I'spose I may as well,' said Mosk, scowling. 'You'll be blaming young Mr Pendle, or the bishop, if I don't; an' as the fust of 'em's goin' to marry my Bell, I don't want trouble there.'

'Won't you confess from a sense of your sin?'

'No, I won't. It's my gal and not repentance as makes me tell the truth. I want to put her an' young Mr Pendle fair and square.'

'Well,' said Baltic, getting ready to write, 'confession is a sign that your heart is softening.'

'It ain't your religion as is doing it, then,' sneered Mosk. 'Now then, fire away, old cove.'

The man then went on to state that he was desperately hard up when Jentham came to stay at The Derby Winner, and, as he was unable to pay his rent, he feared lest Sir Harry should turn him and his sick wife and much-loved daughter into the streets. Jentham, in his cups, several times boasted that he was about to receive a large sum of money from an unknown friend on Southberry Heath, and on one occasion went so far as to inform Mosk of the time and place when he would receive it. He was thus confidential when very drunk, on Mosk reproaching him with not paying for his board and lodging. As the landlord was in much need of money, his avarice was roused by the largeness of the sum hinted at by Jentham; and thinking that the man was a tramp, who would not be missed, he determined to murder and rob him. Gabriel Pendle had given — or rather, had lent — Mosk a pistol to protect himself from gipsies, and vagrants, and harvesters on his frequent night journeys across the lonely heath between Beorminster and Southberry. On the Sunday when the money was to be paid at the crossroads, Mosk rode over to Southberry; and late at night, about the time of the appointment, he went on horseback to the crossroads. A storm came on and detained him, so it was after the bishop had given the money to Jentham that Mosk arrived. He saw the bishop departing, and recognised his face in the searching glare of the lightning flashes. When Dr Pendle had disappeared, Mosk rode up to Jentham, who, with the money in his hand, stood in the drenching rain under the sign-post. He looked up as the horse approached, but did not run away, being rendered pot-valiant by the liquor he had drunk earlier in the evening. Before the man could recognise him, Mosk had jumped off his horse; and, at close quarters, had shot Jentham through the heart. 'He fell in the mud like a 'eap of clothes,' said Mosk, 'so I jus' tied up the 'oss to the sign-post, an' went through his pockets. I got the cash — a bundle of notes, they wos — and some other papers as I found. Then I dragged his corp into a ditch by the road, and galloped orf on m' 'oss as quick as I cud go back to Southberry. There I stayed all night, sayin' as I'd bin turned back by the storm from riding over to Beorminster. Nex' day I come back to m' hotel, and a week arter I paid m' rent to Sir 'Arry with the notes I'd stole. I guv a ten of 'em to young Mr Pendle, and two fives of m' own, as he wanted to change a twenty. If I'd know'd as it was dangerous I'd hev gone up to London and got other notes; but I never thought I'd be found out by the numbers. No one thought as I did it; but I did. ''Ow did you think 'twas me, guv'nor?'

'You were always drunk,' answered Baltic, who had written all this down, 'and I sometimes heard you talking to yourself. Then Sir Harry said that you had paid your rent, and he did not know where you got the money from. Afterwards I found out about the pistol and the notes you had paid Sir Harry. I had no proof of your guilt, although I suspected you for a long time; but it was the pistol which Mother Jael picked up that put me on the right track.'

'Ah, wos it now?' said Mosk, with regret. 'Th' 'oss knocked that out of m' 'and when I wos tyin' him up, and I 'adn't no time to look for it in the mud an' dark. Y' wouldn't hev caught me, I s'pose, if it hadn't bin for that bloomin' pistol?'

'Oh, yes, I would,' rejoined Baltic, coolly; 'the notes would have hanged you in any case, and I would have got at them somehow. I suspected you all along.'

'Wish y' 'adn't come to m' house,' muttered Mosk, discontentedly.

'I was guided there by God to punish your sin.'

'Yah! Stuff! Gimme that confession and I'll sign it.'

But Baltic, wary old fellow as he was, would not permit this without due formality. He had the governor of the gaol brought to the cell, and Mosk with a laugh signed the confession which condemned him in the presence of two witnesses. The governor took it away with him, and again left Baltic and the murderer alone. They eyed one another.

'Now that I know all — ' began Baltic.

'Y' don't know all,' interrupted Mosk, with a taunting laugh; 'there's sumthin' I ain't told y', an' I ain't agoin' to tell.'

'You have confessed your sin, that is enough for me. God is softening your hard heart. Grace is coming to your soul. My brother! my brother! let us pray.'

'Sha'n't! Leave me alone, can't y'?'

Baltic fell on his knees. 'Oh, merciful God, have pity upon this most unhappy man sunk in the pit of sin. Let the Redeemer, Thy only begotten Son, stretch out His saving — '

Mosk began to sing a comic song in a harsh voice.

'His saving hand, oh God, to drag this poor

soul from perdition. Let him call upon Thy most Holy Name out of the low dungeon. Cut him not off in the — '

'Stop! stop!' shrieked the unhappy man, with his fingers in his ears, 'oh, stop!'

'His sins are as scarlet, but the precious blood of the Lamb will bleach them whiter than fine wool. Have mercy, Heavenly Father — '

Mosk, over-wrought and worn out, began to sob hysterically. At the sound of that grief Baltic sprang to his feet and laid a heavy hand on the shoulder of the sinner.

'On your knees! on your knees, my brother,' he cried in trumpet tones, with flashing eyes, 'implore mercy before the Great White Throne. Now is the time for repentance. God pity you! Christ save you! Satan loose you!' And he forced the man on to his knees. 'Down in Christ's name.'

A choking, strangled cry escaped from the murderer, and his body pitched forward heavily on the cold stones. Baltic continued to pray.

36

The Rebellion of Mrs Pendle

'Thank God!' said the bishop, when he heard from Gabriel's lips that the criminal, who knew his secret, had promised to be silent, 'at last I can breathe freely; but what a price to pay for our safety — what a price!'

'Do you mean my marriage to Bell?' asked Gabriel, steadily.

'Yes! If she was undesirable before, she is more so now. So far as I have seen her I do not think she is the wife for you; and as the daughter of that blood-stained man — oh, Gabriel, my son! how can I consent that you should take her to your bosom?'

'Father,' replied the curate, quietly, 'you seem to forget that I love Bell dearly. It was not to close Mosk's mouth that I consented to marry her; in any case I should do so. She promised to become my wife in her time of prosperity, and I should be the meanest of men did I leave her now that she is in trouble. Bell was dear to me before; she is dearer to me now; and I am proud to become her husband.'

'But her father is a murderer, Gabriel!'

'Would you make her responsible for his sins? That is not like you, father.'

The bishop groaned. 'God knows I do not wish to thwart you, for you have been a good son to me. But reflect for one moment how public her father's crime has been; everywhere his wickedness is known; and should you marry this girl, your wife, however innocent, must bear the stigma of being that man's daughter. How would you, a sensitive and refined man shrinking from public scandal, bear the shame of hearing your wife spoken about as a murderer's daughter?'

'I shall take steps to avert that danger. Yes, father, when Bell becomes my wife we shall leave England for ever.'

'Gabriel! Gabriel!' cried the bishop, piteously, 'where would you go?'

'To the South Seas,' replied the curate, his thin face lighting up with excitement; 'there, as Baltic tells us, missionaries are needed for the heathen. I shall become a missionary, father, and Bell will work by my side to expiate her father's sin by aiding me to bring light to those lost in darkness.'

'My poor boy, you dream Utopia. From what I saw of that girl, she is not one to take up such a life. You will not find your Priscilla in her. She is of the world, worldly.'

'The affliction which has befallen her may turn her thoughts from the world.'

'No!' said the bishop, with quiet authority. 'I am, as you know, a man who does not speak idly or without experience, and I tell you, Gabriel, that the girl is not the stuff out of which you can mould an ideal wife. She is handsome, I grant you; and she seems to be gifted with a fair amount of common sense; but, if you will forgive my plain speaking of one dear to you, she is vain of her looks, fond of dress and admiration, and is not possessed of a refined nature. She says that she loves you; that may be; but you will find that she does not love you sufficiently to merge her life in yours, to condemn herself to exile amongst savages for your sake. Love and single companionship are not enough for such an one; she wants — and she will always want — society, flattery, amusement and excitement. My love for you, Gabriel, makes me anxious to think well of her, but my fatherly care mistrusts her as a wife for a man of your nature.'

'But I love her,' faltered Gabriel; 'I wish to marry her.'

'Believe me, you will never marry her, my poor lad.'

Gabriel's face flushed. 'Father, would you forbid — ?'

'No,' interrupted Dr Pendle. 'I shall not forbid; but she will decline. If you tell her about your missionary scheme, I am confident she will refuse to become your wife. Ask her by all means; keep your word as a gentleman should; but prepare yourself for a disappointment.'

'Ah, father, you do not know my Bell.'

'It is on that point we disagree, Gabriel. I do know her; you do not. My experience tells me that your faith is misplaced.'

'We shall see,' said Gabriel, standing up very erect; 'you judge her too harshly, sir. Bell will become my wife, I am sure of that.'

'If she does,' replied the bishop, giving his hand to the young man, 'I shall be the first to welcome her.'

'My dear, dear father!' cried Gabriel, with emotion, 'you are like yourself; always kind, always generous. Thank you, father!' And the curate, not trusting himself to speak further, lest he should break down altogether, left the room hurriedly.

With a weary sigh Dr Pendle sank into his seat, and pressed his hand to his aching head. He was greatly relieved to know that his secret was safe with Mosk; but his troubles were not yet at an end. It was imperative that he should reprove and dismiss Cargrim for his duplicity, and most necessary for the rearrangement of their lives that Mrs Pendle should be informed of the untimely resurrection of her husband. Also, foreseeing the termination of Gabriel's unhappy romance, he was profoundly sorry for the young man, knowing well how disastrous would be the effect on one so impressionable and highly strung. No wonder the bishop sighed; no wonder he felt depressed. His troubles had come after the manner of their kind, 'not in single spies, but in battalions,' and he needed all his strength of character, all his courage, all his faith in God, to meet and baffle anxieties so overwhelming. In his affliction he cried aloud with bitter-mouthed Jeremiah, 'Thou hast removed my soul far off from peace; I forget prosperity.'

In due time Mrs Pendle reappeared in Beorminster, wonderfully improved in health and spirits. The astringent waters of Nauheim had strengthened her heart, so that it now beat with regular throbs, where formerly it had fluttered feebly; they had brought the blood to the surface of the skin, and had flushed her anæmic complexion with a roseate hue. Her eyes were bright, her nerves steady, her step brisk; and she began to take some interest in life, and in those around her. Lucy presented her mother to the bishop with an unconcealed pride, which was surely pardonable. 'There, papa,' she said proudly, while the bishop was lost in wonder at this marvellous transformation. 'What do you think of my patient now?'

'My dear, it is wonderful! The Nauheim spring is the true fountain of youth.'

'A very prosaic fountain, I am afraid,' laughed Mrs Pendle; 'the treatment is not poetical.'

'It is at least magical, my love. I must dip in these restorative waters myself, lest I should be taken rather for your father than your — ' Here Dr Pendle, recollecting the falsity of the unspoken word, shut his mouth with a qualm of deadly sickness — what the Scotch call a grue.

Mrs Pendle, however, observant rather of his looks than his words, did not notice the unfinished sentence. 'You look as though you needed a course,' she said anxiously; 'if I have grown younger, you have become older. This is just what happens when I am away. You never can look after yourself, dear.'

Not feeling inclined to spoil the first joy of reunion, Dr Pendle turned aside this speech with a laugh, and postponed his explanation until a more fitting moment. In the meantime, George and Gabriel and Harry were hovering round the returned travellers with attentions and questions and frequent congratulations. Mr Cargrim, who had been sulking ever since the arrest of Mosk had overthrown his plans, was not present to spoil this pleasant family party, and the bishop spent a golden hour or so of unalloyed joy. But as the night wore on, this evanescent pleasure passed away, and when alone with Mrs Pendle in her boudoir, he was so gloomy and depressed that she insisted upon learning the cause of his melancholy.

'There must be something seriously wrong, George,' she said earnestly; 'if there is, you need not hesitate to tell me.'

'Can you bear to hear the truth, Amy? Are you strong enough?'

'There *is* something serious the matter, then?' cried Mrs Pendle, the colour ebbing from her cheeks. 'What is it, George? Tell me at once. I can bear anything but this suspense.'

'Amy!' The bishop sat down on the couch beside his wife, and took her hand in his warm, encouraging clasp. 'You shall know all, my dearest; and may God strengthen you to bear the knowledge.'

'George! I — I am calm; I am strong; tell me what you mean.'

The bishop clasped her in his arms, held her head to his breast, and in low, rapid tones related all that had taken place since the night of the reception. He did not spare himself in the recital; he concealed nothing, he added nothing, but calmly, coldly, mercilessly told of Krant's return, of Krant's blackmail, of Krant's terrible end. Thence he passed on to talk of Cargrim's suspicions, of Baltic's arrival, of Mosk's arrest, and of the latter's promise to keep the secret of which he had so wickedly become possessed. Having told the past, he discussed the present, and made arrangements for the future. 'Only Gabriel and myself and Graham know the truth now, dearest,' he concluded, 'for this unhappy man Mosk may be already accounted as one dead. Next week you and I must take a journey to some distant parish in the west of England, and there become man and wife for the second time. Gabriel will keep silent; George and Lucy need never know the truth; and so, my dearest, all things — at least to the public eye — shall be as they were. You need not grieve, Amy, or accuse yourself unjustly. If we have sinned, we have sinned innocently, and the burden of evil cannot be laid on you or me. Stephen Krant is to blame; and he has paid for his wickedness with his life. So far as we may — so far as we are able — we must right the wrong. God has afflicted us, my dearest; but God has also protected us; therefore let us thank Him with humble hearts for His many mercies. He will strengthen us to bear the burden; through Him we shall do valiantly. 'For the Lord God is a sun and shield; the Lord will give grace and glory; no good thing will He withhold from them that walk uprightly.''

How wonderful are women! For weeks Bishop Pendle had been dreading this interview with his delicate, nervous, sensitive wife. He had expected tears, sighs, loud sorrow, bursts of hysterical weeping, the wringing of hands, and all the undisciplined grief of the feminine nature. But the unexpected occurred, as it invariably does with the sex in question. To the bishop's unconcealed amazement, Mrs Pendle neither wept nor fainted; she controlled her emotion with a power of will which he had never credited her with possessing, and her first thought was not for herself, but for her companion in misfortune. Placing her hands on either side of the bishop's face, she kissed him fondly, tenderly, pityingly.

'My poor darling, how you must have suffered!' she said softly. 'Why did you not tell me of this long ago, so that I might share your sorrow?'

'I was afraid — afraid to — to speak, Amy,' gasped the bishop, overwhelmed by her extraordinary composure.

'You need not have been afraid, George. I

am no fairweather wife.'

'Alas! alas!' sighed the bishop.

'I am your wife,' cried Mrs Pendle, answering his thought after the manner of women; 'that wicked, cruel man died to me thirty years ago.'

'In the eyes of the law, my — '

'In the eyes of God I am your wife,' interrupted Mrs Pendle, vehemently; 'for over twenty-five years we have been all in all to one another. I bear your name, I am the mother of your children. Do you think these things won't outweigh the claims of that wretch, who ill-treated and deserted me, who lied about his death, and extorted money for his forgery? To satisfy your scruples I am willing to marry you again; but to my mind there is no need, even though that brute came back from the grave to create it. He — '

'Amy! Amy! the man is dead!'

'I know he is; he died thirty years ago. Don't tell me otherwise. I am married to you, and my children can hold up their heads with anyone. If Stephen Krant had come to me with his villainous tempting, I should have defied him, scorned him, trod him under foot.' She rose in a tempest of passion and stamped on the carpet.

'He would have told; he would have disgraced us.'

'There can be no disgrace in innocence,' flashed out Mrs Pendle, fierily. 'We married, you and I, in all good faith. He was reported dead; you saw his grave. I deny that the man came to life.'

'You cannot deny facts,' said the bishop, shaking his head.

'Can't I? I'd deny anything so far as that wretch is concerned. He fascinated me when I was a weak, foolish girl, as a serpent fascinates a bird. He married me for my money; and when it was gone his love went with it. He treated me like the low-minded brute he was; you know he did, George, you know he did. When he was shot in Alsace, I thanked God. I did! I did! I did!'

'Hush, Amy, hush!' said Dr Pendle, trying to soothe her excitement, 'you will make yourself ill!'

'No, I won't, George; I am as calm as you are; I can't help feeling excited. I wished to forget that man and the unhappy life he led me. I did forget him in your love and in the happiness of our children. It was the sight of that student with the scarred face that made me think of him. Why, oh, why did I speak about him to Lucy and Gabriel? Why? Why?'

'You were thoughtless, my dear.'

'I was mad, George, mad; I should have held my tongue, but I didn't. And my poor boy knows the truth. You should have denied it.'

'I could not deny it.'

'Ah! you have not a mother's heart. I would have denied, and lied, and swore its falsity on the Bible sooner than that one of my darlings should have known of it.'

'Amy! Amy! you are out of your mind to speak like this. I deny what is true? I, a priest? — a — '

'You are a man before everything — a man and a father.'

'And a servant of the Most High,' rebuked the bishop, sternly.

'Well, you look on it in a different light to what I do. You suffered; I should not have suffered. I don't suffer now; I am not going back thirty years to make my heart ache.' She paused and clenched her hands. 'Are you sure that he is dead?' she asked harshly.

'Quite sure; dead and buried. There can be no doubt about it this time!'

'Is it necessary that we should marry again?'

'Absolutely necessary,' said the bishop, decisively.

'Then the sooner we get it over the better,' replied Mrs Pendle, petulantly. 'Here' — she wrenched the wedding ring off her finger — 'take this! I have no right to wear it.

Neither maid, wife, nor widow, what should I do with a ring?' and she began to laugh.

'Stop that, Amy!' cried the bishop, sharply, for he saw that, after all, she was becoming hysterical. 'Put the ring again on your finger, until such time as I can replace it by another. You are Krant's widow, and as his widow I shall marry you next week.'

As a drop of cold water let fall into boiling coffee causes the bubbling to subside, so did these few stern words cool down Mrs Pendle's excitement. She overcame her emotion; she replaced the ring on her finger, and again resumed her seat by the bishop. 'My poor dear George,' said she, smoothing his white hair, 'you are not angry with me?'

'Not angry, Amy; but I am rather vexed that you should speak so bitterly.'

'Well, darling, I won't speak bitterly again. Stephen is dead, so do not let us think about him any more. Next week we shall marry again, and all our troubles will be at an end.'

'They will, please God,' said the bishop, solemnly; 'and oh, Amy, dearest, let us thank Him for His great mercy.'

'Do you think He has been merciful?' asked Mrs Pendle, doubtfully, for her religious emotion was not strong enough to blind her to the stubborn fact that their troubles had been undeserved, that they were innocent sinners.

'Most merciful,' murmured the bishop, bowing his head. 'Has He not shown us how to expiate our sin?'

'Our sin; no, George, I won't agree to that. We have not sinned. We married in the fullest belief that Stephen was dead.'

'My dear, all that is past and done with. Let us look to the future, and thank the Almighty that He has delivered us out of our troubles.'

'Yes, I thank Him for that, George,' said Mrs Pendle, meekly enough.

'That is my own dear Amy,' answered the bishop; and producing his pocket Bible, he opened it at random. His eye alighted on a verse of Jeremiah, which he read out with thankful emotion, —

'And I will deliver thee out of the hand of the wicked; and I will redeem thee out of the hand of the terrible.'

37

Dea Ex Machina

As may be guessed, Captain Pendle, now that the course of true love ran smoother, was an assiduous visitor to the Jenny Wren house. He and Mab were all in all to one another, and in the egotism of their love did not trouble themselves about the doings of their neighbours. It is true that George was relieved and pleased to hear of Mosk's arrest and confession, because Gabriel was thereby exonerated from all suspicion of having committed a vile crime; but when reassured on this point, he ceased to interest himself in the matter. He was ignorant that his brother loved Bell Mosk, as neither Baltic nor the bishop had so far enlightened him, else he might not have been quite so indifferent to the impending trial of the wretched criminal. As it was, the hot excitement prevalent in Beorminster left him cold, and both he and Mab might have been dwellers in the moon for all the interest they displayed in the topic of the day. They lived, according to the selfish custom of lovers, in an Arcadia of their own creation, and were oblivious to the doings beyond its borders. Which disregard was natural enough in their then state of mind.

However, George, being in the world and of the world, occasionally brought to Mab such scraps of news as he thought might interest her. He told her of his mother's return, of her renewed health, of her pleasure in hearing that the engagement had been sanctioned by the bishop, and delivered a message to the effect that she wished to see and embrace her future daughter-in-law — all of which information gave Mab wondrous pleasure and Miss Whichello a considerable amount of satisfaction, since she saw that there would be no further question of her niece's unsuitability for George.

'You deserve some reward for your good news,' said Mab, and produced a silk knitted necktie of martial red, 'so here it is!'

'Dearest,' cried Captain Pendle, kissing the scarf, 'I shall wear it next to my heart;' then, thinking the kiss wasted on irresponsive silk, he transferred it to the cheek of his lady-love.

'Nonsense!' said Miss Whichello, smiling broadly; 'wear it round your neck like a sensible lover.'

'Are lovers ever sensible?' inquired the captain, with a twinkle.

'I know one who isn't,' cried Mab,

playfully. 'No, sir,' removing an eager arm, 'you will shock aunty.'

'Aunty has become hardened to such shocks,' smiled Miss Whichello.

'Aunty has been as melancholy as an owl of late,' retorted Mab, caressing the old lady; 'ever since the arrest of that man Mosk she has been quite wretched.'

'Don't speak of him, Mab.'

'Halloo! said George, with sudden recollection, 'I knew there was something else to tell you. Mosk is dead.'

Miss Whichello gave a faint shriek, and tightly clasped the hand of her niece. 'Dead!' she gasped, pale-cheeked and low-toned. 'Mosk dead!'

'As a door nail,' rejoined George, admiring his present; 'he hanged himself last night with his braces, so the gallows have lost a victim and Beorminster society a sensation trial of — '

'George!' cried Mab, in alarm, 'don't talk so; you will make aunty faint.'

And indeed the little old lady looked as though she were on the point of swooning. Her face was white, her skin was cold, and leaning back her head she had closed her eyes. Captain Pendle's item of news had produced so unexpected a result that he and Mab stared at one another in surprise.

'You shouldn't tell these horrors, George.'

'My love, how was I to know your aunt took an interest in the man?'

'I don't take an interest in him,' protested Miss Whichello, faintly; 'but he killed Jentham, and now he kills himself; it's horrible.'

'Horrible, but necessary,' assented George, cheerfully; 'a man who murders another can't expect to get off scot-free. Mosk has only done for himself what the law would have done for him. I'm sorry for Baltic, however.'

'The missionary! Why, George?'

'Because this suicide will be such a disappointment to him. He has been trying to make the poor devil — beg pardon — poor wretch repent; but it would seem that he has not been successful.'

'Did he not confess to Mr Baltic?' asked Miss Whichello, anxiously.

'I believe so; he repented that far.'

'Do you know what he told him?'

'That he had killed Jentham, and had stolen his money.'

'Did he say if he had found any papers on Jentham's body?'

'Not that I know of,' replied George, staring. 'Why! had Jentham any particular papers in his possession?'

'Oh, I don't know; I really can't say,'

answered Miss Whichello, confusedly, and rose unsteadily to her feet. 'Mab, my dear, you will excuse me, I am not very well; I shall go to my bedroom.'

'Let me come too, aunty.'

'No! no!' Miss Whichello waved her niece back. 'I wish to be alone,' and she left the room abruptly, without a look at either of the young people. They could not understand this strange behaviour. Mab, woman-like, turned on Captain Pendle.

'It is all your fault, George, talking of murders and suicides.'

'I'm awf'ly sorry,' said the captain, penitently, 'but I thought you would like to hear the news.'

'Not the police news, thank you,' said Mab, with dignity.

'Why not? Something to talk about, you know.'

'You have me to talk about, Captain Pendle.'

'Oh!' George sprang forward. 'Let us discuss that subject at once. You deserve some punishment for calling me out of my name. There, wicked one!'

'George,' very faintly, 'I — I shall not allow it! You — you should ask permission.'

'Waste of time,' said the practical George, and slipped his arm round her waist.

'Oh, indeed!' — indignantly — 'well, I — '
Here Captain Pendle punished her again, after which Mab said that he was like all men, that he ought to be ashamed of himself, etc., etc., etc. Then she frowned, then she smiled, and finally became a meek and patient Grissel to the unfeigned delight of the superior mind. So the pair forgot Mosk and his wretched death, forgot Miss Whichello and her strange conduct, and retreated from the world into their Arcadia — Paradise — Elysium, in which it is best that all sensible people should leave this pair of foolish lovers.

Miss Whichello had other things to think of than this billing and cooing. She went to her bedroom, and lay down for ten minutes or so; then she got up again and began pacing restlessly to and fro. Her thoughts were busy with Mosk, with his victim, with Baltic; she wondered if Jentham had been in possession of certain papers, if these had been stolen by Mosk, if they were now in the pocket of Baltic. This last idea made her blood turn cold and her heart drum a loud tattoo. She covered her face with her hands; she sat down, she rose up, and in a nervous fever of apprehension leaned against the wall. Then, after the manner of those over-wrought, she began to talk aloud.

'I must tell someone; I must have advice,'

she muttered, clenching her hands. 'It is of no use seeing Mr Baltic; he is a stranger; he may refuse to help me. Dr Graham? No! he is too cynical. The bishop?' She paused and struck her hands lightly together. 'The bishop! I shall see him and tell him all. For his son's sake, he will help my poor darling.'

Having made up her mind to this course, Miss Whichello put on her old-fashioned silk cloak and poke bonnet. Then she fished a bundle of papers, yellow with age, out of a tin box, and slipped them into her capacious pocket. Biting her lips and rubbing her cheeks to bring back the colour, she glided downstairs, stole past the drawing-room door like a guilty creature, and in another minute was in the square. Here she took a passing fly, and ordered the man to drive her to the palace as speedily as possible.

'I trust I am acting for the best,' murmured the little old lady, with a sigh. 'I think I am; for if Bishop Pendle cannot help me, no one else can. After thirty years, oh God! my poor, poor darling!'

In the Greek drama, when the affairs of the *dramatis personæ* became so entangled by circumstance, or fate, or sheer folly as to be beyond their capability of reducing them to order, those involved in such disorder were accustomed to summon a deity to accomplish what was impossible for mortals to achieve. Then stepped the god out of a machine to redress the wrong and reward the right, to separate the sheep from the goats and to deliver a moral speech to the audience, commanding them to note how impossible it was for man to dispense with the guidance and judgment and powerful aid of the Olympian Hierarchy. Miss Whichello's mission was something similar; and although both she and Bishop Pendle were ignorant that she represented the 'goddess out of a machine' who was to settle all things in a way conducive to the happiness of all persons, yet such was the case. Impelled by Fate, she sought out the very man to whom her mission was most acceptable; and seated face to face with Bishop Pendle in that library which had been the scene of so many famous interviews, she unconsciously gave him a piece of information which put an end to all his troubles. She had certainly arrived at the eleventh hour, and might just as well have presented herself earlier; but Destiny, the playwright of the Universe, always decrees that her dramas should play their appointed time and never permits her arbitrator to appear until immediately before the fall of the green curtain. So far as the Beorminster drama was concerned, the crucial moment was at hand, the actor — or rather actress — who was to remedy all things was on the scene, and shortly the curtain would fall on a situation of the rough made smooth. Then red fire, marriage bells, triumphant virtue and cowering guilt, with a rhyming tag, delivered by the prettiest actress, of 'All's well that ends well!'

'I come to consult you confidentially,' said Miss Whichello, when she and the bishop were alone in the library. 'I wish to ask for your advice.'

'My advice and my friendship are both at your service, my dear lady,' replied the courteous bishop.

'It is about Mab's parents,' blurted out the little old lady.

'Oh!' The bishop looked grave. 'You are about to tell me the truth of those rumours which were prevalent in Beorminster when you brought Miss Arden home to your house?'

'Yes. I daresay Mrs Pansey said all sorts of wicked things about me, bishop?'

'Well, no!' — Dr Pendle wriggled uneasily — 'she spoke rather of your sister than of you. I do not wish to repeat scandal, Miss Whichello, so let us say no more about the matter. Your niece shall marry my son; be assured of that. It is foolish to rake up the past,' added the bishop, with a sigh.

'I must rake up the past; I must tell you the truth,' said Miss Whichello, in firm tones, 'if only to put a stop to Mrs Pansey's evil tongue. What did she say, bishop?'

'Really, really, my dear lady, I — '

'Bishop, tell me what she said about my sister. I will know.'

Reluctantly the bishop spoke out at this direct request. 'She said that your sister had eloped in London with a man who afterwards refused to marry her, that she had a child, and that such child is your niece, Miss Arden, whom you brought to Beorminster after the death of your unhappy sister.'

'A fine mixture of truth and fiction indeed,' said the old lady, in a haughty voice. 'I am obliged to Mrs Pansey for the way in which she has distorted facts.'

'I fear, indeed, that Mrs Pansey exaggerates,' said Dr Pendle, shaking his head.

'With all due respect, bishop, she is a wicked old Sapphira!' cried Miss Whichello, and forthwith produced a bundle of papers out of her pocket. 'My unfortunate sister Annie did run away, but she was married to her lover on the very day she left our house in London, and my darling Mab is as legitimate as your son George, Dr Pendle.'

The bishop winced at this unlucky

illustration. 'Have you a proof of this marriage, Miss Whichello?' he asked, with a glance at the papers.

'Of course I have,' she replied, untying the red tape with trembling fingers. 'Here is the certificate of marriage which my poor Annie gave me on her dying bed. I would have shown it before to all Beorminster had I known of Mrs Pansey's false reports. Look at it, bishop.' She thrust it into his hand. 'Ann Whichello, spinster; Pharaoh Bosvile, bachelor. They were married in St Chad's Church, Hampstead, in the month of December 1869. Here is Mab's certificate of birth; she was christened in the same church, and born in 1870, the year of the Franco-German war, so as this is ninety-seven, she is now twenty-seven years of age, just two years older than your son, Captain Pendle.'

With much interest the bishop examined the two certificates of birth and marriage which Miss Whichello placed before him. They were both legally perfect, and he saw plainly that however badly Bosvile might have behaved afterwards to Ann Bosvile she was undoubtedly his wife.

'Not that he would have married her if he could have helped it,' went on Miss Whichello, while the bishop looked at the documents, 'but Annie had a little money

— not much — which she was to receive on her wedding day, so the wretch married her and wrote to my dear father for the money, which, of course, under grandfather's will, had to be paid. Father never would see Annie again, but when the poor darling wrote to me a year afterwards that she was dying with a little child by her side, what could I do but go and comfort her? Ah, poor darling Annie!' sobbed the little old lady, 'she was sadly changed from the bright, beautiful girl I remembered. Her husband turned out a brute and a ruffian and a spendthrift. He wasted all her money, and left her within six months of the marriage — the wretch! Annie tried to support herself by needlework, but she took cold in her starving condition and broke down. Then Mab was born, and she wrote to me. I went at once, bishop, but arrived just in time to get those papers and close my dear Annie's eyes. Afterwards I brought Mab back with me to Beorminster, but I kept her for some time in London on account of my father. When I did bring her here, and I showed him the marriage certificate, he got quite fond of the little pet. So all these years Mab has lived with me quite like my own sweet child, and your son is a lucky man to win her love,' added the old maid, rather incoherently. 'It is not everyone that I would give my dear Annie's child to, I can tell you, bishop. So that's the whole story, and a sadly common one it is.'

'It does you great credit, Miss Whichello,' said Dr Pendle, patting her hand; 'and I have the highest respect both for you and your niece. I am proud, my dear lady, that she should become my daughter. But tell me how your unhappy sister became acquainted with this man?'

'He was a violinist,' replied Miss Whichello, 'a public violinist, and played most beautifully. Annie heard him and saw him, and lost her head over his looks and genius. He called himself Amaru, but his real name was Pharaoh Bosvile.'

'A strange name, Miss Whichello.'

'It is a gipsy name, bishop. Bosvile was a gipsy. He learned the violin in Hungary or Spain, I don't know which, and played wonderfully. Afterwards he had an accident which hurt his hand, and he could not play; that was the reason he married Annie — just for her money, the wretch!'

'A gipsy,' murmured the bishop, who had turned pale.

'Yes; an English gipsy, but like all those people he wandered far and near. The accident which hurt his hand also marked his cheek with a scar.'

'The right cheek?' gasped Dr Pendle, leaning forward.

'Why, yes,' said Miss Whichello, rather astonished at the bishop's emotion; 'that was how I recognised him here when he called himself Jentham. He — '

With a cry the bishop sprang to his feet in a state of uncontrollable agitation, shaking and white. 'W — was Jentham — Bos — Bosvile?' he stammered. 'Are — are you sure?'

'I am certain,' replied Miss Whichello, with a scared look. 'I have seen him dozens of times. Bishop!' Her voice rose in a scream, for Dr Pendle had fallen forward on his desk.

'Oh, my God!' cried the bishop. 'Oh, God most merciful!'

The little old lady was trembling violently. She thought that the bishop had suddenly gone out of his mind. Nor was she reassured when he stood up and looked at her with a face, down which the tears were streaming. Never had Miss Whichello seen a man weeping before, and the sight terrified her much more than an outburst of anger would have done. She looked at the bishop, he looked at her, and they were both ashy white, both overcome with nervous emotion.

After a moment the bishop opened a drawer and took out a bundle of papers. Out of these he selected the marriage certificate of his wife and Krant, and compared it with the certificate of Pharaoh Bosvile and Ann Whichello.

'Thank God!' he said again, in a tremulous voice. 'This man as Bosvile married your sister in 1869, as Krant he married Mrs Pendle in 1870.'

'Married Mrs Pendle!' shrieked Miss Whichello, darting forward.

'Yes. She was a Mrs Krant when I married her, and as her husband was reported dead, I believed her to be his widow.'

'But she was not his widow!'

'No, for Krant was Jentham, and Jentham was alive after my marriage.'

'I don't mean that,' cried Miss Whichello, laying a finger on her sister's certificate, 'but Jentham as Bosvile married Annie in 1869.'

'He married my wife in October 1870,' said the bishop, breathlessly.

'Then his second marriage was a false one,' said Miss Whichello, 'for in that year, in that month, my sister was still alive. Mrs Pendle was never his wife.'

'No, thank God!' said the bishop, clasping his hands, 'she is my own true wife after all.'

38

Exit Mr Cargrim

Once informed of the welcome truth, Dr Pendle lost no time in having it verified by documents and extraneous evidence. This was not the affair of hours, but of days, since it entailed a visit to St Chad's Church at Hampstead, and a rigorous examination of the original marriage and death certificates. Also, as Bosvile, *alias* Krant, *alias* Jentham was said to be a gipsy on the authority of Miss Whichello, and as the information that Baltic was in the confidence of Mother Jael had trickled through Brace and Graham to the bishop, the last named considered it advisable that the ex-sailor should be informed of the actual truth. Now that Dr Pendle was personally satisfied of the legality of his marriage, he had no hesitation in acquainting Baltic with his life-history, particularly as the man could obtain from Mother Jael an assurance, in writing if necessary, that Bosvile and Jentham were one and the same. For the satisfaction of all parties concerned, it was indispensable that proof positive should be procured, and the matter settled beyond all doubt. The position, as affecting both the private feelings and social status of Bishop and Mrs Pendle, was too serious a one to be dealt with otherwise than in the most circumspect manner.

After Miss Whichello's visit and revelation, Dr Pendle immediately sought out his wife to explain that after all doubts and difficulties, and lies and forgeries, they were as legally bound to one another as any couple in the three Kingdoms; that their children were legitimate and could bear their father's name, and that the evil which had survived the death of its author was now but shadow and wind — in a word, nonexistent. Mrs Pendle, who had borne the shock of her pseudo-husband's resurrection so bravely, was quite overwhelmed by the good news of her re-established position, and fainted outright when her husband broke it to her. But for Lucy's sake — as the bishop did not wish Lucy to know, or even suspect anything — she afterwards controlled her feelings better, and, relieved from the apprehension of coming danger, speedily recovered her health and spirits. She was thus, at a week's end, enabled to attend in the library a council of six people summoned by her husband to adjust the situation. The good bishop was nothing if not methodical and thorough; and he was determined that the matter of the false and true marriages should be threshed out to the last grain. Therefore, the council was held *ex aequo et bono*.

On this momentous occasion there were present the bishop himself and Mrs Pendle, who sat close beside his chair; also Miss Whichello, fluttered and anxious, in juxtaposition with Dr Graham; and Gabriel, who had placed himself near Baltic the sedate and solemn-faced. When all were assembled, the bishop lost no time in speaking of the business which had brought them together. He related in detail the imposture of Jentham, the murder by Mosk, who since had taken his own life, and the revelation of Miss Whichello, ending with the production of the documents proving the several marriages, and a short statement explaining the same.

'Here,' said Dr Pendle, 'is the certificate of marriage between Pharaoh Bosvile and Ann Whichello, dated December 1869. They lived together as man and wife for six months up to May 1870, after which Bosvile deserted the unhappy lady.'

'After spending all her money, the wretch!' put in Miss Whichello, angrily.

'Bosvile!' continued the bishop, 'had previously made the acquaintance of my wife, then Amy Lancaster, under the false name of Stephen Krant; and so far won her love that, thinking him a single man, she consented to marry him.'

'No, bishop,' contradicted Mrs Pendle, very positively, 'he did not win my love; he fascinated me with his good looks and charming manners, for in spite of the scar on his cheek Stephen was very handsome. Some friend introduced him to my father as a Hungarian exile hiding under the name of Krant from Austrian vengeance; and my father, enthusiastic on the subject of patriotism, admitted him to our house. I was then a weak, foolish girl, and his wicked brilliancy drew me towards him. When he learned that I had money of my own he proposed to marry me. My father objected, but I was infatuated by Stephen's arts, and became his wife in October 1870.'

'Quite so, my love,' assented her husband, mildly; 'as an inexperienced girl you were at the mercy of that Belial. You were married as you say in October 1870; here, to prove that statement, is the certificate,' and the bishop passed it to Baltic. 'But at the time of such marriage Mrs Bosvile was still alive. Miss Whichello can vouch for this important fact!'

'Ah! that I can,' sighed the little old lady, shaking her head. 'My poor darling sister did not die until January 1871, and I was present to close her weary — weary eyes. Is not that the certificate of her death you are holding?'

'Yes,' answered the bishop, simply, and gave the paper into her outstretched hand. 'You can now understand, my friends,' he continued, addressing the company generally, 'that as Mrs Bosvile was alive in October 1870, the marriage which her husband then contracted with Miss Lancaster was a false one.'

'That is clear enough,' murmured the attentive Baltic, nodding.

'It thus appears,' resumed the bishop, concisely, 'that when I married — as I thought — Amy Krant, a widow, in September 1871, I really and truly wedded Amy Lancaster, a spinster. Therefore this lady' — and here the bishop clasped tenderly the hand of Mrs Pendle — 'is my true, dear wife, and has been legally so these many years, notwithstanding Bosvile's infamous assertion to the contrary.'

'Thank God! thank God!' cried Mrs Pendle, with joyful tears. 'Gabriel, my darling boy!' and she stretched out her disengaged hand to caress her son. Gabriel kissed it with unconcealed emotion.

In the meantime, Dr Graham was examining the bishop's marriage certificate with sharp attention, as he thought he espied a flaw. 'Pardon me, my dear Pendle,' said he, in his crisp voice, 'but I see that Mrs Pendle became your wife under a name which we now know was not then her own. Does that false name vitiate the marriage?'

'By no means,' replied the bishop, promptly. 'I took counsel's opinion on that point when I was in London. It is as follows' — and Dr Pendle read an extract from a legal-looking document. ''A marriage which is made in ignorance in a false name is perfectly good. The law on the subject appears to be this — If a person, to conceal his or her identity, assumes either a wrong name or description, so as to practically obtain a secret marriage, the marriage is void; but if the wrong name or description is adopted by accident or innocently, the marriage is good.' Therefore,' added Dr Pendle, placing the paper on one side, 'Mrs Pendle was not Bosvile's wife on two distinct grounds. Firstly, because his true wife was alive when he married her. Secondly, because he fraudulently made her his wife by giving a false name and description. Regarding my own marriage, it is a good one in law, because Mrs Pendle's false name of Krant was adopted in all innocence. There is no court in the realm of Great Britain,' concluded the bishop, with conviction, 'that would not uphold my marriage as true and lawful, and God be thanked that such is the case!'

'God be thanked!' said Gabriel, in his turn, and said it with heartfelt earnestness. Graham, bubbling over with pleasure, jumped up in his restless way, and gave a friendly hand in turn to Dr Pendle and his wife. 'I congratulate you both, my dear friends,' said he, not without emotion. 'You have won through your troubles at last, and can now live in much-deserved peace for the rest of your lives. *Deus nobis haec otia fecit!* Hey, bishop, you know the Mantuan. Well, well, you have paid forfeit to the gods, Pendle, and they will no longer envy your good fortune, or seek to destroy it.'

'Graham, Graham,' said the bishop, with kindly tolerance, 'always these Pagan sentiments.'

'Ay! ay! I am a Pagan suckled in a creed outworn,' quoted the doctor, rubbing his hands. 'Well, we cannot all be bishops.'

'We can all be Christians,' said Baltic, gravely.

'Ah!' retorted Graham. 'What we should be, and what we are, Mr Baltic, are points capable of infinite discussion. At present we should be smiling and thankful, which,' added he, breaking off, 'Miss Whichello is not, I regret to see.'

'I am thinking of my poor sister,' sobbed the old lady. 'How do I know but that the villain did not deceive her also by making her his wife under a false name?'

'No, madam!' interposed Baltic, eagerly. 'Bosvile was the man's true name, therefore he was legally your sister's husband. I wrote down a statement by Mother Jael that Jentham was really Pharaoh Bosvile, and, at my request, she signed the same. Here it is, signed by her and witnessed by me. I shall give it to you, my lord, that you may lock it up safely with those certificates.'

'Thank you, Mr Baltic,' said the bishop, taking the slip of paper tendered by the missionary, 'but I trust that — er — that this woman knows little of the truth.'

'She knows nothing, my lord, save that Bosvile, for his own purposes, took the names of Amaru and Jentham at different times. The rogue was cunning enough to keep his own counsel of his life amongst the Gentiles; of his marriages, false and true, Mother Jael is ignorant. Set your mind at rest, sir, she will never trouble you in any way.'

'Good!' said Dr Pendle, drawing a long breath of relief. 'Then, as such is the case, my friends, I think it advisable that we should keep our knowledge of Bosvile's iniquities to ourselves. I do not wish my son George or my daughter Lucy to learn the sad story of the past. Such knowledge would only vex them unnecessarily.'

'And I'm sure I don't want Mab to know what a villain her father was,' broke in Miss Whichello. 'Thank God she is unlike him in every way, save that she takes after him in looks. When Captain Pendle talks of Mab's rich Eastern beauty, I shiver all over; he little knows that he speaks the truth, and that Mab has Arab blood in her veins.'

'Not Arab blood, my dear lady,' cried Graham, alertly; 'the gipsies do not come from Arabia, but, as is believed, from the north of India. They appeared in Europe about the fifteenth century, calling themselves, falsely enough, Egyptians. But both Borrow and Leland are agreed that — '

'I don't want to hear about the gipsies,' interrupted Miss Whichello, cutting short the doctor's disquisition; 'all I know is, that if Bosvile or Jentham, or whatever he called himself, is a sample of them, they are a wicked lot of Moabites. I wonder the bishop lets his son marry the child of one, I do indeed!'

'Dear Miss Whichello,' said Mrs Pendle, putting her arm round the poor lady's neck, 'both the bishop and myself are proud that Mab should become our daughter and George's wife. And after all,' she added naively, 'neither of them will ever know the truth!'

'I hope not, I'm sure,' wept Miss Whichello. 'I buried that miserable man at my own expense, as he was Mab's father. And I have had a stone put up to him, with his last name, 'Jentham,' inscribed on it, so that no one might ask questions, which would have been asked had I written his real name.'

'No one will ask questions,' said the bishop, soothingly, 'and if they do, no answers will be forthcoming; we are all agreed on that point.'

'Quite agreed,' answered Baltic, as spokesman for the rest; 'we shall let the dead past bury its dead, and God bless the future.'

'Amen!' said Dr Pendle, and bowed his grey head in a silence more eloquent than words.

So far the rough was made smooth, with as much skill as could be exercised by mortal brains; but after Dr Pendle had dismissed his friends there yet remained to him an unpleasant task, the performance of which, in justice to himself, could not longer be postponed. This was the punishment and dismissal of Michael Cargrim, who indeed merited little leniency at the hands of the man whose confidence he had so shamefully abused. Serpents should be crushed, traitors should be punished, however unpleasant may be the exercise of the judicial function; for to permit evil men to continue in their evil-doing is to encourage vicious habits detrimental to the well-being of humanity. The more just the judge, the more severe should he be towards such calculating sinners, lest, infected by example, mankind should become even more corrupt than it is. Bishop Pendle was a kindly man, who wished to think the best of his fellow-creatures, and usually did so; but he could not blind himself to the base and plotting nature of Cargrim; and, for the sake of his family, for the well-being of the Church, for the benefit of the schemer himself, he summoned him to receive rebuke and punishment. He was not now the patron, the benefactor; but the judge, the ecclesiastical superior, severe and impartial.

Cargrim obeyed the summons unwillingly enough, as he knew very well that he was about to receive the righteous reward of his deeds. A day or so before, when lamenting to Baltic that Dr Pendle had proved innocent, the man had rebuked him for his baseness, and had given him to understand that the bishop was fully aware of the contemptible part which he had acted. Deserted by his former ally, ignorant of Dr Pendle's secret, convinced of Mosk's guilt, the chaplain was in anything but a pleasant position. He was reaping what he had so industriously sown; he was caught in his own snare, and saw no way of defending his conduct. In a word, he was ruined, and now stood before his injured superior with pale face and hanging head, ready to be blamed and sentenced without uttering one word on his own behalf. Nor, had he possessed the insolence to do so, could he have thought of that one necessary word.

'Michael,' said the bishop, mildly, 'I have been informed by Mr Baltic that you accused me of a terrible crime. May I ask on what grounds you did so?'

Cargrim made no reply, but, flushing and paling alternately, looked shamefaced at the carpet.

'I must answer myself, I see,' continued Dr Pendle, after a short silence; 'you thought that because I met Jentham on the heath to pay him some money I murdered him in the viciousness of my heart. Why should you think so ill of me, my poor boy? Have I not stood in the place of your father? Have I not treated you as my own son? You know that I have. And my reward is, that these many weeks you have been secretly trying to ruin me. Even had I been guilty,' cried the bishop, raising his voice, 'it was not your place to proclaim the shame of one who has cherished you. If you had such wicked thoughts in your heart, why did you not come boldly before me and accuse me to my face? I should then have known how to answer you. I can forgive malice — yes, even malice — but not deceit. Did you never think of my delicate wife, of my innocent family, when plotting and scheming my ruin with a smiling face? Alas! alas! Michael, how could you act in a way so unworthy of a Christian, of a gentleman?'

'What is the use of crying over spilt milk?' said Cargrim, doggedly. 'You have the advantage now and can do what you will.'

'What do you mean by talking like that?' said the bishop, sternly. 'Have the advantage now indeed; I never lost the advantage, sir, so far as you are concerned. I did not murder that wretched man, for you know that Mosk confessed how he shot him for the sake of the money I gave him. I knew of Jentham in other days, under another name, and when he asked me for money I gave it to him. My reason for doing so I do not choose to tell you, Mr Cargrim. It is not your right to question my actions. I am not only your elder, but your ecclesiastic superior, to whom, as a priest, you are bound to yield obedience. That obedience I now exact. You must suffer for your sins.'

'You can't hurt me,' returned Cargrim, with defiance.

'I have no wish to hurt you,' answered the

bishop, mildly; 'but for your own good you must be punished; and punish you I will so far as lies in my power.'

'I am ready to be punished, my lord; you have the whip hand, so I must submit.'

'Michael, Michael, harden not your heart! Repent of your wickedness if it is in you to do so. I cannot spare you if I would. *Bonis nocet quis quis pepercerit malis*; that is a true saying which, as a priest, I should obey, and which I intend to obey if only for your own benefit. After punishment comes repentance and amendment.'

Cargrim scowled. 'It is no use talking further, my lord,' he said roughly. 'As I have acted like a fool, I must take a fool's wages.'

'You are indeed a fool,' rejoined the bishop, coldly, 'and an ungrateful fool to boot, or you would not thus answer one who has your interest at heart. But as you take up such a position, I shall be brief. You must leave my house at once, and, for very shame, I should advise you to leave the Church.'

'Leave the Church?' echoed Cargrim, in dismay.

'I have said it. As a bishop, I cannot entrust to a guilty man the care of immortal souls.'

'Guilty? I am guilty of nothing.'

'Do you call malice, falsehood, dissimulation nothing?'

'You cannot unfrock me for what I have done,' said Cargrim, evading a direct reply. 'You may have the will, but you have not the power.'

Dr Pendle looked at him in amazement. 'Yours is indeed an evil heart, when you can use such language to me,' he said sorrowfully. 'I see that it is useless to argue with you in your present fallen condition.'

'Fallen condition, my lord?'

'Yes, poor lad! fallen not only as a priest, but as a man. However, I shall plead no more. Go where you will, do what you will, although I advise you once more not to insult an offended God by offering prayers for others which you need for yourself. Yet, as I am unwilling that you should starve, I shall instruct my banker in London to pay you a monthly sum of money until you are beyond want. Now go, Michael. I am bitterly disappointed in you; and by your own acts you have put it out of my power to keep you by my side. Go! Repent — and pray.'

The chaplain, with a look of malice on his face, walked, or rather slunk, towards the door. 'You magnify my paltry sins,' he flung back. 'What of your own great ones?'

'Dare you, wretched man, to speak against your spiritual head!' thundered the bishop, starting to his feet, vested with the imperious authority of the Church. 'Go! Quit my sight, lest I cast you out from amongst us! Go!'

Before the blaze of that righteous wrath, Cargrim, livid and trembling, crept away like a beaten hound.

39

All's Well That Ends Well

'Bell! Bell! do not give me up.'

'I must, Gabriel; it is my duty.'

'It is your cruelty! Ah, you never loved me as I love you.'

'That is truer than you think, my poor boy. I thought that I loved you, but I was wrong. It was your position which made me anxious to marry you; it was your weak nature which made me pity you. But I do not love you; I never did love you; and it is better that you should know the truth before we part.'

'Part? Oh, Bell! Bell!'

'Part,' repeated Bell, firmly, 'and for ever.'

Gabriel's head drooped on his breast, and he sighed as one, long past tears, who hears the clods falling on the coffin in which his beloved lies. He and Bell Mosk were seated in the little parlour at the back of the bar, and they were alone in the house, save for one upstairs, in the room of Mrs Mosk, who watched beside the dead. On hearing of her husband's rash act, the poor wife, miserable as she had been with the man, yet felt her earlier love for him so far revive as to declare that her heart was broken. She moaned and wept and refused all comfort, until one night she closed her eyes on the world which had been so harsh and bitter. So Bell was an orphan, bereft of father and mother, and crushed to the earth by sorrow and shame. In her own way she had loved her father, and his evil deed and evil end had struck her to the heart. She was even glad when her mother died, for she well knew that the sensitive woman would never have held up her head again, after the disgrace which had befallen her. And Bell, with a white face and dry eyes, long past weeping, sat in the dingy parlour, refusing the only comfort which the world could give her weary heart. Poor Bell! poor, pretty Bell!

'Think, Gabriel,' she continued, in a hard, tearless voice, 'think what shame I would bring upon you were I weak enough to consent to become your wife. I had not much to give you before; I have less than nothing now. I never pretended to be a lady; but I thought that, as your wife, I should never disgrace you. That's all past and done with now. I always knew you were a true gentleman — honourable and kind. No one but a gentleman like you would have kept his word with the daughter of a murderer. But you have done so, dear, and I thank and bless you for your kindness. The only way in which I can show how grateful I am is to give you back your ring. Take it, Gabriel, and God be good to you for your upright kindness.'

There was that in her tone which made Gabriel feel that her decision was irrevocable. He mechanically took the ring she returned to him and slipped it on his finger. Never again was it removed from where he placed it at that moment; and in after days it often reminded him of the one love of his life. With a second sigh, hopeless and resigned, he rose to his feet, and looked at the dark figure in the twilight of the room.

'What are your plans, Bell?' he asked in an unemotional voice, which he hardly recognised as his own.

'I am going away from Beorminster next week,' answered the girl, listlessly. 'Sir Harry has arranged all about this hotel, and has been most kind in every way. I have a little money, as Sir Harry paid me for the furniture and the stock-in-trade. Of course I had to pay f — father's debts' — she could hardly speak the words — 'so there is not much left. Still, I have sufficient to take me to London and keep me until I can get a situation.'

'As — as a barmaid?' asked Gabriel, in a low voice.

'As a barmaid,' she replied coldly. 'What else am I fit for?'

'Can I not help you?'

'No; you have given me all the help you could, by showing me how much you respect me.'

'I do more than respect you, Bell; I love you.'

'I am glad of that,' replied Bell, softly; 'it is a great thing for a miserable girl like me to be loved.'

'Bell! Bell! no one can cast a stone at you.'

'I am the daughter of a murderer, Gabriel; and I know better than you what the world's charity is. Do you think I would stay in this place, where cruel people would remind me daily and hourly of my father's sin? Ah, my dear, I know what would be said, and I don't wish to hear it. I shall bury my poor mother, and go away, never to return.'

'My poor Bell! God has indeed laid a heavy burden upon you.'

'Don't!' Her voice broke and the long-absent tears came into her eyes. 'Don't speak kindly to me, Gabriel; I can't bear kindness. I have made up my mind to bear the worst. Go away; your goodness only makes things the harder for me. After all, I am only a woman, and as a woman I must w-e-e-p.' She broke down, and her tears flowed quickly.

'I shall go,' said Gabriel, feeling helpless,

for indeed he could do nothing. 'Good-bye, Bell!' he faltered.

'Good-bye!' she sobbed. 'God bless you!'

Gabriel, with a sick heart, moved slowly towards the door. Just as he reached it, Bell rose swiftly, and crossing the room threw her arms round his neck, weeping as though her overcharged heart would break. 'I shall never kiss you again,' she wailed, 'never, never again!'

'God bless and keep you, my poor darling!' faltered Gabriel.

'And God bless you! for a good man you have been to me,' she sobbed, and then they parted, never to meet again in this world.

And that was the end of Gabriel Pendle's romance. At first he thought of going to the South Seas as a missionary, but his father's entreaties that he should avoid so extreme a course prevailed, and in the end he went no further from Beorminster than Heathcroft Vicarage. Mr Leigh died a few days after Bell vanished from the little county town: and Gabriel was presented with the living by the bishop. He is a conscientious worker, an earnest priest, a popular vicar, but his heart is still sore for Bell, who so nobly gave him up to bear her own innocent disgrace alone. Where Bell is now he does not know; nobody in Beorminster knows — not even Mrs

Pansey — for she has disappeared like a drop of water in the wild waste ocean of London town. And Gabriel works on amid the poor and needy with a cheerful face but a sore heart; for it is early days yet, and his heart-wounds are recent. No one save the bishop knows how he loved and lost poor Bell; but Mrs Pendle, with the double instinct of woman and mother, guesses that her favourite son has his own pitiful romance, and would fain know of it, that she might comfort him in his sorrow. But Gabriel has never told her; he will never tell her, but go silent and unmarried through life, true to the memory of the rough, commonplace woman who proved herself so noble and honourable in adversity. And so no more of these poor souls.

It is more pleasant to talk of the Whichello-Pansey war. '*Bella matronis detestata*,' saith the Latin poet, who knew little of the sex to make such a remark. To be sure, he was talking of public wars, and not of domestic or social battles; but he should have been more explicit. Women are born fighters — with their tongues; and an illustration of this truth was given in Beorminster when Miss Whichello threw down the gage to Mrs Pansey. The little old lady knew well enough that when George and Mab were married, the archdeacon's widow would use her famous memory to recall the scandals she had set afloat nearly thirty years before. Therefore, to defeat Mrs Pansey once and for all, she called on that good lady and dared her to say that there was any disgrace attached to Mab's parentage. Mrs Pansey, anticipating an easy victory, shook out her skirts, and was up in arms at once.

'I know for a fact that your sister Ann did not marry the man she eloped with,' cried Mrs Pansey, shaking her head viciously.

'Who told you this fact?' demanded Miss Whichello, indignantly.

'I — I can't remember at present, but that's no matter — it's true.'

'It is not true, and you know it is an invention of your own spiteful mind, Mrs Pansey. My sister was married on the day she left home, and I have her marriage certificate to prove it. I showed it to Bishop Pendle, because you poisoned his mind with your malicious lies, and he is quite satisfied.'

'Oh, any story would satisfy the bishop,' sneered Mrs Pansey; 'we all know what he is!'

'We do — an honourable Christian gentleman; and we all know what you are — a scandalmongering, spiteful, soured cat.'

'Hoity-toity! fine language this.'

'It is the kind of language you deserve,

ma'am. All your life you have been making mischief with your vile tongue!'

'Woman,' roared Mrs Pansey, white with wrath, 'no one ever dared to speak like this to me.'

'It's a pity they didn't, then,' retorted the undaunted Miss Whichello; 'it would have been the better for you, and for Beorminster also.'

'Would it indeed, ma'am?' gasped her adversary, beginning to feel nervous; 'oh, really!' with a hysterical titter, 'you and your certificate — I don't believe you have it.'

'Ask the bishop if I have not. He is satisfied, and that is all that is necessary, you wicked old woman.'

'You — you leave my house.'

'I shall do no such thing. Here I am, and here I'll stay until I speak my mind,' and Miss Whichello thumped the floor with her umbrella, while she gathered breath to continue. 'I haven't the certificate of my sister's marriage — haven't I? I'll show it to you in a court of law, Mrs Pansey, when you are in the dock — the dock, ma'am!'

'Me in the dock?' screeched Mrs Pansey, shaking all over, but more from fear than wrath. 'How — how — dare you?'

'I dare anything to stop your wicked tongue. Everybody hates you; some people are fools enough to fear you, but I don't,' cried Miss Whichello, erecting her crest; 'no, not a bit. One word against me, or against Mab, and I'll have you up for defamation of character, as sure as my name's Selina Whichello.'

'I — I — I don't want to say a word,' mumbled Mrs Pansey, beginning to give way, after the manner of bullies when bravely faced.

'You had better not. I have the bishop and all Beorminster on my side, and you'll be turned out of the town if you don't mind your own business. Oh, I know what I'm talking about,' and Miss Whichello gave a crow of triumph, like a victorious bantam.

'I am not accustomed to this — this violence,' sniffed Mrs Pansey, producing her handkerchief; 'if you — if you don't go, I'll call my servants.'

'Do, and I'll tell them what I think of you. I'm going now.' Miss Whichello rose briskly. 'I've had my say out, and you know what I intend to do if you meddle with my affairs. Good-day, Mrs Pansey, and good-bye, for it's a long time before I'll ever cross words with you again, ma'am,' and the little old lady marched out of the room with all the honours of war.

Mrs Pansey was completely crushed. She

knew quite well that Miss Whichello was speaking the truth about the marriage, and that none of her own inventions could stand against the production of the certificate. Moreover, she could not battle against the Bishop of Beorminster, or risk a realisation of Miss Whichello's threat to have her into court. On the whole, the archdeacon's widow concluded that it would be best for her to accept her defeat quietly and hold her tongue. This she did, and never afterwards spoke anything but good about young Mrs Pendle and her aunt. She even sent a wedding present, which was accepted by the victor as the spoils of war, and was so lenient in her speeches regarding the young couple that all Beorminster was amazed, and wished to know if Mrs Pansey was getting ready to join the late archdeacon. Hitherto the old lady had stormed and bullied her way through a meek and terrified world; but now she had been met and conquered and utterly overthrown. Her nerve was gone, and with it went her influence. Never again did she exercise her venomous tongue. To use a vulgar but expressive phrase, Mrs Pansey was 'wiped out'.

Shortly before the marriage of George and Mab, the tribe of gipsies over which Mother Jael ruled vanished into the nowhere. Whither they went nobody knew, and nobody inquired, but their disappearance was a relief both to Miss Whichello and the bishop. The latter had decided that, to run no risks, it was necessary Mab should be married under her true name of Bosvile; and as Mother Jael knew that such was Jentham's real name, Miss Whichello fancied she might come to hear that Mab was called so, and make inquiries likely to lead to unpleasantness. But Mother Jael went away in a happy moment, so Miss Whichello explained to her niece and George that the name of the former was not 'Arden' but 'Bosvile.' 'It is necessary that I should tell you this, dear, on account of the marriage,' said the little old lady; 'your parents, my dearest Mab, are dead and gone; but your father was alive when I took you to live with me, and I called you by another name so that he might not claim you. He was not a good man, my love.'

'Never mind, aunty,' cried Mab, embracing the old lady. 'I don't want to hear about him. You are both my father and my mother, and I know that what you say is right. I suppose,' she added, turning shyly to George, 'that Captain Pendle loves Miss Bosvile as much as he did Miss Arden!'

'A rose by any other name, and all the rest of it,' replied George, smiling. 'What does it matter, my darling? You will be Mab Pendle soon, so that will settle everything, even your meek husband.'

'George,' said Miss Bosvile, solemnly, 'if there is one word in the English language which does *not* describe you, it is 'meek.''

'Really! and if there is one name in the same tongue which fits you like a glove, it is — guess!'

'Angel!' cried Mab, promptly.

George laughed. 'Near it,' said he, 'but not quite what I mean. The missing word will be told when we are on our honeymoon.'

In this way the matter was arranged, and Mab, as Miss Bosvile, was married to Captain Pendle on the self-same day, at the self-same hour, that Lucy became Lady Brace. If some remarks were made on the name inscribed in the register of the cathedral, few people paid any attention to them, and those who did received from Miss Whichello the same skilful explanation as she had given the young couple. Moreover, as Mother Jael was not present to make inquiries, and as Mrs Pansey had not the courage to hint at scandal, the matter died a natural death. But when the honeymoon was waning, Mab reminded George of his promise to supply the missing word.

'Is it goose?' she asked playfully.

'No, my sweetest, although it ought to be!' replied George, pinching his wife's pretty ear. 'It is Mab Pendle!' and he kissed her.

Brisk Dr Graham was at the double wedding, in his most amiable and least cynical mood. He congratulated the bishop and Mrs Pendle, shook hands warmly with the bridegroom, and just as warmly — on the basis of a life-long friendship — kissed the brides. Also, after the wedding breakfast — at which he made the best speech — he had an argument with Baltic about his penal conception of Christianity. The ex-sailor had been very mournful after the suicide of Mark, as the rash act had proved how shallow had been the man's repentance.

'But what can you expect?' said Graham, to him. 'It is impossible to terrify people into a legitimate belief in religion.'

'I don't want to do that, sir,' replied Baltic, soberly. 'I wish to lead them to the Throne with love and tenderness.'

'I can hardly call your method by such names, my friend. You simply ruin people in this life to fit them, in their own despite, for their next existence.'

'When all is lost, doctor, men seek God.'

'Perhaps; but that's a shabby way of seeking Him. If I could not be converted of my own free will, I certainly shouldn't care about being driven to take such a course. Your system, my friend, is ingenious, but impossible.'

'I have yet to prove that it is impossible, doctor.'

'Humph! I daresay you'll succeed in gaining disciples,' said Graham, with a shrug. 'There is no belief strange enough for some men to doubt. After Mormonism and Joseph Smith's deification, I am prepared to believe that humanity will go to any length in its search after the unseen. No doubt you'll form a sect in time, Mr Baltic. If so, call your disciples Hobsonites.'

'Why, Dr Graham?'

'Because the gist of your preaching, so far as I can understand, is a Hobson's choice,' retorted the doctor. 'When your flock of criminals lose everything through your exposure of their crimes, they have nothing left but religion.'

'Nothing left but God, you mean, sir; and God is everything.'

'No doubt I agree with the latter part of your epigram, Baltic, although your God is not my God.'

'There is only one God, doctor.'

'True, my friend; but you and I see Him under different forms, and seek Him in different ways.'

'Our goal is the same!'

'Precisely; and that undeniable fact does away with the necessity of further argument. Good-bye, Mr Baltic. I am glad to have met you; original people always attract me,' and with a handshake and a kindly nod the little doctor bustled off.

So, in his turn, Baltic departed from Beorminster, and lost himself in the roaring tides of London. It is yet too early to measure the result of his work; to prognosticate if his peculiar views will meet with a reception likely to encourage their development into a distinct sect. But there can be no doubt that his truth and earnestness will, some day — and perhaps at no very distant date — meet with their reward. Every prophet convinced of the absolute truth of his mission succeeds in finding those to whom his particular view of the hereafter is acceptable beyond all others. So, after all, Baltic, the untutored sailor, may become the founder of a sect. What his particular 'ism' will be called it is impossible to say; but taking into consideration the man's extraordinary conception of Christianity as a punishing religion, the motto of his new faith should certainly be '*Cernit omnia Deus vindex!*' And Baltic can find the remark cut and dried for his quotation in the last pages of the English dictionary.

So the story is told, the drama is played,

and Bishop Pendle was well pleased that it should be so. He had no taste for excitement or for dramatic surprises, and was content that the moving incidents of the last few weeks should thus end. He had been tortured sufficiently in mind and body; he had, in Dr Graham's phrase, paid his forfeit to the gods in expiation of a too-happy fortune, therefore he might now hope to pass his remaining days in peace and quiet. George and Lucy were happily married; Gabriel was close at hand to be a staff upon which he could lean in his old age; and his beloved wife, the companion of so many peaceful years, was still his wife, nearer and dearer than ever.

When the brides had departed with their several grooms, when the wedding guests had scattered to the four winds of heaven, Bishop Pendle took his wife's hand within his own, and led her into the library. Here he sat him down by her side, and opened the Book of all books with reverential thankfulness of soul.

'I called upon thy name, O Lord, out of the low dungeon.'

'Thou drewest near in the day that I called upon thee: thou saidst, Fear not!'

And the words, to these so sorely-tried of late, were as the dew to the thirsty herb.

We do hope that you have enjoyed reading this large print book.

Did you know that all of our titles are available for purchase?

We publish a wide range of high quality large print books including:
Romances, Mysteries, Classics
General Fiction
Non Fiction and Westerns

Special interest titles available in large print are:
The Little Oxford Dictionary
Music Book
Song Book
Hymn Book
Service Book

Also available from us courtesy of Oxford University Press:
Young Readers' Dictionary
(large print edition)
Young Readers' Thesaurus
(large print edition)

For further information or a free brochure, please contact us at:
Ulverscroft Large Print Books Ltd.,
The Green, Bradgate Road, Anstey,
Leicester, LE7 7FU, England.
Tel: (00 44) **0116 236 4325**
Fax: (00 44) **0116 234 0205**

Other titles published by Ulverscroft:

THE MYSTERY OF A HANSOM CAB

Fergus Hume

Mr. Royston is driving his hansom through the night-time streets of Melbourne when he is hailed by a man supporting a slumped, intoxicated figure, and requesting that the cabman take the unfortunate fellow home — before proceeding to drop his burden and make a rapid exit. Bundling the drunken man onto the seat, the cabman is startled by the reappearance of the good Samaritan, who joins his acquaintance inside — but jumps out before the end of the journey. And when Royston, receiving no response to his inquiries about directions, peers into the cab, he finds that his passenger is now a corpse . . .

VICE VERSA

F. Anstey

Mr. Bultitude is unmoved by the pleading of his fourteen-year-old son Dick that he be spared from returning to Grimstone's tortuous boarding school. During his harangue on the free and easy life of youth, Mr. Bultitude unwisely expresses the wish that he himself might be a boy again — whilst clutching the magical Garudâ Stone, which is all too ready to oblige by transforming his outward appearance into that of his son's. To add insult to injury, Dick swiftly seizes the stone — and with it, the opportunity not only to assume his father's mature and portly form, but also gleefully pack Mr. Bultitude off to the hellish halls of Grimstone's . . .

THE AWAKENING

Kate Chopin

The Pontellier family are spending a hot, lazy holiday on the Gulf of Mexico. Nobody expects that Edna should be preoccupied with anything more than her husband Léonce and their small boys. But Edna, restive and achieving fulfilment only in her beloved sketching, finds her allocated bonds of motherhood and wifely duty to be stifling constraints. And when she teeters on the brink of an illicit summer romance with young clerk Robert Lebrun, new ideas and longings are awakened in her . . .